THE WEEKEND WARRIOR

BY LINTON ROBINSON FOR ADORO BOOKS

**Published by Adoro Books
A Division of Escrit Lit LLC
South Carolina, USA
Copyright 2011**

Copyright 2011 By Linton Robinson
First Edition

1. Literature 2. Satire 3. Media 4. San Diego 5. Non-actionable
6. Works of huge literary importance that might not seem so at first blush, but actually are, trust us on this.

A note to the clueless: This is a work of fiction. About fictional characters and situations. Okay? It means not really true. Jeez.

adorobooks.com

Printed in the United States of America

Available worldwide except in commie countries, total dumps, Islamic extremocracies, and, oddly, Solana Beach, Califonia

TABLE OF CONTENTS

CHAPTER ONE

"Look." Wiley arranged his face and posture into a sub-verbal plea for empathy. "Victims have their problems, I have mine. Where's the compassion?"

It certainly wasn't throwing any pity parties in the back seat of the NineNews Suburban. Caitlin exhibited the same posture towards the two feet of leather-like expanse between them that Israel shows towards border strips. Getting a glance down that monumental cleavage, much less a hand or tongue, looked like long odds. But the day was still young, firm, and confused.

Caitlin's cosmetically perfect face masked her disgust, the way it masked everything else. Wiley didn't really need to trot out his personal museum of nasty character tags and drooling glances to rate her revulsion. He had her from hello. She didn't know what she'd been expecting, but this damaged, fashion-oblivious, grooming-challenged, goat-goateed barfly wasn't it. Wasn't even in the same cell footprint as it. The beautiful face remained professionally neutral as she Inquired, "So what is your main problem, Wiley? In the general sense of the question."

"They won't let me have firearms anymore. Or even blunt instruments."

"I'm glad to hear that." See, she could be sincere.

Wiley's eyes rolled with the smooth orbit of much practice. "You and my parole officer. Well, maybe it's not such a bad idea in my case. But how about you? Decent law-abiding little chunka rape bait who doesn't want to give it up to any AIDS-packing wadmonger who does happen to have a weapon?"

"Gun control cuts both ways."

"Sounds more like doublebit axe control. But, yeah, illegalizing things always works so well. You'll never see drugs or muggings after they make 'em against the law."

"Personally, I carry pepper spray." She'd wanted to work that in, anyway.

"Figures." Wiley put on a snotty bitch accent that didn't sound anything like Caitlin's actual snotty bitch delivery. "Would you like ground pepper on your cornea this evening, Sir?"

Caitlin's mask curled up around the edges for a moment. Wiley saw it, pressed in.

"Listen, Ms. Consumer Affairs...ever hear of environmental sensitivity? The rest of us out here might like to keep breathing. Not to mention it's an aerosol, right? Or do you think of the hydrofluorocarbon propellants as sort of salt in the wound if you're macing an environmentalist or some other ozone fancier?"

In the driver's seat, Mike caught Linsey's eye, keeping his grin out of Caitlin's line of fire. He'd been surreptitiously taping the whole thing ever since they left the station. You never knew when you'd get paydirt. She nodded to him, turned around over the seat with her mini-cam. Caitlin shot her a look.

"Might as well get max footage, since we don't know where it's going." Linsey shrugged. "Little verité, "Cops", live action type stuff."

Caitlin let it alone, turned back to Wiley, who was fooling around with the window control. "Linsey has a point. What are we doing in this segment? Why am I interviewing you?"

"My guess? They're starting to realize you're boring, honey. By now everybody's figured out that no matter how it looks, your jugs aren't going to fall out on the air. So they're losing interest."

Eye into the cam, Linsey showed nothing to the back seat, but her left foot kicked a delighted tattoo against Mike's right thigh. He turned up the gain on his microphone.

"Hey, don't shoot the messenger," Wiley demurred with spread hands. "I'm just hypothesizing. You people came to me. I'm supposed to put the "hard" back in "Hard Look," right?"

Linsey was disappointed. Caitlin didn't detonate; just froze into a platinum sculpture. Didn't even twitch a hand towards the pepper spray or Wiley's eyeballs like you know she wanted to. Damn. Instead she reached up to pat the impervious umbra of her expensive blonde job, a gesture the entire staff had decoded as a fetish of reassurance. No point in gutting this shlub until she got to the bottom of the whole dreary incident. She was dying to know why star On Air Talent and the audio-visual A team was driving around with this balding, tatty field rat.

So she spoke calmly. More or less. "But how? What are we doing? Where is this thing going?"

"Butch's Gun World." Wiley peered around SUV critically. "Why don't you get a van? Flasher lights, siren, recliner swivel seats. They should bring me in as a consultant."

"*Gun* World?" Caitlin did verbal double-takes when agitated. "Gun *World*?"

"And gun-like accessories for the modern urban habitat," Wiley nodded. "You yuppies all want loft living and lofty goals, but don't want to observe the protocols. The over-ride in the under-brush, see what I'm saying?"

Caitlin leaned towards him to scowl, "This show doesn't do gun segments."

Wylie peeked when she lunged forward, settled back as she withdrew. "Hey, whose fault is that? Thing is, "awareness" shows like this are dropping the ball on the whole weapons issue. If Consumer Reports tested the B-1 Bomber or, you know, Star Wars, we might have saved a brazillion or two. Hard to imagine them rating the Stealth Bomber as a Best Value." He framed both words with two-fingered "quotation marks".

Caitlin dragged her locus of loathing from the ruin of his fingernails to the bland assurance on his face. She leaned forward , cupping her head in her hands. Wiley reached out for a reassuring pat on the back, but caught Linsey's frantic headshakes and called it off. Copping back is a zero anyway.

Caitlin muttered, "They must have lost their damned minds."

Butch's might not be a world, but it stakes out some highly uncontested territory of the "Guns R Us" variety. Every prospect pleases the eye with blued, peened, chromed examples of how the West was won...and continues to re-win itself. The gaze falls on highlights that inspire inner thoughts such as, "Jesus, is it really legal to own that thing?" or, "*No* background check?" To Caitlin it was like moving through a creepy cavern lined with toothy vampire bats that might suddenly wake up and chatter into a grisly feeding frenzy. To Mike and Linsey it was "op of the month" and they quickly hooked up their feed cameras and booms, cruising the deadly wall décor with unfeigned delight and no visual irony.

Butch himself, who augmented his rangy cowpoke look with jeans, snap-button shirts, and a vintage Colt revolver, watched the preparations with a smile. His salesmen, both packing flamboyant heat, hung over the far counter, elbows resting on glass beneath which schools of pistols hovered like barracuda in an aquarium. The tall one looked like James Coburn playing a mercenary, the chubby one looked like Chris Penn playing a guy nobody dreamed would turn into a serial killer whose seven state rampage brought premature bereavement to hundreds.

They dug the camera, the novelty and the close-up view of Caitlin's justly famous and professionally displayed bosom. Especially as it heaved in exasperation during her emotion-laden chat on her cellular phone. They normally agreed on very little other than the multi-faceted life advantages of superior firepower, but came to accord on the proposition that if that Jap the Padres picked up from Cincinnati could pitch a slider as nicely as Caitlin could pitch a fit, the results would be Goodbye cellar, Hello home field advantage in Petco Park.

Meanwhile, Wiley flirted with the camera. He held a massive, Star Wars-class electric stun gun on his palm by his face, mugging like a spokesmodel pimping hair rinse or boutique coffee. Motioning Mike in closer with the omni-directional boom, he purred, "Note the slim black polycarbonate case, the sexy steel studs protruding like penis piercings but delivering one hundred eighty thousand volts of persuasion. Perfect tool for the third millennium, wouldn't you say, Butch?"

"I think of it like my TV remote, buddy. You point it at the program you don't like and Zaparoonie! Hassles deleted. It's really just a mute button for real life."

Wiley nodded, appreciating the wisdom of the remarks and aptness of the analogy. "But what people want to know, podnuh, is if this gizmo will actually blitz some molester back to the stone age, or not. They're betting their buns on it, is my point."

Butch found the very idea of doubt amusing. "Here at The World we stand behind every product we sell."

The chubby salesman chimed in, "You wanna stand in front of 'em, that's your lookout."

Hard to argue with that one, either. Wiley moved on to more technical grounds. "But has it ever been tested on real, live crash dummies? Nobody ever does that with weapons." He leaned close to the camera with a confidential, wised-up look. "You starting to figure out that's what we're here for?"

Wiley's seduction and impregnation of the lens was interrupted by a curt snap from Caitlin. "Okay, cut!" His image flicked off the viewscreen, replaced by Caitlin, striding purposefully towards them, holstering her cell phone as if she'd just twirled it and blown smoke off its barrel. She obviously felt much better about the whole procedure.

4

"Listen up. I just spoke to Barry and I've got it figured out."
She turned to Wiley with a "jig's up" demeanor. "I don't know
why I got that email about you being a special guest producer.
Though I have my suspicions."

Wiley stepped slightly back, moved the Stun Gun slightly
forward.

"What they are actually thinking back in the office is a sort of
George Plimpton/Geraldo Rivera reality thing. You stun yourself
and we see what happens, then you tell us about it. Or, I'll be
happy to stun yourself for you."

Wiley seemed mystified by this information. "*That's* what
they're thinking? What is this, Jackass: The Electrocution?"

Almost imperceptible changes in the muscle tone of her face
would have indicated to a close observer that Caitlin was starting
to enjoy it. "They're thinking that for a reason. Namely because
you told them that's what you were going to do." She rolled right
by Wiley's feeble dismissive hand flutter. "And that is what we'll
be paying you to do. Or not paying you not to do. So I intro you,
you zap yourself with that gadget, I interview the remains.
Ready, Freddy?

Butch was impressed. "Wow. That's more commitment than
you'd get at Consumer Reports".

Wiley quickly sorted through the narrowing tree of responses
and escape routes. "Let me tell you something I learned from
those experiments they do with rats."

Caitlin, her control restored, savored the luxury of humoring
him. "And what did you learn?"

"Don't be that rat."

The chunky salesman nodded to endorse the wisdom in that
little caveat. Adding, "Being the deer sucks, too."

"So does being in charge of this segment," Caitlin snarled,
ramping back up to command. "So Wiley. Are you ready? On
your 'X'? Got your motivation?"

Wiley leaned his head over, slapping his ear as if he had a
malfunctioning hearing aid, or perhaps an invasive mosquito.
"Hello? Incoming? It's getting pretty clear to me that it's not my
calling in life to, what would you say? Mortify my flesh? In
order to edify some freeloader watching a show without even
Paying Per View. What I most need here is some creative space
for observation."

Once again Caitlin felt control slipping through her expensively maintained fingertips. What the hell was it with this Wiley guy? And how could she put him up on blocks? Or stuff his head for her wall? "What? Are you babbling about?"

"About pure street cred, honeybuns. About the American male at large, the face of the crowd, the impact demographic, point of purchase sensibility. I'm Street Corner Talking, here. I'm all about, like, Bus Stop."

Actually, it turned out to be a pretty upscale, concerned commuter, type bus stop. The sign on the bench advertised a sushi bar. The waiting passengers wore suits and carried slim leather cases. They looked at the camera incuriously. The men checked out Caitlin a little more acutely, but played it cool behind their Wall Street Journals, not at all affected by the proximity to celebrity. The women scanned her quickly, registered the peculiarly female admiration/hatred, and subtly turned away.

Mike and Linsey had their gear on line and ready to position, but there's always some hold-up. In this case Wiley, remonstrating with Caitlin in a somewhat pushy bid for understanding and a little slack. "They told me it's probably because when I was two I stuck my little dingus into a lightbulb socket. Might be another one of their apocalyptic stories."

"Apocryphal stories."

"If you'd been there you might have thought it was Apocalyptic Now. And I gotta admit, it sounds like the sort of thing I would have done. But you can see where it would breed all sorts of phobias, if you follow me."

"Do I look like somebody who follows your trainwreck of thought?"

"I'm talking about boinking a light socket. Come on, you're supposed to be a professional information hunter/gatherer. Let's focus up a little, right?" Wiley pointed at the suits at the bus stop. "Look at those cellphone-toting, corporate insider briefcase bearers. I could, you know, just stroll up behind them and twang my magic twanger on their asses while you roll tape. Hey, the latest in communication technology, yuppie scum. The medium is the message and the message is medium rare."

Caitlin kept her eyes on him as she barked over her shoulder, "Mike, if he makes a move towards them, take out his kneecaps."

Deeply offending Wiley's sensibilities. "Oh, man. I wasn't going to actually *do* it. I doubt my PO would be too impressed by the whatchacallit, scientific imperative. No, we do this the capitalist way: wait for our guinea pig, then offer to pay. Surely you remember those bygone days, 'Will work for money'?"

Caitlin inspected the skyline, then the mild damage her silk-wrapped nails had done to the luxuriant skin of her palms. What she whispered was almost a prayer: "Somebody has to die for doing this to me.

Even Wiley's synthetic bravado was getting worn a little thin after the passage of fifteen strained minutes. "Christ, zip for four," he bitched. "It's enough to topple your whole belief in the exploitation theory of capitalism. If it hasn't keeled over already. What good is it having all these desperately poor, homeless dipshits running around loose if you can't get them to do just about anything for a few bucks?"

Caitlin dripped disdain. "Oh, I think you might have conned the wino into it if he hadn't thrown up."

Wiley waved his non-fool-suffering hand. "Useless for our purposes, baby. What I was trying to tell you: the man was already stunned." Suddenly his brow cleared, his posture straightened like a Setter spotting a grouse. "Hey! Pick up on the tweaker. Coming right this way. Beautiful!"

Sure enough, a muscular young speed freak named Chad was jittering down the sidewalk towards them, enthusiastically scoping out everything in view and much, much more. At the sight of Caitlin, his eyes widened and pants tented. He headed over, also emulating a bird dog, in his case a Pointer. Wiley hastened to intercept him.

Watching Wiley's gesticulations while negotiating with the amphetamine fan, Caitlin weathered another freshet of damaged reality. If you can't control things, what could they *do* to you? Not an inviting area for investigation. She motioned to Mike and Linsey, "This is so out of hand I'm going on autopilot for awhile. Just shoot anything that moves and we'll sort it out later."

Linsey was already storing images of the speeder. "Jesus, he's more interested in the jolt than the money."

"That's his problem. Set up and I'll see if I can get them up against the wall."

Which she eventually managed to do. She eyed Wiley standing in front of the peeling posters for rock concerts and psychic healers, thinking that having him up against a wall was a tragic waste of a firing squad op. Standing a safe distance away from the vibrating Chad, she leaned over so he could speak in her hand mike. "So how are you feeling, Chad?"

"Me? Yeah! I feel great. Fucking excellent."

Oh good, Caitlin thought. I love asking questions to get answers we can't broadcast. "And you're ready and willing to experience the effects of the Dynamix 180 Stun Gun, then tell us about it?"

Chad stared at her with eyes like mating jellyfish, confusion feathering off into irritation. "What? Yeah, sure I'm ready. That's what's going down here, right? Hey, man! You said twenty bucks. What is this shit?"

"Actually," Caitlin said soothingly, "He should have said fifty dollars." She couldn't keep the venom out of, "Isn't that right, Wiley?" Chad's mercurial gaze wobbled between them, so she dialed back to the Soothe setting. "Don't worry, Chad. You'll get paid. Are you ready?"

Chad answered by pulling up his grubby T-shirt to reveal a six pack stomach, all fat long since burned off by the buzz. No doubt about it, Caitlin thought, this guy really says Street Crime in capital letters. Wiley might be a pustule on the butt of progress, but his plan's working out. Chad caught her stare at his midriff, made the obvious misinterpretation, and leered with badly receded teeth. And he knew exactly how to impress this bitch. "Beam me up, dewd," he told Wiley.

Wiley favored the camera with a "here I go" take, then placed the studs of the Dynamix 180 up to Chad's washboard navel and pulled the trigger. Chad launched backwards into a heap as if snatched by an invisible hand. Wiley stared at the stun gun with new respect, as did Caitlin. Mike and Linsey were already covering Chad's twitching body.

Wiley stepped over to Linsey and gently pulled the lens up to take in his close-up and announcer voice. "The results of the application were extremely gratifying, especially to a longtime connoisseur of cat cartoons. Our subject stiffened and jolted in a true Tom and Jerry fashion.   His eyes slammed up in his skull like Sylvester and he fell down in a very satisfying heap like the Coyote."

Linsey wrested the camera out of his clutches, returning it to Chad's unconscious form. Wiley continued as a remote voice over. "Unfortunately his skeleton did not light up and flash like an X-ray and he didn't break up into bouncing little chunks when he hit the pavement, as we've been led to expect. Life turns out to be a fairly shabby imitation of Art after all, it appears. We probably should have ordered the stunner from Acme."

Chad's eyes opened with a pretty good impression of the flipping roller shade effect so common in Toontown. He sat up and Caitlin squatted beside him, Wiley zeroing in on her skirt sliding up succulent thighs. She genuinely cared about Chad. It was her job. "How do you feel, Chad? Getting it together?"

"Or at least," Wiley chimed in, "As together as you had it before I zonked you?"

Caitlin managed to say, "Shut up, Wiley!" and "Are you okay, Chad?" in the same breath with different tones.

Chad was emphatic. " Man, that was filthy! What a fucking rush!"

"So you were immobilized and incapacitated? Incapable of aggression?"

"Fuck yeah!" Chad's eyes jitterbugged over to the Dynamix 180. "Hey, can you only set that on 'Stun'? Any other settings?"

From off camera, Wiley came through.   "The mail order Acme model has 'Puree', 'Zombie' and 'St. Vitus Slam Dance'. But these guys don't know from going first class.

Chad shook his head admiringly at the stun gun. "What do those things cost?"

"But wait," Wiley piped in, "Don't answer yet. You also get this lovely pepper spray dispenser. Just give him the thing, Ms. Consumer Coddler. They'll find him in a dumpster zapping himself shitless and selling plasma for more C cells. Power to the people."

Caitlin rose and swiveled in the same smooth movement. She put her perfect face inches from Wiley's highly imperfect one and yelled, "Wiley, you shut the *fuck* up!"

Wiley stepped back from this manifestation, but not without getting a scan down the bodice. Linsey and Mike looked at each other, shocked. They'd never heard Caitlin swear before. She did it a decent job of it.

"Shut up and pay him, Wiley." She caught herself, visibly hauled back on the reins of reason. Wiley hunched a shoulder, shot his eyes sideways, inviting her to step away from Chad. Dumbfounded, she did it.

"Listen," Wiley said in a suave undertone, "If he's incapable of aggression, he's not really in any position to collect, is he? He got his free jazzing..."

Caitlin's expression and body talk made Linsey snap the camera from Chad to her, anticipating valuable footage of mayhem or homicide. It made Wiley take a step back.

"Kidding! I'm joking, okay? Christ almighty. I'm going to give him the money. What do you think I am?"

As devastating as Caitlin looked in flesh and blood, she was even more so on a television screen. A glance told you that this was a young woman destined to fulfill even her own gaudy vision of her future. She looked sexy and on top of things sitting beside Chad on the bus stop bench, the HARD LOOK logo winking below to her left. She spoke into her mike with professional cool.

"Incapable of aggression. At the touch of a button. We can do so many things at the touch of a button in our society: delete mail, call police, launch nuclear war. Isn't it worth eighty dollars to be able to push a button and stop street crime?"

She turned to Chad, her voice creamy and caring. "Thanks so much, Chad, for volunteering to help us give electric protection a Hard Look."

Then back to the camera, slick and automated, "I'm Caitlin Vanderkeller, On The Street. Now back to Barry and Corelle at Channel Nine Newscenter."

Barry and Corelle made positive sounds, surrendered their airspace to a commercial for talking geckos. Jerome the bartender reached to turn down the volume, then returned to stacking glasses. Specifically, the cheap, chipped glasses provided so the undiscriminating clientele of The Mimosa Club could convey alcohol from bottle to mouth. Most would have happily skipped the glasses and gone straight to the bottle, but that wasn't considered in the best interests of the management or public health.

The Mimosa was no longer a retreat for sailors whose memories of Subic Bay had lent an affection for tropical details and small, loose women; it was now a dingy, if not actually grubby, filling station for the permanently disaffected, disenfranchised and generally dysfunctional. If it had a theme song, it would be, "How would you like to go where everyone knows your alias"?

The room was too gloomy to even see the walls: a good thing, all told. The bar itself, however, was big and luxuriant. It had once been a peculiar American cultural item known as an "organ bar", where funlovers could place their drinks right on the instrument while singing along to skirling licks from forgotten airs. The bar was spacious because the organ had been removed and sold to stave off economic decline. Several of the regulars' organs had suffered sacrifices. The Mimosa had once been described as part of a system to convert blood plasma into alcohol. At varying rates of exchange. When a person sells their blood to eat, they've entered a rapidly narrowing loop, like that of a lasso. Selling blood to drink isn't quite like that. It's more a metaphor than anything.

Wiley sat at the pregnant bulge of upholstered front rail where the organ had once wurled. It was as close as he got to a home. And the Mimosa's habitués and sons of habitués were his closest approximation of a family. Even if they weren't all there, they were there for him. His drinking and news-watching companion, a dented denizen called Jasper, still gawked at the silent screen.

"I thought you said the show was about you?"

"Not *about* me," Wiley told him with the world-weary resignation of misunderstood celebrities everywhere, "I was the producer. You know, behind the scenes. You saw me in those shots, though, didn't you?"

" Looking good," Jasper nodded sloppily. "You really shock that punk's ass?"

"Duh? Why do you think call it 'reality television'? Of course, there's special effects, editing, technical stuff, involved.

"Know what I think?" Jasper asked this question a lot, apparently unaware of its absurdity. "I should get one of those things. Stun blaster jobs."

11

Jerome the bartender, who thought of the term "long suffering" as a job description, glanced up and issued another of his gravelly, no-bullshit, warnings. "Don't bring it in here, or you'll be out on your ass."

Wiley and Jasper avoided comment and eye contact by tossing back shots.

"All I need," Jerome groused, "You assholes start electrocuting each other."

Jasper waited the respectful pause before changing the subject. "So you really made it with that Caitlin piece? Yikes! Those knockers real?"

CHAPTER TWO

Rollie Moon was not ashamed to watch television. He'd devoted his life to print periodicals ("flushed" was the verb he currently preferred) but had no snobbery about electronic media. News is news is news, was his idea. And fluff is fluff and TV has no monopoly on that. Besides, he was a guy and most guys enjoyed Channel Nine News. MammoPorn, Rollie called it. Just out of the shower, he brushed his long hair dry while watching Jammi Jamison's athletic boobs bounce around in front of the weather map, ran a despairing hand over the fading tan on his slackening surfer abs while admiring the soft curves and vixen face of co-anchor Corelle Pauls, brushed out his beard while awaiting the ice-sculpture perfection of Caitlin Vanderkeller on Hard Look. Which he actually did watch for mostly professional reasons. He wouldn't mind having a consumer advocate column at The Week, but hadn't been able to get it past The Egg Man. Might hurt advertising. Might get complicated. Might work.

Caitlin, probably number one on San Diego males' local Must Fuck lists, didn't grab Rollie's groin to any major extent, but he did have a sort of perverse interest in her. He admired perfection, and she was about as pristine a phenotype as you'd ever be exposed to. He didn't realize that was exactly what was keeping Caitlin down in the sub-minor leagues of San "Dago": she was just too perfect. Those who choose faces to go national know Americans have a hard time relating to the immaculate. They like their phosphor idols to hint at the possibility they might live next door to somebody who didn't need bodyguards to keep people off their beach. They like flaws, prefer the ninety second percentile. True in Rollie's case: he didn't respond to Caitlin because he didn't see her as being in his mating pool, maybe even his gene pool. But she shone as an icon. And maybe a symbol of the perfection he was denied at work.

His interest rose markedly when Wiley showed up. He couldn't believe anybody so media-dysgenic would be featured amid the gloss, glitz and titz of Channel Nine. He's dressed worse than me, Rollie thought. Maybe they've decided they need more Everyshlump appeal. But as the segment went on, Wiley impressed him. Who would have thought? Definitely more fun

13

than those yammering chipmunks on the rest of the show. More fun than anybody he was running in The Week, for that matter. Rollie found himself wishing he could see what they'd edited out of that bit, then caught himself at it and laughed. He clicked off the set and put on a CD. Zappa and the Mothers, "We're Only In It For The Money." Back when shaggy, unkempt and crazed paid off.

J. Danforth Scorment IV also watched Channel Nine News. Never missed an airing, as a matter of fact. He had a fatherly fondness for the women who brought the news to him. Well, sort of an incestuous father fondness, but it was genuine and massive. He adored Corelle's soft, yielding mystique, worshipped at the altar of Caitlin's porcelain hauteur, squirmed in delight at Jammi's prancing and nickering. He loved his girls to sweet, gummy little pieces and felt like they were his very own. Which, since he owned Channel Nine, was close to the truth.

Actually, "own", if closely examined, turned out to be a lot more complex than our usual sense of the word. Although we live in a society in which people think they "own" all-terrain Porsche's which would revert to the bank any month they couldn't come up with a sum equal to about half their rent, or that they "own" a condominium in Maui for two weeks each year, or that they "own" a sports franchise just because the team they root for defeated it three times in a row.

J. Danforth (known to the society pages and country club associates as "Dan the Fourth") had in fact been given the controlling share in the station by his mother, briefly grieving widow of billionaire Danforth the Third, who had bought the paper during his Media Collecting Period, fueled by the massive purchase clout of power utilities originally hegemonized by his father, Dan Junior, to the enrichment of stockholders and lawmakers but the general detriment of the often-maligned voters of California.

His father had been a cagey steward of energy billions, and his widow even shrewder, having brought to the table a gold-digger cunning that she began developing even before the appearance of her weapon-grade breasts and legs. But it was obvious to all that the bloated carcass of Fourth did not harbor a business mind. In fact, it was hard to discern much mental activity at all.   He'd been a handsome youth;   textbook illustration of the dying breed known as "Playboys", and darling of Del Mar racing, Newport yachting, New Zealand skiing, as well as increasingly disturbed International Star Fucking.

It turned out that even money sticks to a fool longer than control over media. The jackals, vultures, and crocodiles of the financial veldt stalked Fourth from waterhole to den to lair, nibbling off parts of his fortune like cheetahs culling a herd of wildebeests. At the point in time when he wallowed in a Jacuzzi in front of his sixty inch set he had become a classic front, sock puppet to a nameless, faceless conglomerate of high-rolling Japanese, Las Vegans and Zurich Gnomes who interfaced with him only through the person of an accountant who had left Hong Kong in the knick of time, taking him with looted capital that would only have withered away under Communist tutelage.

He still held some stock, but nothing approaching control, and was under strict orders not to vote it on his own whim under penalty of dire setbacks.   At over five hundred pounds of poorly disciplined flab, J. Danforth would not thrive on the street. In fact, he had regressed from "Playboy" to more of a "Playinfant". He would have been best served by wearing diapers in a huge "Playpen". Which was not too far from actuality. He floundered up our of the hot, foamy water, wrapped an enormous custom towel around his stomach collection, and waddled over to a phone on the Louis Fourteenth sideboard. (He'd lost his cellular phone and servant pager in the burbling water, along with a waterproof vibrator, a string of one-inch beads and two martini glasses.)

He punched a number, waited with eyes on the screen, blurted, "Hey, Boo! You watching the news? Did you catch that guy zapping the kid in the breadbasket? Cracked me up! That's what we need more of, boy howdy." He didn't listen to the reply, just dropped the phone and thudded over to a double-door refrigerator that clashed violently with the tasteful, overpriced décor of his den. He threw open the refrigerator and freezer doors, rummaging happily. As he did, he idly worked his other hand deep into a certain fold in his flab where he knew from long experience there was, securely hidden, a penis.

At the other end of the one-ended call, Stevenson Yao, late of Hong Kong and the Pacific Rim school of business ethics, smiled ruefully at his wireless handset and replaced it precisely on his desk. Of course he'd watched what he thought of as De Tails at Eleven. Not only was the station his direct responsibility (and therefore also the maintenance, manipulation, housebreaking, and buttwiping of J. Dan the Fourth) his obsession with Caitlin Vanderkeller was of a higher and consuming stratum than the low-level, childish lusts of Occidentals. He idolized her at a level so spiritual it occasionally disappeared into thin, *feng shui-*modulated air. She was a goddess to him, like the lustrous white shapes he had first seen as a child among the crags of Tiger Balm Gardens. A willowy white Kuan Yin. He would have sold his soul to pose her like that, nude in a depilated, Noritake china way, perhaps delicately morphing into enamel, then spotless polished metal: a cyberYin like Sorayama's robot girls (of which he owned several large signed proofs and many smaller editions.) Hair in a goddess bun, fingers entwined in a serene mudra, a lotus held just so. Calm, colorless, motionless; free of all clamor, corruption, and traps of Birth. Ready for Stevenson Yao's worship and corruption.

But his soul was no longer his to sell. It was tangled in buyouts so complexly leveraged that it presented another of those bottomless "ownership" questions. He had masters, and they were powerful. Which made him powerful. And power was his favorite pull toy. He had perverse tastes in power politics. One example was his name. He had a perfectly good name, several in fact. Like many parents in parts of Asia well within the Western orbit, his parents had given him two names. To them he would always be Chang Jen. Or however the Commies decided to spell it, and the Western media idiots craven enough to adopt. But just as valid was the toney Western name for use at cram school, the Ivy League, office suites, clubs, and mah johng games where power and money flowed: Stevenson. His mother had a thing for intellectual politicians in the Lü Buwei and Han Fei mold and Adlai was the closest roundeye she could find.

But he insisted that all underlings, minions, and coolies in American call him "Boo" for obscure reasons perhaps understood by speakers of Chinese. He spoke Cantonese and Mandarin, of course, but also Japanese, English, and a great deal of German, which he thought of as "Swiss". But spoke to them in a crude pidgin, mischievously mixing Japanese and Chinese tropes to produce a patois he thought of as Gobbledy Gook. He wore nerd glasses and funeral suits to heighten the effect. He was starting to consider getting Yakusa body tattoos and wondering if he could spare a finger joint. He owned every Charlie Chan and Mr. Moto film ever made and intensely admired Peter Sellers. Who he somewhat resembled in an Asian way.   To his superiors he spoke impeccable English. Or Japanese or Swiss or whatever.

He saw Wiley's bit and had been at a loss over what to make of it. But now he knew.

Before Yao even checked in the next day, the Station had received a half-dozen calls complaining about the StunGun segment. It would have been much worse if they'd shocked an animal instead of a nominal human, but still. They also got over three hundred phone calls, letters, and emails demanding more Wiley.

Somebody who jumps in there and relates to things the way real people do, was a lot of the gist. Others were quite impressed by somebody actually, on camera, assaulting a street criminal and knocking him on his goldurn ass. They wanted more about personal security. They wanted more reaching out and touching somebody. They wanted more Wiley. The big question around Channel Nine was: how do we give him to them?   Nobody seemed to know where Wiley worked, lived, or hung out. Caitlin showed them his emails from generic servers, shrugged. She didn't like the looks of management trying to get hold of him. They didn't look angry or deadly enough for it to be a good thing. She hoped they didn't find the phone number he'd slipped to Linsey on their way back from the StunGun fiasco.

CHAPTER THREE

Wiley was, by Mimosa Club standards, over-dressed. He had on a suit-- more or less--socks, laced leather shoes. Mustache and goatee somewhat trimmed, Men In Black shades. Yet he sat among them bummed out. Jerome, the bartender, sensed his heavy mood and set two shots of whiskey in front of him unasked. Wiley fired one down with a reflex elbow jerk.

Jasper, the club mascot, leaned closer to Wiley, mumbling, "Hey, so what, Wiley? So what, man? Fuck 'em if they can't take dictation, huh? You've been kicked on your kiester by bigger dickweeds than them."

A wheelchair ricocheted out of the narrow passage to the men's room, expertly maneuvered by a legless combat vet everybody called Strack. He sized Wiley up with his typically dope-glazed, world-weary eyes and wheelied over. In his deep, hoarse rasp he said, "So, you still on there, troop?"

"Nah," Wiley sighed. "I went in expecting to line out some new ideas for shows, go for a drive with Caitlin, case things. They cut me a check and told me to get lost."

Down the bar, Cathilda spoke up. A massive, blowsy, Black bawd, Cathilda was a conversational force to be reckoned with in the Mimosa. She was rumored (rumors mostly traceable back to herself) to have been a model and dancer. A rival rumor sprang up from a co-barfly, who claimed she'd been a bargain basement prostitute. He countered her stridulent challenge to this claim by mentioning a certain distinguishing feature in an undistinguished part of her anatomy and that if she could demonstrate him wrong about it he would withdraw his claim and pay her a thousand dollars. So far she had not taken him up on it. She had, in fact, punched his lights out with a longnecked Miller Lite. "I might not have good taste," she announced while he was resuscitated and helped to his feet, "But I sure as hell ain't less filling." In the Mimosa, she had claimed her true calling: a shrill, loudmouthed busybody. Her input came down to, "Hey, you got a check?"

That called for the checkee to buy a round, which Wiley signaled to Jerome with a twirl of his finger.

Strack spun back to his accustomed spot, where two stools had been removed to accommodate his chair. A big man with powerful arms and corded neck, Stack could just see over the bar from his chair. If he needed more optical advantage, he was capable--and had proven it--of slapping his hands on the bar and vaulting up to stalk along it on his leather-shod stumps. "Hit me easy, Jeronimo," he rasped. "I'm driving."

Next to him, Goody lifted his refreshed highball glass in a salute to Wiley. A rather natty drinker in his seventies, Goody shaved close and used bay rum. He picked up a black plastic device the size of a cell phone and pushed it to his throat. When he hit the trigger, it vibrated, transferring those vibrations into his paralyzed vocal cords to create a croaking simulation of speech. Sounding like Donald Duck playing a mob heavy, he said, "Thanks, kid. Needed to wet my whistle." He sipped, replaced the vibrator at his throat, quacked out, "Sorry about your job."

"Fuck it," Jasper said. "Fuck jobs." This was a sentiment widely applauded in the Mimosa, especially when somebody who had somehow managed to get hired got, as so frequently, fired. "You don't need them, Wiley. Fucking day jobs. You're the man, Wiley. Wotta guy, wotta babe. Wotta grifter, hot damn."

"Yeah, if nothing else, I got paid for no good reason," Wiley said, philosophically sopping up his second shot and reaching out for a refill.

"Got to shock that little dickstick right in the yarbles," Strack reminded him.

"Got to screw that chick with the tits," Jasper added. "Wow, pow, halleluiah."

"Careful, mutt, there's a lady present," Cathilda cawed.

"Smoking" Joe Gasperetti, a burly bounty hunter who favored the Mimosa as a sort of vacation from the even worse bars he normally frequented, mouthed the obligatory, "Where? Got her stashed under that Mao-Mao muumuu?"

"Yo MaMa," Cathilda snapped reflexively, tugging at her voluminous design by Omar de la Tentmaker.

"Ah, well," Wiley sighed. "It was a slice."

Jerome picked up the phone, shoulder-cradling it while pouring ersatz tequila into a glass of lemonade to produce Cathilda a margarita ala Mimosa. "Hey, Wiley. It's for you, bro. Stop giving out this fucking number."

Wiley craned to reach the phone, leaned over the bar to listen. He grinned. He beamed at the glaring Jerome and twirled his finger again. Ring a ding ding.

Despite her beauty, knockout figure, intelligence, and authoritative presence, Caitlin was not universally loved by her co-workers. Go figure. One of whom was thoughtful enough to make sure she was in the circulation loop of a viewer's letter which suggested, in vivid and memorable terms, that consumers would be better served by Wiley's aggressive, hands-on attitude. And that Caitlin could be of significant value if applied in a Vanna White capacity: dressing nice, smiling, and sticking her chest out.

After a few hours of alternating rage and insecurity, Caitlin stood outside the glass of the broadcast booth, mouthing Barry Covington's stock line as bitterly as a Satanist who can't forget his rosary recitations. "And That's The Way It Looks From Here." God, who dreamed that one up, Caitlin asked of the thick glass. It especially rankled employees who knew the more apt phrase would have been, "The way the teleprompter looks over there." He might see himself as Rather meets Morrow meets Buckley, and the Station might be reluctant to tell him different, but Caitlin wasn't alone in seeing him as an idiot savant programmed to recite input in the narrow windows of lucidity between his drinking bouts and orgies of tailor therapy.

The Station was apparently unaware of how Barry was seen by viewers. The only male "name" on the NineNews marquee, he was once thought of as a sort of pompous Charlie, pimping the Station's pulchritudinous Angels. But currently regarded as a pain in the ass who should just shut the hell up. His "Way It Looks" tagline had become a popular San Diego buzz-phase for inability to get the picture.

Corelle Pauls (nee Nata Speriolaphoris) was the latest, and longest-lived, of his pert foils, a risky position that Caitlin adroitly avoided. She saw working with Barry as a promotion toward firing. Not to mention her interpretation of Corelle's co-anchor position as "second banana to a chimp". Corelle's tenure was not entirely because of her soft, inviting beauty and understated lush body reminiscent of Jacqueline Smith--AKA

The Loveliest Angel. There was also her personality or, as Caitlin saw it, lack thereof.

Corelle had come to TV news not from journalism or "communications" departments, or even from the sham personality schools advertising as Broadcast Academies, but from modeling. Spotted in a Robinsons May sleepwear ad by Scorment. Under the chatty on-air personae she was sweet-natured and placid, a combination that made her easy to work with and caused Caitlin to classify her as a "cud muncher".

Gazing through glass at these two bozos doing what she could do far better but seemed unable to get her hands on, Caitlin felt mocked by the booth glass. Glass ceilings were one thing, and sort of understandable if you looked at them from above. But the invisible barrier that relegated her to a sideshow in the two-bit local circus while these clowns boffed around the center ring had her stumped, frustrating and feeling the effects of the most horrible narcotic to which she was prey: self-doubt. Worse, she needed to talk them out of something hideous.

"It's all about consumer awareness," Barry told her, angling towards being able to give her some fatherly/brotherly physical contact. "And you're the go-to gal for that."

Caitlin was mostly aware of how much Barry had consumed and angled away from his breath. And hands. "So let me do the segment by myself. Or let him do it."

Barry gave her an avuncular laugh and shook his distinguished coiffure. "The Brass want this guy. Been getting mucho calls. He's hot. He's back."

Caitlin experienced another moment in which the world seemed to have shifted polarity, leaving everything butt over teakettle. Wiley was hot. Might as well open up the big guns, lower her gunsights towards the fly of that exquisite worsted suit. "So you don't have enough juice to deal with this mope off the street?"

Barry's laugh was less genuine, but who could tell? "Not me, babe. Try talking to Justin." Yeah, right, Caitlin thought, talk to Justin. Which is just what she ended up doing the next morning.

Justin Watkins, the nominal station manager, was also among her least favorite colleagues to talk to. Justin ran the station with a harassed demeanor and a profound belief that there's no such thing as a good decision. His yearbook quote would have been one that Mike happened to get down on tape one afternoon: "Lead? I can barely manage to manage." His "least likely to" would have been: Get enough balls to fire his wife Sherree, the human resource from hell. The slacker ethic of the station often got termed, Justin Time. His ass-covering maneuvers were referred to as the Justin Case.

But it got worse. Yao himself was at the meeting, as well as that treacherous fungus Barry. Attempting to psych her up for the wonderful possibilities of working with Wiley again. And better yet, as a more or less co-host of her segment. Very stimulating concept, they attempted to assure her, could create some major TV, the kind of two-person team that worked so well for Siskel and Ebert, Burns and Allen, Cosell and Ali. We just can't wait to see how well you pull this off.

Caitlin reacted to that final sentiment by having a mild panic attack, followed by a spa session and shopping. The first time she'd chosen a blouse based not on what she thought of as "professional presence" but what she reluctantly termed "prick tease factor." It was obviously a trench war between her and Wiley at this point, hand to hand combat for home, virtue and the way of life she held dear, no holds barred. He creamed her.

Caitlin had chalked out a response to the absurd, debasing scheme they had broached to her. She dialed on some enthusiasm in order to seize the initiative, announcing she would do some research to figure out what topic would most appeal to viewers. Her research consisted of hours of brain-cudgeling, augmented by what for her was quite a lot of drinking. She came up with the perfect ploy. Something she could sell on glitz and noise, but would be a quagmire for Wiley and the station, threatening people right where they lived. While hopefully bogging him down in some boring research.

"It's perfect," she told them at the next meeting. "People love their cars. They like gadgets and attracting attention. They're obviously concerned about security and see Wiley as having a handle on that."

Barry enthused, winking at her as always. "You've nailed it, Caitlin. Perfect. I can already see some great ways to introduce the segment." You'll see them better after Sean and Belinda write them up and give them to you, Caitlin thought.

"I rike," Yao said, nodding like a wind-up monkey. Which was all it took. Except fending off Yao's continued campaign to expose her to art.

They saw the possibilities clearly, a clever and aggressive plea for awareness and helpful tips on selecting the best protection for your beloved automobile. What they got was Wiley walking around a pay lot, kicking the cars into a cacophony of angry bleats and raving about it while Caitlin cringed on the sidelines in her new whore blouse, trying not to look aghast. Nobody ever described television as an exact science.

After a frantic editing session that must have resembled Hirohito's high command trying to put a positive spin on alleged developments in Hiroshima and Nagasaki, two results were hammered out. One was that Wiley was once again fired. The other was a segment that tried desperately to avoid cars being kicked and focus on the finer things in life, like Caitlin's blouse. And the following vocal performance by a bloodshot Wiley:

Volumes have been spoken about the annoyance of auto alarms. But not nearly enough. For one thing, we're still having to listen to the damned things shatter the night with their wretched repertoire of squeals and squalls and snide wah-wahs like police sirens in old Eurotrash movies. This is because the topic has so far been confined to how rude and invasive it is to drench neighborhoods with the sound of electronic katzenjammer just because a cat jumped on your car or you were too stupid to open the door correctly. Or even because you're stingy about who possesses your damned stereo system, a matter which is hardly the problem of everyone within earshot.

At first blush, it might seem that a more effective form of discussion would be trying to educate alarm owners to the fact that their noise toys are completely useless. Nobody pays any attention to them. In fact, if I saw some enlightened footpad trying to steal a car with its alarm

23

bleating, I'd help him out, just to get the damned thing out of the neighborhood quicker. Unfortunately, you learn that "alarmists" aren't really concerned with preventing theft. They're interested in making noise and drawing attention to their cars—something that gets harder to do as all cars move towards looking exactly alike.

So it becomes necessary to move the entire discourse to the obvious next level: discussions of how to discourage or get rid of alarms. Let's approach the problem calmly and professionally, tailoring our response to the relative gravity of the situation. The use of steam rollers, high explosives, and noise-seeking missiles, in other words, should be reserved for the absolute last resort.

Communication is always the first consideration in conflicts between our right to tranquility and some other dipnoid's obsession with inflicting manic shrieks and squawks. A best first step is a friendly note to the offender, drawing his attention to the problem and perhaps citing the salutary effects of quiet on the suburban organism. The note should be left in a spot where it will be easily seen, such as the roof or hood. The medium is clearly the message in such cases, so select your writing implement with care. I rather like using the awl attachment on my Swiss Army knife, held so that it protrudes between my clenched fingers. The "church key" type of can opener is also popular, but hard to control. Actually, it's hard to beat the plain old sixteen penny nail. And the price is right.

Of course there are now alarms that verbally accost innocent passers-by, making written communications beside the point. They are an example of what this is all coming to because they violate the very basic principle that cars should not talk smack to people. We rejected sexy Japanese girl voices telling us our fluid levels are low and don't really find even television fantasies of talking cars very funny (witness "My Mother the Car"). Uppity autos have no place in real American life. Even Christine managed to kill people without giving them any of her lip. If we ignore this development we'll certainly end up chatted up by smarmy homosexual cars like the one on "Night Rider".

The important thing in conversing with auto alarms is to be firm and to the point. If they say, "You are standing too

24

close to this vehicle" (which they do in a really bitchy manner) just ask "You mean this new Targa with the lighter fluid dripping off it and the guy fondling the Zippo?" We should point out that converting a car into a fireball is an excellent way to get it towed away. Flames are a fun and festive way to make a point. Just ask anyone in the Ku Klux Klan or Department of Alcohol, Tobacco, and Firearms.

If the alarm's opening gambit is, "Move away from vehicle at once," Just ask how far away you should be when the tires explode. Another remark that alarm-equipped cars seem to consider a nifty ice-breaker is, "System is armed". I wouldn't have it any other way. It would be truly unsporting to pump a clip of nine millimeter rounds into an unarmed system. We should be fair about these things, even though it's an obvious case of Man versus Machine, not to mention sheer Moloch Materialism. The important thing to keep in perspective is that even the lowest criminals among us have the right remain silent, so we should offer our neighbor's pretentious car the same right. In fact, we should insist.

The segment ran mostly because nobody was around by the time they got it edited, they had nothing else to go with, and Barry and Caitlin figured out it was the easiest way to make sure they never had to deal with Wiley ever again, ever.

"How hot will he be now?" Caitlin asked Barry.

"He's roadkill," Barry intoned, slurring only slightly. "Frisbee cat. History. Glad I'm not working the switchboard when the bitching comes in."

And as a matter of fact, the segment did light the switchboard up like a Tijuana disco. Drew more crazed email than sending your address to a Rolex retailer. Most of it positive.

It turned out everybody hates car alarms, even people who own them. One call from some lunatic, who sounded like Mel Blount doing a Daffy Duck version of the Terminator, demanded that Wiley demonstrate the fireball effect. All demanded more Wiley. But viewers, Justin pointed out to Yao, are not the same as advertisers. We have to keep in mind where our bread is buttered. Yao nodded, replied with a similar metaphor involving yakisoba.

Thom Barker, for whom Advertising Director was not only a lead position, but a calling, was emphatic that Wiley was a booster shot for Black Plague. "Do you know how many ads we sell from that whole sector?" he yelled at Justin. "It's not just alarms. Those same nice folks--who used to buy our time--also install stereos and accessories, do detailing, maybe also windows and trick rims and neon lighting, all kinds of stuff. It's a major industry, and we just told people to set fire to it!"

Justin had already told him that Wiley had been fired, this time for good, so he just held up a frail finger against the tirade of trouble, answered his insistently blinking phone. He listened, went into a puzzled trance, punched hold while telling his secretary to give the caller what he asked for. He returned a rather vacant gaze to the blustering Barker. Who raved more before realizing he wasn't getting through. "Who the hell was that?" he demanded.

Justin stared at the phone. "Oh, some guy named Hudson from Auto Sound Hut."

"See?" Barker screamed, "It's starting! You want alarms? I'll show you alarm on my sheet next week!"

The Mimosa ecosystem had a sound level that reacted to intruders just as any jungle reacts. The same way that a hardwood copse falls silent as a lithe predator glides through its undershadow, or a rainforest canopy erupts into the warning screeches of exotic birds and boisterous monkeys, the Mimosa was never unaware when a new phenotype entered their sphere.

The guy in the sharp suit didn't trigger more than the usual apprehension, but conversations fell to the level that allowed eavesdropping as he questioned Jerome. Who kept looking at the guy's face as he announced in a too-loud voice. "Who, Wiley? Well if he's expecting you, he'll probably be around pretty soon."

The guy hastened to explain that he hadn't made an appointment, exactly, just wanted to talk some business. While Wiley, four stools to the guy's left, raised his head from the cradle of a forearm damp with slopped-over mixer and brought his ever-shattered attention to bear on the guy in the suit. His motion drew the guy's glance and they made eye contact. Wiley slammed upright on his seat.

"Ack! Hey, look, Hudson, don't jump to conclusions, man. Tell Mel that sunroof thing was just sort of a trial run. I'm awaiting results right this minute. I was going to get it back to you this week." As the guy moved toward him, he invoked his ultimate invocation against harm, "We can work this all out."

"Good," the guy said. "Because Mel's got a contract for you. With One Shot."

CHAPTER FOUR

Rollie Moon slumped at his desk, plucking at his beard. He was bitching and whining on the topic, No longer much fun being editor of Southcoast Week, and arguably even worth it. He was getting no argument from Karin Chones. Called "Casey" around the Week, for obvious reasons as well as the generally accepted concept that she was the go-to editor when a story was a complete train wreck. Like so many female editors working under energetic chiefs, she was completely sold on Rollie and loyal to him unto death or even worse fates.

Attractive in a wholesome, pleasant way in her mid-thirties, Casey was tough as nails on the business end: ruthless with a blue pencil or telephone. Efficient, dedicated, and brassbound were words chosen by colleagues to describe her operating shell. Below that was a layer of soft, chewy nougat that many a social worker would scoff at as too candy-assed heart-bleeder. She would have taken whole countries home with her to mend their wings, breast feed them, and cry at their inevitable funerals. Deeper in was something harder to make fun of: the way-too-single heart of a childless mother hen.

She took care of the Week and wanted to take care of Rollie, but could see no way to do it without taking care of Hollis Ovarón. Or having him "taken care of", like they say. She nodded sympathetically as Rollie told her what she already knew, convinced her of what she had already stitched onto the red satin banner of her embattled conscience.

"Okay, he killed Bar Of The Week. And put in that church review column. I can live with that," Rollie allowed.

"Easier than I can live with him suddenly deciding he's an editor," Casey said, grimly. "Every time he 'improves' a piece by switching the lead paragraph down the page I want to break his fingers."

"Or shitcans a perfectly good title and replaces if with a line at random from the body of the text?"

"Or one of his idiot quotations," Casey nodded. "Who can forget, 'Go To The Ant and Consider His Ways', on that welfare cheater's confessional?"

"I keep coming back to, 'Put Away Childish Things', on the pedophile piece. Where does he *get* that stuff?"

Casey involuntarily scanned the wide windows that separated the editor's office from the cubicles of Editorial. Staff moved around the grey cubicle maze lazily, as though embedded in aspic. She told Rollie, "I hacked his computer. Password's 'Jehovah', by the way. He's got a program like a thesaurus, but if you put in a word, it returns a phrase from the bible or some come-to-Jesus meditations book."

"Jesus Christ."

"Too many responses to sort, I'd guess. But if you put in 'child abuse', that headline is the first thing that pops up. You also get 'Suffer The Children To Come Unto Me'. So it could have been worse."

"I don't understand it. Things were going fine for him. Kyle has the money side of the paper running like a clock, I had the content on a par with any weekly in the country. Why'd he suddenly decide to get hands-on?"

"Right after he got Born Again."

"Are there any term limits on Abort Again? He's killing articles we've already agreed to pay for. For no reason."

"Worse. There are reasons. Just not shown to mortals."

"What does that mean?"

"He killed the one about the community center because the councilman who proposed it opposes notifying girls' parents about abortions."

"You're kidding."

"Not one iota," Casey said grimly. She didn't kid around about her research. "There's an invisible minefield. Any connection he spots, however tenuous, to evil democrats or abortion and condom providers or companies linked to Satan."

"Wait, wait. Satanic companies? Like Starbucks and Microsoft?"

"No, like Proctor and Gamble. There's a whole underground of people who spot Beelzebub's holding companies. He's on several internet forums about it."

"That reminds me, Case. You're reprimanded for spying on the owner's computer. Don't you know too much Knowledge of Him could give you brain cancer?"

Casey smiled slightly. "Well, his screwing around with content and looting of the revenues to finance his church stuff is going to give us unemployment, anyway."

"Why do you think I'm sniveling about this? Editors are unemployable. I'm too old and spoiled to survive on the streets."

"And I'm too much of a ball-breaker to be a prostitute."

She and Rollie shared collegial smiles. But... Rollie went on, "What can we do about it?"

Casey shrugged, "Catch him in bed with a gerbil circus?"

"Hey, Wiley's on TV again like he said," Jasper chirped. "But it's in Spanish."

"Cause it's Channel Eighteen, ya dumbass," Cathilda laughed. "Beaner news."

"Switch over to Twelve," Strack grated. "Get the white man version."

"Say *what*?" Cathilda evoked a deep sense of personal and racial outrage. "Excuse *me*? Who you callin'?" She was running out of openers without coming up with a message, so she knocked it off as the channel clicked over to a string of commercials on NewsNight Twelve.

Five minutes later, Wiley appeared on the screen, just as they'd heard. He was standing in an urban parking garage, looking at the camera with bleary distrust.

"You know how I feel about noisy alarms," he said. "But the main thing is, they're useless. Observe." He stepped to a nearby Cadillac Escalante, hoisting a baseball bat he'd been holding below the range of the camera. With a leer at the lens, he slugged the bat down on the windshield of the Caddy, reducing it to a starburst of gleaming cubes. The soundtrack was inundated by the shriek of a car alarm.

"Hmmm," Wiley mused. "Doesn't keep me from doing this." He took a Barry Bonds swing, blitzing the side mirror off and into a line drive across the garage, where it hit another car, setting off more alarms. "Let's see what happens," he smirked.

A speeded-up clock graphic at lower right showed the elapsing of fifteen minutes while Wiley spoke to the camera in a forthright, engaging manner, "Wouldn't it be better to have some sort of remote alarm that, oh, say... rings in your pocket, instead of out here where you can't hear it and it just ticks people off? Something like this.."

He stepped over to a glossy Mercedes and rattled the door handle. Then he pointed to a logo on the windshield. A close-up read: ONE SHOT REMOTE ADVISORY.

"We'd better chill," Wiley said in a confidential undertone, and sat down behind another car, bat between his knees. He addressed the camera from that position, man to man. "Because you see, One Shot Remote doesn't make any noise. It doesn't have to. It lets you know wherever you are--in the office, in bed, in the movies--that somebody's messing with your car. You can even set it to vibrate instead of sound. It's a two stage alarm, the second stage activates if a door is opened."

A handsome, muscular young man in a suit entered, holding a small, elegant remote in his hand. He looked the car over, beeped it with the remote, patted the hood lovingly. Wiley stood up and looked into the camera. "One Shot: The kind of system even I can get behind."

Jerome clicked the set to mute while the bar applauded. Wiley stood up on the footrail, arms spread to accept their accolades. He raised a glass to friends present, tossed it off to more clapping and clinking of glassware. Jerome kept on working behind the bar, rolling his eyes at Wiley's performance. The phone rang and he picked it up.

"Hey, Limelight, " he yelled at Wiley. "It's for you. Some dweeb, says he's Justin."

Wiley sat, and none too comfortably, behind his own custom "desk", wearing make-up and an incandescent Hawaiian shirt. A screen behind him displayed the "Wiley's Weekend Warning" type and logo. As he addressed the microphone, the screen switched to a segment title, "Morning Becomes Electric". Thus spoke Wiley:

"So it's the Monday to set your clocks forward, yada yada yada. The government taking a little slice out of your sleep time again. I'll tell you how to give a little setback to a clock, but first let's examine our context here." His delivery had been understated, even wooden, but he was warming up.

"For those who haven't figured it out yet, this show mostly deals with things to do on weekends. And there's no doubt that many of you dutifully go out and knock yourselves loose doing all these strenuous and dubious activities. But really, when you get right down to it, what is the greatest benefit of a weekend?

"You got it: Sleeping In. Rolling over to pound the other ear instead of getting with some cockamamie program. Snoozing away secure in the hope that the six o'clock alarm will never ring. Knowing you don't have to shave when you do get up. And it would seem so little to ask of life; merely to sleep, perchance dream a little. But there are those that actually interfere with the simple and unalienable pleasures of sleeping in."

Suddenly Wiley, or something he'd ingested, was on. His face became pliable and expressive, his gestures fuller. He was cruising. Only three people knew that he was extemporizing. No script, just Wiley live.

"What sort of fiendish scum would do this--wake you before you are ready to go-go? Set pitfalls in the path of the beautiful dreamer? Let's examine several of these foul forces, devious devices, and eye-opening conspiracies--preparatory to calling for their speedy and brutal annihilation."

As he continued, a superimposed graphic informed viewers they could order a transcript of the show to read at home. A transcript that went on to say:

> Let's make it clear that we're not talking here about merely waking up in rude circumstances. That can be easily arranged. The easier you are, the more likely you are to wake up rude and rueful. But we're not blaming the victim here, we're after real culprits: outside agitators with no commitment to knitting up of your raveled sleeves. Disrupters, preemptors, agents provocateur of insomnia: Dreambusters.
>
> Take the simple alarm clock. Take it and bash it up against the wall. Good show. These ugly little devices, handy enough for ticking away the moments that make up a gray day, have forgotten their place in the scheme of things. They are trying not merely to tell time, but to make time, to arrange time, and with alarming frequency to seize the

time. Are you, a human being and the clown of creation, to be ordered about by a tiny (if noisy) pack of gears or quartz? I certainly hope not.

There are plenty of ways to put an uppity clock in its place. Some can be learned at hard-nosed martial arts dojos, many can be purchased over the counter along with the requisite ammunition. Or you can be creative: feed the clock to an alligator, stick it in a Polynesian dancer's navel, put it in a Russian Easter egg, run a few mice up it and see who salutes. Just don't take any crap off it.

The simple doorbell, while not as intrinsically treacherous as the phone or clock, can be coaxed into the ploy, made an unwitting instrument of some cabal opposed to the much-remarked wisdom of letting sleeping dogs lie. I'm sure you've experienced the following example of such behavior. You slowly claw your way into some form of consciousness, seeing without really comprehending that your clock said 5:25 right before you obliterated it to bits. You're not really integrated enough to grasp that it's Saturday morning, your stomach and mind are flitting queasily away from memories of Friday night--just three hours ago.

You dribble half your furniture over to the door and open without thinking (And why not, you've been doing everything else so far without doing what anyone would call thinking). There stand two drab women and three snot-nosed brats, chattering into your reamed ears that they are Jehovah's Witnesses. Eyewitnesses at that. Not an innocent bystander in the bunch. They hold a newspaper up to your parboiled eyes and what is splashed across the front page in red, 24 point type? "AWAKE!" Talk about fast-breaking news, huh? Their other paper is called "Watchtower" by the way...the same one Jimi Hendrix warned you against all along. These people are a menace.

Best way to defend against them is sleep nude and answer the door naked. This sometimes produces side benefits. Another household hint is to keep a stock of Hare Krishna, Mormon, and Satanist pamphlets by the door to pass out to such disruptors. But we're talking a sorry state of affairs. Namely, Rude Awakenings.

Your television set, which you generally regard as a pal--a bit pushy, perhaps, but essentially an entertaining, jolly good fellow--can get wicked on you. For instance, you nod off during Horrible Horror Theater and the National Anthem. You are blowing yourself some sweet Z's when a piercing tone brings you alertly to your lips. Just in time to hear them say they are leaving the air. But not to worry, they'll be back at 5:30 tomorrow morning. With a test pattern. Thus giving a rude awakening to some other fool.

Telephones are the worst yet. They can turn on you with no warning, jangling your entire nervous system just to sell you phone service. People call you up to tell you you're the wrong number and don't even tell you what the right number is. They enlist you in a sad and wide-eyed lottery of the lost. You can't be too careful with phones; they're like having a little doorway into your world where any deranged somnophobe can pop by and weird out right into your ear. They are surrealistic by their very nature, as we can illustrate with this telling anecdote. Your waterbed, ordered a month ago, finally splashes down in town. Therefore setting up a routine fiasco in which you grovel up from sleep to mug the phone in time to hear, "Hello, this is Dreamland."

Hello, this is Dreamland. The study of rude awakenings approaches the understanding of dreams. Since we are Americans, this treats of (need I say it?) the American Dream. The American Dream is, in many ways, merely to be allowed to continue dreaming. But the slumber party is being crashed. If this seems frivolous, let's not forget that the two-day weekend was first dreamed up right here in America. Earlier and elsewhere people slaved six days then went to church all Sunday. Sleeping in may indeed *be* the American Dream. And as the rude awakenings remind us, it is not a right but a privilege to be defended as zealously as any other perc. What other use is being part of a privileged class, eh?

As an American you have a right to the American Dream, so guard it carefully or you might just wake up one fine day and find yourself wide awake. Don't laugh, sleeping in is very political. Every four years we have some yo-yo coming on with the latest variation of "Wake Up, America!" Sometimes he offers the smell of coffee, other times nothing but the bleak shores of consciousness, as

34

though it was all a good thing, and somehow better for you than snoring off.

Forget these terrorists. The first sign of a fascist is a desire to raise your consciousness. Let's keep our heads, everyone: consciousness sucks. No cause for snooze alarm. Do not go gentle, fight against the dying of the night. Extremism in the defense of forty more winks is no vice. Guns don't kill people, but dropping by before noon on Saturday certainly should. Tune out, turn in, drop off. Dare to dream. Only trouble is--gee whiz, you'd be dreaming your life away. And the only way to deal with trouble like that is to sleep on it.

Talk about striking a chord. Nobody had ever heard anybody defend their right to goof off and sleep in before. Much less sanctioning violence in the matter. Wiley was in like Flynn's milkman and starting to look like a Great American. A dingy, erratic new star shone over the Station. He was washed in notoriety and media attention, overpaid by reflex, mentioned by jealous comedians. But did he take advantage of his new clout? Use it for evil or selfish gain? Come on, what do you think?

CHAPTER FIVE

Wiley's integration (or "worm-in" as Caitlin characterized it) generated different levels of approval in different sectors.

Caitlin clearly hated his guts. To include all offspring, inhabitants, liens, ancillaries and wholly-owned proceeds of said guts. Her loathing, in short, was complete and irreversible. She didn't confront him with a crucifix or anything, but the thought of a stake through his heart often infused her with bitter cheer.

Barry, when sober enough to think about it, merely thought it showed a lack of class and décor sense he had already detected in management and was kind and conscientious enough to memo Wiley some suggestions of tailors he thought might fit the income and comprehension range of a man who would appear on television with an off-rack, probably even pre-owned, tweed blazer over a knit shirt.

Mike and Linsey considered him the Cultural Attaché from Planet Fun, and loved committing his wacked-out remotes to digital archives. This infuriated Caitlin, who considered the team to be under her personal tutelage (a relationship Linsey expressed to Wiley as "her downriver AV niggahs") and saw their increasing assignment to Wiley as an act of outright theft.

Corelle, a genuine sweetie in a sea of phony intrigue, was receptive to Wiley's offer of pal-ship and willing to help him learn the business. The latter was of little help, since she didn't understand it much herself, mostly because she was, albeit in a lovely and gracious way, pretty stupid. The receptiveness was tested as soon as she let her guard down after a friendly beach walk led to stopping by the bar at World Famous and sampling some tequila shooters. Results inconclusive and not even very clearly recalled.

Yao, although bullish on Wiley futures, was violently averse to any sort of contact with him: physical, vocal, visual, or even whatever the adjective is for email. Wiley gave him the willies. Okay, Wirey gave him the "wearies". There.

This polarization of acceptance, camaraderie and *esprit* led Wiley to concentrate his drive to become an acquired taste in one direction where he sensed that his estimation could be increased: pert, pointy weathergirl Jammi Jamison.

Wiley took an oblique approach to that reversal. Jammi presented as squirrelier than Balboa Zoo on free peanuts day, but would be worth some angling because she walked around every day in a Five Alarm body. She might not have been the brightest girl ever to breach the walls of fame armed with raw ambition, a cute smile, and a highly-tuned, drool-friendly, aftermarket-equipped frame...but she pretty obviously knew what she wanted. Which was the usual: More. Wiley had already figured out that under the steely curves and airbrushed tan she was punched around by a clamoring briarpatch of neuroses. And that she was mainlining Exposure. It was just a matter of tinkering.

Wiley took the obvious shot of discussing her participation on his segment, and could see she wasn't biting. No problemo, it had just been a gambit. When she said she knew what he was after, he came back with, "Maybe what you should be thinking about is what *you* want?" That stopped her cold. She didn't remember a guy ever thinking about that before. In fact they generally dismissed the things she did want, while lunging towards her sleek and shinies.

Not Wiley. He produced her secret lusts like rabbits from a hat and waved them in her face. Preparing to go into production. Product placement with cute infomercial hostess. His own show with co-hostess. But then he said he could tell she liked doing weather and just walked off.

This was nothing Jammi's oddly under-sexed life had prepared her for. She was used to gym guys casing to see if her buff was as hard as theirs and unlikely to present any un-pretty sights during coitus. Since her pre-teen fumblings with boys, she'd kept naked males in the Ewwww! category, preferring a workout on the bars or mats to thrashing in back seats. The body she got the most pleasure from was always her own.

Of course she'd slept with suits to break into TV. Duh. But she hadn't fully explored the aspects of using men, and the idea that a guy she could screw for advancement might still offer something for her own nasty thrills was a novel one. And Wiley, she quickly realized, was a Star. It would be like fucking Barry or Caitlin, except messier and more normal.

It was three days before she managed to happen across Wiley's path and finagle him into paying her attention. His product thing was going pretty well, actually. He was evaluating one now that he thought was going to be the one to go with. Why

37

didn't she co-host his segment, see how it went?   Since she saw the offer more as a gesture of faith than bed bait at that point, Jammi agreed. And looked smashing in a white apron and cute, cocked chef hat while Wiley did a bachelor kitchen bit. She did things like open the microwave while Wiley scowled inside, commenting along the lines of:

As a technophobe and general reactionary, I bitterly resisted owning a microwave oven but finally got one when I found out they're not only faster, but healthier and energy saving as well. This seemed so counter-instinctual as to be Faustian. It was like learning that chocolate chip macadamia cookies are better for you than okra or tofu or similar members of the Nasty Slime Nutrient Group. Which is true, by the way; and you can tell any diet fascist who sticks their nose into your eating pleasure that you saw it on television so it must be a factoid. Hey, you watch my show; I can do that much for you.

So what happened after I got totally hooked on instant radar cooking? My microwave broke down. What does one do about *that*, I ask you? Replace the reactor core? Rebyte the hard-bitten drive? Reset the phasers? Call Dionne Warwick? I just threw it away—without ever having found out if it would really explode a poodle. And immediately went into cooking withdrawal.

How the hell do you get anything to eat without it, huh? Where do you buy stuff that the little trays won't melt in an oven? Who's got the time? No fear: I figured it all out and have prepared instructions for other bachelors who find themselves cold-turkey with only a conventional oven to heat it with.

1. Get hold of some meat, an edible substance constructed from used animals and widely available—in a range of colors and weights—at marked supermarket sections or special meat boutiques.

2.   Place the meat in a suitable container. "Suitable" mostly means "won't melt in an antiquated oven", but also, "won't leak hot grease".

3. Add vegetables if desired. The kind from cans are good, especially white or yellow ones, but not lettuce or that general kind of light-duty vegetable.

4. Here's your chance to get creative. Pour some liquids over the meat. The best liquids come from bottles stored in cabinets above eye level. These are edible, often tasty, and go very well with meat. Anything marked "Campbells" or "Picante" would be a good place to start. Never use liquids from cabinets below waist level with reindeer names like "Ajax", "Blitz", and "Comet"—they are frequently inedible and almost never tasty.

5. Turn oven on until there is a glow inside it. The switch that lights it up immediately turns out to take a long time to cook the meat, so use the round one, which takes longer to light up the oven but cooks faster in the long run. It has settings like "Bake" and "Broil", but no really fun ones like you'd find on a blender. Neither appliance can be set on "Stun". Not deliberately anyway. You can select numbers for your cooking. When faced with numbers, I usually choose the familiar ones associated with cars. Being a Chevy man, I've found 350 to work well. A friend has had less luck with 460, but that's Ford for you.

6. As with microwave cooking, the meat will be done when you hear electronic beeps, except that with so-called "conventional" ovens the beeps come from a remote detector on the ceiling. which mysteriously detects doneness. If your kitchen doesn't have such a timing device, you can use old fashioned methods, such as waiting for a canary to pass out.

7. Take the meat out of the oven, being careful to use a meat-lifting device (I like vice grips myself). The oven will usually have another switch just to blow the smoke away and let you see what you've been cooking (not always worth it). Allow the meat to cool: if you're in a hurry, just run it under cold water for a minute. Some sinks have neat little hoses like miniature hubcap-cleaner sprayers that make this easier and more fun. Cut the meat into sizable chunks and place the chunks on plates, the plates on tables. Kitchens are full of implements to deal with them from that point on. Dig right in.

Once basic techniques for baking (or broiling, if you selected that option) are mastered, it's easy to whip up dessert. Ovens are great for brownies, cookies or cakes— it's how the pros make them. Simply buy a box of readymix in the supermarket "Cake" aisle. Grease the pan if you have any grease laying around. (I usually find plenty inside the oven). Pour the powder into a pan and wet it down. Add some eggs if you find any. Put the pan back in the oven (which you have left on as a cleansing process that burns away any residue of the meat) and cook on 427 or 283 or whatever until it resembles the picture on the box.

Single guys liked the show but so did women, who saw it as an indication of the sort of things they're always whining about anyway. The ad department liked it because they'd pre-sold lines of appliances and TV dinners. Jammi liked it because it got a great rating, possibly due to promos showing her in the frenchy apron leaning over to peek inside an oven.

Wiley again avoided her until she stalked him down. She didn't realize that she was practically begging him to show her the new product he said would make him the new Ronco. He reluctantly worked her into his only spare moment. He'd be available for a few minutes after a location shoot. Just a film test for the product. He'd line up a spokesmodel if he decided to push this contraption. Get a good name for it. Brands like Pocket Fisherman and Kitchen Magician don't just fall out of the sky.

Jammi wasn't sure about the location, a spa motel called Jacque Coozie that notoriously provided rooms with hot tubs and generally conducive atmosphere. She noticed light stands and a tripod left in the room, assumed that the object on the floor draped in dark flannel was the Mystery Product. Wiley let her in, immediately returned to scanning panels of negatives, shaking his head and ignoring her. "The steam messes it all up," he groused. "We should have done it over at Borrego Springs."

"Hot tub stuff," Jammi asked, once she got his attention. "Is that it?

Wiley laughed dismissively. "Old hat, honey. This is just a location. Bad one at that. Drove me nuts trying to get decent shots." He returned to his skeptical examination of the proofs, then remembered Jammi was present when she sat on the table beside him. "Oh, yeah. Hey listen, did you bring a swimsuit like I said?" She nodded warily.

"Okay, okay," Wiley sighed, rubbing his neck. "Look, there's no model shot going on right away. I just wanted to see how you looked with the thing. Any more shoots get done elsewhere, maybe just in a studio. What the hell."

She looked at him expectantly. "So, yeah," he said while taking another look at the negs. "Why not slip in there and change? We'll see how you look."

When Jammi moved to the bathroom, checking the lock as she went in, Wiley stood and pointed to the other door. "Look, I'm all in knots. I'm going to take a soak before I do anything else. Join me if you like. We can talk for a minute while I unwind."

Jammi was double wary by the time she came out of the bathroom with an extremely minimal bikini plastered to her incredible form. She slipped into the hot tub enclosure to see Wiley lolling and rubbing his shoulders on the rim like a man with work cramps. As she entered he lifted a plastic glass and toasted her.

"Slither on in, the water's fine. I left you the best jet over there." He pointed with the glass. "This is great, actually. It'll get you, like, psycho/physio/spiritually prepared for the product itself."

It did look nice. Jammi slid into the water cushioned by her conviction that her strength, stamina, and kickboxing training would allow her to trounce Wiley's ass if he tried anything. Wiley rubbed some more, sighed. "Feels much better. Feel good for you, too?" He smiled, she nodded. "Great. But let's talk about where you want to feel good five years from now."

Jammi slowly relaxed. She noticed bubbles blowing out of holes in her seat, but kind of liked the feeling. The longer she laid there, sipping some sport drink Wiley had graciously handed her, the better it felt.

"What's in this MetaboLite, anyway?"

"Date rape drug," Wiley laconically replied.

"You put Roofing in my drink, you scumsack?"

"Nope, an Old School classic. Alcohol."

Actually, "caña", Mexican sugarcane alcohol of close to 190 proof; odorless, tasteless, and ever clear. No need to be subtle with Jammi, though. Essentially a clean-living athlete, she was a total, if not quite teetotal, lightweight. What you'd call a cheap date.

She indignantly started up out of spa, but slipped and bellybustered back into the water. The splash soaked Wiley, turning his cigarette into a limp paper turd stuck on his lip. She couldn't help but laugh. She splish-splashed some more, then told him, "Boy, when I sober up, I'm gonna kick your nuts off."

"Relax," said Wiley, totally unnecessarily. "Grab a shower. The product's in the next room waiting for your full, fine-tuned attention."

When she came out of the shower, wrapped in a big fluffy white towel, Wiley held up a robe for her like a perfect gentleman. When she slipped into the sleeves he cinched the belt around her waist. The shower, permanently set to warm and steamy, had done nothing to dispel the alcohol vapors that were hanging soft pink flock and strewing cushy pillows throughout the spongy lace halls of her medulla oblongata.

Wiley whisked the veil off The Product, which looked like a luxurious Harley Davidson saddle of sexy black fabric sitting on the floor. It was slit longitudinally like an old-fashioned bicycle seat. Even a saddle horn, with a circular ring around it to be gripped like a steering wheel. She examined it curiously.

"Is this another corny abs workout gadget? They all suck." She tapped her own tight six-pack to indicate what could be done with equipment Not Seen On TV.

"Not really," Wiley said, showing her a remote control device. "Watch this."

He touched the control, the saddle hummed, an inch-thick rod with a familiar bulbous taper emerged slowly from the center slot, extended to a height of about four inches, then withdrew into the slit.

Jammi goggled, then giggled. "Hey, that's obscene! You'll never get that on the air, Mister." Which was a pretty hilarious thought, sending her into sloppy laughter.

"Just on cable channels, where the real money is. You know, like Playboy."

Ah, that was a name to conjure with. Jammi's interest in The Product soared.

"But it has to be experienced to be truly appreciated," Wiley purred. "You're looking at the next great exercise fad. You must be dying to give it a test drive."

Well, matter of fact. Out of sheer curiosity, if nothing else. Jammi stepped over to the device, hesitated. What do you do with this thing? Wiley moved to her, positioned her astride it and gently sat her down. She knelt, then settled onto the saddle, the robe curtaining her legs. At Wiley's urging she leaned forward and grasped the pommel ring.

"It's all in this patented control box," Wiley spieled. "I've already dialed in lubrication, so..." He touched a button and Jammi eeped as the rod slid smoothly up, bumping against her bare pudenda.

"You're probably noticing the fail-safe feature," Wiley continued, "Just like an elevator door. Wouldn't hurt a flea."

Jammi wriggled a little to accommodate the gently insistent dildo and oohed as it slid into her. Then out. Then back in, without the pause this time. Slowly but surely.

"This blackbox has more control parameters than a 747," Wiley told her. "You can replace the business end you're currently experiencing with whatever differently sized and shaped interfaces you care to face up to. You can also modulate the thrust amplitude..." He touched the box and Jammi felt the next cycle of the rod move into her much deeper. She was starting to think this gizmo might sell a few copies.

"Oops, don't overamp that thrust," she tittered. She could envision the infomercial possibilities of this little item, all right. This was how sex was meant to be. No teamwork needed, no sweating and slobbering. Just another body workout on a machine. The Naughtylus, they could call it. Or how about SoloFux? She chortled.

"That about right for you?" Wiley asked solicitously. Jammi nodded, her head staying down after the nod. "And there's this popular parameter, labeled Frequency."

At his touch the rod started moving faster. Not too fast, though. And not too slow. Just fucking right. After a minute or so she decided a little faster might be better yet. She was leaning forward against the "steering wheel" by then, eyes closed, the robe slipping off her shoulders.

"How many speeds has it got?" she asked in a soft moan.

"Enough to get the job done," Wylie assured her quietly. He moved the frequency up another notch and when Jammi gasped, he stepped to her and gently tugged away the robe, tweaked away the towel. He hung them over a chair and sat down in it, lost in contemplation of the hard, glistening glory of Jammi's high-maintenance body. He dialed on a few more rpm's, which seemed to do her a power of good.

In a low, calm voice he said, "Then there's things like the degree of twist." Another touchwheel tweaked and Jammi's eyes popped open, swimming. She glanced at him without seeing him. She'd never felt anything remotely like that before. Wiley decided to leave it on Twisteroo for awhile. SpiroGyra and Corkscrew could wait.

He lounged in the chair fiddling with the remote like a kid with a radio controlled airplane, sending Jammi's wondrous little frame through loops and spins and interior immelmans.

"This is the Double Time cadence," he announced as she whimpered. "And here's the Deep Burn sequence. Or how about, Long Climb To Summit?"

Jammi drifted in and out of consciousness, powergliding through golden clouds of sensation. And started feeling something else she wasn't used to and therefore hadn't yet learned to recognize as the swelling chords of a powerful orgasm. When it washed over her the reaction of her springy muscles almost drove her right off the machine, but Wiley had learned a lot about the remote by then and worked her like Hemingway playing a lunging marlin. She felt another orgasm build, then break over her like a thunderstorm. A few more burst pyrotechnically in her brain and she slumped forward, one cheek on the carpet, her hips still twitching in an absent-minded rhythm. She felt so good she just wanted to cry. No man she'd ever been with had ever cared how she felt about the whole shennanigans, if *she* got off. As Wiley shoved the saddle aside, knelt behind her, and slished into her, she felt her automatic response and could only think, "This is just so *sweet*!"

Wiley, plundering her hard, chiseled curves, was thinking pretty much the same thing.

The next morning she woke up from the deepest sleep she could ever recall. She stretched like a creamed cat, feeling wonderful beyond her experience. Then she touched Wiley and realized she'd awakened with a colossal pain in the ass.

No: literally. She had a good idea what the twinge she felt "back there" meant and shook Wiley awake with accusatory abruptness. "Did you do what I think you did? *Where* I think you did?"

Wiley shrugged, "I'd have asked permission, but you'd passed out."

Her luxuriant aura forgotten, she started whacking him anywhere she could reach. But he surprised her--yet again--by moaning, "Could you use that whip over there?"

That stopped Jammi in her tracks. She'd heard of such things, of course. But... "You mean you enjoy this?"

"Not *this*, so much, but the general idea."

Jammi went and got the whip and came back to the bed, where Wiley had rolled on his stomach and pulled the sheets down to expose his rump. She hesitated.

"Is there any special way you're supposed to do it?"

"Just follow your instincts, kid."

She gave an experimental lash, which Wiley responded to, but not all that gratifyingly. She tightened her grip, moved to bring more personal-trained muscles into play and laid a stinging cut across both buttocks. There was no mistaking his reaction to that. Jammi paused, delectable little naked morsel with big black whip, and pondered.

"So that hurt?"

"Oh, yeah, come on."

"And you like it?"

"What gave you that idea?"

"Well, then" she said, dwelling of the unauthorized ache in her own nether regions, "You're just going to *love* this."

Later she found out she liked it, too. All in all, it was a pretty impactive twelve hours in Jammi Jamison's sex ed. Even Wiley learned a few things. Like how it feels when somebody doesn't respect your orifices less traveled.

The odd thing was that their affair continued for several months. Less surprising is that it just got nastier, kinkier, and more damaging. Who knew?

(Ans: Anybody Wiley could get to listen.)

CHAPTER SIX

Naturally, Jammi wasn't the only starstruck young hottie to experience the full benefits of Wiley's peccadilloes. His weekend segment was drawing a larger audience share (with concomitant ad rate engorgement) and expanding under its own momentum. The sales staff pressed for more restaurant reviews, consumer products reeled under Wiley's bleary gaze, interviews with celebrities created more of the catastrophe that viewers were learning to love. As a new local icon, Wiley was finding that attractive women would go out of their way (if not minds) to be seen dining, sporting and smiling with him. His attempts to take advantage (curb your shock) of this advantage led to mixed, even scrambled, results, but a degrading time was had by all. His ideal segment during his honeymoon with the public eye would be something like a free dinner in a great restaurant with some cheerleader or bikini contest winner, followed by trench warfare. One dreary example: the segment he called "**Thai Dai**."

In case it hasn't been brought to your attention before, restaurant critics are jive. Taking on fuel is vital to weekend funquests and the restaurant reviews help you find edible food about as well as those movie critic cretins help you find a flick worth watching. For one thing, restaurant critics are totally ignorant of the three basic food groups: intoxicants, bodily fluids, and chocolate chip cookies. Secondly, they are always suggesting weird stuff to eat instead of normal, muscle-makin' fun foods. For instance, they are big on ethnic restaurants. Not your normal ones either; there is, after all, a well-defined line between the exotic and the alien.

Well, we aren't going to start a restaurant reviewer review here, because somebody would just review *that*, then there'd be a review to the fourth power and where would it all end, I ask you? But neither are we going to waste your time mentioning eateries like the newly opened Sock Mow Yo Ying, featuring authentic Vietnamese dishes from the sixties. Like what? Cold Rice Dinky Dau, Black Market K Rations Fu Loi, and Rat Napalme? Nor will you presumably be bummed to miss out on a critique of that new Somali restaurant. No menu there, folks. You get nothing to eat and have to have a rock concert to pay for it. Forget the all-tofu spread at No Fun Chow. We'll also slide over the new wave of hybrid cuisine, like kosher Japanese at Sosumi or Mexican soul food at Nacho Mama.

Where we will go is to House of Bangkok. Now a mature, sophisticated writer like myself wouldn't think of making funny little puns on a name like that. Nor would we spin out a bunch of lame japes like "Thai one on", the sort of thing you constantly see the reviewers from the daily papers doing. Food is serious business, old chump. Without it, where would you be? You are what you eat and, need we add, if you don't you ain't.

My dining companion drew the usual stares. She was, after all, voted Miss Tarzana, California not too many years back. Back before she fell into reduced circumstances, diminished alternatives and (I hasten to add the obvious) disreputable company. Not that being a restaurant reviewer groupie is the end of the line or anything, but hardly what we would desire for our own loved ones, is it? Nevertheless she gets by quite fine, thank you, except for the obnoxious little trait of occasionally swiping food from my plate after distracting me with gambits like telling me a wrecker just drove by followed closely by my car, or pretending to spot celebrities like Vanna White. Which wouldn't be so bad, except that she often replaces the remnants of such portions if they don't suit her jaded tastes. Which in turn wouldn't be so bad if she didn't wear thick coats of raspberry lip gloss.

She also disappointed me severely when I discovered that she had no tiger skin lingerie. Apparently Tarzana, the city, has nothing whatever to do with Tarzan, the former matinee idol (and a seminal influence on my own philosophy and table manners.) Of course these minor failings are a small price to pay for getting to eat (not to mention sleep, shower and inventory lingerie) with a former beauty queen. But enough of my companion's shortcomings, on with the chow.

We began by noshing (now there's a Yiddish word for you, like snot-about-town Marlys Langdon and all those hipper-than-thou New York transplants over at the Union Tribune might use at any time. We're not completely uncultured over here in Electronicland you know). Noshing, as I say, on a chilled plate of celery and carrots (cunningly carved to resemble orange french fries, though this is probably done with some Occidental device like a Kitchen Magician or router) dippable in a delicious mixture provided for that purpose. A mixture, so they tell me, of peanut butter, oil, and other ingredients the nature of which I was too wise to press them for. Oil and peanuts or not, it's exceptionally tasty. Make sure you get some. If they fail to provide some, make a scene. Loudly mention the name of a reviewer for NPR, or even the mucoidal Ms. Langdon. See what it gets you.

Every time I go to a Thai place I mean to order something new, but I never do. I always get Nam Man Hoi because it's so fine. I recommend it. In fact, I insist. It's in oyster sauce, which is one of those Eastern ideas that works out much better than it sounds, like Tantric sex. And contains mushrooms, bamboo shoots, scallions, either chicken, beef, or pork, and those scrumpy little tiny corn on the cob dealies that used to fascinate you back before you lost your capacity for fascination—ones you snitch piles of from salad bars every chance you get. And if that doesn't do it for you, for a buck more you can get it with shrimp. Need I say more? How many in your party? Smoking or non?

My faithless companion, the queen of former beauty, had the Paht Grapow (and, I've reason to believe, a substantial share of my chicken.) It's a choice of chicken, pork, shrimp or (of all things) squid, cooked in a garlic and mint sauce with red chilies. She seemed to like it, judging by the sounds she was making, but I can't tell you for sure because she was too stingy even to give me any. Can you believe it? Hell with that bimbo, just get the Nam Man Hoi. Or perhaps the huge shrimp in garlic, pepper and curry sauce. Or when was the last time you had duck salad, complete with lemongrass dressing and cashews? All reasonably priced, probably due to the fact that life is cheap in the Orient. (Or anywhere for that matter.) And they have fried bananas and coconut ice cream for dessert. Can you stand it? Now that's exotic. (An alien dessert would be squid ice cream. There's a place for each mollusk and every mollusk should be in its place, I always say. Frequently, anyway.)

One major point at the Thai places (and I want to stress this) is not to miss out on the Thai Iced Tea. It's way better than Caucasian iced tea. For one thing, it has cream in it. Never thought of putting cream in iced tea, did you? That's because you haven't been around for thousands of years and Thai culture has. Not that it would make any difference if you had been, because you'd probably have spent those formative thousands of years hanging around McDonalds and Video Arcades anyway and ended up just as uncultured after all. But that's your problem. There are other ingredients in the tea, one supposes. They are secrets. And inscrutability counts heavily in Asia. The point, however, is simple and well-taken. Namely, *do it*...get the damn tea. Why is that so hard for you to grasp?

Don't expect fortune cookies. The Thais do not make them. Neither do they make televisions or tennis shoes or boomboxes or motorcycles. No crackbrain management theory books either, come to think of it. Nor do they subject us to sneak attacks, religious fascists, or military embarrassments like some Oriental countries I could mention. For Asians, the Thais are really not a bad sort at all.

If I had even one small complaint about the House it would be that some of my chicken seemed a bit nibbled and had a pronounced raspberry taste, which clashed with the other flavorings. And now that I come to think of it, I also wonder what made me think that Vanna White would be doing in a restaurant full of names nobody could possibly spell.

The trouble was, although Wiley liked running with foxy stuff, he was finding that though they might bask in his fame, laugh at his remarks, tolerate his touch, and just cream on paparazzi and club ropes falling away as easily as shoulder straps, they often balked later on. Like when they saw him naked. Or, when dark enough or drunk enough to get by that, many would bail out as soon as he proposed some of his more refreshing ideas of what to do to them. Narrow-mined twits, was his assessment: all show, no go. They shouldn't wear thongs if they've never seen a vibrating butt plug before.

At a level somewhat removed from such monkeyshines, however, it was hard to tell if Wiley was having his beastly way with the ghost in the machine that was Channel Nine's management, or vice versa.

His value as pied piper to disaffected, prime-aged news viewers considerably cheered "Boo" Yao, but it was not unalloyed cheer. He had seen Wiley's potential and glommed him up, not without an eye to cutting himself in, probably with some sort of syndication scheme. But more immediately, it would take five months for the increased viewership to show up on the sweeps and translate into ad dollars. And Wiley was just one bright spot, standing alone on a burning deck.

The station was doing all right, as stations go, but Yao was in charge of making it do better. And, being an accountant, he didn't know how to increase quality of output or generate markets. What he knew how to do was cut costs. He was unapologetic for his professional myopia. "If somebody doesn't count the beans," he often intoned in purest Pidgin, "Nobody get to make any dip." He'd already figured out how to juice the bottom line at Nine. And they weren't going to like it.

It wasn't a totally new concept, but Yao had more or less figured it out himself. He greatly admired the phenomenon of automated radio stations. No people around, maybe one person on duty at a time, the rest just feed being transferred and repeated. A CPA's dream: no personnel, no moving parts. Yao himself listened to computer-based broadcasts of elevator music and Chinese classics. He had once paid a technician to set up a program that generated loops of samisen music and Taiko drums.

He had recently been made aware, through inquiries, that the technology was at hand to automate TV stations. All national feed and syndications, everything handled by software, national ads and infomercials sold by internet quotes and automatic responders. A station that would literally run itself. The ideal destiny for the independent station: total dependency. Sayonara expensive management types, production staff, all those useless drones. Direct jack-in of viewers to The Market.

He'd convinced the shadowy owners of his scheme, but they were now, ironically, hung up on the possible potential of Wiley to turn the station around. And there was the matter of having to have a news desk. A local news show has almost nothing to do with informing people of anything. It serves two functions: entertainment and providing the channel a reason to exist. The only thing distinguishing a network station in Boston from one in San Diego is that the news show is different. And what's different about it is the personalities of the news readers. The news is the public face of a station. Yao fumed that the faceless station of his dreams had to be so mired down in the smell of greasepaint, but it seemed to be a reality he had yet to overcome.

He was seeing that the national news is a feed, requiring no local input. But local events and sports needed to be handled locally and reported through personalities that could be pimped to viewers desperate to relate to the world through the synthetic families and neighbors conjured up on their screens. TV news helped keep the personality of the *viewer* from merging into statistically randomized smoke.

He'd explored having robots like the ones in Disneyland read the news. He'd investigated having local news fed by scraggly street stringers and read by vocalization programs over pre-filmed composites of actors. He was working on it.

Oddly enough, the events that would kick Yao into high gear in his plans to liberate Channel Nine from the bother of paying wages and withholding were taking place across town in the austere offices of Southcoast Week, one of those "hip free weeklies" that every city has, sucking up ad revenue like sponges while cluttering the streets with the inevitable litter of anything given away for free in big stacks everywhere.

The jump from impending "improvements" at an electronic medium to internal struggles at a print news organ might require a little background. Fortunately, the history of the paper and the convulsions that soon would wrack it are readily available.

Southcoast Week was started up in the early eighties, part of the wave of free publications that swept the country during that odd, stunted decade. As ad buyers stopped laughing at "readership" figures offered instead of paid circulation, piles of tabloids in every outlet provided passers by with the opportunity to become secondary litterbugs, and circulation departments no longer had to fool with carloads of pocket change: the handout urban tabloid carved out a nice slice of the American Eyeball and charged through the American Nose to access it.

Eudora Ovarón conceived the idea of launching a weekly in San Diego after a Sunday Brunch at the Hotel Del Mar, during which East Coast friends scoffed at the ludicrous quality of the San Diego Union Tribune, not-so-arguably the worst big city daily in the country. Possibly, her sophisto buddies theorized, in several countries. "The only Sunday paper I've ever been able to read in less than ten minutes," one Brahmin sneered. "You must have done the crossword puzzle?" her New York chum inquired solicitously. And further snotty remarks of that general complexion. Humiliated by proxy, and fired with that menopausal itch To Do that afflicts many women recently widowed by overbearing, tedious millionaires, Eudora decided to become a latter day Media Mogul.

Her nitwit son, Hollis, the only fruit of her acerbic loins and such a disappointment that her deceased hubby had not only estranged but disinherited him, had also borne heavily on her mind of late, an equally fertile source of humiliation. He had found that his chosen career as a motivational speaker was stony ground for an insecure, dithering nebbish, and had developed a tendency to mope. And not pay bills. Surveying the structure of the Union Tribune, Eudora come to the obvious conclusion that being a publisher would not be beyond her son's grasp.

Her shrewd survey of the publication world also led her to realize, as many editors never do, that an urban weekly is not really a newspaper, but a magazine. The whole slate of features and departments is more like the classic monthly and there is no way a weekly paper can compete at news dissemination with a daily paper, much less television and internet. She also realized that the work itself would quickly bore both her and Hollis, so she made two key hires and told them to set up a paper.

Kyle Albedo came highly recommended as a personable, efficient, ruthless guy who could run an advertising staff in his sleep and lusted for total control over the financial end of an enterprise. That, and his aunt was a member of her meditation circle, back when she was into that instead of media barony. She told him what she wanted, he nodded and told her he was all over it. And he was.

Rollie Moon came to her attention because his meandering route through the media world had led to a stint editing Vision Quest, the local new age forum. Fresh out of Berkeley with radical ideas, a thirst for news, and a taste for high-grade marijuana, Rollie dropped into San Diego because it was close to prized surfing haunts in the Baja. He worked for some weekly papers, but drifted along the stream of his interests, editing a surf paper called RipCurl, then one named Baja Highway. By the time he got caught by that treacherous undercurl striking free spirits when they start wanting to be able to rent their own place and date women their own age, he moved from X Stream to Jox! to Vision Quest, selling newsbreaks on the side and writing water sports for national mags.

When she asked him how he might go about creating a weekly paper for San Diego he told her, "Copy the LA Weekly, but dumb it down." She hired him on the spot, installed him and Kyle in a storefront with a luxurious office for herself and Hollis. Southcoast Week came forth as a weekend events calendar and blossomed into a stylish money machine under Rollie's talent and Kyle's solid husbandry. Leaving Eudora free to follow her muses; gallivanting off to Oahu, Sedona and Santa Cruz as a Buddhist of the Dalai Lama/Naropa stripe.

Hollis also turned to religion, leaving the mundane affairs of the paper to others while immersing himself in his wife's stern, hysteric faith. A fetching, stubborn girl who came to his door with rants and pamphlets regarding her Church of the Devine Covenant: Victorious, she essentially badgered the publisher into marrying her and knocking her up fairly continuously. And into devotion to the ephemeral and subterranean springs of her collection of loosely-linked churches of direct revelation. Everything was fine until the latest in her string of spiritual coaches harangued Hollis for not using the power of the vessel the Lord had entrusted unto his hands in order to further the Good Work. At which point the inevitable clash with his staff would not be long in coming.

Meanwhile, across town, fiscal types at Channel Nine had given up on controlling Wiley himself: they recognized a force of nature with upstairs juice when they saw it. They were trying to firewall him away from infuriating, and thus alienating, their advertising base and viewership in general while diverting his destructive genius into something more like a smelting furnace and less like a brushfire.

That the aging staff had lost touch with that base was made obvious by early July. San Diego was no longer Omaha by the Sea, populated by retired admirals, rich widows, mellow surf pappies, and descendents of Okies and Wetbacks. The real estate crunch was fueled by an exodus of young people escaping the horrors of the Rust Belt, then whining because they couldn't get good pizza or bagels or off-Broadway or nihilism out here in paradise. The old Spanish homes were giving way to condos crammed with two childless wage-earners: a spoiled and fickle lot. They wanted their media features and nobody was giving it up on TV, so they shopped for it. Many had liked Caitlin and Jammi, watching them with the volume off while listening to Enya or blues or Bulgarian Chicken Chokers or whatever was hip. They dug Wiley and no other station in San Diego had anything like him.

Nevertheless, the staff had serious conniptions over Wiley's inimitable take on children in a segment he termed "**I Kid You Not**". He started off grousing about kids running amok in restaurants, then zoomed off into:

> So before you even go into that whole "Well, of course, you're a single guy...." thing, let me dismiss the concept that the presumably childless rate low on philoprogenitiveness, while marrieds dote on them. That pedophobes are all bachelor types like me and W.C. Fields (a patron saint of kidmudgeons) and Ted Bundy. Not so. If you really want to hear the lowdown on just how lowdown kids are, talk to parents. The typical mother will go on for hours about exactly and specifically how rotten her brood can really be.
>
> The only people who like kids are grandparents. In fact, I get the impression that the only thing kids are good for is to produce grandkids. Well, fine, it gets the crumb-crushers and fuddy-duddies together and hopefully shuffles them off to Seaworld or an alligator petting park or wherever...out of the hair of us funlovers. Over the river and through the woods with them, I say.

Many parents, however, are too foolish either to have arranged to have grandparents or to lateral the rug-rats off to them. They haul their progeny into restaurants, theaters, and whatall, inflicting upon the rest of us the sounds, odors and sights of their interior functioning. There they are, cramming stuff into the kids, oblivious to the fact that it will inevitably come out again, in one or more of several nauseating forms.

What happened to babysitters? I remember them from my own youth (and I hasten to add that I was not like kids today...I was a screaming little pox, such as to shame the current state of badness.) Fraulein Dachau, clad in black Spandau Spandex and somatizing us with Teutonic detachment. Mary Poppings, the teeny popper next door who just showed up, turned on and dropped off, often leaving her stash within reach. Good old Nanny Goat, the mustached softball jock who fungoed us around the flat at any hint of insurrection. Ah, where have those dear ladies gone when we need them?

Still, there *are* methods of making kids quiescent: it requires only the sand to employ them. I myself prefer taxidermy, the ultimate seen-and-not-heard treatment, reducing the tykes' needs to an occasional dust and wax. But a bit extreme, evidently, for today's permissive parents. Next best is to reduce the little rodents to a state of stark terror, shaking lest their next breath be sufficient to cause them unimaginable grief and butchery. This gets harder to do with each generation, but parents with the proper mettle will pull it off. Try reading this column to them and mentioning that I run a summer camp for the young, incorrigible, and edible.

Another nostrum that works wonders is drugs. Something mild like morphine or St. Joseph's Kwayludes for Kidz. The right dose produces a comatose calm and zombielike compliance that is marvelous to behold. Of course there are those wienies who object to giving kids narcotics, but if they don't learn about it at home, they'll just pick it up on the streets.

And speaking of the street trade, kids can always be sold off. There are still plenty of buyers out there who will pay a good price for kids in decent condition, particularly Arabs, white slavers and cults that worship Charlie Sheen.

You can expect to get less from dog food manufacturers and the little nippers are impossible to unload at garage sales, church bazaars or eBay.

The beach offers excellent advantages to disciplining the age-challenged. For instance, it is literally child's play to entice a child to dig a big hole in the sand. And it takes no more than a hint to get the child in the hole. Some of them snivel a bit at the idea of then having the hole filled in up to their necks, but most can be made to stand still for it, either with imaginative role-playing games or threats--they are, after all, very small and in the bottom of a hole. Once this is accomplished it is easy to monitor the child's movements. If it gets bored, tell it a story. A good choice might be something about the awesome powers of nature. Tides, for instance. Any blubbering, wailing or gnashing of gums at this point is easy to counter. Upend an icechest over the kid's head and have a seat. This will ward off sunburn as well as unseemly behavior.

It is just as easy, actually, to bury the little buggers butt upwards, and use them as bicycle rests, since kickstands don't work very well on the sand. But that's getting into material reserved for my upcoming book, "Uses for Dead Kids". It's a big break for the little snifflers...could do for them what a similar book did for cats.

For more ad hoc control situations, I recommend sporting a shoulder holster containing a squirt gun loaded with my special blend of equal parts household ammonia, itching power, laughing gas, and Navy surplus shark repellant. Write to the address on the screen for a copy of "Wiley's Arsenal of Misogyny."

But there is no final solution to the kids problem. Some of our most cherished activities, such as drinking, driving, and sex, create them. Like herpes, they can't be cured, only controlled. So would whoever is in charge of the little bastards please CONTROL THEM?

It wasn't like nobody had seizures over the segment, or called in to protest at the Station, the cops, the state legislature, the FCC, the Council of Churches. But by and large the buzz was highly positive. Yuppies and lofties prided themselves on not being Ward and June. They were actually closer to Ozzie and

Harriet than Ozzie and Osborne, but didn't permit themselves to realize it. They were the first generation in history to be terrified of turning into their parents and at some level they realized that the quickest way to do that would be to have children. Anti-kid rhetoric thrilled them; a klaxon call to freedom. Bloggers were elevating Wiley to God-like status and a punk band named themselves Wiley Wiley Bobiley. The Demographic Side was strong with that one, and the station was starting to own it. And figuring out how to sell it.

CHAPTER SEVEN

Just go diddle a few little boys under your spiritual care and nobody ever wants to let you forget it. Much less move quickly on to the healing process. Nevertheless, you have to try whatever spin control you can pull off. That was the situation, however vicarious, that faced Hollis Ovarón when a cute little nipper attending day care at his Church of the Almighty Embrace became so filled with holy spirit that he decided to save his little sister's soul. When his parents found the two of them naked in an empty bathtub performing some extremely unwholesome acts with wide-eyed piety, then got back under enough control to interview them sensibly and find out these activities were considered sacraments down in the Church basement, they reacted predictably. Leading to several serious assaults, multiple arrests, batteries of attorneys and, worse yet, battalions of journalists.

There wasn't much Ovarón could do to comfort his afflicted brethren--his lawyers went so far as to say he'd be out of his mind to even contact with them--or to stop the flow of televised pictures of pederast deacons being perp-walked and sinister upshots of the church façade. But he could bygosh keep it from happening in his own paper.

Rollie had scored pretty well on the story, gaining interviews with overlooked ex-menial workers (aided, true, by Casey's looting of their chief's computer) and connecting the local outrages to the Church's national organization and missions abroad. Jazzed on having an inside hook to a national scandal, Rollie wrote an article on the preliminary evidence and plunged into deeper investigation. Imagine, then, his reaction upon coming in the morning after a late night salvage session by Ovarón, flipping on his computer, and scanning a front page layout on which his story had been removed in favor of the rambling confessions of a gambling addict who pissed away his life at the Viejas tribe casinos but found it again in Jesus. Casey described that reaction as "intercontinental ballistic" and she was right up there with him in geosynch orbit. Rollie's first coherent remark to her was, "Stop the presses." What they actually stopped was Everything.

Hollis Ovarón was about as oblivious as people can get without weeding themselves out of posterity by walking into traffic, but when he entered the Week offices at his usual straight-up ten, clutching his morning newspaper and double-tall pumpkin latté, even he tumbled to the fact that something was awry. Far from bending to tasks on their monitors, the staff clustered in sullen clumps, treating him to hostile stares. Roland Moon was standing at his office door like a Western gunslinger, flanked by Casey, who had the look of a woman who has whiled away hours whetting a kitchen knife in anticipation of her faithless husband's return from a tawdry tryst. His staff formed into a double cordon, creating a gauntlet of eyewitnesses leading from the front door to Rollie. He had no idea what was going on, but felt a deep desire to turn around and flee.

Nevertheless, he walked the gauntlet of pissed-off personnel, approaching Rollie in a showdown scenario so stereotypical that he imagined he heard a drum roll and Morricone flute bleats. He was at a loss for an opening comment ("Fill your hand, varmint," seeming appropriate to the mood and choreography, but not the costume and set). He was spared fumbling for his end of the toughguy dialogue when Rollie, in a calm and neutral voice, told him that he had reset the front page and sent the paper to the printers. Being incapable of decisions, he had fortunately faced few decisive moments in his life. But he had a quick glimpse of a forking of paths, one of which was a yellow brick lane marked Least Resistance Ave. and available by merely nodding pleasantly and schlepping off to his office. Instead he drew himself up and said, "I changed that page for a reason. Call the printers and tell them to wait for new boards."

Rollie showed a better grip on terse talk: he just said "No."

Which ground Ovarón's gears to a halt. What do you do when an inferior refuses your orders? Have them shot? Option them up and have them torn down? It was just unthinkable. He stared at Rollie, noting for the first time subtle earmarks of a man who has pandered his soul to the forces of darkness. He had to be strong in the face of it. He tried to be offhand as he said, "Fine. I'll call them myself. We need to talk in my office." God knows what he would say in there. What was wrong with everybody today?

Casey flashed up his face like a highway flare. "You don't censor the news, Hollis!" she yelled, setting him back a step. "You don't try to keep people from finding out what happens. This is a newspaper."

"It's not like people aren't watching it on the tube, anyway," Rollie pointed out. "Your best bet is to roll with it, not make things worse by having a fascist attack."

A chorus of grumbles and dissent from the staff, who had closed into a semi-circle like junior high boys waiting for a fistfight to jump off, backed Rollie up and alerted Ovarón for the first time that he was in the middle of a major conflict. He grasped for mutiny-breaking techniques. Captain Bligh had good ones; but where did it get him? What had the Citizen Caine guy done about this sort of thing? He took a breath and intoned, "I am the publisher... and owner, don't forget... of this paper. I have final say over content. We will go with the gambling story. Please get back to work at once."

"Forget it, Hollis!" Rollie snapped. "We're professionals. Unlike you. We can't work like this, covering things up to save your babyraper buddies."

Well, there it was. Ovarón hadn't actually heard it put that way yet, though he should have known it was coming. Those fine men of God being tarred and feathered, and he himself drawn into vile accusations. He jerked from reflex. "You are fired, Moon. Everybody else... get back to work or you'll be out the door right behind him. I won't tolerate this sort of false witness."

"Fine with me, " Casey snapped. "I'm with Rollie on this. We all are. If you want to even *have* a paper, you'd better get off your high horse and start using your head for something besides a halo roost."

The staff, stiffened by her stance and caught up in solidarity, shouted similar sentiments and started moving forward. No specific purpose, just the amoeba logic of a mob. They pressed in around Ovarón, yelling insults and demands. They touched him! He reacted to that in the way his whole life had trained him to: he lost it. He spun free of the crowd, running away towards his office with his paper and coffee. In another mob reflex, they moved after him, their voices louder and shriller. Ovarón had the impression of torches in their hands, stakes and hammers. Probably even sickles. With the shrewd instincts of born prey, he ran right into a blind corner. Surrounded and stymied, he exercised another prerogative of mindless flight, moving higher. He jumped on a chair, then a desk. It wasn't enough.

Standing on the corner file cabinet, gaping down at the baying mob, Ovarón trembled as he spoke into his cell phone, "Mother? They're after me again."

That remark silenced the staff, incredulity over-riding their laugh reflexes. They listened, intrigued, as the pallid, shaking publisher poured out a version of his situation that seemed to reference a subtext of schoolyard bullying. Regaining a little composure, Ovarón looked down at his staff like Charles Laughton from a poop deck and announced, "All right, now we'll just see."

Immediately the phone on the desk rang. Rollie picked it up to hear the crisp, patrician tones of Eudora Ovarón tell him to put her on speaker. He flipped the switch, gave Ovarón a derisive glance and turned to watch the reactions of the staff.

"While I appreciate the excellent work you've all done to make this paper what it is," she stated without preamble, "I'm afraid this behavior is unacceptable. You are overlooking something important here, so let me remind you. This paper belongs to Hollis, not you. He can do with it as he pleases. If you have grievances, there are channels to express them."

Rollie spoke up respectfully, "Thank you, Eudora. But those channels have been exhausted. This paper is going down the tubes and we're being asked to do things that are unethical."

"By the ethics of whom, Roland? I would think an owner's religious convictions count more than your canon of journalism conventions. I'm sure you realize I'm right about that."

"We just want to do our jobs without harassment," Casey put in from the ranks, supported by a swell of grumbles.

"Hello, Ms. Chones. I admire the way you've tossed a loaded word like 'harassment' into this discussion, but it sounds to me like pure insubordination."

From his file cabinet perch, Ovarón suddenly broke in, "Maybe they have a point, Mother. I could just..."

"Hollis!" she snapped, "This is your enterprise. Show some backbone and take control of this thing. Exercise your incumbent authority."

Rollie's shoulders slumped. Casey saw it and wanted to cry. They'd lost, hadn't they? Damn!

From the speakerphone, Eudora Ovarón said, "Rollie, would you be kind enough to hang up now? And please stop hounding my son. He serves high purposes and does as much good as he is up to."

Putting down the handset, Rollie muttered, "For all the good it does anybody."

Ovarón straightened up from his defensive crouch, the cell phone to his ear. Clearing his throat, he spoke forcefully to the staff. "The office is closed for the day. I'm going to decide whether to retain the paper or sell it off."

The staff chanted in unison, "Sell, sell, sell!" Rollie abstained. He knew the probable buyers, mostly chains, wouldn't be any improvement.

Startled by the chanting, Ovarón listened to the phone, then spoke. "Okay, listen. I will open as usual tomorrow morning. Anybody who shows up will still be employed. But I won't tolerate any more of this. Try to remember who pays you."

"And you try to remember who brings the money in," Rollie said.

"That's an easy one." Kyle Albedo, business manager, had not joined the pack, but lounged on a desk watching the fiasco play out. He was lucky because even at his most cocksure, Ovarón had never dreamed of getting involved in the numbers end of things. He had the business and advertising purring like a Swiss watch. He wouldn't mind if Ovarón knocked off plundering the cash flow for his idiot crusades, but considered the editorial staff a necessary nuisance at the very best. He said, "I do."

But his trademark Panatela almost fell out of his mouth into his hand-stitched shirt pockets when Ovarón started jumping up and down on the file cabinet, shrilling, "No, I do, I do, I do!" He jumped down to the desk, the staff falling back in the universal deference for the obviously insane. Stamping his foot, he yelled, "I hired you, I paid you! It is from me, *me,* that all your blessings flow!"

Rollie stared up at him scornfully. "Don't crap your pants, Hollis. Your mom can't wipe that up over the phone."

"That's enough of that!" Ovarón screamed. "The doors will be locked in fifteen minutes. Anybody inside at that time will be trespassing. The police will be called!"

He leaped off the desk and broke through the mob, running across the office while they stared.   He bolted past Kyle, lounging on the desk blowing smoke rings and otherwise keeping his shirt on, ran into Rollie's office, slammed the door and locked it.

The staff followed, pressing up against the big windows which, as a matter of policy, had no blinds. They howled at him, wrote obscene taunts on the glass with magic marker, blew smeary kisses on the windows. He quaked, babbling into the phone, until they all drifted away. He slammed the phone on his desk, drained, and slumped in his chair. A pair of sharp raps on the window made him look up. It was Kyle.

"Don't worry, boss," he called out through the glass. "We'll get through this just fine. No problems on the business side, where it matters."

Bucked up somewhat by this support, Ovarón asked him, "But what if they all quit?   There has to be something the people can read."

"Let them read ads," Kyle grinned, but realized it was an overhead shot. "We can slap in wire service, hire temps. I'll run more ads to fill space. It'll work out."

"You're probably right, Kyle. Thank you for you support. I've always admired the quality of your contribution here."

Then how about a raise, Kyle thought: I'd say there's a big one in the bag before this snafu's over with. He also thought: Like people pick this paper up to read it.

Favoring the bunkered-down Ovarón with a wave that stopped just short of patronizing, Kyle moved back to his own office and quickly got all five of his salesmen on a conference call. His message to them was:

"Mayday blitz. We're selling an additional fifty percent space this week." He paused to let them subside, chuffing on his cigar, then went on, "Stop pissing and moaning, dammit.   I'm upping your commissions ten percent on the overage and you can give some deep discounts.   Tell anybody already in it's a 'good customer' rate of half off if they double their space. Any new business you're working on, give 'em the discount as an intro offer. Got it?" He paused perfunctorily, then barked, "Attaboys! Fetch!"

He hung up, immediately speed dialed a house account. "Listen, Stan. I've got something going on here I want to let you in on." Maybe Ovarón thought he'd have one hundred percent staffing tomorrow morning, but Kyle was better at reading people and he knew a walkout when he saw one.

The pier break at Ocean Beach wasn't exactly pumping, but there were some good swells to reward those patient enough to wait. And Rollie had seldom been more patient in his life. He would gladly have stopped time at that exact moment, bobbing in a sunlit chasm between green sea and blue sky. Straddling his board, facing away from the lying traps of land, he was merging. And in no hurry about it.

A rasta-coifed blonde dewd paddled up beside him, possibly to make sure he was alive and awake.

"Yo, Moon dog. Long time, no sea."

"Way too long," Rollie answered slowly.

"What I'm saying, brah. Short board, there. For a geezer. "

"It's a shred kind of day."

"I love that kind."

"Yeah, but I hate decisions."

"What's to decide?"

"If I didn't go to work today because I quit or got fired."

"Dude! Does it matter?"

"Not really" Rollie kicked into a decent wave, moved into position and shot the pilings, a move so sloppy and just plain nuts that even the jaded hotdogger raised a fist in salute, thumb and little finger pointing out and up.

Ovarón quickly learned to come to the office through the parking lot entrance, where a hastily hired security guard kept wolves from the door. He wouldn't have come in at all, except the paper needed to be put out and there was nobody to do it, and he'd been advised that mutiny didn't generally signal a sellers' market.

But the first morning after his mom put down the insurrection he made the mistake of having his wife drop him off at the coffee shop as usual, then walking up to the office, latté in hand. Since he read the morning paper as he walked, he didn't know he was in the thick of the some sort of fray until he got jostled by a heavyset woman carrying a sign reading, "Southcoast Weak on Liberties".

Looking up, he was stunned to find himself surrounded by a mob. Worse, a mob full of photographers and TV crews. Casting his startled gaze around the gadding crowd, dazed by flashguns and thrusting microphones, seeing scorn and fury in the eyes of his former workers, he backed against the wall. Big mistake-- that was right where they wanted him. Trying to make sense of it all by reading the signs, he came up with his usual conclusion: End Times.   Placards screamed, "Liberate The News," "Ovarón Represses Truth," "Right To Work Unhassled." An old reflex lefty freelancer waved a faded, vintage placard proclaiming, "No Scabs On Us."

Ovarón had no idea what that meant, but it sounded nasty, diseased, and reproductive. That tenor of thought was supported by the grisly banners of two pro-abortion protesters who had snuck in to take advantage of the publicity. An independent photographer wore a red T-shirt tight across her bulging bosom: "To Hell With The Evangelical Right." Linsey and Mike craned for advantage, he in his Che Guevara shirt. Putting it all together with lightning speed, Ovarón realized he was being attacked by shock troops of the anti-Christ. And reacted accordingly.

Holding his forearms in a cross in front of his face (a maneuver which splattered his latté and tossed his paper to the wind) he plunged for the office door, screaming, "Get away from me, you filthy animals!"

A chorus responded: a post-modern refrain involving their right to jobs, free expression, coffee breaks, and women controlling their bodies. As he fumbled with the keypad lock, he turned for the second time as many days to face a pack baying for his throat. "You're doing Satan's sabotage!" he shrilled. "God is not mocked!" Several press people later claimed to have come in their pants at that moment, without even the benefits of particularly impure thoughts.

Inside the door, shaken but safe enough to be defiant, he yelled the most financially and legally significant utterance of his life: "Atheist scum! No wonder you all got fired!"

The following "Week" issues (marked by shortened dink roll editions, drafty pages jammed with boilerplate and syndicated mediocrity) would feature longwinded editorials decrying the situation, whining about ingratitude and lack of love from pampered underlings, beseeching the support of the community in a time of crisis and wickedness, and--above all--taking pains to describe the absent staff as sulking, vindictive slackers who *quit*. Not by any stretch of the imagination employees fired without cause, and certainly not out of religious discrimination. No, no, no, no.

But those denials didn't make it on the news at eleven, did they? Whereas, you bet your sweet ass, the concept of firing people for being Atheist Satanists did. A standup comic at the La Jolla Comedy Store did a bit on the problems of being both an Atheist and Satanist: observing that Atheists have nobody to talk to during orgasms. Nobody ever screams, "Oh Satan, I'm coming." Meanwhile, there it was, all over the news: Hell's Atheists Locked Out.

Good old "Boo" wasn't paying his usual attention to his phone conversation with the lawyer in New York who provided his main contact with the amorphous Ownership of Channel Nine. He had already heard all this about the station numbers. And he had proposed the staff cuts in the first place. But now he was stalling, trying to figure out the Wiley perplex. There was money in the little creep. Major numbers and growing listener identification, but he really did look like day-old crap on the air. What's more to the point, Yao kept thinking, there's no way I can cash in on the guy if he's locked into the station like this. His boredom with the discussion led to him click his universal remote, which unlike most "universal" remotes, actually controlled everything he owned--which was a whole lot of cool/geeky stuff that supported remote control, and vice versa. Flicking through cable channels as idly as drumming his fingers, he suddenly stopped, totally ignoring the London gasbag as he worked back a few channels to a breathless remote from the Southcoast Week office. He spoke to the phone more brusquely than usual, "Hang on, let me hear something here." Thirty seconds later, he said, "Let me get back to you, Adrian. I might have a really elegant solution for this whole thing."

With the glass doors between himself and the ravening crowd of bloodfeasters, Ovarón took a moment to pull himself together before turning to face his empty offices. Maybe he hadn't thought things through all that clearly.

In total agreement with that concept was Karin Chones, who walked out of the press room and treated him to a cold, clinical stare. Ovarón jumped at the sight of her, landing back against the doors and triggering a cacophony of laughter, jeers, catcalls and photoflash from the mob outside. His first interpretation of her presence was that the hordes had found another entrance and would swarm in, drag him out and lynch him on an inverted cross. Chones had been pretty tight with Moon, as he recalled, and very unlikely to be missing the boycott/pandemonium. His every orifice clenched as she walked towards him.

In fact, Casey had been the first of the staffers to express loyalty to Rollie and vow to walk off any conceivable pier on his behalf. Rollie had asked her not to; had in fact held a meeting for the entire editorial staff in a Pacific Beach surfer dive, asking them to hang tough and not worry about him. They held an impromptu vote and called a general walk out. The vote was immediately followed by a general drunk-out.

But Casey, the staffer most attached to Rollie, had stayed. She'd had no intention of doing so, but Rollie himself had talked her out of leaving. He knew her deep attachment to the paper at the integral levels where publications actually exist: the white fibers of concern and experience running through the tissue of money and words. Walking out and seeing the paper flounder would affect her like sitting and watching a baby drown in the bath. While the rest of the staff frolicked and groped in the heady high produced by change, rebellion, and shoreleave illusions of freedom, she leaned against Rollie in a back booth, sobbing. "I can't go in there tomorrow, Rollie. I can't let you down. But..."

But it's your life, Rollie thought. It's all you've ever been, you raised the damn thing. Nursed it and changed its diapies. "You should stay on," Rollie told her.

She pushed away, staring at him in shock. Rollie went on, "It's the right thing to do. I admire you for seeing that."

Involuntarily, Casey's gaze flicked to the staffers, immersed in frivolity. Rollie followed her look, then brought her back to his eyes. "Fuck them," he said. "What they think or say about you for staying on is meaningless, Casey. They're drones, wage earners who earn less to feed their egos. You're wired in at a different level."

"Deeper than you?" she whispered. "You hired me, Rollie."

"Because the paper needed you. And it still does."

She started to protest, but he put a finger over her lips, pulled her in and kissed her on the forehead. He felt the flutter run through her. She had a crush on him. Like they all get crushes on the editor or doctor or CEO. The important thing was...

"It's not a dry goods store, Casey. It's an information source. Somebody has to keep it real. I lost my job trying to do that: you keep yours for the same reason."

Casey felt the tears come; gently turned and walked out. Bitter in the throat of a lifelong leftist is the realization that sometimes you reject spicy struggles and gestures for the day to day drudge of survival and results. Some can step up and swallow that load. But it leaves a mark.

Which Ovarón must have seen, because he somehow knew better than to discuss anything. Just take Casey's presence as a gift from God and try to sort this mess out.

Casey also realized that it would be pointless to recap the obvious. All she said was, "One condition."

Ovarón blinked rapidly, awaiting the offer of a mess of pottage or bread made from stones. Casey waited, too. Finally he stammered, "What condition, Ms. Chones?"

Casey grabbed a layout sheet and held it up to his face. Even in his nervous condition he could tell that the headline, "Think Locally, Grope Globally", indicated that the diddler piece had been restored. Behind the layout, Casey barked, "Don't fuck up!"

It took a long moment, but Ovarón finally nodded, waving his hands weakly at the story in wretched approval. Advertisers expected (in a legally binding way) that the paper would be out the next day and he had no idea how to do that. He couldn't think of any other way out of this pickle and his mother had told him to deal with it like a man. So he began by taking orders from a woman.

"Good," Casey snapped. "Now take off that coat and tie. We've got to work to do." She spun on her low, sensible heels and stalked off towards the composition terminal. "Oh, yeah. Kyle said the business staff will be in later. After the circus out there has wound down a little."

Ovarón glanced at the doors, triggering a burst of outrage and scorn. He hurried after Casey, shucking his coat and tugging at the knot his wife had put in his necktie.

At the end of the day, all we have is what we did. To Hollis Ovarón, slumped at the editor's desk in a fatigued funk, it was far from clear what he'd accomplished. There was so much meaningless scutwork in this business. He'd spent nine hours phoning people up to discuss matters he didn't fully understand, looking over copy that seemed to be written for self-obsessed harlots on Xanax, shuffling obscure advertisement layouts from one spot to another, taking calls from asylum escapees, checking facts for stories that were apparently made up from whole cloth, writing headlines without recourse to his God-sent ScriptureQuest program, putting reporters from other papers on terminal hold.

Was this what he'd wanted to do with his life? He lapsed for a minute into his favorite daydream: fighting through the Nazi Romans, plucking His Savior from the rude cross and carrying him to an airy upper room where he could salve his wounds with Gilead balm, nurse him back to health, walk in his strengthening footsteps, fawn at his right hand. He lolled in the chair, squirming and ready to bolt.

Kyle Albedo stopped by on his way home, popped his cheerful head in the door. "Nothing like a little fire baptism, eh, Brother Ovarón? Buck up, it'll get better. This issue's out and we'll have temps in tomorrow to start taking over some of the work."

Grateful, but ashamed, Ovarón nodded his head silently and went back to his brooding in the cheerless dim of Rollie's office, now his by default. Casey walked by the windows--he was going to have to get some blinds for them soonest--and glowered at him. She could glower, that woman. But where would he have been without her? It was getting very confusing, trying to sort friend from foe without a scorecard.

He heard Casey talking in the hall, somebody with a low voice. He stiffened. Had they come for him? Had she suckered him in for some devilish ruse? He heard Casey snort, "What does it matter where he is? Or even if?" More muttering, then Casey, loud enough to benefit his ears, said, "No, just walk right in. Kick in the door. Piss in his coffee. Make yourself at home."

That alarmed him, but in a subdued way. His freakout mechanisms were overtaxed and flagging. He continued to slump in the chair: let them come take him if they would. He probably deserved a good scourging.

Anti-climatically, the apparition that darkened his door was a diminutive Asian dressed in a stiff suit; deferential in geek glasses, bearing a clunky briefcase. Who entered his office diffidently, bowed jerkily, and said, "Excuse. Prease?"

CHAPTER EIGHT

"I just don't understand why Hard Look would get the ax. I pull my numbers, bring in awards, increase views." Caitlin shook her head, a woman trying to get the world back in its rightful groove. "Why are you doing this? You've got my picture all over those expensive bus ads, for Christ's sake."

Yao inscrutably lowered his epicanthial folds before replying, "Not you fault. Big company do comprete lestlucture of station. Bling national feed, syndicate shows. News now one houah world news and sports. News team now just leeding sclipts flom networks. Not need rocal shows."

"That's insane. Automated radio stations work, but not TV."

"Evelybody get same news. People onree care about faces of news team, personarities. Gimmicks."

"They like my face, don't they? I was told I was being groomed for anchor and I don't even rate being at the desk?"

"Glooming ovah. You so leddy now."

"What? Make sense, would you? Can we get a translator or something?"

Yao pushed his fake Tojo glasses up his nose with his middle finger, giving a wide coolie smile. "You talk boss-man now."

Caitlin gaped at him, her thoughts turning to her pepper spray grinder. (*Dispenser*! Damn that Wiley.) It wasn't the first time she'd fantasized about kicking the crap out of Yao. Use her Tai Bo training to smash his glasses, yelling "Lemember Tien An Men Square, Chinkyman!" But this particular reverie, probably the closest ever to spilling over into reality, was interrupted by the most unlikely intrusion she could have imagined. In the station context, that is.

"We have bigger things in mind for you, Caitlin," wheezed the voice of J. Danforth Scorment. She turned to stare. Had the "owner" ever set foot in the station since she'd been there? Had any staffer actually met the man? He had always been envisioned as the closest to earth of the dimly perceived corporate hierarchy that owned the station, a lower level sub-angel or demi-urge so mundane as to actually have a face and name. And now she was seeing that face, speaking that name.

"Mr. Scorment. What a surprise to see you."

To say the very least. It was surprising the man could walk. Much less through a door. Scorment's appetites were legendary, and what she could see not only confirmed those legends but amplified them. The mortal remains of myriad pastries, multi-course gluts, expensive liquor, and midnight pudding orgies wreathed him in bulk. His face bore the stamp of spoilage and debauchery so graphically it made her envision a secret vault somewhere with a portrait of him as a slender young man swaddled in dorian innocence. She'd seen lust pour from men's eyes before, but it never made her want to scrub herself. Scorment was like a statue carved in suet, entitled, "Mommy's Money Shot To Hell".

"And a pleasure to see you, my dear. In the... ahem... flesh." The scrubdown urge hastened on to muriatic acid.   Scorment juggernautted over to a chair. Yao jumped up, did a highspeed Mandarin bow, and helped him achieve an angle of repose.

"Bigger things, my lovely. A girl should aspire to... bigger things."

Ewww, gross.   She was trying to remember what Carrie Fisher did to Jabba the Hutt, but only recalled something about being digested for a thousand years, which made her fight a gag reflex. "Bigger things, Sir?" was what she came up with. Made her want to spit on herself, but it worked. He glowed and-- unthinkably--swelled up.

"Oh yes. Oh yes. This whole anchor thing will seem like nothing to you when you start to realize what it is to be an Editor In Chief."

She was baffled by that one. Editors were little dweebs doing tech scrabblings on videotape back in some morlock catacombs. They were serfs, how could they have a chief? She pushed out a pawn, desperate for an inkling. "A new position?"

"As a matter of fact, it will be. You keep up on things, don't you?" He beamed at her with a proprietary air that made her think of stripping and running through a car wash. "You'll be the first in that seat, so to speak, that The Week ever had."

She'd wanted an inkling and got FreakSpeak. What the hell was on this puffball's mind? Well, sounding stupid always worked for titsy blondes. "The Week, Sir?"

"Editor in Chief of Southcoast Week. Full charge. Full perks. Full..."

"You're saying I should be a newspaper editor? Are you firing me? Is one of us losing their marbles?"

Yao and Scorment laughed long and loud over that one, Yao chortling behind his hand with a kamikaze squint, Scorment generating great waves that rippled around his flab like adipose tsunamis, coming together at odd places to form double-amplitude interference peaks. The effect was far from a jolly bowl of jelly: more like a malignant tumor in the throes of metastasis.

"Dear girl," Scorment gasped, a second before Caitlin would have bolted for the door, "We wouldn't fire you. We're promoting you. Full charge, did you hear me? Maybe you should sit closer, here."

"But... why me?" The eternal cry of the unsuspecting victim. In this case linked to some fairly major logistical ramifications.

"Why not you?" Scorment bellowed, jowls jouncing like pink pigs in rut. Yao tittered behind his Yale ring. "You're wonderful."

"But... newspaper editor?"

"Now don't even think of selling yourself short in front of big fans like me and Boo." This was the first time Caitlin had heard Yao's nickname, which heightened the surrealism of pretending to talk logically with these grotesque lunatics. "You have a lot of qualifications. I mean look at you." He leered, then raised a finger like a manicured kielbasa to intone, "But above all, loyalty. We need somebody over there whose loyalty we can absolutely count on."

Is he kidding me, Caitlin thought? Or just himself? She wrote it off to the personal holocaust Scorment had visited on his brain cells. "So *I'd* be loyal?"

"Sure you would, honey," Scorment brayed, "Because you'd kill widows and babies to get back over here and anchor."

Oops, he had her there. Assuming the station was still around. She managed to say, "Ah."

"You betcha, ah. Besides, it'll look good on your résumé."

"I suppose. Diversity and all."

Scorment snorted. "No, no, no. Diversity is hiring fags and jigs and wetbacks. Hiring blonde hotties just makes good business sense."

Caitlin always cringed when other people used derogatory epithets. She had burned an aversion to racial prejudice into her own psyche at a young age. She had known from the start that

73

she was a superior individual, far above normal humans. So to mark out any of the inferior drones that crawled around below her for special abuse seemed not only pointless, but a cruel thing to point out. Calling her a "blonde hottie" was merely crude and, as a matter of secret technicality, inaccurate. Best way to deal with such attitudes is sticking with verifiable facts.

"I don't know how to, you know, edit. Publish. Print things."

"Sure you do, you edit your segments everyday, choose topics and material, write your own commentary. And on a tighter deadline."

She studied him, her mind scrambling for purchase. There might be something to what he was babbling.   The chief characteristic of an Editor In Chief would mostly be superiority and attitude. Ability to delegate scut and divert responsibility.

"I'll tell you a little secret, " Scorment continued as she cringed at the very thought. "Magazines are run by women, same way the Army's run by sergeants. If it won't run through a woman's head, nobody gets to read it. And I'm talking about women like you: tall, tough, decked-out, built, hot. They lead by looking commanding and classy. Plus, of course, they usually sleep their way up. Hint, hint."

Okay, now he *had* to be kidding. Somebody. "Well, what can I say but 'Thank you, Sir?' I'll do my very best to justify your faith in my abilities and god-given hotness."

A series of ripples raced around Scorment's global torso, preliminary shocks to the major tectonic disturbances of his attempts to stand up. Yao tried to make his assistance look casual but Caitlin saw and enjoyed the strain on his face. Scorment lurched out of his berth like a newly-christened dirigible. He trundled over to Caitlin, who blew her chance to stand up--not from respect or etiquette, but to feel less like a bug menaced by a bowling ball--chuckled, and patted her knee, a sensation like being licked by a temple dog. That does it, Caitlin thought: it's the spa this afternoon.

"I think you'll find your new position has it's own rewards, challenges, and satisfactions," he wheezed.   Then he was negotiating the door, and gone. Yao gave her a final celestial smirk, then disappeared in his wake. She knew she was going to have to pull some strings to get into the spa in fifteen minutes, but it had to be done. She thought best when buried in scented mud, anyway.

CHAPTER NINE

The fruits of his somewhat loopy conversation with Ovarón in the Reichsbunker atmosphere of the Week offices had gratified Yao immensely. But even immenser was his surge of glee and gloat when he presented his findings and strategy to those involved. Danforth Scorment had absorbed it with somewhat less than the concentration he'd give to incorporating a baked Alaska, but he had definitely been impressed and showed it with various seismic temblors.

Yao had made certain to seat Scorment on the reinforced chair across from him at the beautifully polished table in his conference room. He was glad to keep distance. The choice of phone call versus video conference with a "real" owner had been a conscious one.

"It's not really a take-over," Yao stressed. "We're White Knights."

"The good guys, eh?" Scorment wobbled out. "Saving the homestead? I love it."

"Well," Yao allowed, "More like Stealth Hostile White Knights."

"Hostile White Knights?" Scorment dissolved in undulant cackles. "Ku Krux Kran, that what you're telling me? Excellent, Boo. Bloody excellent."

A terse tick from the speakerphone reminded them both of a third party to their conversation, some remote minion of the Ownership, monitoring their giggles. "Will this Ovarón sign off, though?" the phone wheedled in a chill Germanic tone. "He sounds like a bit of an idiot and an equivocator."

"If I'd had a contract, he'd have signed on the spot," Yao crowed. "Now I've got the contract."

"I'm looking at the fax right now," the phone replied, with a hint of the idea that it could just as easily look at their IRS records, used underwear under the bed, or status in Santa's Big Book. "This sounds too good to be true."

"That's what's so good about it," Scorment bellowed. "He really needed cash, and staffing: we're giving it to him. Maybe less than he thinks. He gets five percent stock in my station."

"Is that wise?"

"Oh yeah," Yao trumpeted. "We get forty-nine percent of Week Publications. Forty-nine!"

"And they keep forty-nine percent. With two percent held by an independent accounting firm so that neither party will be able to vote the other one out."

"What I'm sayin'!" Yao enthused. "*My* company. Solid!"

"Yes, very sound. We control without seeming to. I'm sure you've hidden away the connection. But why do we give half of our stock to Mr. Scorment himself?"

"FCC regulations, I gather," Scorment told him. "Neither of us can hold half because we control other media. This way works just fine."

"Clever, no?" Yao asked the phone.

"Well done, Mr. Yao. But what will the health of the newspaper be like after all this?"

"Not a problem. We're laying off station staff, we can send them over. Camera, editor, research." It's beautiful, Yao thought. Those outplaced drones can't hit us for unemployment, and the Week will carry them on salary. We increase their revenues by more ad sales... and the salespeople all work straight commission. I'm a frigging genius.

What he said was, "I'd like to bring somebody into the room to speak to you." The phone clicked an assent. Yao had wondered if there were sometimes artificial intelligence programs on the line with him instead of people.

He stepped on a button under the rug beneath the conference table and almost immediately Kyle Albedo stepped into the room. Yao motioned him to a chair near the telephone speaker, spoke in fluent pidgin.

"Mistah Luckahs, this Mistah Kire..."

"Kyle Albedo, Mr. Ruchers. Business manager of Southcoast Week. I'm thrilled to be getting your support and am sure I can show you a profitable return very quickly."

"And how is that, Mr. Albedo?"

"We haven't been saturating all possible markets here. If I may explain something, this city is riding a massive demographic shift that has not been noticed by current management. The old admirals and retirees and Okies are dying off, alzheimering out. What good are ads that won't be remembered five minutes?"

"It's nice to talk to somebody who speaks plainly, sir. What new areas would you pursue?"

"The huge influx of yuppies fleeing the East and L.A. but not cool enough to take on San Francisco. Hip, metrosexual, childless, scared. They love Wiley and his amoral take on things. Think it makes them sophisticated. Same way they like Dan Savage's "Hey Faggot!" column. Who we are already picking up. And anything like that we can get our hands on. Linda Barry, Life in Hell, Tom Tomorrow, all that "edgy" stuff. Show me edgy and I'll show you somebody who can be stampeded into buying things."

"Buying what sort of things?"

Albedo leaned back and smiled at Yao and Scorment, who returned it with inscrutable and unpalatable grins, respectively.

"Beauty, security, status, sex, sin. All off the rack. That tw... Mr. Ovarón wouldn't take sex ads, can you believe it? Weeklies are *owned* by sex, tobacco, booze, bars, personals."

"You mean *personal* personals? Ads for escorts, phone sex, that sort of thing?"

"That and tobacco-sponsored shows, booze, the whole plastic surgery, spa, lengthening sort of thing."

"Things people buy in order to get sex, in other words."

"Exactly. All of that falls in with the younger, newer ad base we're pursuing. All paid for on commission. And we can't really do this above the table, but with the station and paper both, we can probably do some swinging."

"Swinging?" Yao and Albedo both caught the interest beneath the austere monotone.

"Swing ads. Customer gets coverage in both at a discount."

"Oh."

And that was that. Everything went into motion so smoothly that Caitlin's conversation with Scorment and Yao had sprung upon her without the usual heralds of rumors, whispers and requests for denials.

Fleeing the aftermath of that same conversation, in the enclosed comfort range of her Lexus, Caitlin modulated the volume of her Kitaro CD and touched a button that caused her sun roof to slide sensually open. A she ramped out of the parking structure and looked up at the blue California sky she smiled... just as her mind got crunchingly encroached by Wiley's latest commentary. Pleasure draining from her like the warmth seeping from the pores of a person trapped in a freezer, she gritted her teeth and glanced at the surrounding traffic. Damn, most of them looked like maniacs. Why did Wiley get under her skin like this? Worse, the insane rant he'd spieled off from the depths of a clanging, gnashing hangover had drawn a barrage of favorable calls. He'd called the segment: **The Thinking Man's Guide To Playing In Traffic.**

Unless you're a total couch spud or have a serious exercise addiction, sooner or later you are going to decide that you can get your weekend jollies more efficiently by driving somewhere in an automobile. Trouble is, everybody else is using the same strategy. This can be a hassle, especially with all the recent restrictions on methods of reducing crowding and general overpopulation (the AK-47 assault rifle as an excellent example).

So you could sit in the gridlock, cursing and stewing. You could do what an increasing number of right-thinking young Americans do--rage like a methedrine-crazed maniac. Or you could center yourself, relax, and consider the ancient wisdom that holds the journey as important as the destination. Especially if you know a few little games I've especially designed to alleviate those tiresome moments spent stalled in a bumper crop of bumpers.

"Urchin Gooning" is a swell game; educational, action-packed, and involving a lot of audience participation. Play is simplicity itself. When logjammed at stoplights, search out cars full of kids and start making faces at the little trolls. This is fairly jolly in itself. I usually start off with elementary ploys like oscillating my tongue and Grouchoing my eyebrows, then move on to intermediate, hand-assisted gestures, such as pulling my eyes and mouth into grotesque and loathsome shapes. By now the kids are raptly attentive, seldom exposed to such behavior from the nominally adult. When the little gargoyles start responding with faces and gestures of their own, I move into advanced moves like picking my nose and flipping imaginary boogers in their direction. The intervention of windows, you see, preventing the launching of real boogers.

This generally activates a primal trigger that pushes them past some obscurely defined juvenile limit and they start responding noticeably enough to attract their parents' attention. The parents respond by battering them senseless, right in front of my gleeful eyes. But the best is yet to come, because the little ankle-biters, not yet realizing the full enormity of their seemingly innocent playmate's scheme, invariably try to weasel out by claiming that I started it. If you can imagine anyone lodging such allegations against a respected journalist and pillow of the community. Certainly their parents can't, especially when I fix the lot of them with a steely stare that clearly implies, "Who has abdicated control of those nasty little ragamuffins?" That usually settles their hash until late in the (dinnerless) evening. I especially relish the imploring, spaniel-eyed gazes they throw me as they are driven off into the sunset, unable to accept the fact that an elder of their own species would set them up so coldbloodedly under the guise of friendly fun. As I mentioned, the game is quite educational.

I have also found it worthwhile to keep a few props around, especially a pair of white plastic vampire teeth. This can produce spectacular results with very young kids in very close cars. The hat trick of this sport is to cause a tyke to wet his pants and therefore the upholstery. I buy the teeth cheap right after Halloween, of course; the same way I stock up on those little candy hearts with nitwit sayings on them after Valentines day. Which you do, too, right? Come on, admit it. Just like you also wait until right after Easter to close out on a few of those ghastly candy chick and bunny Peeps, mostly for the atavistic joy of biting their adorable little heads off. Wow, real mature, man. Ozzy Osborne on a glucose jag, hey. You go for cheap thrills, you get what you pay for.

Another little goody picked up most easily at Halloween time (a fantastic holiday for jacking little kids around, by the by, but more on that in it's own season) is a rubber face mask. Preferably the almost realistic humanoid kind that gives you that queasy look of borrowed flesh, sort of like Roy Rogers right after a facelift. Some sort of hat, even cheap sunglasses, aid the disguise, which could do double duty for bank robberies, but is all you need to play "Defensive Pass Interference". This is a high-speed, fast lane game. Rather, a next-to-the-fast-lane game. Start by putting the mask on the back of your head. Add hat, glasses, costume jewelry, a touch of make-up and spritz of cologne, whatever you think best, I'd be the last to condemn your taste in such matters, believe me.

You are now equipped, so just toad along, waiting for some hot shot, preferably in a Porsche or Samurai or some other intrinsically hypercompetitive car to get behind you. Slow him down, mousetrap him, get him impatient. Then, when he gets a chance to pass, reach around to your left ear with your spread right hand, stick your head out the window right in front of him and waggle your fingers. I wouldn't be above a little friendly weaving and yawing at this point, myself. You have to put yourself in the passers place to appreciate this one (not generally a good thing to do in these little pastimes, unless you are a pretty hard core rotten egg). He merely sees the head of a drooling idiot pop out the window of the car he's passing, evidently looking back and therefore more oblivious than most folks to the prevailing road conditions. This can be disconcerting. You can, in fact, disconcert some impatient hotshot's ass right off the road. If that is indeed what happens, you score double.

One other little seasonal purchase can add some fun to waits in the gridlock. Every Fourth of July, squirrel away a little stash of fireworks. Some of these, like Roman candles and bottle rockets, need no explanation when it comes to creating havoc, mayhem, and frivolity on the freeway. But also try to have a handful of cherry bombs and Saturn Missile Batteries in the glovebox for staving off boredom. The name of the game is "Sun Roof Bombing". You can romanticize it as much as you want...be a Beirut Druze terrorist, an IRA nationalist, or an Iraqi chortling, "This SCUD's for you." All it takes is an M-80, a lighter, and proximity to a car with a sun roof.

First of all, note the driver of the sun-roofed vehicle--the smug complacency with which he faces life (Or she, I hasten to add; there is nothing sexist about arriviste smugness. But then Sun Roof Bombing is also strictly equal opportunity calamity). Sunroofs tend to go with certain vehicles, and certain lifestyles. Surely you will be dealing here with a full-bore Yuppie; a tanning booth customer, a drinker, perhaps, of Diet Perrier, the kind of person who works it into conversations that they actually read "Satanic Verses". In short, a schmuck. Hopefully even an attorney. Sitting there on his sheepskin seatcovers, listening to a Windham Hill CD, thinking about convertible debentures, when a sputtering little bundle of bang arcs in through the factory sun roof and propounds an opposing point of view. This is what aficionados term the Moment of Truth.

An even more ruthless truth spews from the multiple maw of the Saturn Missile Battery. A small paper box with 25 pencil-sized plastic rockets ready to launch sequentially, this is the MIRV, the Star Wars, of Sun Roof Bombing. The Smart Bomb for Dumb Detonation Tricks. The effect upon the recipient is hellish in the extreme, probably even somewhat deleterious. Especially if he (or she, let's not forget) has the gears engaged and is holding in the clutch. But tell me, what did your Driver's Education teacher specifically say about that practice? It's certainly a lesson worth mulling over while sitting in a once-luxurious automobile surrounded by two dozen rockets behaving like killer bees in a feeding frenzy. And, podnuh, the smell of gunsmoke. You drive off chuckling, secure in the probability that your playmate momentarily has a priority of thoughts that puts a very low emphasis on memorizing license plate numbers. You, on the other hand, drive on refreshed, ready to try more of ol' Wiley's gridlock grins.

Damn that man!!!! He could reach out and twist her off when she was miles away from wherever he was currently slithering around. She jabbed the button to safely batten her sunroof. The soothing new age environmental sounds no longer soothed. She sped up, heading for the last minute appointment she'd browbeaten Roman Holiday into giving her, dying to sink into nice, clean mud. The only thing good about this unforeseen wrench in her career was that she wouldn't have to put up with Wiley anymore. Or so she assumed.

CHAPTER TEN

Wiley didn't much care for sitting in Caitlin's new office. For one thing Caitlin was there. And looking at him with an expression he'd seen on people who examined the interior of his refrigerator. She was no longer a mark to be taken down, or a competitor to be nerfed into the rail as he finessed his way past her. She had somehow become his boss. And she didn't care for it any more than he did. Shame they couldn't get together and work it out, reach some mutually suitable sham. Preferably in a bathtub full of Gerber's Strained Peaches. Well, sooner or later she'd have to tell him what she wanted from him, which would give him an angle.

What Caitlin desperately wanted from Wiley was a disappearance. If he'd spontaneously burst into flame it wouldn't be too soon or drastic to suit her. Trouble was, he was more important to the schemes of ownership than she was. So she had to stand for Wiley's ogling and gutter surrealism. She'd considered buttoning up her blouse for this interview, but had thought better of it and actually arranged her bosom for even more spectacular view. Eat your hard out, you scuzzy cockroach, was the general idea. Well, she'd hauled him in, she'd have to say something.

"You know we both got shipped over here by the owners. Part of their partnership."

Wiley nodded noncommittally. Take your time, baby. I got all day.

"They have some exciting plans for this paper and you're a big part of it."

"I just hope I can contribute up to their expectations. It's a team sport."

Yes, Caitlin thought. But you pitch the shit and I have to catch it. For now. She said, "Your column is a major thing. They hope to syndicate it to other weeklies." Incredible, ghastly, but true.

"Gee, that's great. I've dreamed of this. But, if you don't mind, what column?"

"The weekend thing, same as you've been doing on the air."

"You mean, write it down? Type it, like?"

"Well, I think there's a word processor at your work station."

"Work station? Oh, desk, right? Cubicle. My little cube in the corporate icetray. Okay, Babes. I mean, Boss. Trouble is, I don't really write that stuff. I just jam. You know, turn on the mike and trip out."

"Well, maybe you can tape your... trip... then transcribe it."

"So I'll have a secretary?"

"Yes." Caitlin said it without grinding her teeth. Even though she, as yet, had no secretary of her own. And her files had apparently been sacked and looted by the one that quit. "Your deadline. You know what I mean, right?"

"I have it written by then or I'm dead?"

If only. "Well, you'd be frowned on, let's say."

"And I can't recycle my TV stuff?" There was always waste in these things.

"Hardly. Original material, first one due on Tuesday. For Thursday's issue."

"Great. You got it. I'll knock it out this weekend." He ventured a conciliatory smile. "Henceforth the name."

She didn't seem to see the smile, much less raise it. "One thing."

Oh, shit, Wiley thought. They always say that. It's like "but.." only worse. Oh, by the way, there's this iceberg. One thing, there's a jillion hostile Indians. Oh, did we mention we're putting you people in ovens?

"Just one?" Venture the smile again. What the hell? Something ventured, nothing gained. She continued blandly, "We're going to need a sort of pilot."

Oh shit, oh dear! Like most scammers and third-rate conmen, Wiley had taken a few flyers at the soft technicolor undercarriage of Hollywood. And one thing he learned there was "We need a pilot" is Hollycode for "Your ass is out". But she'd said, "sort of", right? See one, play one.

"Sort of?"

"I don't know what they call it here. A first column that explains what it's all about, who you are, what you're doing. A weekly column about weekend activities. But, you know, an example of what they're going to get. Where you're coming from."

Wiley had one of his flashes of insight. She didn't know what she was doing. And was insecure about it. Excellent! No real help on this one, but a good thing to stash away for later. But what did they want from him here?

"You're talking about a first episode, sort of?"

"Exactly." She hid her relief, but not from Wiley.

It hit him. Oh yeah. "An Origins Issue."

"I'm not sure I follow you."

"Yeah, you know, like you've got Superman or Batman or somebody, then you go back and do a backstory on them. Parents killed by criminals, Krypton explodes, magic lantern. It's the origins of the characters."

Caitlin nodded carefully. Good, good. See if he can pull it off. And I'd really like to see an Origin on Wiley himself. In fact, that might be worth a little money to look into. She smiled for the first time. "I think you nailed it, Wiley. Remember, Tuesday noon." Scorment, of all people, had been right about this job not being without its rewards and satisfactions.

"Look, all I'm asking is for a little help from my friends," Wiley whined. "I've paid my dues in this dive and just want a little love, a little kickdown, a peck on the cheek of comradely cooperation. Can I get some?"

The sodden faces so characteristic of the Mimosa at five to two in the morning reflected little in the way of bonhomie and desire to step into a breach. They barely reflected the sudden harsh lighting associated with Last Call. Many of them, in fact, were plastered to the bar or dirty tables.

"Come on, people," Wiley wailed. "I'm on my way to stardom here and all I have to do is turn in an article in a couple of hours. I need your inspiration, your local color, your sagacity, your moxie, your unique supply of the American spirit. Whattaya say?"

Jerome flexed his biceps in anger, knitted his brow in frustration. His hard fingers drummed on the bar as he glared spitefully at the shitfaced Wiley. Finally he shrugged, pulled a thin plastic bindle of white powder from his back pocket and tossed in on the bar in front of Wiley.

Wiley's face was wreathed in gratitude and relief. He snatched up the baggie and made a pass at Jerome's hand, which was snatched back in a pet.

"Oh, bro, this is what I'm talking about. Love, baby. Support. Male biped solidarity. Can I put it on my tab?"

Jerome snarled, "I've told you not to use that offensive term in here." He thrust out a brawl-calloused palm for payment.

When Casey came in at eight she saw the cassette taped to her computer screen first, then noticed Wiley crashed under her desk wearing gray underpants and one sock. She surveyed him for signs of life, made coffee, booted up, put the cassette in her recorder and pushed play. She'd typed for a minute, then looked through at Caitlin, appearing harassed in her glass office, and laughed her ass off.

The Way Of
THE WEEKEND WARRIOR

Incredible as it may seem, I was once as lame as you are. A real turkeybait from nowheresville. Worse, from a little berg just south of Nowheresville. I had a nice house, a wife, a family, a cool car, a swimming pool. But somehow it wasn't enough. It never is. Then one day I realized how meaningless it was. (I think it was while listening to a Talking Heads album.) I mean there I was, a middle-class, middle-income white male, practically the dominant species of the planet, and I was having no fun. So, for some reason, I decided to deal with it by seeking the Meaning Of Life.

I tried Zen, sitting around with my eyes at half-mast while some old fart out of a Kung Fu flashback whacked me with a stick as I tried to figure out the sound of one hand clapping. When I finally got it, I booted the old dharma dhumb-ass in his satoris and continued on my Way. (Ans: Clap in one hand and wish in the other and see which comes tlue, glasshopper.)

Over the years I tried Buddhism, nudhism, Kundalini Yoga (which I had thought had something to do with oragenital sex), shamans (namely Sam the Shaman of East LA), LSD (I decided it was crazy to take something to

85

make you crazy, but I'm still a little confused on that one), channeling (all I got was public access channels), Krishna, Scientology, the teachings of Don Juan the brujo (you seen Juan brujo you seen 'em all). I learned I had to seek My Way by becoming a Warrior. But I had not yet found My Way. (I thought I did for awhile, but it turned out to be a creepy identification with Frank Sinatra).

Then one day, as I sat beneath a tree by the river, reading a Classic Comic of Sidhartha and listening to "Let Me Hear Your Bodhi Talk" on my Walkman, I heard someone say, "What are you doing this weekend?" My heart (or perhaps it was my Walkman) skipped a beat: I didn't know! I resolved to answer for myself that timeless question: What good is it to gain inner peace if you don't even have a date for the weekend?

This, then, is the Way of the **WEEKEND WARRIOR**: whence he came, whither he goest, whath he dooth. (NOTE: Collectors! This is an "Origins Issue". Double sack it and wait 10 years for a major payoff.) From my initial enlightenment, I moved out into the world; learning, experiencing, challenging, landing on my lips. I sought the heart of Saturday night, learned what was coming down on Sunday morning, thanked God for Fridays. I found The Truth. The Meaning of Life. Which is, that life should be enjoyed. I was stunned. "That's *it*?" I asked, "The truth of the universe is Have a Nice Day?" The Universe didn't bother to reply. So I dealt with it. I became The Weekend Warrior™. All I needed was a silly costume and a secret identity. A nearby Banana Republic took care of the first requirement (a bit sillier than I'd hoped, and no cape, but very Bogart.) I solved the identity crisis in the traditional way--I became a mild-mannered reporter.

Here at Southcoast Week, slaving away under the Scrooge-like thumb of Caitlin Vanderkeller, I could appreciate weekends. And with the lavish pay, use of the company plane, and all the opportunities for graft and abuse of power, I was able to begin my mission: to have a blast every weekend and report this lore to the reader. In short, to serve you. Yes, *you*. Who else is reading these very words, someone over your shoulder? This is that old fashioned media that actually communicates, pal: print. This is not MTV. This ain't no disco. Ain't no fooling around. We're both backed up against a cognitive wall, eyeball to eyeball. There is nothing, no one, to come between me and you. And between me and you, your haircut sucks. But you probably know that.

What you probably don't know is what goes into having a good time. You probably think you do, just because you can't remember your most memorable experiences, or because you keep a detox center on retainer. Well, there's more to it than that. For instance, there are training exercises. We are constantly bombarded with propaganda stressing the importance of conditioning to a healthy lifestyle. Well, how much more important it is, then, to a lifestyle of total dissipation and hedonism. If you're going to achieve not knowing who or where you are, you'd better at least know what the hell you're doing. The path to diversion is literally and liberally littered with the remains of the half-assed, half cocked, and half-priced. But perhaps we should draw a veil over that subject. A black velvet curtain, embroidered "Not a pretty sight."

My years of seeking have taught me the wisdom and methods for proper preparation. Just the sexual training I do is dumbfounding. (Well, some have found it dumb.) I do curls that would curl your hair, pushups in positions so unthinkable you'd never think of them, crunches so unmentionable I hate to mention them. Just as a warm-up I flip over a dime in the bottom of a coke bottle with my tongue. Five sets of twenty reps. Sex is too important to be left to amateurs. It is, profoundly, a game of inches.

Of course, I build my mind, as well. I've learned to scan menus in any language, computing tips in pesos, piasters, and pushniks. (Before landing this ridiculously overpaid job at The Week, I generally gave tips like "Horny Harriet to place in the Third at Del Mar"). I have learned to compute the heat of meat, the angle of dangle, the blood content in my alcohol, the edge of tomorrow, the point of no return (I don't see the point, I used to make a living recycling bottles and cans.) But I'm sure you get the idea. And will want to get each month's wisdom as **THE WEEKEND WARRIOR©,** with help from a hand-picked staff of merry men and unmarried women, gives you the skinny. We will answer all your questions before they even occur to you.

We are in favor of dancing, prancing, cometing, vixening. We approve of head trips, side trips, loose ships, loose lips, tight tits, rude bits, all-nighters, one-liners, high-siders, lowriders, dirt-bikers, hitch-hikers, sunburns, u-turns, street fairs, discreet affairs, zipless sex, oedipus wrecks, bicycle treks, bicep flex, curls, squirrels, and all the girls in the world.

We stand opposed to Monday Mornings, small craft warnings, workaholics, jammed hydraulics, jobs, snobs, mobs, the elite, the effete, the compulsively neat, the banal, the anal, the varicose veinal, dieting, rioting, quieting.   Inhibition,   prohibition,   malnutrition, repression, depression, school in session. We take a dim view of authority, seniority, rule by minority. Frown upon gummers, bummers, overcast summers.

So if you have questions, complaints, or suggestions on how we could serve you better, have the freaking courtesy to keep them to yourself.   Don't make the common mistake of confusing us with anyone who gives a rat's ass about anything except hedonistic romps, self-serving ploys and unalloyed pleasure. We are out for max kix and don't care much about the niceties.   We will therefore resort to sexism, racism and ageism if we feel like it, and maybe throw in a little capitalism, barbarism, surrealism, and priapism. (Look it up.   Do you expect us to do *everything* for you?)

Of course you're entitled to your opinion. Stuck with it actually. What you need to do, sport, is start religiously reading **THE WEEKEND WARRIOR®** which will appear in The Week whenever I damn well feel like it. That will be all.

CHAPTER ELEVEN

The golden California summer basked languidly along while Caitlin transitioned into a new career not of her choice. She was a quick study, picking up what odds and ends of lore and technology were required of an editor. She realized that much of what she was learning would stand her in good stead in her real career once she could locate enough widows and orphans to sacrifice for her return to grace. She acquired a wider sense of the community taste, a heightened sense of grammar. Little things like knowing better than to use a noun like "transition" as though it was a verb. Or using "was" instead of "were" in the subjunctive case.

She had garnered little resentment around the office so far, mostly because the staff had all been fired and replaced with temps, jitterbug j-school scabs, and a few others jettisoned by the auto-castration of Channel Nine. The lack of broad resentment was more than made up for by the depth of Casey Chones' antipathy, however. Her feelings were betrayed eloquently by every movement, utterance, glance and breath. Not a big deal: Caitlin had experience at ignoring umbrage smoldering in the breast of lesser females. She settled in, poked around, tried her muscles, shook out her wings, and allowed running the second largest periodical south of Los Angeles to grow on her.

The more she morphed into an editor, however, the more she became aware that a certain thorn in her paw was sticking in her craw and just generally riding up her crack. Same shit different job: the fly in her anointment was Wiley. Apart from her personal distaste for him, she was concerned that his columns, though perhaps humorous to the young, brainless and shameless, were also unsavory and possibly even evil. Not much of a shock, but she now was in charge and had to do something about it. The upside was, she was in charge. At least, that was her impression at the time.

She had compiled a collection of questionable clips, neatly pinned on her bulletin board, that deepened her resolve that Something need be Done About that damn Wiley. The lead for a column entitled The Decline and Fall of the American Bosom read:

This is what we hotshot pro journalists refer to as a "Scoop". You'd wondered why until now.

One of the early Weekend Warrior columns had been a history of American weekend entertainment. It included lines she found jejune and disgusting:

> The three day weekend--hat trick of America's contribution to goofing off and the ultimate in TGIF--has been a tradition since Robinson Crusoe got off on Friday. In fact the first Thank God It's Friday party was thrown by Crusoe in 1821. This led to the invention of the Happy Hour, which was also thrown on Friday, who was actually far from happy about it.

Her hackles were further raised by a piece on sailing that she, a fan of Windjammer afternoons on the Bay, had actually suggested herself:

> It's edifying to note how many old nautical expressions are still in the common language. Fore and aft, learning the ropes, cut of his jib...all come into a new focus as one hangs on to a sloop or lurches the deck of a southern yawl.

> "Three sheets to the wind", a handy phrase for Weekend Warshipmates, suddenly becomes sensible, even as objects of the description become insensible. My favorite turn of tarry phrase is, of course: There She Blows. Or, "thar", whatever, so long as she blows.

She'd corrected or deleted some of those outbursts, but they mysteriously returned in the final printed version. She suspected that Chones drone, who obviously kept a doctrinaire distrust towards her for supplanting Moon and always took the side of writers against management. You could tell by the decorations and mementos in her office she was a commie-wannabe and malcontent.

Caitlin definitely remembered cutting the "i" out of a phrase which returned in print as the original: "Well, gentile readers." And although letters from the public were mixed, but mostly positive, she was also starting to get feedback from readers regarding replies Wiley sent to their missives protesting his columns. His answers were leading to less amicable correspondence. Some it from attorneys.

She was looking at one from an incensed Catholic girl in Tierra Santa, who'd complained about his referring to the Holy Trinity as "Daddy-o, Laddy-o, and Spook." How could he take people's beliefs so lightly, she had implored. Wiley's reply had not smacked at all of "Yes, Virginia." In fact, it had been,

"That's a very good question, honey. I'm glad you asked that question. Hey, sit on that question. Next question?"

She had attempted to tighten her reins on Wiley early on. She'd called him in and told him he needed to build a backlog, a term she'd just learned. Having several columns on hand in advance would not only make editing safer, ensure he didn't space deadlines, and allow her to get a forecast of his pissing in the punch. He'd agreed surprisingly easily, then turned in four columns the next day. Caitlin didn't know that he'd barfed them all into a cassette recorder during one all-night druggy/drunkie session in a Mimosa denizen's Toyota mini-motorhome. She considered them useless. But he had, after a fashion, complied.

She decided there was only one way to tighten up on Wiley, spike Casey's sabotage, and clarify the lines of authority. She hadn't been an editor long enough to learn any better, so she called a meeting. Herself, Chones, Ovarón. Kyle Albedo had memoed her that he would also attend, if that was all right. She thanked him for his interest and waited for the meeting, subtly honing her nails.

Wiley's jump to The Week had been less noted around the office than Caitlin's arrival and deployment. Largely because he was seldom in his nice new office and when he was, he was often unconscious, or at a level of consciousness to which "un" could only rank as an improvement. He stealthed in under Caitlin's glamour boss umbra and started gestating. Out on the street it was another story. He was catching on like a fire in the ratlines. Yuppies and cyberserfs, hipsters and students, beachboys and partydolls; all read Wiley and saw their chance to get in on something like The Tick, Duckman, Dr. Gonzo, The Simpsons, Kids in the Hall... but on the ground floor. Not to mention Ground Zero, since Wiley was starting to pop up in other urban weeklies--courtesy of syndication controlled by the canny Yao. He was San Diego's Own iconoclast and drawing a bigger following than a wounded tapir in the piranha tank.

And "following", in circulation and ad rate circles, is synonymous with "clout".

The meeting was comfortable enough in the refectory-style conference room that reminded Caitlin of the Hall of the Salem Elders, but getting nowhere. She just couldn't get across the degree of evil that Wiley was creating. Ovarón was oblivious and the Chones troll spitefully spiked every suggestion on the "artistic freedom" petard. Finally she played the "revenue card", an issue on which Ovarón had been burned once and now examined with ostrich-eyed acuity.

"Have we even measured what this is doing to our advertising sales?" she asked them all. Chones continued glareful, Ovarón glanced idly towards Kyle Albedo. "I think it's something that we have to keep in mind. Ads pay the bills."

Kyle's attention had been wandering around loose and getting into trouble until that moment, but he suddenly focused on her. Well hello, he thought. Who have we here? He formed the thought that the new editor might be more valuable as an ally than as a live action pin-up.

"Nice of you to think of us. Refreshing."

Casey scrambled onto the issue. She was furious that Editorial had actually taken the side of Ads, upsetting the natural order of things. You throw them a bone with special editions for real estate and restaurants and such: you don't let them dictate policy. Which real newspaper people are well aware of. She swung around on Kyle.

"So have you been losing ads lately, Kyle?" She knew he would never admit it if he had.

Kyle grinned, tapped his cigar ash. "Ad staffs are used to having to live with your attitudes," he told her, giving her just enough handsome smile to take the sting off. "What we do; if life hands us horseshit, we flog methane and orchid fertilizer."

Caitlin realized from Casey's triumphant posture that she had just lost a few points. She turned straight to Kyle. "We carry a lot of cellular phone space, don't we?" Kyle chuckled: there were cell ads all over the paper, the feeding frenzy of the times.

She tossed a stack of photocopies on the table then read aloud from her own:

This is a decade in which hand-held cellular phones are status symbols. Wow, electric slave bracelets. Why not just wear a collar and leash so the world of work and worry and weirdness can just snatch you up and jack you around at its leisure (since you no longer have any of your own).

Before Casey or Kyle could try spin-doctoring that decidedly anti-advertiser paragraph, she asked Kyle, "Since it's summer, I assume you have a bit of gardening and lawn care accounts?" Kyle nodded. "Don't we have some major space from Home Depot?" Another nod.

She read from her page as Kyle picked up a copy from the stack.

> A man's home is his old lady's castle so you'd best keep the lawn spiff. Right off the bat you're going to need a whole range of over-priced implements from Home Despot. Like a giant, gas-guzzling, power rider mower, equipable with snowplows, leaf-blowers, and rocket launchers. You will also need a neighborhood kid that you pay fifteen bucks to break the thing for you. I know, it sounds weird, but it's the way these things are done.

> Consider green paint. Or brickbats. Even bark, though it's much worse than bite. Don't mess with seeds: put in a few bulbs. Plant them in straight rows and they'll grow into track lighting. And don't plant the wrong ones. You know how many gardeners it takes to change a bulb? Answer next week.

She looked around to gauge the reaction to this strike against their ad buyers. Ovarón's brow was furrowed at he scanned his copy. He looked up, puzzled. "What does he mean, 'You can't get crabgrass off a toilet seat.' ?"

Kyle was chuckling. The rest looked at him so he shrugged, read:

> Forget those cruel, inhuman traps. Especially if you want to get anywhere with Bridget Bardot or Kim Bassinger. Around my spread we deal with moles in a kind manner. We kind of kill them, then we kind of eat them. You should try my Mexican Specialty, Pollo in Mole Sauce. *MMMMuy bueno.*

Great, Caitlin thought, I try to help your department out-- even though for selfish reasons--and you undermine me with cheap snickers. Some of this must have leaked through her porcelain poker face, because Kyle gave her a weak smile.

"Hey, we can always sell to paint stores and Mexican restaurants."

But he realized he had miffed her, and that any possible alliance there was worth a little assertion. He leaned forward in his seat and slipped in his oar.

"Look, Caitlin. I think you're missing something here." She regarded him with a blankness only subtextually hostile. "You aren't some assistant anchor anymore. You're the editor. If you say something gets cut, it gets cut. End of story."

Everybody in the room looked at him, with different reactions. Ovarón thought, Then why didn't that work for me? Casey glared at Kyle, who she had always viewed as a parasite perched on the editorial haunches and sucking off their hard-fought blood. Caitlin gave him a long, appraising look that Kyle read as a hand extended to seal a pact.   She tapped the table twice with an exquisite fingernail, then said, "Of course you're right, Kyle. Thanks for reminding me. I'm editor, I control content."

She cast a benign, wide-eyed look at Ovarón.   "Correct, Hollis?" Ovarón, though thinking that the matter would take some thought to sort out, nodded. Caitlin turned a much less gentle eyeball to Casey. "Correct, Ms. Chones?" There was nothing Chones could do but nod her head. For the moment, anyway.

Caitlin carefully picked the first article over which to break Wiley's--and by extension, Casey's--chops. She waited for a slam-dunk. It came soon enough.

She'd managed to trap Wiley and haul him into her office, but there was something inconclusive in the way he regarded her, slumped in a chair in his yardsale chic, leaning his head in one hand for gingerly support, his eyes wide and unblinking as though painted on his lids to fool the history teacher. She finally decided she had as much of his attention as was currently available and shoved a copy of his most recent column towards him. He gave it a cursory inspection without moving. She had the feeling that his mannequin-like external calm cloaked some

94

horrendous clamor of neural nastiness within. And she was right about that.

She went right to her One-Punch, a paragraph she'd highlighted in baby blue, early on in the seminal article, "How To Quit Breathing. (Smoke)". She read it aloud:

> One scheme with which I had mixed success (mixed, that is, with total disaster and a touch of nitrous oxide) followed from the logic that one cannot smoke when someone is sitting on his (or her, I suppose) face. It remained only to line up a nonstop telethon of face-sitters, brave girls who variously occulted my lips and nasopharynx in two hour shifts for over three days, during which I smoked only one cigarette. How I managed that will have to remain shrouded in innuendo, I'm afraid, having been a little disgusting and possibly impossible. Suffice it to say that it would not have worked had the girl been a virgin.

If she had communicated to Wiley the depth of her concern about the suitability, printability, fitness and suggestiveness of the piece, she failed to see evidence of it dawning on his face.

"Wiley," she said. He continued to stare. "This just isn't acceptable. I think you know that, actually. You're trying to test the limits of the situation, aren't you? Well, here they are. We aren't going to print anything sexually suggestive or degrading while I'm editor here. I know you can clean this up and it will still be funny and... well, whatever it is that you do."

Wiley had finally moved, but no towards enlightenment. He was now making an in-depth survey of his fingernails. Probably not for the public health reasons one would surmise. Caitlin found herself speaking in measured tones we use with recalcitrant kindergarteners or retarded security guards.

"I hope you understand what I'm saying here, Wiley. I'm hoping that in the future I won't need to interfere with your work."

"Me neither." He had spoken. Good. Very, very, good. Now...

"So let me point out a few things about these paragraphs," she said, pointing to the Two-Punch section, also emphasized in Tarheel Blue. Wiley made no move to read along , so she read it aloud: more didactic techniques from kindergarten and rent-a-cop academy.

The pack of cigarettes is attached to one end of a length of dental floss, piano wire, or some such thin, strong material, and the other end is looped around the penis, just behind the legendarily sensitive glans. This method is very effective for compulsive worker/smokers, given to snatching out the pack in the heat of computations. Gradually, aversion is built. Of course women are handicapped in this method since they don't have penises, but perhaps can figure out a way to get by. I've never understood how women get along without penises anyway. They are fun, decorative, and affectionate, but also essential to many basic activities. I have spent hours trying to imagine pissing off a tall parking garage onto a busy street without a penis and am a loss at how to do it. Or rather, "they" are at a loss. Well, *viva la difference.* You've come a long way baby, but are strictly a local operator when it comes to pissing off. I'd be envious, too.

"Now, come on, Wiley." She tried to soften things up with a nice smile, showing that she knew that he knew that such things just don't fly. No dice. She paused, looking for whatever footwork would work on this roach from the woodwork.

"I'm only interested in applying normal standards here," she said. "Really, I just want to make this less hassle for both of us."

Wiley lurched to his feet, catching himself on edge of her desk. Leaning closer than she had ever, ever wanted to be to him, he said, "Less hassle's cool."

Caitlin's mixed relief was brief, because he pushed off the desk and tottered to the door muttering, "Let's start right now."

At the door her turned, said, "I just soooo fucking quit," and caromed out the door and through the desks of the outer office.

Caitlin fell back in her chair, staring out at the closing street door. She felt her limbs relax, her head falling back on the ergometric support, her shoulders shrugging off a weight, her breath exploded out of her like a sprinter's finishline gasp. Her arms flapped to the side and she lay back as though crucified staring at the ceiling in rapture. From somewhere, syllables of praise and joy bubbled up to her lips and she murmured, "Hallelujah!" Then she shouted, "Hallelujah!" This brought glances from the cube pits to her wide window, so a lot of people saw her leap to her feat, throw back her head, raise her arms and handle the whole chorus.

CHAPTER TWELVE

Rollie would have thought he'd never see the day. At least not again. After almost fifteen years at one of the most prestigious positions in town, he was back to applying for one of the scraggly excuses for journalism jobs that San Diego County offered. Depressing. But necessary for peace of mind, he reminded himself. He wouldn't mind dragging out surfing all fall. Fortunately, that's the way it usually worked in his field anyway. Slim pickings was the special every day.

He was talking to Jonathon Toppen out of sheer efficiency: Toppen owned the biggest string of weekly papers in the County and was usually looking for somebody to work on them. Generally somebody young, energetic, hungry, and likely to stay that way awhile. Entry level to nowhere, was how Rollie termed it. Like getting in on the World Trade Center at the ground floor. Toppen was sympathetic. And worse, voluble.

"You remember the Sixties, Rol?" he asked, leaning back in a rickety chair with his feet on a pathologically disarrayed desk. Twenty years older than Rollie, Toppen didn't look like much of the sixties had stuck to him. He was a very trim, clean, sleek individual from his high-gloss shoes to his shining bald pate. Rollie's memories of that decade consisted mostly of watching guys Toppen's age flip out and wishing he'd get old enough to join in before it all blew up and drifted away. No such luck. Even Berkeley wasn't really that way by the time Rollie got there.

"Don't they say if you can remember the sixties you didn't do it right?"

"Or didn't do enough," Toppen snorted. "But what I mean is, how'd you like to have been a whore back then? All of a sudden you have to compete with younger stuff that can be picked up free at any coffee house?"

"Hard to compete with freebies," Rollie agreed, lounging on a moldering sofa. "It's like freelancing when people can just pick stuff up free from people trying to build syndication."

"Exactly. I built up this chain for years, totally independent. Nine community papers from the beach to the high desert. Anywhere you go in this county, there's those little streetcorner soldiers with the latest local Direction under glass."

True enough. In fact, Rollie had a copy of the Pacific Beach Direction in his pocket as he spoke. And already knew the Direction this conversation was headed.

"Then along comes old dribbleglass with the Southcoast Wack and all of a sudden you can pick up a more expensive paper for free," Toppen ranted. "Well, you get what you pay for. But who really pays for it is the entire community."

"I agree," Rollie said, suspecting it wouldn't do any good.

"Who were those dingbats with the 'Freedom Isn't Free' song?"

"Moral Re-Armament," Rollie supplied.

"Yeah, what happened to them?"

"I guess they disarmed. Morality just has to fight it out hand to hand."

"It's an irony nobody seems to get a clue about," Toppen plunged on. "You look at the economy as an election, the candidates that get the most money stay in, right? Well these free papers pre-empt your 'vote' in the matter, don't they?"

Whoa. Rollie had never thought about it quite that way before. "How can it be a rip-off if it's free?"

"And ironically, that's what costs you your freedom. Where would evolution be if the weak didn't die, just kept on reproducing anyway? If you don't like what the Week does, you can't boycott it, can't cancel your subscription. They don't need your money."

"But they need your eyeballs."

"They need your eyeballs to be out there. There's no way to prove you aren't reading it anymore. So they do whatever they want and the public can't have a say in it, can't get rid of it."

"Well, there's only a free press if you own a press," Rollie said. "I can say whatever I want these days and nobody hears about it."

"Not everybody gets to write editorials, Moon. Say whatever we want. But I'm responsible to my readers. I have to speak for them, not my own whimsy or my advertisers' interests. Or they'd stop sticking quarters in my little soldiers."

"I see what you mean. If you don't pay for something there's no contract with you, not even symbolic. No transaction or relationship."

"You got it, kiddo. No contract. Their only love life is with advertisers."

"Wow, Jon, that really is pretty ironic."

"You bet your ass. And it gets worse. How many other "free" things are there like that? It's kind of like the problem with socialism. If everybody owns it, nobody owns it. You get socialized medicine, you can't vote with your wallet anymore. They give you a free house, you can't vote with your feet."

"Scary words for citizens of the Free World."

"Now you're getting the picture, Rol. Sorry to trouble your day."

"Well apart from my old job being an evil conspiracy to enslave people's minds in a profit-driven commie plot, I guess this means you're not flush enough to hire me."

"Boil it down, that's what we come up with. Sorry, man."

"Two words." Rollie stood up and headed for the door, winding through old furniture buried under stacks of paper products. "Surf's up."

If Caitlin had thought her previous meeting had been stupid and useless, well, this one also had "Boo" Yao present. With his usual knack for making her feel warm and fuzzy all over. This time he was telling her she'd screwed up making Wiley quit. And she hadn't killed him yet.

"Look," she said, keeping her homicidal bent under wraps unless it became absolutely imperative, "We already had this meeting. And I was told that I'm in charge of the editorial content of this paper."

"Oh, you ah, you ah," Ovarón gushed, patting the air in front of him like a man checking the resilience of a trampoline. "But not personner. Wirey varuable resoulce."

"But he *quit*!" Caitlin almost screamed. "I didn't fire him. I just told he we take a dim view of articles about sticking cigarettes up vaginas or whizzing on people's heads for recreation."

Ovarón blinked at that, trying to get some sort of picture of what she'd said and how it would get into his paper, then concluded it was one more time when he just didn't quite get it, but would weather its blowing over.

"Tlouble is," he told her. "Wirey tarent."

"Wirey's *whul*?"

"He tarent. Ahtistic. He lite, we pubrish, people buy. How it wuhk."

"All the writers are talent. But we edit them. *That's* how it works. I don't like all those ads for strip clubs and homophone whores that Kyle's bringing in, but you know what...that's his department. And he does a great job."

Kyle, carefully keeping out of things this time, nodded his thanks for the prop. Caitlin sat as erect as possible, both hands on the table to intone her closing argument. "So I don't go over there and tell him to clean up his shop. And editorial is my shop."

Yao was unscathed by her picturesque conviction. "But you rost Wirey," he insisted. "No good."

Caitlin, casting wildly about for alternatives to outright murder, hit upon an unlikely source of support. "Casey," she said, keeping the plea out of her voice, "You have much more experience than I do. What do you think about editing the writers? Let them do whatever they want?"

Casey had to admire the way Caitlin had put her on the spot. She thought about it a minute, then said, "The thing is. With artists... and Wiley isn't really like the guys who write news or calendars, he's an artist... you can't really hack and slash and compel."

"Then how do you edit?" Caitlin demanded.

"Talent is like a natural force," Casey told her, warming to her lefty/artsy analysis. "You don't just stop rivers or get rid of them. You don't stop floods or wildfires. You have to work with them to an extent. Control without containing." She was pleased with that speech, looked mildly at Caitlin to see if it sunk in.

Caitlin leaned forward to speak and froze, her mouth half opened. The sight of her leaning forward with her lips parted caused Yao to shift his legs around and Ovarón to launch into one of the interior scriptural monologues that were his subconscious guards against intrusions of The Flesh.

The pause was getting a little nervy when Caitlin snapped her mouth and leaned back in her chair, gears obviously lined up and awaiting the kiss of the clutch. She smiled at Casey and said, "Then I assume you would be capable of controlling Wiley?"

Casey jerked visibly as the trap snapped around her. The toothy jaws she had just smugly created, set and baited. Dammit. But there was no real choice but to play up. She looked

Caitlin right in the eye and said, "Yes, of course. It's what I've done for years."

Caitlin shifted her gaze to Yao and very sweetly murmured. "So he's her responsibility?"

Now it was Yao's turn to take a pause for thought. Which he did, with his usual abacus clickety-click of mind. He squinted and smiled around the table, then said. "So we got agleement now?"

Caitlin and Casey nodded with varying degrees of warmth, Ovarón pulled himself out of a mental recitation in which each resounding iron phrase began with, "Seek ye not..." and gave the quick cursory nod of a student caught napping and trying to fake an answer to unheard questions. Kyle, who'd been replaying the back nine of Torrey Pines in his head, gave a debonair shrug. Yao wouldn't stop grinning.

"Ret Wirey be Wirey," he beamed.

Wiley hadn't had a drink in almost five minutes. There was an ersatz tequila right by his elbow on the curvaceous bar, but he was involved in a nose-to-nose harangue with Cathilda about Safe Sex and too busy ranting and dodging spit to pick it up.

"You got a position, Wiley," she was yapping, her massive mams lunging around like burly retainers just waiting for her to unleash them on Wiley and the world in general. "You gots to serve and protect."

"That's the *cops*, you dusky dimwit," Wiley shouted, "I'm a columnist. I'm supposed to confuse and piss off."

"Well, you're pissin' me off, you honky-ass ho. You needs to get your Weekend Warhorses to stop spreading killer jizz around the sistahood. I ain't foolin witchoo."

"Sure, sure," Wiley smirked. "How about a nice little how-to for kinder, gentler drunk driving and date rape?"

"I *know* you didn't just say that," Cathilda bawled, a common windup for her to move arguments to a more physical plane. "I'll show you what us workin' niggers think about that drunk rape shit."

But we will never know exactly how sentiment runs in those quarters because Jerome's blunt voice hammered through the discussion like a referee's whistle. "Wiley, phone for you. At least I think it's for you."

Glad to be out of Cathilda's crosshairs, Wiley turned to his long-neglected drink. "Who did they say they want?"

"Said, 'Wirey, prease.' And stop giving out this number!"

Wiley cupped his hands beside his mouth and yodeled, "Lassie, come home." He put the phone to his ear, staying blank as he panned the arc of expectant faces. Still expressionless, he raised a finger. The suspense built. Wiley tossed the receiver to Jerome and spun the finger like it a circus plate juggler. A cheer rose from the bar.

"In fact," Wiley crowed. Then lifted both forearms and spun them counter-rotationally. Jerome smirked, reached for another bottle on the backbar. Wiley started doing the woof, woof Arsenio chant and the whole bar took it up, flushed with joy for their colleagues happiness over whatever it was. And, of course, getting free rounds.

Strack wheeled out of the restroom scanning the celebration of waving and woofing. "Who let the dogs out?"

"THEY did," Wiley howled. "Cats outta the bag, mutts off the leash, cow humped over the moon, bear shit on the Pope. I came, I saw, I conquered, I came twice for good luck. YEOWWW!"

Jasper picked up his free drink and blinked at Wiley. "Does this mean you have to go back to work?"

CHAPTER THIRTEEN

"Hey... back at work!" Kyle spoke those words but Wiley, pasted deep into his chair by a congress of demons, registered only the sounds emanating from the dapper suit leaning in his open office door. He didn't connect them with any particular semiotic significance. The suit was a big waxy cartoon guy with a Dick Tracy jaw, like on those little comix they used to wrap around bubblegum. He was smiling, his teeth sparkling with rhinestones, his herringbone shirt writhing with glowing sagas of sci-fi depravity. He leered and drooled at Wiley, sagged against the door like a melting chocolate Santa. Wiley sagged deeper. This, too, would pass.

"Glad you're back on board, my man," Kyle continued cheerfully. "I appreciate what you've been doing for us. And just wanted to let you in on something. We're doing a special fashion number in August. Not too early to be thinking fashion, right?"

Wiley's fritzed neurons nimbly interpreted those remarks as a series of electronic crackles and pops, somewhat like a bug zapper eating a bowl of dry cereal.

Kyle winked, pointed a pistol finger and mouthed the word "Fashion" before moving away. For some reason known only to the poltergeists that inhabit the frontier between cognition and perdition, Wiley caught that one word. Right in his teeth. He bolted out of his chair and dived across his desk, skimming a wake of papers and detritus. Two long rubbery Plastic Man strides took him to the door. He slithed down the hall with his head bumping the suspended ceiling, avoiding glances at the ambiguously patterned carpeting, which had already tried to trap him into a maelstrom of treacherously fascinating hellfire. Barging into the Ladies' Room, he ignored a mousy Latina temp who shrieked, quailed back into a stall and locked it, feverishly crossing herself.

The Wiley in the mirror was not the insubstantial, wavery Wiley who leaned over the sink. Not the Wiley made of India rubber and hastily wrapped in stiff bondage by fabrics made of alien materials and held together by fiendish devices. Not the Wiley whose eyes moved slowly forward out of squirming flesh, in search of answer from the solid, God-like Wiley he saw before him. *That* Wiley was clad in radiance and relevance, in clothing contrived by squads of ancients to sheathe every line of his elegance. The Wiley who stared out from deep eyes that swirled back to the beginnings of illusory time, and spoke from a mouth that could chew down mountains. And said the word, and the word was "Fashion", and he saw that it was good. Wiley was on a mission.

Fortunately he had already written his piece for the following week, so being found comatose and naked in the bathroom accompanied only by a Señorita keening prayers to Saint Euphemia, Patron of Hysterical Virgin Rapee Dontwannabes--and the subsequent legal and medical procedures--didn't disrupt the smooth flow of Wiley to the masses.

"It's such a winner I can't believe we never did it before." Fresh from informing Wiley of the upcoming Back To School Fashion Issue, Kyle was trying to impress Caitlin with how clever it was. And therefore that he was. "We can kiss off the school kid stuff. These people don't care from kids. Wiley showed us that."

Yea, a light unto our feet, Caitlin thought.

"But hitting this time of year as a fashion season is perfect. We get the jump on all the autumn showing stuff, hit the students and juniors. We don't have any sort of reputation with the boutiques and outlets. Haven't had, anyway."

Caitlin glanced at him, thinking she heard him approving of the way things were going. Kyle shrugged. "Everybody is fired up for doing a special fashion thing for that issue. Even that sports idiot. I even got Wiley on board, believe it or not." Which did little to impress Caitlin, since she could see the street from her office window and what she saw was Wiley, strapped to a gurney, being trundled into an ambulance. She gave a radiant smile. Kyle felt his futures increasing.

"That reminds me, Kyle," she said casually, still savoring the glow from seeing Wiley boxed up and shipped out, "I wanted to show you the galleys for his next column. We've got some time for a change and I thought you should know what's hitting the fan."

Kyle rapidly scanned the sheets she handed him, initial consternation replaced by a rascally smile.

"I appreciate your showing this to me. It's a nice switch to have editorial concerned over us poor schmucks who just pay the bills and salaries."

"I didn't want it to mess up any accounts you have going. Or at least warn you."

"So you're definitely running it, no matter what I say?"

"You know how it is now. He's a creepy jerk, but he's our creepy jerk."

Kyle pointed a finger vaguely upwards. "Not to mention 'their' creepy jerk?"

"Did I mention that?"

Kyle gave her his best smile and perched a hard flank on her desk. Caitlin immediately stood up. "Since you want my input, I'll say this. We take the high road on this issue. No censorship just to save our bottom line." His glance took in the line of Caitlin's bottom as he spoke. "We treat him like the featured artiste he is and just live with however the chips fall."

Caitlin smiled and nodded as he moved towards the door. "Great, Kyle. I think you're right. Thanks for the feedback."

Kyle tipped a hand in salute. "Thanks for putting me in the loop. For once."

Caitlin mused as Kyle closed the door. The references to previous treatment of ads by editorial had not been lost on her. Was it possible she was actually doing a better job here? She thought it just might be.

Kyle sprinted to his office, grabbed his phone with one hand and started thumbing his pager with the other.

Responding instantly and at times illegally to Kyle's page, Phil Newburne blasted up I-5, threading his Dodge Viper through temporary holes in the traffic with death-inspiring dash. Goosing the snarling V-8 into a turbo whine, he stood two cars on their noses taking the 52 exit, blitzed by soccer moms onto the La Jolla Parkway and floored it up the canyon. Power slaloming down Torrey Pines Road, he entered downtown La Jolla at warp speeds, skidding through little-known sidestreets and alleys until he could line up his final lunge into the parking lot. He took an extra second to pull around behind the dealership before piling out and zipping inside. The Porsche guys didn't want customers seeing his mighty Mopar and he didn't want them seeing it.

His homicidal driving had paid off: he popped past Karl Loberg's secretary and into his office while Karl was still on the phone with Kyle. He always answered his wife's objection to his purchase of the rubber-dusting horsepower overkill of the Viper with full performance package by saying, "I want that power to be there if I need it to save my ass." That day had finally come and the Viper had definitely viped ass.

Karl looked up, waved at Phil and put the call on speakerphone. "Guess who just steamed in the door, Kyle. Without knocking, either."

"Some manners, Phil. Look I was just telling Karl about Niekro pulling his ad for next week. I thought it might be a chance for him to really kick butt."

"Good thinking, Karl. You can move in on those guys right here in The Week, where it counts with your best age and income group. Can we support him, some way, Kyle?" Delicate stuff here, since Phil had absolutely no idea what Kyle was talking about.

Kyle chuckled over the hollow speaker. "We already are. That's why Niekro's pulling out. We've got an article coming out pointing out some deficiencies of those Beemers. Supposed to be pretty powerful. So I figured, Who'd want to take a shot at that market, pick up a few buyers who might be changing their minds and, hey, here's an ad right here for a *real* sports car."

Karl squinted at Phil, but spoke to Kyle. "Now when you say, 'right there'?"

"Absolutely, buddy. Very same page. And not back in autos, either. Right up in editorial, underneath the Warrior column."

Karl smiled, "The weekend thing? Say, that's not a bad approach."

"Sorry, I can only give you an eighth page there. You understand, the placement. But you could follow up with something back in the auto classifieds, pound it home."

"I like it. You sure BMW's pulled out?" Karl looked at Phil to confirm, got a sweeping palm of insouciance and readiness.

"He said to cancel. He might change his mind, but I'm not counting on it. He hated an article and over-reacted," Kyle's tone made it clear that the kind of man who would jump the gun by pulling advertising was too embarrassing to even discuss.

"How much does a one-shot there work out to?"

"Oh, you could do a lot better with a multiple. But what am I taking your time for? Phil knows all that better than I do, and he can put you right on this."

"We'll see what we can come up with. Thanks for calling, Kyle," Phil smiled at Karl with the air of a man tying a napkin around his neck.

"We like to work with people. Talk to the gentleman, Phil. I'll let you guys get to it." And Kyle rang off.

"You're showing some initiative, Karl. We've never had a dealer go up front like that before. I've got an idea how we can whipsaw 'em front to back section, then follow up next week. Plus, I can give you a break on insertions because Kyle's making an exception..."

Kyle didn't even wait for the whole contract to emerge from his fax machine. Way to fire, Phil. He immediately turned to his computer monitor, which displayed the list he'd just made up of numbers to dial automatically. He moved the cursor to the list: Jaguar, Lexus, Mitsubishi, Rover... When the first number highlighted he hit the mouse button and heard the ringing in his headset.

"Yo, Ronnie! Kyle Albedo at The Week. How's it hanging? Listen..."

Smiling smugly, Karl Loberg pushed the paper across his desk towards his three salesmen. Wow, they thought, quarter page up front. Nice support. Help us get some asses in these saddles. One of them read quickly, spoke up. "Ah, the Warrior column's about cars this week. Smooth move, Karl."

"That's not a column," Karl beamed. "It's a paid hit."

AUTO-PSYCHOMETRY
By The Weekend Warrior

You can't pick up a magazine published for women (or whoever else does their reality check at supermarket checkstands) without having some nitwit quiz analyze your personality (and more frequently the character of whoever is stuck with you) by scoring traits like your favorite foods or sexual positions. Men generally disdain this amateur pyschodiagnosis since we've long known how to judge people's characters without messy inkblots, quirky graphanalysis, heady phrenology, or having to add up scores. Just get a look at their car. End of story.

But only the beginning of this article, which will go on to say that our wheels are central to establishing our mistaken identities. Some years ago a drinking acquaintance of mine, who does valet parking at a UTC monolith that will remain as nameless as it is already faceless and graceless, told me something I've never forgotten. "Drivers of gold Audis," he confided, "Should be buggered to death." I wouldn't dream of questioning data from such an authoritative source and in fact years of hitch-hiking (circa 1974-1981) taught me that he spoke the literal truth. If anything, you could include drivers of any gold car.

Once it is realized that cars are barometers of their owner's personality it becomes more meaningful than astrology or any idiot Kulture Kwiz. Some such analyses are easy: people who drive Audis, Opels, Pacers, or Hummers are obviously idiots. Those in Cadillacs tend to be swine and those in the modern tiny Cadillacs are idiot swine. We can tell what drivers of red or black cars are trying to say almost as easy as those with sloganized VW's and jalopies.

But some traits are less evident, such as the deep-seated financial insecurities of those with purple or yellow cars (or, oddly enough, any make of DeSoto or Saab). Pickup drivers are easy to read, but what kind of mentality pilots a four wheel drive Jeep with gold trim? Or better yet, a Land Rover--an even more overpriced and useless mall mountaineering vehicle imported from the rugged terrain of England? (That Hummer owners are that much more stupid, piggy, and deluded seems to obvious to mention: but just in case...) Are SUV drivers showing machismo fantasies or mini-van fashionability run wild? Easy to answer that one: the driver is either a man or a woman.

Speaking of which, some cars are made only for women. And not just the boutique Camaros and Vettes with automatic trannies and decor--the kind often referred to as "wive's cars" but which you probably associate with coke dealers from Leucadia. We're talking about cars made for single women. Starting with early models like the Triumph TR6, continuing with the Fiat X 1/9, and Pontiac Fiero, leading up to the Miata. Women who drive these cars tend to be racy, either independent or co-dependent, and either divorced or working on it. Men who drive these cars are less than men and secretly know it. This makes them devious, unpredictable, and suicide-prone. Don't get between an overpass abutment and a male in a Fiero. Especially if he's smoking menthol cigarettes, but that's another article.

Some cars change their character indications over the model years; note the difference between the jolly folk who drove old rounded Mercedes and the empty slicksters in the new square Japanese-looking ones. Same goes with Volvos. Especially Volvo wagons and most especially blue Volvo wagons. Don't ask why, but don't trust these people or follow them too closely. You've been warned.

Most men used to be able to quickly tell the make and year of any car, but today they're so alike it's hard to even guess the country of origin. This would seem to indicate that people's personalities are also starting to converge. You may jump to your own conclusions--unless "co-incidence" is one of them.

Consider also the change in personalities in drivers of fun cars and convertibles. Show me a guy in a 1968 Bonneville ragtop and I'll show you a party in transit. Just add liquids and stir. But the current crop of sport-drivers? Well, maybe it's not their fault that we live in a sobersided decade in which a "Beemer" is regarded as a fun car. Preposterous. Have you ever heard of anyone fornicating with their feet out the back window of a BMW? Of course not. Nobody bulldogs calves from the fenders of BMW's, nobody drives them into golf course ponds to see if they'll float, pukes out the doors, runs over a row of lane marker cones, or gets cornholed over the hood. Just try to imagine some MBA hanging a BA out a BMW window. Even if you wanted to, you couldn't because of the passive restraints. You don't need any pop-psych phrase more telling than that one: passive restraints. Also available with passenger-side airbag.

The new "sports car" BMW is a symptom in itself. Ugly and nerdy looking, but you saw James Bond drive it in a movie cunningly not titled "Beemer Promo Clip" so you think driving one will make you cool. Well James Bond also drove around the street in a modified Venetian gondola and you don't do that, do you? Editorial note: it's a freaking movie, you morons! If you don't realize that, it says a lot about your state of mind. See? Our psych quizzes actually work.

Caitlin mused deeply on the total affects of the auto Rorschach column, which had turned into a pricklepatch of disturbing ramifications. Apparently Wiley could do no wrong. Furthermore, what wrong he did increased sales. Her only ally on the staff was on her side because she could bend editorial to the will of income. The income went into the coffers of Ovarón's mission work, which she was starting to see as offshoring babyrape. Editorials might enlighten people, but they read the paper in order to be more shallow and sluttish. She was starting to see the ecology of the paper in it's entirety, a bramble of double-edged conundrums. And the entire system served the dual purpose of supporting and protecting Wiley. Who was therefore beyond her control.   And she was well beyond strategies of controlling Wiley. There was a time for controlled backburn, but this was the time for Scorched Earth. Don't verminate, exterminate.

Ovarón was still publisher, and she had seen his Achilles heel from the start. It was why she was here in the first place, indirectly. He wouldn't think twice about sacrificing income on the altar of religious obsession. She didn't like back-stabbing, but when you are threatened by evil enemies who attack you ass-first, it has its place in the modern corporate arsenal. And one thing you could say about Ovarón: he might be an ideological idiot, but he *could* read. It was time to put the blocks to Wiley from On High.

CHAPTER FOURTEEN

Ovarón was deeply ambivalent about Casey Chones. As with so many other things. On the one hand, she was the one who had stood by him and rescued him in his sorest trial. Well, actually there were sorer trials pending on various court calendars, but sufficient to any given month the evil therein.

On the other hand, she apparently hated his guts and worse, made no bones about it. But he had few confidantes (his mother currently not taking calls due to immersion in sensory deprivation vats and Tantric studies) and he sensed something maternal about Casey. So he laid his troubles before her, enduring her smirks, sneers and occasional explosions into non-nurturing language. The current matter was only one scrawled letter from a marginally literate reader, but it disturbed him. So he felt it wise to see if it would disturb somebody else. The letter perturbed him; brought forth the possibility of snakes in his bosom, of his paper serving two masters, of promulgating work of Darkness.

Casey took his troubles in hand, furrowed her brow and read. She then burst into sardonic laughter and lofted the crumpled letter into her trash can with an impressive hookshot. "San Diego has a population of over a million people, Hollis. Do you realize how many idiots that includes?"

He gaped; obviously hadn't given it much thought. Despite being their Mayor, Casey thought. Better dumb it down. "More than most cities this size, let me tell you."

"But if we are printing Godless evil, corrupting children..." He stopped just short of her uplifted eyebrow. Woops, not a good idea to go there. "It just sounds very unwholesome," he whined. "What can I do to..." He petered out, looked at her.

"Tell you what, Boss." She always made that word sound so nasty and ridiculous. But what was she saying? "I'll look into this for you. Straighten things out. But you have to quit reading those letters. Anybody who would take this paper seriously enough to write us is obviously a serious yanker crank."

"Uh, yeah. Well thanks, Casey. I knew I could count on you."

You can barely count on your fingers, Casey thought. You couldn't count to twenty and a half, naked. But she did think about the letter denouncing Wiley's diabolic softening of the moral fabric. She knew Ovarón hadn't actually read the columns, and that his control over content had been snipped off and put out to pasture. Largely her own doing. On the other hand, he was still Publisher and majority stockholder. And who knew what his relationship with the other owners was like? She decided to talk to Wiley.

Which turned out easier than usual, since he was lying on his desk staring at the ceiling, quivering with an abundance, or even a surplus, of awareness. She stared at him in a half-hearted approximation of disgust, not knowing she was about to launch their relationship to an entire new level.

"Look, it's probably not a big thing. The screwballs from his church yapping at him. But he pays attention to that stuff. That's how we got stuck with you and that Vanderkeller harpy, remember?"

"No big deal," Wiley toned. What was a big deal, apparently, was the sound produced by repeatedly goosing his electric pencil sharpener into little spritzes of whizz.

"Then it's no big deal to stroke him a little, is it?"

"Stroke?" Wiley looked at her wide-eyed. "I don't do strokes! I might pimp an aneurysm or embolus, but I don't stroke off! Not without a coxswain or hazmat gloves, you understand?"

"Sure," Casey lied. "Why not write something he'll like and I'll show it to him. Read it to him, I'd guess. And he'll blither off on some other crusade against sanity."

"What would he like? The stroke thing is out. Heart attacks, that's what people are wearing. Prostrate cancer. Blow jobs to go. LammyWinks Habitrails. Ventricular felching. Street sertonin. Duck butter. If he's got eyes, I can cop it."

"Come on, you know the drill. God is basically a nice guy, just misunderstood. Jesus is a bro. Honor your parents, say "no" to sin, go to the church of your choice."

"Church, huh? Have you ever been to church?"

"Or course I've been to church," she answered acerbically.

"I never have. I don't think. Does Stonehenge count? Or those saucer people? Oh wait, Notre Dame is a church, right? They worship humpbacks." He swam into focus, swung off the desk. "No, this is great. I've wondered for years. I'll do it. Investigative journalism at it's finest. Infiltration. Deep throat cover. I'll go where no white breeder has gone before, penetrate the whole God frammis and blow it wide open."

"No, you're supposed to be nice. Puff it up. You *can* do that, right?"

"I don't remember."

"Devil bad, God good. I'll give you a few more inches. Next Tuesday. Okay?"

SITTING IN YOUR OWN PEW
By The Weekend Warrior

Even in these days of troubled times, one of the favorite American weekend pastimes is attending the church of your choice. "Church?!" I can just hear you yowling, "Booooring! We wanna catch the football game and go out and wreck some fragile ecosystems with our dirt bikes." No sniveling, we're going to church and that's that. Your scrawny little undeveloped souls need it. How else are you going to grow up into a Soul Man, like John Belushi or Sam N. Dave? No backchat, get dressed and brush whatever it is you did to your hair and we're on our way. But first, for the terminally back-slidden, a brief rundown on why one goes to church.

The primary reason for attending church (and for being fairly uncritical about the propositions put forth there) is simple and monolithic. We're talking about Sin. The Big Book is quite explicit about the wages of Sin. And if you've ever tried making ends make on the wages of Sin, you know where that's at. Of course there are various types of sin. Cardinal Sin, for one; the kind learned in College. Or perhaps St Louis. Then there is your Venial Sin. Venial sins are no big deal and hardly worth the trouble of committing. Sloth and envy and coveting and such. No rep, no rap.

Sins of commission (frequently incurred by salesmen) and omission (also a bugaboo of salesmen) figure in, but not prominently. Some sins are a little archaic, like coveting one's neighbor's wife, ass or ox. When was the last time you looked over the fence at yon greener grass and found yourself thinking, "Whoa, nice ox?" Don't tell me, tell your pastor or Dr. Ruth.

Perhaps the most daunting is Original Sin. Not some offshore knockoff. Not some sleazy signed, numbered edition of 666. Sin in it's original and uncensored version. Like unadulterated adultery. Penal envy. Covert coveting. Billy Idolatry. Some churches will tell you that Jesus died for your sins. I can relate to that—I'm dying for some good sin, myself. I prefer sins of the flesh, if anyone out there's interested—though I also dabble in gluttony and intemperance.

Which leads us to another sticky wicket propounded in Church—Hell. Not the Matt Groening kind with cute rabbits, either. The three-ring, brass-bound, hellacious hell of fire and brimstone (whatever that is). A churning urn of burning theological funk. A bottomless, endless pit of unquenchable fire in which sinners burn painfully through eternity like spiders flicked into a fireplace. Not exactly Club Med, you see. And, they will take pains to inform you, a must to avoid. This is where all the carousers and Hell's Angels end up. You can sin your ass off there, if you want, but you won't like it because you'll be suffering too much. Raw deal but that's the Hell of it.

On the other hand, there is heaven, a place populated by Teen Angels, Earth Angels, St. Peter, Paul and Mary and, presumably, St. Mounds. They are said to have a hell of a band. Between hell and heaven is Limbo, best known in this country as a dance invented for getting into pay toilets. And Purgatory, which was bought by the Aspen Corporation and turned into ski condos. These are half-way houses of the holy, where your soul can be stuck between planes for a temporary eternity. Best way to avoid them is go to a church that never heard of them.

The choice is obvious when put that way, of course; but a lot of people have trouble deciding and if you can't make up your mind by the time of the last trump, you go to Hell anyway. An angel named Gideon blows the last trump. Which, as any bridge player will tell you, can lead to your partner committing a Cardinal Sin. Not that any jury in the world would convict them. In fact, you'll note that Gideon has been assigned to the ignominious task of placing Bibles in motel rooms.

Fortunately God, when not otherwise occupied with green apple production and irrigating Indianapolis, is said to have devised methods for getting ringside tables in Heaven and avoiding off-season bookings in Hell. The best bet being Grace. No, not Grace Jones. I knew some oddwad would come up with that. Get serious, dammit, we're talking about your immoral soul here. No, we refer to Amazing Grace, the only kind with any real pull in the hereafter. So better figure out what you're here after or you'll be here after the last trump.

So, which church to attend? There are two main flavors in this country: Catholic and Protestant. Jews don't go to church—they go to synagogues. Besides, you have to watch what you say about Jews or you get in trouble. Crucified, even. Check out Mel Gibson. Suffice it to say Jews eat kosher, live in Ghettos, and are all trying to move to Zion (which ought to thrill the National Park Service no end.)

Catholics are strong on pomp, circumstance and multiphasic mindfucks. For instance, it is possible for Catholics to sin by despair. In other words (and you'll need to quit your infernal woolgathering and follow this closely) if you totally lose hope of heaven and feel you are too despicable a sinner to ever get it together, you have, in effect, low-rated the powers of Grace and therefore (you're gonna love this) committed *another sin*. Makes Catch 22 look small caliber, doesn't it?

Another theological kneeslapper—the words of the Pope (*ex catheter*) are infallible. Some dimbulb Pope in one of the less inspired centuries declared that this was not so, but it was later decided that (you guessed it) that pope was mistaken because a pope cannot be mistaken. Catholic churches are good for people who like Dungeons and Dragons...or lots of period props and costumes.

Protestant churches, on the other hand are somewhat disorganized, like most protesters. The original sect were the Lutherans, named after Martin Luther; king of the protest thing. God knows what he had to protest in those days. Catholics, mostly. But it also might have been something called the Diet of Worms, which is also understandable.

Then there are Baptists, who celebrate belief by holding people underwater. This is said to create the belief that one is being drowned and may have something to do with the rise of Credence Clearwater Revival. Whereas Catholics believe in celibacy of clergy, Baptists believe in celibacy for *everyone*. And no dancing, card playing or cosmetics, if you please. Baptists girls, who believe they are already damned for having danced, can have refreshingly relaxed attitudes towards further explorations of Sin, by the way.

Methodism was started by Stanislavski, and emphasizes method, as opposed to madness. Descended from Calvinists and Hobbsians, Methodists believe in the doctrine of the elect (even after elections) and in predestination (even without reservations). They have nothing to do with methadrine, methadone, or Calvin Klein. Neither do Baptists.

Episcopalians are formal and tight-assed, and generally called "High Church" by those not yet hip to Rastafarians and Mormons.

Mormons, in fact, are also known as the LSD church; the only American-made church and it shows. These knuckleheads were wandering around the desert trying to escape the problems caused by having more than wife (which right off shows you they were a few bricks shy of a load) and, as you might guess, starving. Eating whatever shrubs or cactus they might find in the desert. You get my drift? Suddenly they have a big vision of Indians giving them some tablets and a bunch of Kosmic Trooths. Does this sound familiar? Or did you sleep through the Sixties? And the best part is, their main dude is called Moroni. They got into Moronic things like building temples to seagulls, forming the Moron Tabernacle Choir and coming on with the Osmond Brothers. Mormons are sobersided, chaste and tenacious. They will not intermarry with Catholics (for fear of ending up with basements full of Original Sin). The thing is, Mormonism works. It's probably the religion you'd want your kids to have—especially if they're girls. Check it out. Get those Indians to lay some tablets on you and if you start seeing seagulls, say "Jonathon Livingston, I presume."

There is also a smorgasbord of smaller, one-trick churches for special needs. Seventh Day Adventists, for instance, have church on Saturday—a good bet for NFL fans. There are Christian Scientists, who believe in prayer instead of doctors (it's also your only hope against lawyers); Muslims, who believe Salman Rushdie's life is worth $2 million; Quakers, who don't believe in war; and Buddhists, who don't even believe in reality.

Or, you can just pick a church by the music. Black Protestant churches are best; great choirs, a lot of soul, and most of all, they've got rhythm. Unlike Catholics, which is probably why there are so damned many Catholics. You can also choose a church with a big, impressive pipe organ, but there is actually no proven relationship between organ size and pleasure.

There is a certain etiquette in church-going. Tip the ushers for a seat up close, on the left so you can see the pianist's hands. Specify Apocalypse or Non-Apocalypse section. When they pass the money plate, try not to grab too much; there is often barely enough to go around. Many churches have little slips of paper in the seats. Write song requests on these and hand them to the ushers so they can take them to the organists. Periodically everyone will stand up and start singing songs you've never heard of. Just fake it with anything appropriate you know. "Stairway to Heaven" is a natural, but would be in poor taste sung backwards. Say something to the preacher on the way out to show him you stayed awake through his sermon. Let him know you share his concerns about current immorality, but don't offer to give demonstrations. Don't be too cute—ecclesiastics almost never say things like, "Let's do communion."

Religion provides the opportunity to profit from the thoughts of a unique blend of wise, loving saints and dangerous, genocidal psychos. In recent years, it has lost prestige; people preferring to believe in politics, nature, magic, and science—disciplines even more dangerous, fascist, lethal and loony. Church still appeals to those with more confidence in God than their senators, shrinks or bank accounts. No black Sabbaths, white weddings, or screaming blue messiahs; no first causes, second comings or third worldisms—just folks hooked on a feeling and high on believing. So, until next week, may the lord bless your pointy little heads.

Casey couldn't believe it when she got the piece. Trashed and hierogylphicked as usual, but just what the doctor ordered. She transcribed it into Human, printed it out, stalked Ovarón to his office, sat him down and read him the whole thing. And thus did manifest two miraculous conversions.

Ovarón, while failing to comprehend most of the references, managed to grasp that the maligned Wiley was in fact a champion of things Godly and ecclesiastic. A paradigm really. He felt proud to have him on board. In his righteous glow he asked Casey how Wiley felt about false witness born against sins of the flesh. She left immediately, so he had to call the receptionist to send Wiley a basket of hams and cheeses crammed full of religious tracts about mission orphanages.

The other reader who suddenly swerved into Wiley's camp was Casey herself. She had transcribed his previous missives on automatic, the typesetters' blindness to copy content that allows print people to remain off the front pages of crime sections and admission books to closed observations wards. Aided by her resentment of his person, his style, and his usurpation. Reading aloud had brought her to an awareness of something. The guy could actually write. And had a nice wry wit. And handled subtext as ably as any cosmetic surgeon.

She stayed at her desk after work, reading the past columns, and transcripts of his TV show. She was dumbfounded. Morning Becomes Electric? Whoa. She was working with a major writer and her admiration brimmed over. Like most educated populists, she assumed artistic talent--and wasn't writing really the Queen of the Arts?--to be geniuses and positive beings. She was the type who listened raptly to the pronouncements of Bob Dylan or Joan Baez and assumed they made sense. Who took Bono seriously. Who would vote for Martin Sheen. To say nothing of Warren Beatty.

All that rapturous undergrad reading of Bukowski and Burroughs and Thompson was bound to catch up to her some day. She was impressed by Wiley, sucked into the maelstrom of his descent. She'd acquired no immunity to the Wiley bug.

One reader not swayed into the Wiley Fan Club upon reading the column was Caitlin Vanderkeller. It only took her a couple of paragraphs to figure out why the column had been written, deduce who was behind it, and assume it worked. Shit. Even God liked Wiley. She might just be stuck with him. Maybe she should become a Catholic and start praying him away. Wait a minute, wasn't there a little Santeria store up in Normal Heights? Maybe they'd have a spell to entice Darkness to come claim its own.

CHAPTER FIFTEEN

Rollie Moon was hardly what Caitlin had expected. Her only exposure to print media people had been writers from sections with idiotic names like "What's Happening" and "Street", that interviewed her because she was a media figure. Who gave great glossies. Sycophants glutting on glamour and sniffing for blood in the water, they responded very predictably to handling. Other than some dweeb from a short-lived "coastal living" mag, Rollie was the first actual editor she'd ever met. Maybe they were all like this. She was starting to get a little intrigued.

Not a bad-looking guy. In an unstudied way. But she sensed something odd about him, even eerie. Shaggy mop of sun-streaked hair and a beard edging out from straggly towards unruly. He wasn't exactly disheveled, but was far from the level of shevel she was used to. He had a rangy beach build; the long, smooth muscles of swimming, surfing and volleyball. Approaching forty and spending hours at a desk wasn't doing his physique any favors, but was adding "character" to a face that had always been a shade too intelligent to write off as SoCal Beach Boy.

He wore the sockless deck shoes, aloha shirt tucked into faded jeans, and unstructured cotton sport coat he considered his work clothes. His comfort attire would have been knee-length swimming jams, weathered Ughs and maybe a towel. He wore a wide-brimmed white straw hat, too. On the back of his head, which her mother always told her was a good sign. But, she figured out, the odd thing wasn't the way he looked: it was that he obviously didn't care about it, probably never thought about it. This was so strikingly opposed to the attitudes of the men she'd known and dated and worked with that it had a subliminal impact on her, like meeting a coyote when you've only known show dogs. She'd decided he might look fuzzy, but was a little dangerous.

The interview was pathetic, of course. Here was the guy who had sat in the chair she was sitting in. Well, the ugly one she'd replaced with the current luxury/power model. And applying for a staff writer job. One of those left vacant by people who'd quit to support what he'd started. She could almost understand that normally, but this didn't seem, somehow, like a guy who'd do that. She couldn't say why.

After five minutes of pattycaking each other, she'd tried to move into the sorts of questions Scorment and Yao had emailed her when they heard about his application and told her to interview him and sound him out on issues like possible impending lawsuits or union trouble. He parried them effortlessly, but didn't move on into pressing the case for hiring somebody who'd been canned as a trouble-maker.

She didn't realize it, but she was impressed. She wasn't used to meeting guys like Rollie. It's as if somebody who had eaten only on Formica tables all their life suddenly inherited an antique walnut drop-leaf. A few nicks, non-linear pattern, less carefree. But you could see how they might grow to love it and never again be truly satisfied with plastic imitations. Caitlin had only reached the stage where she realized that Rollie would be harder to wipe off and polish.

What really grabbed her attention was that he seemed to speak casually, without any spin or premeditation. His questions to her were also very disingenuous. How could she run the paper without experience? How about staffing? She could feel the difference between her contrived questions to him and his genuinely curious ones. She decided to try giving him a dose of his own medicine. Honesty. See how *he* liked it.

"Mr. Moon. I don't know why you chose to apply for this position. You can see a few of the problems, I'm sure. But mostly, to be frank, I don't get the impression you really want me to hire you."

He smiled, leaned back in his chair for the first time, looked at her in a disconcerting way. As if he was addressing her not as a potential boss or hurdle to advancement, or object to be craved and connived for, but as a fellow human being.

"Ya caught me. I'd rather be tied to a tree and peed on than work for your jerkoff bosses. I just have to be able to say I did it."

Now that hooked her. This was a serious man, but he'd just applied for a job he didn't want. And didn't seem to be panting after her, either. Well, there were plenty of tragic explanations for good-looking men not going for her. But the job thing was enigmatic. "Very interesting, Mr. Moon. May I ask why you took up your time and mine to interview for it?"

"I'm sorry. I hadn't considered your time. I shouldn't have come in." He stood up to leave, reaching for his résumé. Caitlin moved it out of reach, motioned him to sit. He hesitated, then perched on the forward edge of his chair. She leaned forward slightly with a serious look.

"No need to apologize. It's been interesting meeting you. But for my own curiosity, why did you come?"

Rollie looked embarrassed, but met her eye. "My girlfriend isn't comfortable with me not having a job."

Caitlin smiled slightly. "And you'd really rather work on your novel?"

Rollie settled back, returned the smile. "Most editors are failed writers, but not all. I've been looking into financing for my own publication. Maybe even a website. Real news, real features. No fluff or BS." He grimaced ruefully. "Gee. Wonder why there isn't a big line of backers clamoring to get in on it?"

Caitlin kept her mouth from falling open, but gave him a wide-eyed stare. This guy's ego was just running around naked, waving its impotence in your face. Amazing. A true independent, straight out of some sappy Capra movie. She couldn't help asking.

"If you'll forgive a personal question, you seem like a man who calls his own shots. I understand that you don't mind going to the mat for your own vision."

"Is that a question? I guess it is. I think of myself that way, but look how long I stayed at The Week. Or was that what you were asking?"

"I don't think so. What I was wondering was why you would do something you don't want to do because of your girlfriend's comfort level."

Rollie stared at her a moment and started to say something automatic. Then she could see him starting to say something aggressive. Incredible: you could just read the guy's feelings right off his face, like a child. Then he shut his mouth, stood up, and walked towards the door.

Oh, nice going, Caitlin. Ferret out his failure, then bite his balls. And he seems so nice. She jumped up, "Mr. Moon! I'm sorry, I didn't mean to..."

At the door he turned back and gave her a smile that hit her right in the heart, an area not accustomed to even lightweight hits. He said, "No, you're right. Being right means not having to say you're sorry." And he was gone.

Through her office window she watched Moon winding through the cubicles. Some of the remaining skeleton staff waved. Some pointedly turned their backs. Casey Chones ran up to him and spoke animatedly. He replied in kind, smiling down at her.

Watching them, Caitlin suddenly realized: she loves him. Maybe is even in love with him. Maybe they'd all been, back before The Troubles. Caitlin frowned at the affectionate scene. Thinking, If she's got his back so bad, why didn't she quit? Daughter in an iron lung or something? She slowly sat down, picked up the résumé without really focusing on it. So that was Roland Moon. A new one on her.

Caitlin clicked out of the street door of "Week", her powerful stride in tall expensive heels beating the usual tattoo of power and fullcourt press. Which is worth a little sideline commentary to head off possible reader frustration. This is not the sort of book that glories in dropping *au currant* brand names of smart clothing and footwear. If that disappoints you, you might be more comfortable reading Brett Easton Ellis or Jay McInnery or somebody in that whole Eighties Vapid School. It was decided that books should be about imaginary people and contrived situations, not label placement. So if you're hip to shoes and designers and such, just project your own names onto the costumes. You'll probably do better than we could.

Her sleek, shimmering progress toward what she thought of as a "parking structure" was interrupted by a young woman who burst from the neighboring Starbucks to accost her. (Upon reflection, we decided it's okay to use passé brand names of stupid corporate clones.) The woman, who Caitlin instantly classified as College-Ruined Surf Party Girl, braced Caitlin, whose reflexive thoughts regarding the location of her pepper spray were punished by a quick flash of that damn Wiley's comments. The little weasel could even piddle on a person's instincts towards self preservation.

Hand subtly inserted in her stylish clutch, Caitlin raised a bland, interrogatory eyebrow at Gidget Goes Undergrad. Who was studying her, and detesting what she saw. Caitlin was used to that. She moved to pass, but her newest fan snapped out of it.

"What did you say to him, you plastic-ass witch?" Putting her thoughts into words, even cryptic ones, seemed to organize her assault. She pushed in, thrusting a home-done nail with off-the-rack polish into Caitlin's face. "You're a really cheap, obvious piece of work, aren't you? After-market tits and face job? Is that it? Has he lost his mind enough to start fucking Barbie dolls?"

Obvious? *Cheap*???? Caitlin figured that her outfit, shoes, nails, hair, and facial cost more than this twit's car. But she was a journalist now, and the Five "W's" came first. Most notably:

"Who?"

"What?" Surf Chick didn't follow.

"No, that can wait, with the When, and Which and all that. You keep mentioning "him".

"Oh, cute. You've got no clue, right?"

"I get a little sick of that 'blonde equals clueless' thing. But I have to admit I'm stumped on this one."

"Roland fucking Moon! That's Who. And Why. And What the Fuck."

Ah, the ball-breaking girlfriend. Now Caitlin did a little studying. While carefully moving the pepper spray off the "Safe" detent. She hadn't really thought much about what Moon's uncomforted GF might look like. (Yeah, right. But that's her story and she's stuck with it.) But "if she had" (smirk, wink) it would have been some anorexic artsy type with long straight hair and a rapacious sexuality smoldering behind her ennui. But this chick wasn't all that bad. Looking, anyway. Slim, outdoorsy. Okay, atrocious mullet. But cute with hints of spirit. In other words, boring.

"All I remember saying to Mr. Moon was that he had wonderful qualifications, but we couldn't use him at The Week. Is there some kind of problem?"

Well, yes. There did seem to be. Her mild remarks seemed to have sent Beach Babe up and over some inner wall. She trembled, speechless, her pointing finger curling into a claw, her other hand into a fist. Flushing, nostril's dilating. Caitlin thought, Would you care for ground pepper? *Screw* that Wiley!

Whatever had detonated in the woman's psyche hit its limits, imploded. She calmed, dropped her finger, looked sad and depressed. Resigned. "The Week used him plenty before you got there, Barbie. Overused him, abused him, tossed him in the dumpster. But he didn't come home from his interview, get his stuff, and clear out because you wouldn't hire him back."

Caitlin openly gaped. "He left you?" She wasn't even slightly qualified to assess the assortment of emotions that hit her. She snapped shut, went on Corporate Auto. "Sorry. But I have no idea. All we discussed was business. He did mention that he was applying because his girlfriend wanted him to. I gather that's you."

More collapse. She seemed stricken to hear that, but nodded her head shakily, as if expecting it. "And what did you say?"

Caitlin paused, decided to try something new she'd recently seen demonstrated to good effect. The unvarnished truth. "I said he didn't seem like the kind of man who'd do something he didn't want to because somebody else made him."

Demolition complete. A hint of tears, even. Caitlin normally rather liked backing people off and making them cry, but this didn't feel very good at all. She heard more tears in the voice, "He isn't. At least he wasn't until those Week assholes..." Her head snapped up, face tortured. "Yeah, and me. Okay. Okay. Look, sorry. Good luck with those fuckers."

She stood still, moping, as Caitlin edged by, stifling a surprising impulse to pat her shoulder.

When Caitlin pulled out of the "structure" in her creamy Lexus, Moon's apparent ex was still standing where she'd left her. Not a happy camper. A thought crossed Caitlin's mind and, without thinking it through, she whispered the window down and called out, "So are the address and phone number on his résumé still valid?"

With a startling suddenness, the woman spun and charged at her, clenched fists pumping. Caitlin suddenly grasped the concept that unified her adversary, brought her together and explained her whole pose. Beach volleyball. She punched the Lexus off the sidewalk into traffic, did a risky pass in the oncoming lane, and made her getaway.

CHAPTER SIXTEEN

Caitlin was starting to appreciate Kyle Albedo. He was smart and efficient. He ran the paper, carrying many of the staff, including the publisher and maybe even Caitlin herself, without having a puffy ego about it all. He seemed to appreciate her work and gave her the feeling that she was learning fast and doing well. Aside from that, she definitely thought of him as her only peer and ally on the Week. So she was always glad to co-operate with him, and increasingly glad to lunch with him. He made it clear that he'd love to massage her scalp with his headboard, but was also a gentleman about it all. And he was definitely inventive, she thought. Creative and "out of the box". Maybe one of those headboard sessions would be fun and educational. If she didn't have an ironclad rule against fishing off the company dock.

So she felt relaxed and professional lunching at a sidewalk table in front of one more Little Italy bistro that blatantly pined for the faraway hills of some ersatz, virtual Sorrento. And, rather than apprehensive, was intrigued to see what Kyle would come up with after he read the latest Wiley opus she'd handed him.

Kyle had mentioned to her that the public seemed to like Wiley's take on the automotive side of life. Caitlin, having figured out something of what was going on beneath the surface, had dropped the hint to Casey. Who had pitched it at Wiley. Who had either slashed it out of the park or blooped it up into a nest of nuclear terrorist hornets. She realized by now that she couldn't really tell.

THE WAY TO DOGSTYLE DEATH
By The Weekend Warrior

One of America's favorite pastimes is cooking with gas,
Pinchin' some ass, Drivin' too fast.

The Flying Burrito Brothers

126

And a burrito that flies never lies. There are no two ways about it: Driving Too Fast is either one of our most genocidal social problems or an exhilarating rite of passage for American youth. The problem is: What, exactly constitutes "Too Fast"? Well, Einstein might not have been a Flying Burrito, but he pretty much pegged anything over the speed of light as being Too Fast. And he knew his onions. But there are other people who cling to the theory that Too Fast merely means "at a greater velocity than the officially posted speed limits". People from a demographic cross-section technically known as "Pussies".

Speed limits, once you strip them of their cultural bias and punch them up with a few well placed .30-06 holes, are essentially just laws. And why are laws made? Exactly: to be broken. It's the American way. This country was founded by breaking laws, avoiding taxes, brandishing firearms and heading West in a hurry. If you have any doubts at all, ask yourself this leading question: If the speed limits really are The Limits, why do they sell radar detectors? And why put all those three-digit numbers on your speedometer?

So should we consider safety as the border of Too Fast? That Driving Too Fast would be driving at speeds unsafe given the vehicle and road conditions? Seems like a good place to start. The act of taking your life and others' into your hands. Those are the table stakes, all right. If you're too stupid to know that, stick to bumper cars and roller coasters, sport.

Which underscores the importance of selecting the proper vehicle to Drive Too Fast. It might seem, to the naive, that a fast car would be the way to go--but it ain't necessarily so. Doing two hundred is no big when you're low slung, sweet swung and expensively sprung in a Lamborghini or Mostachioli or some such. On the other hand, I've owned cars in which doing fifty five was an exercise in flash-frozen terror. Just let fear be your speedometer, if not co-pilot. As such diverse thinkers as Einstein and Jerry Lee Lewis might say, it's all relative. I was scared stupid doing forty down the block in my first drive in my old man's hotwired '58 Dodge. Note that, since I wasn't allowed to drive at all, even one measly mph was Driving Too Fast. The ideal to strive for was put forth by (of all people)

Ralph Nader, when he ranted the motto: "Unsafe at any speed." Which naturally brings us to the discussion of motorcycles.

What motorcycles offer is the simplistic purity of the one-track mind. And a very clean definition of Too Fast--namely, when you have killed yourself. They offer instant death, none of that lingering, Lifetime Channel Disease of the Week Movie crap...you just vaporize like in an arcade game, and find out how many lives you've got left. In that crouched-over, defecatory position favored by Cafe racers, you meet death doggie style, humping along like Pluto until the last thing that goes through your mind is Uranus. And all this without killing an unacceptable number of innocent bystanders.

From the Humongoose 1500, ideal for racing jets on the airstrip, to tiny, pipey dirtbikes like the Fastazz Sunbichi 125, perfect for wedding reception slaloms and indoor work, there is a size of bike just right for your personal aspirations. It's interesting to note that the Japanese, who make all these Kamakazis, Yomamas, SuziQ's and such, prohibit bikes of over 500 cc displacement in Japan. Which lets you know what's going on. It's like, "Enjoy your motorcycle, Lound Eye. Lemember Nagasaki."

Which brings geography into the question. You have to pick your location. It's difficult to Drive Too Fast on an interstate highway. But extremely easy on, for instance, a day care playground. Or perhaps a bar mitzvah in a place with a lot of big windows. The more people around, the easier it is to Drive Too Fast.

To be fair, we should mention a whole different slant on Driving Too Fast, which is that it is impossible. Just as Masters and Johnson said that the only unnatural sex act would be the impossible act, it could be argued (and probably will be after a few sufficiently venal defense attorneys read this) that there is no such thing as DTF. A fascinating hypothesis that begs for experimentation. So let's experiment.

Or rather, let's *you* experiment. Try this: mash your accelerator down as hard as you can for as long as you can. What did the car do? The limit right? You took it to the limit, like the Eagles. Not over the limit, right? Need I say more? Except to ask; did you survive this experience?

In one piece, or a number of pieces that can be expressed by a single integer? I rest my case.

Here's an even more conclusive experiment. Find somebody who has never driven a car in his life. Loan him a car (I won't patronize you by adding, "Somebody else's car".) Then stand well back to watch what he does. Almost instantly he will be driving Too Fast. It could be said that humans learn to Drive Too Fast before we even learn how to drive. It's probably hard-wired into our brains like language or drinking until we puke.

Which reminds us that alcohol and drugs are generally cited as aids to Driving Too Fast. Especially amphetamines, also known as "speed" (fancy that). But then, depressants like beer and seconal seem to work equally well at producing the dramatic results we associate with Driving Too Fast. The only possible conclusion is that driving *less* than Too Fast is only possible within a fairly narrow window of the psychopharmaceutical spectrum, and could thus be considered an aberration of nature. Of course, drunk drivers are homicidal scrotes and all that. But then, who isn't, in this day of overpopulation, pollution, and mass extinction? And it's all between consenting adults, right? It's like, hey, You don't wanna get AIDS, then walk the line, don't pull the twine. Same way, you don't want to be a highway fatality, don't take the highway. Remember; cars don't kill people, uncontrolled deceleration kills people.

Aside from intoxicants, overpopulated areas, and faulty equipment, there is no better aid to Driving Too Fast than having a woman present in your vehicle. The aphrodisiac qualities of speed are justifiably legendary, of course. But the vice works versa, too. Not to mention that sex at high speeds is instructive in and of itself. There is just nothing to put a fine edge on careening around a corner on two wheels like having a curly little head bobbing around in your lap at the time.

If anything can heighten the danger of slamming a slalom through the trees on some idiot golf course, it's feeling teeth being whipped back and forth against your driveshaft by those sudden changes in direction. We're talking big stakes here, sport; fates worse than death.

Somebody putting their mouth where your money is. You've got life, death, birth control and infinity all in one sweet package, baby driver. Yo, Thunder Road.

So is there a maximum speed for having sex while driving? If that figure can be determined (and I would volunteer to perform experiments in that direction if suitable volunteers and grants could be finagled) then one can easily move it out another notch. Sex is another thing that is unsafe at any speed. You might actually be safer doing someone *en passant*, as it were, than home in bed. For one thing, at 100 mph, it is unlikely that anyone's significant other is suddenly going to walk in at a significant moment and blow you into insignificant rubble. On the other hand, one wrong spasm and you're history. But then that's the name of the game, isn't it? Snuffed in mid-orgasm. What a way to go! And who, other than your graveside eulogist, is going to say you went Too Fast?

Probably Bruce Springsteen put it best, in his immoral words:

Wrap your legs around my velvet rims
And strap your arms cross my engine.

Well that one might actually be too kinky to even visualize, but you can tell the Boss had his head in the right place. Or maybe you can't. Somewhere down around her turbocharger, sounds like. But that by the way. The important thing is, keep the gin in your generator, the "mo" in your motor, and the piss in your pistons and all will be well as long as you keep reading **THE WEEKEND WARRIOR®**. Preferably at excessively high speeds.

Her first indication that she really, really, truly had no clue about Wiley's appeal was the sight of Kyle laughing so hard he choked and had to repel the ministrations of two white-jacketed "Italian" waiters from Mexicali who were dying to try out the Heimlich Maneuver. Maybe, she thought as she pushed a glass of water towards him, it's a guy thing. It was obviously not one of those "It's kind of a no-no for public media to advocate drunk driving, drugged vehicular mayhem, and underage sex" things.

With Kyle restored to emotional and respiratory equilibrium, and the waiters nursing Hispanic pouts, she detailed some of her apparently boring and non-funny concerns. Kyle listened with an encouraging, intelligent expression. In his head he was composing a phone conversation to several men of his acquaintance, starting with the owner of a five-outlet Kawasaki franchise. Just a draft, but along the lines of, "We both know, Bill, that the whole 'meet the nicest people', 'motorcycle fancier' stuff is bullshit. Most of the guys you want in your shop are dying to be Bad and flaunting their close terms with death."

But suddenly he tore his attention from his spiel and focused on Caitlin so intently that she stopped in mid sentence. She looked at him somewhat askance, ran a quick tongue across the front of her teeth, "What?"

"Can you run that by me again?" Kyle asked her, "Starting with that 'ought to be a special zone' thing?"

"I mean just for Wiley," she recapped, "A sort of walled-off preserve for him to rage with his disciples and not mess up ordinary people. Sort of a Danger Zone, like they have around volcanoes and warlords."

Lyle held up his hand and Caitlin watched, puzzled, for several strained minutes. At one point she nodded off a waiter approaching with a pitcher. More MexiSulks. Finally Lyle put his hand down, then reached out for hers. She slipped her hand into his wondering if he was going to propose marriage, swear to jail Wiley, or proclaim himself the Ancient of Days. What he did was shake her hand and give her a thumbs-up.

"The Red Zone," he tolled out in bold type and drumrolls. "The Red Zone."

"Oh, right. The volcano area. That's what they call it."

"You're one sharp blonde, Vanderkeller," Kyle told her with a manly sparkle. "We don't just call it that, we have a ten point red border on the page. Maybe even the whole page set in red. I'll check with Charlie about that."

"I don't think we're on the same page," Caitlin said. "Whatever color it is."

"The Wiley spread!" Kyle expostulated, making Caitlin envision a perverted ranch somewhere in the Ozarks. "His column on the right page, tie-in ad underneath. And across from it a full page of selected ads."

"Selected for being dangerous to society?" Caitlin asked. "Only readable with special glasses for adults and non-idiots?"

"Specially selected for the Danger Factor. A loosely defined, macho, edgy quality that Wiley defines."

"Is continuing to define," he added, slapping the proofs in front of him. "Not For Wimps. The killer bikes, the suicide chili sauce, the rape-me boutiques, the leather crypts. This is going to be major. You're too much, boss baby."

Now it was Caitlin who sat and stared for several big ticks of the ormolu clock from Napoli. "Thanks Kyle. I appreciate that. But it was all your idea, actually. And what it says to me is: Wiley gets two whole pages with nothing but him and advertising. In the front of the book."

"Amazing, huh?" Kyle crowed. "Unprecedented. We're going to make out like bandits."

"In other words," Caitlin asked in a hollow tone, "Wiley can insult advertisers, degrade women, advocate unwholesome and illegal sex, promote homicidal driving and theft...and *nothing* he does will get him the hell out of my hair?"

"Who cares?" Kyle chortled. "We're doing great. *You're* doing great. You're going to be running this paper for a long, long time."

Caitlin didn't let him see the hole that remark had blown in her soul. She smiled and congratulated him. It was now absolutely imperative to abolish Wiley herself. Kyle wasn't going to help, but she had thought of somebody who just maybe could.

CHAPTER SEVENTEEN

Caitlin just didn't feel right barefoot. There were reasons she owned forty pairs of shoes. Feet are the Achilles heel of female appearance, and there they just were. Feet. But walking in the deep sand of the beach volleyball courts on South Mission would look pretty stupid in footwear, particularly footwear with flair. She also felt overdressed. She was the only woman around wearing shorts, much less culottes. Her top looked very casual and kicky in her cheval mirror, but contrived and prudish among women wearing the bare decent minimum in which to compete athletically.

She watched them playing for awhile. Wow. Lithe, lean, bronzed, agile as eels. And powerful. And beautiful, really. She could see a segment backed with abstract footage of these girls diving, pouncing, spiking, slapping each others' butts. Of course, having sand adhering to your skin by sweat didn't look all that great. But still. It was like being at a zoo or aquarium featuring some hybrid of dolphin and Jack Russell Terrier. She spotted Rollie's girlfriend tossing the ball in the air and soaring up to unwind on it like a glove leather spring. Ms. Sideout didn't spot her until the game was over. Then walked away; her tight, rippling tail twitching in disdain. Caitlin forced herself to follow.

The Ex cooled down in a bivouac of folding chairs and icechests. Caitlin found herself wondering how the coolers would rate in a competitive test. Then fought the impulse to pound herself on the brow. Listen, *screw* that damn Wiley! She glanced at the nearest chill chest and sure enough, recognized the brand name: Igloo 36 Quart Legend. Losers, she thought, should have sprung for the Steel-Belted Coleman 54. One more worthless engram squirmed into her long term memory courtesy of SuperCreep.

THE WEEKEND WARRIOR CHILLS OUT
By The Weekend Warrior

If there's one thing left everyone can agree on, it's that weekends are not made for lukewarm drinks. When you need coolin', baby you're not foolin'.

Fortunately we live in a high-tech age and can buy devices known as "coolers" to keep our reagents at proper temperature. But which of the many coolers on the market is best for weekend partying? Hang on, willya, we're getting to that. With the Official **WEEKEND WARRIOR®** Cooler Shoot-Out.

The test got rigorous right off the bat when the volunteer testers turned out to be my chums from the Old Vets and Beatniks Rod And Roscoe Club. This almost always complicates things. The idea was to test the coolers under field conditions by loading them with food and beverages (I'm almost positive there was some food in one of them somewhere) and then setting out on an expedition to do what many people enjoy on weekends, namely slaughtering smaller fellow living beings whose only crime was to occupy a lower rung on the food chain, and then eat their corpses. The coolers would be graded for capacity, durability, and whatever you'd call the ability to keep something cold.

The coolers tested were:

"Goodtime", solid white foam	$1.19
"Lil Playmate", swivel lid	$18.00
"Chill" Soft Cooler , fabric	$14.99
"Igloo" 36 Quart Legend	$24.99
"Rubbermaid" 54 Quart	$44.99
"Coleman" 54 Quart "Steel Belt"	$60.00
"Igloo" 128 Quart Marine Legend	$189.00

The testing crew consisted of "Smokin" Joe Gasparetti, the Doctor himself—"Doc" Hardesty, Tiny Tim Markham, and a couple of other anglers/pirates who prefer anonymity.

Old hounds, sea dogs, the sort of men who go down to (and often under) the sea in ships.

As is usual in such maneuvers, the first night was devoted to softening up of the local community through light-hearted havoc and horseplay while avoiding as always the responsible authorities. Frankly, authorities give me a rash and this feeling runs high in OV&BR&RC circles. Somewhere along the line, and fulfilling another tradition, several misguided young women attached themselves to our party (some in shockingly innovative ways) and were thus shanghaied into the upcoming Cooler Test. As the sun rose, we drank a toast to Steve McQueen in honor of his role as The Cooler King in "The Great Escape". Then, Jolly Roger hoisted on a diesel cruiser and coolers in hand, we embarked.

The young women who accompanied us were of short acquaintance, deep thirsts, limited vocabularies, and brief wardrobes. They could barely scrape up enough scraps of fluorescent pink and green fabric to cover their essential goodness. No problem. The OV&BR&RC is ever a friend to the homeless, hapless, underfed, and underclothed. Supply lines secure, we turned to the tests.

Right away we detected a failure in several of the larger units. The 54 quart model, for instance, would not accept 54 quarts of beer, no matter how they were stacked. I was prepared to downgrade all such items, until Tiny Tim pointed out that it probably would hold 54 quarts if they were emptied into it. He was prevented from trying this theory out.

Tests went well at first. The coldness tests were excellent from all units. People kept repeating the tests, exclaiming, "Wow, check out how cold this is!" and demonstrating on various warm-blooded parts of various anatomies. All units passed. As time went on we noticed poorer performances from the smaller units. For one thing, they got empty.

Tiny Tim tried to do more technical temperature tests, but the thermometer had disappeared. Probably in the hands of Doc and one of the girls we hadn't seen in quite a while. He had muttered about the importance of ovulation temperatures. So Smokin' Joe tested the effectiveness of the Igloo 36 by sticking his toe in the gelid, stagnant water in which floated a few odd beverage cans, scraps of food, and a pre-tested condom. This did not yield professional results, apparently, so he tried his wrist, then his elbow, and finally his face. He seemed to like this sensation and remained that way, gathering in-depth data, evidently relishing the cool white solitude of the view. Unfortunately, Doc liked the view of Joe's rump up in the air, so he gave him a friendly boot. This created tension. I was afraid these two deadly warriors would start fighting. Or worse, singing.

But Doc suddenly told Joe to "cool out" and began a deep meditation on motion and alimentation by leaning over the rail for a prolonged period. This practice, which he called "chum-baiting the fish", involved passing previously digested pieces of fish back into the water like a true sportsman. One more of the great cycles by which nature works her wonders.

Joe was experiencing a very literal mindset at the time and took Doc's advice to heart, as we found out when one of the girls refused to get any live bait on the grounds that it was in the Rubbermaid cooler, which was now also occupied by Joe, sitting nekkid in the icy water, head thrown back at a dangerous angle and complaining of friction burns. I swear, that guy will bitch about anything. Anyway, he left the cooler soon after Tim tossed in a wounded sting ray he had caught. But the girl still wouldn't get the bait. I might add that the Rubbermaid proved a satisfactory container not only for the ice and bait, but also for a pain-crazed sting ray and Joe's keister in similar condition.

By that time the "Goodtime" all-foam cooler was totally demolished, the result of Doc having had his face resting on it while somebody sat on that very face. Let me caution you that coolers are not made for this purpose. In fact I don't believe there is anything specifically made for resting your head on during face-sitting sessions. Pity, too. All that was left of the cheap foam chest was little white spheroids of foam that kept showing up in every little inconvenient cran and nooky, a reminder that those too ignorant to avoid history are doomed to keep eating it. Hey, for $1.19 you don't get bronze monuments to posterity. What you get is beaches covered with little white crud. We'd have to call the "Goodtime" a failure, on ecological, psychological and scatological grounds—smart weekenders come better prepared than that.

At this point Smokin' Joe decided it would be prudent to test the coolers' bullet-proof properties. It would be easy, he pointed out, for some fool to drop a spear gun, which could then go off and ventilate a cooler, spilling lots of quantity. This seemed believable at the time, since he was twirling a speargun, practicing fast draws with it. The test was simple enough. Joe hauled off and plugged the Igloo dead center with one shot. The spear went right through the side, and through a fish inside. Seeing the fish impaled on the spear set Joe's ever-mercurial mind caroming down other channels and he went off to cook the fish over the charcoal...*en brochette.*

So we had no spear to test the other chests. The Old Beats Club seldom lacks firepower, however, and a withering crossfire ensued, which few of the chests survived. When we do a shootout in the column, me bucko, you may believe that a shootout will be had by all. Since the chests had been heaved over the side to give them a sporting chance, the tests terminated at this point—though it should be noted that whereas the Igloo 36 came apart immediately, the Steel Belted Coleman showed some impressive stuff. It even deflected a shot from a .22 some fool had brought along. (But in case it was smug about it, Doc blew the top right off it with a one-handed blast from his sawed-off twelve gauge.)

If anyone thinks this test excessive or hazardous, let me hasten to note that all precautions were taken—there were no beverages left in the chests by the time of the tests. We hauled the survivors back aboard, and Joe plopped down on the Marine Legend which still served as a fine seat despite multiple wounds from large-caliber revolvers. And a stab wound from some berserker. He was joined by a girl from Camp Pendleton, who claimed to be a bit of a Marine Legend herself.

At that point all the coolers had flunked the ultimate test— they were empty. After travails that would have daunted Ulysses we limped back into port flying the JollyRoger and several bold ensigns composed largely of fluorescent pink and green fabric. We decided that all the chill units rated careful consideration for purchase—much more careful than we were capable of at the moment.

A few last minute tests were performed back at Tiny Tim's apartment, including the highly controversial test of being dropped from his second story landing onto the hood of the neighbor's MG (which the Steel-belted Coleman passed with flying colors—mostly chips of British Racing Green). And the crucial Being Kicked To Pieces In a Brute, Blitzed Rage Test, performed by Joe after he turned and tripped over the Rubbermaid with an armful of fish poles. The Rubbermaid would certainly have flunked this test were we not grading on the curve. Smoking Joe, after all is a Black Belt in some kind of crazy Japanese crap.

So that was our conclusive cooler test. The conclusion: Cooler than you'll ever be.

But more pressingly, Rollie's ex-other swilled and spewed spring water from a sports bottle, which she dropped back into the Igloo and brushed sand off her ass with a motion clearly meant to be taken symbolically. A lean, powerful Dewd with braided hair the color of winter wheat and skin the color of a walnut credenza reached up to pick a stray grain off her inner thigh. Another move doubtless freighted with symbolism.

"Look," Caitlin blurted, "I didn't have anything to do with your break-up with Roland. And I don't have the hots for him."

"Why would I care about that?" Her look was as flat and ill-intentioned as one of those Kung Fu throwing stars. "He's like, so past pluperfect."

She glared defiantly, surrounded by other jocks and volley-dollies lolling like a pride of tawny carnivores. It hit Caitlin then. She'd been climbing with Rollie. Over-reaching herself, wanting to be something other than who she was. Now she was back among her species. But she would sure resent any implication that Rollie belonged more with sharp, educated media people than mesomorphic sun priestesses.

"But I need to find him for business reasons."

"You took his job. Will there be anything else?"

"I didn't take it and I don't want it. But I think I can help him." Without waiting for the retort that line begged for, Caitlin stepped up close to the seething volleyjockette and switched to Sympathetic Confidant.

"You know, I've noticed men can sort of lose it when they're out of work. Especially when they've had time to realize they're moving in on forty." She was cribbing heavily from something she'd been told by a wife whose husband she'd been dating, but whose existence she hadn't suspected. "My guess is he's off soaking and drinking or whatever he does, and will get things thought through."

"Why would that matter to me?" she asked, resting her hand on the golden shoulder of the grain-picker. Caitlin checked the guy out and decided it was a pretty valid question. If he'd just lose those "Matrix" sunglasses.

"Then why does it matter to you?" There, that was blunt enough. "I just need to get hold of him for business and you're the only one I know who knows him." Other than the entire staff of The Week, but that wouldn't do at all.

"Beats me." Even her shrug was athletic and efficient, "Shacked up, probably."

"Well, they say the woman is the last one to know anything." Caitlin probed, hoping she didn't turn up a punch in the face.

"I know plenty," Coppertone snapped, "He's hanging around Cocos with some Aussie bitch. But the thing is... I *don't care!*"

"Well, thank you for not caring," Caitlin murmured. She shuffled away, sandblasting her expensive toenail polish to rubbish. The sand on the courts was different. She realized that the constant impact of players spiking and slamming and whatever they did had probably ground the grains together, knocking off the corners. The resulting round grains were like quicksand.

She turned around after a dozen steps, looked back at the girl sitting on the lap of Playa God. She called, "You look good. You look happy. You're beautiful out there. Enjoy it." She met a dozen blank stares, all the skinny sunglasses reminding her of a coven of vampires. She turned and walked off with as much dignity as you can muster when dressed foolishly and sinking to mid-calf with every step.

CHAPTER EIGHTEEN

Even among international beach hostels, Coconuts Cabanas maintains a shady reputation. It's right on the Pacific Beach boardwalk, so passers-by can get a first hand view of its riffraffish collection from corners of the globe. Yes, this was where you would go if you wanted sunshine up your butt, sand in your sheets, controlled substances out of control in your bloodstream, and a continuous stream of domestic and imported sex-mongers. Less so if you were particularly fastidious or liked to sleep at night.

Caitlin found the usual party in full fling on the railed patio. She leaned on the seawall, scanning the variety of exposed skin and jarring accents. She could have built a garden shed from the empty beer cans. Roofed it with empty pizza boxes. Fun-lovers from far corners drinking, basking, talking polyglot shit.

Suddenly she realized that what she had taken for a Mexican peasant slumping in a *serape* and wide, sequined sombrero, was in fact Roland Moon. He looked wasted. But far from wasted on the big blonde who stood by his lounger, shaking her bounteous booty to the strains of "Mambo Number Five". She occasionally called out encouragement and disparagement to other dancing girls and nonchalant guys, her every syllable marking her as Australian. She wore the tiniest thong bikini Caitlin had ever seen. From the rear it converted the girl into Life Support System for Dueling Buttocks. From the front it deepened appreciation for shade meanings of Down Under. The top seemed to be made of fishing line and two bottle caps with Jolly Rogers on them. She was a typical Sheila: laughing and unselfconscious. She looked like a jolly roger indeed.

Caitlin glanced south towards the volleyball ghetto. Moon hadn't moved very far to relocate his amours. In any sense of "far". She hopped up to sit on the rail, then swung her legs over and approached Moon and the Awesome Aussie. Attention swung to her at once, as if she'd broken some invisible plane and was now among them as a bonafide person of interest. The blonde from Oz bent over, an effect better imagined than described, and shotgunned some hand-rolled smoke into Moon's bright red, wide open face. He inhaled noisily, smiled without opening his eyes. Another girl in the neighboring chair and a bikini that showed a lot of aureole held a Dos Equis to his lips and poured. He inhaled again, gargled, smiled. Caitlin wished Linsey was along to record all this. It might make a good consumer warning message about Southern California beach spots. Elective chemo-lobotomy on ten dollars a night.

Caitlin stopped at the foot of the chaise, looking down at what she considered the wreckage of Roland Moon. Not totaled, but definitely sprung.

Ms. Outback offered her a friendly smile and a can of premixed MaiTai. "Tinny of turps?"

Caitlin took the cocktail, pointed it at Moon. "I wouldn't have thought his fashion sense could degenerate any further, but he made me a liar."

The Aussie laughed with the expected perfect white teeth.

"He did look a swaggie when he came in. Then next we know, he's down to his grundies and right stonkered. Couldn't let a cobber burn up his white points, could we?."

She saw that it wasn't just his face that was overly ruddy, though it was confined to every square inch of epidermis. Not too bad, though. Wouldn't need an ocean of calamine lotion. DAMN! that WILEY!!!!! She looked at the Australian girl and immediately thought, "The type of girl that makes you say, 'Lord have mercy, woman—I don't wanna be no *slave*!' " He was more than insidious, he was like some trojan horse virus that took over your cerebral functions to replicate itself. The offending column had run a month ago, and here it was seeping out of her primal mind like Swamp Thing.

THE WEEKEND WARRIOR TANS YOUR HIDE
By The Weekend Warrior

Memorial Day is just a memory, so summer's here and the time is right for tanning at the beach. A good suntan is the perfect summer accent, giving you a healthy glow compared to which pale skin pales in comparison. Acquiring a suntan is not as easy as it might seem. There are tanning traditions which have been built up since tanning started in the Bronze Age (and progressed in the Dark Ages). Tanning occurs when sunlight strikes human skin at the proper angle to cause the secretion of tannin, which either produces a lot of designer-toned Vitamin D and converts your upholstery into rich Corinthian leather, or covers you with unappealing peeling, depending on whether you did it right or not.

It is important to do tanning at the right time; daylight hours are best. Location is also important; pick someplace under the sun. It's good to tan near water so you can occasionally wash off the sweat, crud, effluvia, oils, gunk, mung, drool, and bodily discharges that tend to manifest on people laying out in the hot sun. Locate yourself near a body of water big enough so that you won't leave a ring, okay? I'm sure there's no point in even asking you to pick up your oil slick after you. Dress is optional. Attitude, however, is everything. Your disposition should be compatible with laying flat on your face (or ass) for hours out of sheer vanity. Check? Check.

You will find this flaccid self-indulgence somewhat tedious if lying on a flat concrete slab or a hot sand hazard—unfortunately the exact composition of most places where people tan themselves. I'll save you a lot of brain-wracking; the solution is to get some sort of chair or lounge to sit on. A lightweight, portable one would be swell. They sell them everywhere. Are you with me? If you can't get a chair, try to find a suitable location between a rock and a hard place.

Another handy accessory is a pair of sunglasses. They makes it easier to watch other sunbathers, often without doing so noticeably. They are also invaluable in helping you look cool, which is hard to do while laying around half naked and sweating like a pig in heat. Bring along some cool drinks and something to read, and you've got it made in the shade. That's right, the shade. While you were fussing around with all your junk, the sun moved. Oh no, huh? Surprise solution: You move too. Very good.

So there you are, basking like a cat on the hearth, warming your cockles under that old thermonuclear space heater in the sky. Having your own little Bikini Atoll Beach Party. Doesn't take more than the greatest conglomeration of energy, mass, and radiation in the Solar System to keep you happy, does it? And fortunately all that priceless energy has nothing better to do than traipse ninety three million miles out of its way in order to make you look better in a white swim suit. No meter running, not a cloud on your horizon. Then somebody comes up and tells you should be wearing sunblock. It's enough to make you wonder. Or as my old pal Del Shannon used to say at the drop of Larry's hat, "Wuh, wah, wah, wah, wah wonder". More specifically, it makes you wonder why. (Hit it, Del. "Wuh, why, why, why, why, why?") Why they try to make everything so damn *dangerous* anymore. Suddenly mindless summer sunning, like mindless summer sex, is being accused of downright murder. Bad enough your sex partners are trying to kill you, now the *sun* is out to get you. What is the secret to Safe Sunning? (There is no such thing as safe sex. There never was.)

Easy. Ignore all this cancer crapola. They'll tell you anything causes cancer. If you want the real truth, clothes cause cancer. Run around naked and you don't have to fear the reaper. This is a true fact and can be easily proven. So easily, in fact, I invite you to get off your buns and prove it yourself instead of sitting there nodding like a numskull and waiting for me to do it for you.

Also important to realize is that work causes cancer. If you doubt this at all, check out these known facts: Anywhere you go in the tropics, be it Hawaii, Africa, Phuket, New Guinea, Pago-Pago, Bora-Bora, Atu-Atu, or Walla-Walla, you will find tribes of grinning jungle-bunnies who don't do a lick of work nor wear a stitch of clothes. And they *never* get cancer. In the so-called "temperate zones", however, where everyone is short-tempered, civilizations are made to order, and it's cold as brass monkey's half the time, people wear all kinds of idiotic clothes and work their butts to the bone. And what do they get for their pains? (Other than bony butts and mentioned in "10 Worst Dressed Lists"?) Exactamundo...our favorite Zodiac killer, the Big C.

So wise up, already: this skin cancer scare will blow over, just like herpes and toxic shock and cellulite and the Kardashians. It's all a flimsy fabrication to sell you medicated goo, anyway. Dressed up in fancy pseudo-psientific mumble-jumble about cosmic rays. Hah, that's a hot one! Buck Dharma Rogers zaps your epidermis. Right. And "ozone layers." Come off it. This could only be the work of a bunch of double-domed worry junkies with one head in the ozone, one in the twilight zone and slinging a load of it deep in the end zone. Because you know what really does cause cancer, don't you? Well, being a laboratory rat, for one thing. But more to the point, Worry. Keep furrowing your pasty little untanned brow and you're just laying out the welcome mat to every malignant melanoma, crazed carcinoma, and deranged leukocyte that might want to rock your cell block.

So to hell with these so-called experts; don't worry, be chappy. Get way out, lay out, stay out and ray out. Of course you need a modicum of caution. (There are four modicums in a healthy dose). Just because you're unlikely to end up in the Al Solzenizkin Cancer Clinic doesn't mean you need to do your impression of Uncle Meat, either. If you're a radiation rookie, some sort of fishbelly white individual with the pasty complexion of a sewer snoid, don't try to live your life in one day or you will become a crispy critter with a whole lot of flakin' goin on—in need of an ocean of calamine lotion,.

The trick is to increase your exposure gradually. Start with just your arms and shoulders, then your legs and midriff, then get daring enough to flash some tit or buns before working up to full frontal nudity. By gradually increasing your exposure you will eventually be able to frequent nude beaches without resembling the road company of "Burnt Weinie Sandwich".

As your tan deepens and spreads, you'll naturally want to show it off. This can get very competitive. It is also the kind of competition of the type known as a "spectator sport". As much fun as being seen is seeing others in various states of brown-out. Especially since many showing off tans are young women.

And not just any young women, either. I'm talking about the kind that get you talking to yourself. You might be heard to say things like, "*Got* to be more careful." Or perhaps, "Lord have mercy, woman—I don't wanna be no *slave*." Or words the effect of, "Don't throw it me so strong, gal; I just can't *stand* no more." You know the type of girls I mean. Though probably not as well as you'd like.

But beware, not all are what they appear to be. Tanning is being infiltrated by artificial ingredients. Some of the chocolate shades you see draped fetchingly around the rococo fluting of someone's corpus delectable are not the result of carefree hours under the sun, but synthetic Vitamin D copped in back alley dens where shady tanners slump under cold artificial lamps, fooling Mother Nature. The results are making it more difficult for natural tanners to compete, but there are no tests for synthetic tans (often called Stare-oids) and they continue to glut the market. (It is rumored that artificial tans taste different than real tans. You have the official permission of THE **WEEKEND WARRIOR**® to test this theory.)

There are more advantages to modern tanning than just the visual delights. There are olfactory advantages to having a thousand sexy little sizzlers laying around marinated in coconut oil. Or banana oil. Or various fragrant tropical essences. It gives beaches a bracing odor. Newer oils come in Teriyaki, Mesquite, English Leather, Lemon Pledge, Kama Sutra, and your choice of Ranch, French, or Thousand Islands. Don't be a chump, rub yourself with these yummy items. Who cares if sand sticks to you? It beats after-shave or perfume. And rubbing oil on other people is *the* mating ritual of the new Bronze Age. Again, increase your exposure gradually. And when oiling up your partner, don't take coverage for granted. You never know when that fat old sun will decide to nip right through a flimsy scrap of cloth, so be thorough.

So, you've got your place in the sun. You've got your lounger, your shades, your *au jus de soleil*. You've forgotten your cares, covered your ass, and are ready to turn a darker shade of pale. Is there anything else we are going to bug you to think about before you start your countdown to ecstasy? Only this: set your phase to stun, the indicator to medium rare, the dial to the hippest of hits, and the controls for the heart of the Sun. Then kick back, Jack—it's summertime and the living is greasy.

Caitlin realized she was grinding her teeth. The Australian girl gave her a sisterhood smile and poked Rollie with a toe ringed in silver from Goa.

"Best get a decko of this, Wally." Aside to Caitlin, she said, "The ace journo. Rotten in two hours, and stunned mullet when a lady calls on the old fella."

145

Rollie peered up at Caitlin, who loomed over him backlit by sunflare. "I saw this already," he muttered. "Sandahl Bergman comes back from the dead to warn Conan."

"How are you doing, Mr. Moon?" Caitlin asked. She realized he was blinking and squinting to take her in, so she moved around to perch beside him on the lounger.

"Good question. I'll take a viewer poll. How am I doing, ladies?"

Much of the chorus that answered his polling was in cooking terminology, but was unanimously positive and spirited. Within a statistical error of less than one percent.

"There you have it," he intoned smugly. "But here with an opposing viewpoint is Rollie Moon, from the Coconut Grove. Who opines: No job, no pad, no girl. These are phenomena that frequently arise together.

"There seem to be a lot of girls around here."

Roland took that under advisement, scanned surroundings highly populated by revelations of bosom and thigh. He pondered. "Yeah, I guess. So far so good." He struggled to focus on her. "Listen, Nine News, is there anything else I have that you think I shouldn't? My car, perhaps? Now where did I leave those keys?"

Behind him, the Aussie girl pointed to them lying on a table, tossed a towel over them and winked at Caitlin.

"I don't think it's fair to blame me for your problems."

"It's not? Oh, okay. Who should I blame? Wait, I remember. Ah great. I was drinking to forget it and now I remember. It was That Bastard."

"Could you be a little more specific?"

"The Eggman. Holeass Ovarón is the bastard of the moment. The *illegitimus du jour*, as it were."

The Sheila laughed. "Talks a rage, don't 'e?"

"I should have seen it coming all along," Rollie went on. "No, wait. I did see it all along. Wrote it up, even. It's public record now. Shipped platinum. With a bullet. Cocksucker blues."

"There's also Scorment."

"Okay, Those Bastards. Wait a minute, Danforth Scorment? Why?

They're in cahoots."

"No, that was The Band. Richard Manuel was in it. Garth Brooks. No, wait. What the hell's wrong with me? Garth

Hudson. Rick Danko. Levon and his son Jesus. All in it together. Dead now. Wow. That's heavy."

"Are you sure you're not putting me on?"

"Sure, a little. But it's fun. I am pretty plowed, you know. Do you think there are any plows in San Diego county? Not snow plows, of course, but the usual, you know, sodbuster plows."

"Look, don't take this the wrong way, but would you consider coming with me, taking a shower, drinking some coffee, having a nice siesta, then talking a little?"

"If you want a job, remember how you tossed me out into the cold." He looked down at his pink complexion. "Well, you know. Out. Into elements. Disgrace and shit."

"I think we should talk about how they screwed us both and how we can maybe get unscrewed."

"Hmmm. Do I get to go undercover? Stake anybody out?"

Caitlin looked at him a long time, then closed her eyes and relaxed. She listened to the waves, mindless chatter and Chili Pepper music. She felt a blast of hot air hit her nose and opened her eyes to see Ms. Dip Thong blowing her another foof. She inhaled, looked back at Roland, who was still looking at her.

"You get to stake out some vampires."

"All rightie, then! Transylvanians, eh?"

"Nope, pre-op."

"Hmm." Roland waved to Rectal Floss Girl, who undulated over leaking smoke. "Should I go take a shower and nap with this woman? And, what else? Oh yeah, coffee."

She eyed Caitlin with laughing eyes, knocked her knuckles on Roland's head. "Reckon! You gone ga-ga, mate? Give it a burl before I have to bash you up."

"Well, that settles it. Where are my clothes?"

"That's my line, cocker," Mz. Oz guffawed. "You're wearin' your clobber."

"Okay, then. Sounds like a job for Stupor Man. Shall we?"

Caitlin and two other girls heaved him out of the chair and steadied him. He swept off the sombrero, tossed it to the floor and danced around it. The girl reached for the poncho, but he tore it off and did some bullfighter passes. A muscular German girl lunged at the cape and he passed her with a fairly credible Veronica. He looked down at his pink, hairy torso and said. "I think I've had about as much pleasure as I can stand."

In the parking lot, he fumbled in the pockets of his trunks, dropping change and bits of paper. "I'll drive."

"Sure you will, El Cordobes," Caitlin muttered, wondering why she had thought this was such a nifty idea. "Get in the designated chardonnay Lexus, there."

"Hey, just because I can't walk or focus or do math analysis in my head..."

Caitlin opened the door and hip-checked him through it. He sprawled on the seat, thrashing limply while she got his hand and feet inside and closed the door. When she slipped into the driver's seat, he was fondling her stereo, muttering, "There's gotta be some Flamin' Groovies in there somewhere. Or wait, how about the Rascals? Four Tops. We need beach music, here. Do you know Boardwalk Angel?"

"I know Under The Boardwalk," she said, backing. "And Hotel on Park Place."

Roland nodded owlishly. "I can already tell this is going to work out." Then keeled over and out.

CHAPTER NINETEEN

Rollie woke up lying face down on a Pawley Island rope hammock. He was staring at porous Mexican patio flags laid without grout. Not much information to work with. He looked at a forearm, dangling in his peripheral vision, but recognizably his. Ooo, that's going to peel, he thought. He could see some sort of white cream spread on the pink skin, sniffed. Hmm, Après Soleil. Nice touch. Aloe vera and secret ingredients. He dozed awhile longer, then got around to raising his head. He was staring into a sliding glass door. He could see inside well enough to identify a rather soul-less living area in Scandinavian blonde, but not so well that his own reflection didn't dominate his perspective. Not too reassuring. Although he toyed with the possibly that the diamond pattern of deep grooves the hammock ropes had impressed in his skin might be the next personal decoration fad. The cutting edge has to weary of tats and piercings eventually.

He realized that rolling over would not only be a mistake, but impossible. So he rolled out. Which left his head throbbing, but gave him a new view of his surroundings. A nice umbrella of unbleached muslin had been sheltering him from further solar devastation. The patio had a cute arched roof, presumably somebody else's patio floor. The legs of cast iron chairs and table were painted off-white. A pair of gorgeous calves scissored by his eyes. All he had to do was tie these clues together. He'd get right on it.

Hold on, the legs were back. With a hand. Lowering a big sunny yellow mug in front of his face. He smelled fresh coffee. Things were looking up. Another lovely hand appeared, holding a snifter of brandy. The hand poured a dollop of brandy into the mug, disappeared. He thought it out and committed his resources to reaching for the cup. Which moved slightly out of reach. Aha. He'd suspected as much. Well, two can play.

It took awhile, but he managed to trap the cup between his hands. It wasn't very hot by that time, but he was in no position to snivel. The position he was in was standing upright, guzzling coffee, looking at Channel Nine's Caitlin Vanderkeller, who had never made an appearance in his hangovers before. Or even masturfantasies. Bizarre.

She reached out and took the coffee, not without a bit of a struggle. She draped a nice fluffy Turkish towel over his forearm, then a luxurious terrycloth robe. She walked away, holding the cup out to her side. He moved after it, reaching. She led him to a door, pushed it open. It was a really cool bathroom with custom fixtures and talavera basins. She set the coffee by the sink and withdrew. He walked in, picked it up and swallowed gratefully. The door closed behind him, softly but firmly. A message was starting to emerge and he just about had it figured out.

Rollie held a full cup of coffee under his nose, hoovering up the steam and bouquet. "This isn't Starbucks, I hope? I refuse to patronize those buzzards."

Caitlin, curled in a white "MamaSan" chair with Mayan patterned cushion, waved a dismissive hand. "No. I don't pay attention. It's the big can at Trader Joe's."

Rollie sipped, wrapped in the wonderful robe and perched in a deck chair and surveying the tops of the trees that choked the river through Mission Valley. Below him, the red Euro-look cars of the Trolley slid to a stop and opened their doors. "Whatever, it sure hits the spot. Thanks."

Caitlin nodded politely, keeping an eye on him. He took another slug, scratched at his toasted knee. "But as you were saying?"

"It all revolves around Danforth Scorment."

"Fourth in the hearts of his countrymen. I don't know him, of course."

"Who does? I think you have to ante up a million bucks to qualify to be admitted into the presence of his set."

"But from what I do know, I think we can rule out any machinations on his part. Or even rational thought."

"That's certainly my impression. But he's a front for the real owners of the station. I'm sure of that. Who now own at least half of The Week."

"I don't think that's legal. They'd have to file... Wait, how do you know about this? You couldn't even stop them from shipping you over to the Print Gulag."

"I know, that's all. Okay, I've been having lunch with that old guy who handles the documents and billing."

"Oh, yeah. What's his name? Tyler."

"Taylor. He sits down there doing all that xeroxing. So glad for company it's kind of pathetic. A sweet old guy, actually. And he knows where *all* the bodies are buried."

"Just nobody ever asks him. Impressive."

"I'm a real caution sometimes. But I was hoping you might bring something to the table on this thing."

"I had a pretty cool sombrero, but you took it away. Rushed me up here in my skivvies." He took another jolt of java. "Trader Joe's, huh?   Well, look. The Week is very closely held. But you're saying Scorment bought some of it. So there's going to be shares, shake-up, paper trails. Let me see what I can come up with."

"Now that's what I had in mind. You bring your newshound talents to bear. I'll poke around some more, we pool what we find. Sound good?"

Rollie leaned back, sipped again. It sounded very good, actually. Too bad he was never that into blondes. Or electronic media faces. Still, he could get used to sitting here with good coffee, looking into the serene, ordered countenance of Caitlin Vanderkeller. While scheming to nail Those Bastards.

"Let me get back to you."

She laughed, something else he could get used to. He raised his mug to her in a gesture of toast or salute. "Confusion to our enemies."

She reached her mug out, clinked his. "Wotta team."

"Great," Rollie said after taking a swallow to seal the toast to co-operation and confusion. "That only leaves me a few minor, but somewhat pressing, problems. Like getting some clothes and my car and figuring out how to get home. Is this one of those places where people with long hair and beards get disappeared in the elevators?"

"It leaves you a few more problems than that, doesn't it? Like, 'Home, what home?' and 'Money, what money?' and such."

"Now that you mention it. I could call a cab except for that money thing you brought up. And I doubt any of your clothes would fit me."

"I've given that a little thought."

"Splendido. I've managed to get so forlorn and stupid I have to have blonde TV girls think for me."

"See? You're in deep doo doo. But I've got a plan."

Rollie hunched forward, "Will you have to kill me if you tell me?"

"I haven't decided. First, there's the money."

"I hate the idea of money coming first in life, but you're right."

"How's the job hunt going?"

"I think you might know. There's only one daily paper in town and, A) they hate my guts. Along with B) since the LA Times pulled out of the county there are about thirty over-qualified journalists for every job in town."

"How about free-lancing? With your background..."

Rollie laughed an unfunny laugh. "There's really no such thing. The local magazines don't run writing because it takes up space they could use for color pictures of expensive crap. The Tribune has unions. If they could shop outside, don't you think they'd have something worth reading now and then? The only paper that pays anything for outside work is The Week."

"Which pays pretty well, for some reason. And desperately needs copy now that everybody walked. How are they all going to get jobs, anyway?"

"They're collecting unemployment and hitting the beach while they wait for their class action suit with the Labor Council to force them to re-hire."

"So they didn't jump off a dock to support you, after all? There goes another golden legend."

"They did enough to embarrass me. I mean like, humble me. You know. Am I worth that?"

"They seem to think so," Caitlin said softly. "But here's my point. Think you can come up with any interesting free-lance stories for me?"

"Are you missing the drift here? My byline is eighty-sixed."

"So you'd just have to settle for getting your stories printed. And the money."

Rollie studied her with new eyes. "You're not really blonde, are you?"

"If I wasn't, the last person I'd tell is some snoopy reporter."

Rollie gave her a smile that really nailed her. This was a smile for intimates, an invitation to the inside. He said, "So essentially you'd conspire against your employers to buy features from their disgruntled ex-chump?"

"That's my plan. Well, more like a scheme. And meanwhile, we'll work together on figuring out this whole deal Those Bastards are running and see if we can derail it."

"Wow. You're my hero. Yeah, I've got a few tales I could spin you. Some I've been dying to see in print. That dipshit Ovarón wouldn't... But he's not at the wheel anymore, is he? Scorment is, with his Sicilian ninja investors group."

"In a way. Another way of looking at it, I am."

This time his smile was more than intimate, it was conspiratorial. It was a secret handshake between team-mates, a bond of comrades in arms. Caitlin caught herself wondering what sort of smiles he kept stashed for women he actually... Whoa! Enough of that stuff, girlfriend. You need to be around men more.

Rollie leaned back, said, "Of course, it's not like having my clothes and car."

Caitlin stood up wordlessly and walked inside. She came back carrying a one-piece lime-green polyester leisure suit. "Only color they had in your size. I didn't know boxers or briefs."

"Well, if it's none of the above I'm not going to tell some nosy editor." He took the suit and held it up. "Is this how you see me?"

"I didn't want to leave you in the K-Mart parking lot very long. Especially without an approved safety seat. It'll work until you can get your poncho and sombrero back, Cisco." She tossed him something, which he snatched out of the air. His car keys.

"Good job! Now if I could only remember where I left it."

"The Liquor Barn parking lot by that Coconut place. According to the Aussie."

"Oh, yeah, Jody. She's a good egg."

"Here's five ones and some change. Take the trolley from the convenient stop downstairs. Transfer to Number Nine at Old Town."

He grinned, heading for the bathroom with the leisure suit. "So we keep in touch."

"I'm looking forward to your next story. Sign it Dennis Schumann."

He stopped, puzzled. "Why Dennis Schumann, particularly?"

"Because he's one of those darling gay guys next door, who idolize me and will cash the check for you."

Rollie stood there in his sunburn, bathrobe and plastic flip-flops, staring at her. He hoped he really wasn't thinking, "All this and great tits, too."

CHAPTER TWENTY

If Caitlin retained a shred of doubt that Wiley was her own personal visitation of the Final Plagues, it was dispelled by the first annual Fall Fashion issue. She'd somehow assumed that since it was Kyle's idea--and a really great one, in her opinion-- and that since it was one of those rare occasions when the whole staff directed their attention to a single, unified goal, Wiley wouldn't rub his crotch in their face on this one. For insight into that concept, simply trisect the word "assume".

Wiley had shocked Casey by turning in his column over a week early. He seemed quite passionate about it, filled with an almost messianic verve to see it in print. "The Fashion God," he slurred, "Has spoken. Go and do likewise."

FASHION VICTIMS
By The Weekend Warrior

Opinion is divided on the role of fashion in society: does it function as a conspiracy, an addiction , or merely a loathsome and communicable disease? Never one to overlook a "gimme", **THE WEEKEND WARRIOR**™ will examine that question and field the usual devastating results.

The investigation was furthered by very close questioning of a figure with known fashion connections: a ex-model I dated. She was around the style game for a long time and in fact refers to herself as an "Old Fashioned Girl". Which I will vouch for, though it can take as many as six Old Fashioneds to do the trick. (I happen to know she's also a "Tequila Shooter Girl", but she's a little fuzzy about that incident, which is just as well).

She summed up fashion history for me in one word: "French". It's a word she's gotten a lot of mileage out of, but she's right: fashion would be nowhere without the French Connection. You can see it in the vocabulary. The very concept of "fashionable" is expressed as *ala mode,* which might seem a little weird until you see all those anorexic clone models probably just praying that somebody would slap a scoop of ice cream on them. You can hardly talk about clothes without using terms like *décolletage* (meaning a deficiency of collagen), *derrière* (meaning "from the rear"--many a young model was born in the Midwest, but reared in Paris), *chic* (meaning "to show too much *derriere*") or *in vogue,* (meaning "photographed hanging off some bulimic, grotto-eyed holocaust victim look-alike so as to give a 'daring' glimpse of something carefully constructed to resemble a breast but located where no normal woman would have one").

Of course, not all fashion terms are French: we owe "Vunderbra" to German, "spangle" to Splanglish, "bangle" to Bangladesh, "Heroin chic" to The Auld Moss, and "Prozac chic" to Hillary Clinton. The Italians have a lot to answer for, too. All that Armani, Gucci, Oscar de Low Renta. In fact the very word "fashion" comes from the same Italian root as "fascism". But none of that is important to you right now. What *is* important, according to the Warrior--and you don't get much more important than that--is knowing how to predict fashion trends and avoid their ravages.

Rule # 1 Don't be a woman

Fashion victimizes women almost exclusively. Including women trapped inside men's bodies, of course. Although I don't fully understand that concept. A man trapped inside a woman's body I understand all too well. The last time it happened to me it required a drum of icy Gatorade, a hydraulic jack, two sets of AbMasters, an overdose of Valium and a Papal Dispensation to get loose.

But the important thing is, men (*real* men, anyway) are immune to fashion. We *never* think about our shoes matching our wallets. We never freak out because somebody in the same room is wearing the same outfit. In fact, if you work for an insurance company you might freak if you notice your outfit is *different* from everyone else at the meeting. You can't put some Roman flit's name on a twenty dollar pair of jeans and sell them to us for a hundred bucks. You can't get us to pay a hundred bucks for a haircut. We don't give a lot of thought to our belts or skin coloration or socks seams or if our fellow plumbers in Paris are showing more or less butt crack this fall. Okay, there's the running shoe thing, but those are basically toys or tools or something: fashion is a condition that mostly stalks female victims.

For instance, women pay consultants to find out their Color Seasons--that they are "Winters" or "Springs" and have to buy a bunch of make-up and accessories to work it out. Most men instinctively dress seasonally. In baseball season a Padres hat and cleats will do, in football season an oversized Chargers jersey and black goo under the eyes, during surfing season jams and a lobotomy, and during ice hockey season a plastic face mask and machete. No consultant needed, everything accomplished with common household materials. Why would women and not men get sucked into rampant Fashism?

Magazines, that's why. Women's magazines feature skinny young women dressed up in ridiculous, expensive clothes. In men's magazines the young women are neither so skinny nor so encumbered. Fashion just doesn't raise its botoxed head. Oh, sure there are clothing ads in male magazines; but usually just some kid with a lots of pecs and cheekbone staring into the camera with some vague attitude and unencumbered young women crawling his frame. Except Esquire and GQ, where they think women carry disease or cooties and prefer to depict clean-cut, firm-fleshed young guys. But those International Male types aren't the point: we're talking about breeder males. Who are much less interested in fashion than male things like cars, guns, electronics, tools, and (chiefly) breeding. Men don't care what we wear. Or what women wear, for that matter. Or if. Have you ever heard of a man dressing a woman with his eyes?

If so, he's probably a fashion designer. Fashions are almost exclusively perpetrated by homosexuals out to degrade the women they despise. After a show, they get together to snicker over the stupid stuff they've just gotten those silly little bitches to wear on a raised runway in front of cameras and bright lights.   Then they take turns wearing the stuff themselves. Which is why it's all made for tall, mannish, hipless women with no breasts or body fat. Once you know what's going on, the whole scam is sooooo obvious.

Rule #2 Calculate what Young People are wearing.

It's absurdly easy. I'm surprised there's not a little rotary slide rule to do it for you. All you have to do to be hep with the hot young styles is cruise the thrift shops in middle-aged neighborhoods. Just buy clothes your parents got rid of as being unfashionable. Hippies wore forties funk that fifties people were too slick for, the "New Wave" wore the skinny ties and tight cuffs the sixties people dropped out of, now everyone is wearing Eastern European polyester crap that *nobody* would have. You can almost make out a chart for what spontaneous, creative youngsters will be sporting in the future. Or you can just:

Rule #3 Dress like John Travolta

This rule seems strange, but it's one of the most reliable of our times. For some reason Travolta has been the Fashion God of America for decades. How do these things happen? God knows. You can't choose it, it chooses you. Travolta would probably rather be God of Volcanoes or Rain Forests or Streetcorner Personality Tests, but instead he was picked by the Universe to show Americans how to dress. He did "Grease" and everybody suddenly decided to celebrate those fun fifties with leather jackets, poodle skirts and cosmoline hairdos. Then "Saturday Night Fever" got everybody into three piece poly suits, the Hustle, and more hairgoo. "Urban Cowboy" came out and everybody ditched the gladrags and started wearing boots, Stetsons, and Bull Durham chaws. Then he made a couple of movies where he just danced around practically naked and everybody did *that* (Flea should credit him on his album covers).

Then, for reasons we mortals can only guess at, he did the worst thing imaginable--he didn't make any more movies. It was hell. Nobody knew what to wear. Pathetic souls slumped around in satin tour jackets, cowboy hats, and motorcycle boots—crying out for accessorization, acting out the hurtful need for a direction, a zeitgeist, an ensemble. As a result, the eighties was a shambles, the only decade without its own "look". Okay, parachute pants. Obvious reaction to a disaster situation--or possibly the Bailout era.

Just when things could get no worse (suburban teenagers were starting to sag trou and their parents were wearing Forest Gump drag) The Second Coming saved us all. Travolta returned with "Pulp Fiction", trailing clouds of glory, and everything was back on track. You could *feel* the relief. No more the nagging, the niggling doubts, the hollow look in the mirror: men needed only to get out there with dark stark Eurotrash suits, weird sunglasses, a nine millimeter sidearm, and a discreet but fashionable opiate habit and the nineties just fell into place. Women had but to dress like the Travolta's leading ladies. (Huge syringe protruding from between breasts optional, and not for beginners).

The "dress like Travolta" fashion rule only works because Travolta is infallible and has never abused his Godhood. Think what might have happened if he had played "Gandhi". A million young people wearing loincloths and caste marks. Or if he'd done "Amadeus"? Or The Riddler or Robin Hood or Elvis or Jabba the Hutt (the "young Jabba") or the One Armed Man? It's too frightening to imagine. Fortunately, in a world with so little to believe in, we can have faith that Travolta will continue to guide and watch over the way we dress. Unless the rumor is true that he'll star in the soon-to-be-cast Dennis Rodman Story. With Damon Wayans as Jordan, Wesley Snipes as Pippen, Whoopi Goldberg as Madonna and Jim Carry in the role he was born to play: 100,000 berserk fans. But where were we?

Ah yes, Fashion: Menace or Mindfuck? I think I've said enough to let you draw your own conclusions. But in case you can't, allow me to say that all you really need to wear is simple clothing, like a humble T-shirt. An idea commemorated by **THE WEEKEND WARRIOR**™ Humble T-Shirt, the kind of anti-fashion, anti-ripoff statement all hip people are making these days. Order one while they last, just $49.95 from http://www.southcoastweek.com/giftshop. Plus shipping and handling. Get a few for your friends, too, or they'll feel shabby and left-out. Hey, that's how fashion works.

Casey was delighted with the piece, which reflected her personal feelings about the addictive, parasitic nature of statement clothing. She praised Wiley lavishly, assuming that some of it got through his various stupors and crazes. Kyle was equally pleasured, to Caitlin's astonishment.

"He didn't hock a booger in the fashion issue," Kyle told her, "Just did his thing. And look at the Red Zone. Ads from Catwalk and Retail Slut. Face it, we don't cover that whole ballgown, Reagan-era scene that San Diego Magazine works."

"So that little tantrum actually helped us."

"You bet," Kyle leaned over her desk put his hand on her forearm. "Listen, we're on a huge roll, here. We have to move into new territory, cut new trails: it's the nature of the times. And we're doing it."

"Okay, so he didn't alienate anybody. What did we gain?"

"For openers, a two year contract from Buffalo Exchange."

"That used clothing store?"

"That chain of ten used clothing stores," Lyle replied. "Very big with young spenders. Wiley hit it right on the nose."

Caitlin suffered in silence.

"And," Lyle gloated, "They'll be all over Halloween. Bring in a lot of other stores like that, even those Hawaiian shirt joints out in the beaches."

"If there's a perfect event for Wiley," Caitlin said, "It would have to be Halloween."

CHAPTER TWENTY-ONE

Rollie Moon's Indian Summer Surfing Orgy had not been a case of all play and no work. Freed of the petty tyrannies of the office, he'd had time to circulate, follow-up, suborn and wheedle his way down the trail of several interesting investigations. Corruption is not hard to find in San Diego. We are talking about a town whose bonds were suspended by the SEC, whose credit rating was dropped below that of itinerant winos, and over half of whose councilpersons were under active indictment, if not confinement, by the FBI.

What is hard to find is a newspaper that will mention such things. Rollie took that in hand and was pressing in on several different scandals...including why newspapers wouldn't cover the various stenches under their noses. Incompetence he could excuse, but what he was nailing down went far, far beyond that. In early October Dennis Schumann's first byline appeared in the Southcoast Week.

It was a hell of a story. It first documented, in a rich marinade of ridicule, the various proposals that had been put forth--and endorsed by the Union Tribune--to solve the "problem" of San Diego's airport being located downtown where it was easy to get to.

It was just imperative to build a new one, of course. There were Federal funds for new airports (though not to improve old ones). Projections showed growth which would need more airports...and therefore more real estate, and therefore more ad space. But mostly, it was just old and a good excuse for new concrete.

The solutions included (and Rollie didn't have to tell the locals that he hadn't made any of it up): building a bi-national airport with a runway that crossed the Mexican border, building a new airport in the desert and connecting it with San Diego by means of a tunnel through the mountains to house a mag-lev train, building a *floating* runway in the open sea and transporting passengers to and from land on shuttle barges (if you're not a local perhaps you need more solemn assurance that this was, in fact, a real proposal by an actual mayor and backed by a more or less real newspaper), and convincing the U.S. Navy to drop their whole Top Gun school and national defense fixation in order to give up their strategic Miramar Naval Airbase for civilian use.

The latter proposal, being the least obviously psychotic and the one most rabidly endorsed by the Union Tribune, came under closest scrutiny by the gimlet-eyed "Dennis". The paper had backed millions of dollars worth of studies and ballot proposals about the advisability of occupying land that the owners--who also owned hundreds of warplanes capable of mass destruction--did not want to give up. Dennis trounced the plan, gave evidence that the current field was not obsolete--including a reprint of a Union Tribune article showing how few acres and runways it had compared to other large cities as well as data showing that in spite of that they field handled more landings and passengers than all of them--and examined the paper's shrill claims that trying to evict the Navy would be a better idea than expanding Brown Field at the Mexican border: a field that sat on massive acreage the city already owned. Why would the city and "U.T." be so nuts about Brown Field, Dennis implored his readers...then indicated that answer to that would be forthcoming in subsequent articles.

Dennis caused a minor stir in the conscientious voting populace, a flurry of commentary by television news and talk radio, a major swell of anxiety in city halls and the offices of the UT and the national newspaper chain of which it was the flagship. However, the impact of his initial piece faded in comparison to the mirth, horror and ad sales generated by Wiley's pedophobic tribute to Halloween. The column solidified Wiley's standing with the fed-up childless singles that make up much of the Week's demographic and probably inspired aspiring serial killers all over America.

HELL O WEEN
By The Weekend Warrior

Halloween might seem like a holiday that holds adults hostage to the ravages of children, but a wise reader (with a little help from The Warrior) can find advantage amid the havoc. For one thing, the custom that sends the little clots around dressed up like gruesome bloodsuckers, ghastly butchers, obscene little monsters, grisly slabs of pestilence and slobbering evil incarnate could be seen as truth in advertising concept (Pirandello would have loved it).

Sure, the season also licenses the little hellions to knock at the doors of normal folk and demand "treats" under penalty of playing dirty "tricks" on homeowners if not satisfied, a repugnant form of protection racket for infantile delinquents. But who says the besieged householder can't play a few tricks of his own? All in fun, of course.

For instance, it's loads of fun to watch a four-year-old, tellingly dressed as a pirate, plunge his greedy hands into a bowl in which several pounds of M&M's have been carefully poured over a few mousetraps. Yo, ho, ho, me hearty. Not much of a trick, really. But then hardly a treat, either.

Repulsing these already fairly repulsive little hordes should involve at least as much imagination as they did in outfitting themselves. Sticking a few obviously child-sized skulls on the fence posts can keep the little nippers at bay while maintaining the spirit of the holiday. Of course, there's also the traditional, symbolic version--the Jack O'Lantern. Simple enough to make; all you need is a candle, a sharp knife, a scoop and a trifle-too-trusting tyke named Jack.

It used to be easy just to stop by the drug store for "Ex Lax" and "Pheenomint", which so closely resemble chocolate and chiclets. And it was heart-warming to imagine the little lumps moaning on their potties while their extorted goodies erupted. But today's kids are wise to such tricks, so try adapting another traditional set-up, the apple bobbing tub.

Beginners can merely wait until the little rotters kneel to snap up the proffered fruit, then boot them right in their booties. Okay, it's unsubtle, crude and low-tech, but it makes its own statement. Advanced apple-baiting techniques include tying small but tenacious alnico magnets (available from the back pages want ads where popular mad scientists get all their goodies) to nearly invisible fishing line leading out of the water and over to your favorite trolling rod. When you hear the limpet-like click of a magnet smacking a set of dental braces just snatch up the rod and settle back in your front porch fighting chair for clean fun and macho, Hemingwayesque exercise. If you use a light (20 pound, say) line, even a five year old goblin can put up a darned good fight. I've also found their frantic sunfishing and thrashing around seems to keep other tricksters from approaching.

The average kitchen contains a veritable arsenal of anti-personnel treats. Chocolate-coated Alka-Seltzer tablets create time-delayed havoc: for more immediate foaming sprinkle donuts with oven cleaner. "Mints" from air fresheners are refreshing...but why not just to the address at the bottom of this page for a copy of Freddy Kreuger's Household Hints or (better yet) Wiley's Halloween and Diet Cookbook with icky recipes such as Roach Motel Wafers, alum cookies and Tabasco kisses?   Fans of projectile vomiting might find it worthwhile to lay in a little syrup of ipecac for the occasion.

On some occasions I actually go so far as to give the little rodents real candy, but only cylindrical types like tootsie rolls. These make it easier to hide the firecrackers tipped with tiny slow fuses so they'll go off in the indefinite future. When they explode they reduce the paper sack to confetti (more peripheral festivity) and blow a cloud of candy all over the street in a manner reminiscent of the Mexican piñata. The charges are too small to seriously injure the children. Unless, of course, they have already wolfed them down without chewing or indeed unwrapping them.   But then, parents repeatedly warn children that such practices lead to tummy aches, and I always support parental wisdom when possible, or at least when convenient and/or profitable.

A little thought can turn Halloween from a trial into a really fun affair in which kids actually come to your door and *volunteer* to be guinea pigs in unwholesome psycho-social experiments. Let your imagination run free, if not totally amok. How much trouble would it be to hinge your (heh, heh) "Welcome" mat so a touch of the doorbell would plunge your tender visitors into chambers of spiders, snakes and similar gruesome greeters?   A little informed cooperation could turn your entire neighborhood into a theme park of gory dementia, a sort of Steven King's Candy Cane Lane. Have a happy hosting the horrors, huh?

CHAPTER TWENTY-TWO

The minute she turned from the top step and looked down the hall toward her doorway, Casey felt her goldish glow turn into the dull red smolder of irritation. She'd been out later than usual, attending a rally for Mexican presidential dog-in-the-manger Andrés López Obrador, which had led to tapas and red wine later, part of an admiring circle around a leftist legal dissident who had actually been tortured by a PRI death squad. Well, torture squad, anyway. She was in no mood to deal with somebody leaving a heap of filthy old rags in her hallway.

Building management will hear about this in the morning, she grumbled to herself as she undid her locks and slipped inside. Like most liberals, Casey defied authorities by default, but quickly turned to them to enforce her personal peeves and belief systems. The whole glimmer had gone off the night. It had been so wonderful in the candles and crystal, toasting each other for being among the brave, committed few. She entered and closed the door, grumping at being back in mundane reality with trash in the hall, short sleep before deadline day, and no sign of any copy from that damned Wiley.

Uh, oh!

Her door flew open and Casey stepped out, eyeing the unsavory heap in a mixture of disgust, apprehension and incipient rage. Very cautiously she kicked at it, then harder. It humped as though contemplating cellular division into two identical loathsome lumps, then rolled over to reveal the carpet-bombed face of her star columnist, twitching and gibbering inaudibly under the ravages of some ungodly potion or two.

Returning from a quick trip to her kitchen, she dumped the chilled contents of a Brita filter pitcher on his face. His eyes clanged open like the knell of doom. His lips curled back like an infected mongrel's, revealing what to her were damaged teeth with stems, seeds and body hair wedged between them, but he would have thought of as a friendly smile. "Casey Chones!" he squawked. "Mounted in the cabin. Farewell trippin' to the promised land."

"Wiley you *fucker*!" she screamed. Wiley continued to exhibit his effect of drawing profanity from those who seldom indulged. "What are you doing here? Where's your piece?"

"Right here in my pocket," Wiley slobbed, clawing at his pants. He pulled out a .32 revolver with trigger guard and hammer tang removed by an inexpert hacksaw. "But I'm happy to see you anyway. I'd stand on ceremony, but the flesh is weak."

"It just keeps getting worse, Wiley. I'm writing you off."

"What? Some goody two-gooder you turned out to be. Scorn a man when he's down and trying to be out."

"You've got six hours to get that column in. Or I'm through with you."

"How can I? Look at me. I'm hazardous wasted. Can't move, can't think, can't speak. Can barely see. It's getting dark, Doc. Is this the end of little Rico?"

"You can speak just fine," Casey snapped.

"Sure, *now*. But not for another five minutes, I'd estimate. Much less... how many hours again?"

"Wiley, having talent brings responsibility. Is it so hard to get it together just once a week? At a reasonable hour?"

"Work week, hours, schedule," Wiley groused in a blurred monotone. "The litany of alienation that flays the American male out on a table to measure his manhood by the inch."

"Oh, like you guys don't run around measuring yourselves."

"Chopping us up into bite-sized briquettes of utility," Wiley midnight rambled. "Take away our numbers and give us secret names!"

"Hold it down, please. My neighbors are already pissed off at me."

As evidence for that argument, two doors had opened down the hall, irate faces poked out. Wiley defused their hostility with a friendly wave. Since he waved with the hand holding the Saturday night special, the faces instantly vanished, taking their damn irateness with them.

"You've got to get out of here, Wiley! Now!" She was humiliated to realize she wanted to kick him right smack in the nuts. Grab his unrestricted handgun and pistol-whip him silly. Silli*er*.

"Would, should, no could," Wiley intoned like a sad priest. "I'm blotto. From the planet Lotto. Rolling big losers, *nolo locomotto*."

166

Casey stared at him a minute, then ran inside for her handy-dandy digital voice recorder (with storage for up to seventeen hours of MP3 music). She thrust it in Wiley's face. "You're on a roll. Spill it. Do your trick."

"I thought you said I had to get out of here." Oh, yeah. She jittered, thinking fast. Then ran inside again, this time coming back with a two-wheeled dolly used for moving furniture. What Mexicans call a "*diablo*". Casey thought fast pretty well: she also had duct tape and a roll of nylon cord. She studied Wiley for a second, carefully laid out coils of rope, then used her foot to roll him over on his stomach, on top of the rope.

Mumbling through the runner pile, Wiley commented, "Well, hello dolly. You keep one around just in case? Actually, that one could handle a half-dozen cases."

Casey flopped the dolly on his back and started lashing it to him with the segments of rope that protruded from under him. "I move a lot. Mostly out from worthless men." There was truth to that, Lord knows, but actually she'd had the dolly since college under the advice of Freewheelin' Franklin in her big brother's Freak Brothers comics.

She snatched the gun from him and stuck it in her coat pocket, not without a squeamish squirm of aversion. With a big heave she turned the whole dolly/Wiley construct upside down, Wiley now supine, lashed to wheels and ready for take-out. She tore off quick skritches of duct tape to secure his knees and a few other places that looked saggable, then effortlessly tipped the cart up and started down the hall, Wiley incoherently singing the Doors' version of "Whiskey Bar." She had worried about the stairs, but they took care of themselves. A little slip on the top riser led to Wiley sliding down the whole flight like a big ugly kid on a sled. At the landing, the dolly hit the wall and popped upright, slamming Wiley up against it face-first. "Aieee!" he yelped, "That's gotta hurt."

She repeated the process three times to get him, now more stunned than ever, to the parking level. As she wheeled him through the dark car grotto he raved, "The weirdness on the left has surely past. Yet I remain lashed to the mast. My naked ears all tortured by the sirens sweetly singing."

The sound of police responding to reports of a maniac brandishing machine guns filled the space with ululating whoops of menace.

"See?" Wiley demanded. "Man, that worked out really cool. Let me try something a little harder."

Casey opened the rear gate of her blue Volvo station wagon and tipped the dolly in, head first.

"Blue Vulva, huh?" Wiley sneered. "Figures." Casey took a minute to snatch off another few feet of tape and move to apply it to his mouth.

"Wait, wait," Wiley whined. "You want the column, right?"

Casey paused, she hadn't thought beyond getting the hell outta Dodge.

"There's only one chance in a snowball of hell," Wiley babbled. "Get thee to the Mimosa Club. K and Alvarado. It's a desperate shot, but it just might blow up in our foolish fucking faces."

Casey gave the tape a wind around his head, lifted the wheels, and slid him into the wagon like a paramedic slamming a stretcher into an ambulance. She exited the building carefully and waited two blocks before pouring on the coal for the Mimosa.

CHAPTER TWENTY-THREE

Jerome, wearing his Last Call face and demeanor, looked up dispassionately when Casey entered, slamming both doors open with the dolly to present a spasmodically twitching Wiley with hell in both eyes and foam oozing out from under the silver tape across his mouth. "Sorry, no recycle here. Dispose of him in the proper bin."

The denizens took in Wiley with the Zen calm a night of hammering cheap booze can produce. Jasper ventured, "Service entrance in rear."

Cathilda whinnied, "No in-flight refueling."

Strack rumbled, "That extreme skateboard games shit was last week."

Casey looked around at the Mimosa and its fauna, far from reassured. She set herself up for more self-castigation by being glad she had the gun.

Jasper approached Wiley curiously, examining him like Lord Carnarvon peering at a mummy prepped for cultural looting. "Not a bad ride, Hoss," he decided. "A rig like this could solve a lot of problems for a lot of folks."

Wiley gibbered and gnashed beneath the tape. Coming to the realization, Jasper reached up and yanked it off with a helical *voila* move. Wiley howled like a gutshot coyote. Jasper looked down at the tape, which now depicted a map of Wiley's nape hair, mustache, and soul patch. "Oh, yeah. Sorry Bro."

Turning to Casey, he bowed. "Howdy Ma'am. I'm Jasper. That's Jerome behind the bar about to chuck us all out. And all those damn drunks over there."

"Hi. I'm Casey. Can you help me get this man functional?"

Cathilda wavered over to consult. "I doubt it, honey. That Spanish Fly stuff is bogus and Ginseng takes too long. Have you got any poppers? IV Viagra?"

The irregulars were crowding around Wiley, giving Jerome an opportunity to scoop up all their glasses without a fight. Wiley slavered at them, trying to bite anybody who got too close. One such lunge tipped the dolly and he whammed down on his back again, knocking him breathless.

"Okay," Casey asked wearily, "Now what?"

"Depends on what you want to accomplish," Jerome said. "In the next eight minutes."

Wiley got her attention by shyly booting her in the calf. She leaned over, straining to hear his labored words. Which were: "Calls for decompression. Gotta be done just right or I get the bends. And the kinks and heebie-jeebies."

Casey looked at Jasper with such palpable helplessness that Jasper patted her shoulder consolingly. "It's all right, Lady. This happens all the time."

Despair surfacing in the post-action lull, Casey murmured, "He has to write something for me. Or I'll kill him."

Which reminded her. She pulled out the pistol, causing Jerome to put his hands under the bar and regard her with an animal alertness. The patrons showed little reaction. Jasper shook his head sadly. "Won't work."

Horrified, Casey gasped, "No, no. I'm not going to shoot him. I just want you to dispose of..."

Jasper nodded, "Nope. Like I said, that gun won't work. Smokin' Joe got so cute cutting it down it won't fire anymore. Wiley just carries it to..."

Cathilda stomped on his instep. Jasper yipped, then looked hangdog. "Yeah, right. Anyway. Here, let me take it."

Casey held the gun out, hanging between her fingertips. Snorting, Cathilda snatched it and dropped it into the bottomless sea of her cleavage.

From the bar came the ragged voice of Strack. "You want to get him up and ready for action like right now, affirm?"

"Six minutes, max," Jerome intoned.

"No problem," Strack croaked. "Pure logistics. And ordnance." He wheeled around the bar, one hand spinning his wheels and the other holding a shot he'd hidden from Jerome. He surveyed Wiley's lash-up professionally. "Not bad. Small wheels though. You want to race afterwards?"

Casey shook her head, so Strack shrugged and pulled some arcane paraphernalia from the nylon bag on his useless knees. He held up a convoluted, combat-ready clump of hardware and smiled at it proudly. "Technology. That's what toppled the Russkies. You think they could build something like this?"

Casey doubted it, but didn't yet see why they would want to. The Mimosans all nodded at her, basking in second-hand pride over what had been wrought and was capable of more wroughting on further notice. Flipping levers and valves, Strack walked her through a catechism of his *deus ex megabonk*.

"Okay, the business end here came off a standard respirator." Casey could now see that what she'd thought was some obscene sex gadget was a flesh-colored shroud to fit over mouth and nose. "Connected directly to the Main Chamber here." Which opened like a rifle breech to reveal a burnt interior. Strack touched a stud on the side of the device and a coil in the chamber glowed cherry red. "Electric ignition," he said proudly. "Nine volt". A mutter of praise ran through the crowd. Pulling a tube with enameled dragon from his shirt pocket, he carefully poured some fine grains of what looked like yellow sand into the breech, then sealed it. "Lebanese hash," he commented. "Crumbles up like sandstone."

Toggling open another chamber at the rear, he showed her a screw-down tensioner. "Drop an amyl nitrate cylinder in the Propellant Chamber," he told her, "Lock and load. Or nitrous. Different payload, but you get operating pressure either way."

He whipped what looked to Casey like a CO_2 cartridge out of a cross-breast bandolier, slipped it into the cylinder and ratcheted it down. "Now this," he went on, "is optional, but advisable for this circumstance." He opened another small chamber with polished chrome interior and pulled on a string around his neck to tug a titanium charger engraved with the Special Forces out of his collar. He positioned it over the chrome chamber and tumped in a few righteous jolts of coke. The crowd titter this time had a harder edge on it.

Strack sealed the cocaine chamber and adjusted a small set screw. "The Induction Chamber works on pure carburetion," he said, checking Casey for comprehension. "You know; Venturi principle, all that?" Casey nodded dumbly.

"So," Strack concluded, "Push this button and the hash ignites, hit this one and the amyl blows through the barrel, forcing the smoke out through the aspirator with a fine jet of some damn decent Peruvian toot." He held up the gizmo, which Casey now saw as freighted with catastrophe like a loaded torpedo. "Ta, daaaa. The Bongzilla, reporting for duty."

"Five minutes!" Jerome barked.

Jasper tipped Wiley back up to vertical hold. He looked like home-made dogshit. Strack rolled up, wheel to wheel with Wiley, and extended the mask. Wiley bowed his head as gratefully as any communicant, making a tight seal around his breathing orifices, aided by the remnants of the duct tape.

Strack touched the lighter stud, paused, then pulled the trigger for the propellant. The Bongzilla emitted a low, implosive hiss. Strack toggled the trigger, producing explosive puffs like a steam locomotive. Glancing at Casey, he moaned, "Wooooooo, wooooo! I think I can, I think I can, I think I can..." over the chug, chug, chug. Turning back to Wiley he said, "You're on the Peace Train, now, Brother." Wiley's chest inflated, his eyes bugged out. Casey could have sworn smoke blew out his ears. When he started gagging and thrashing, Strack withdrew his portable gas chamber and observed the results with scientific detachment.

Casey saw no improvement in the situation. Wiley, supercharged from the nuke hit on his plundered store of brain chemicals, was not responding. It was obvious to any experienced observer that the fury of the neurological storm had turned inward, poking tight twisters of havoc into cellars best left unexploded, avidly seeking out the fragile trailer parks of higher reason. She looked a question at Strack, who shrugged, "It's pure science. You want to apply it, you need to have some expectations."

"I need for him to give me a column." She met the circle of uncomprehending eyes, tugged out her recorder and waved it. "I need three thousand words in five hours," she yelled.

"Wrong," Jerome answered her. "Three minutes."

The denizens had it sussed out now. "Oh," they chorused, "A rant!"

Jasper nudged her, said, "You have to pull his chain." Casey glared at him.

"Crank him up," he clarified. "Get him started."

"Yo, Wiley," Cathilda purred mischievously, "What you think about Safe Sex?"

Wiley's eyes snapped open, pools of sardonic venom. "*Safe Sex*!?!?" he screamed. "Don't even get me started on that steaming pile of malicious misanthropy."

Strack leaned over to hit the "On" button of Casey's recorder, which she held up like a contrite Catholic virgin offering a candle to her star-crossed Savior while Wiley raved out of control.

When the gigahit from the clusterbong died out, he slumped in his bonds, his verbal spew trailing off like a Walkman on the last few milliamps of its Energizer AA's. His head lolled forward. Drool dripped on his shoe and bare foot.

Jerome slammed the bar and bellowed, "That's it. Get your raunchy red asses outta here!"

SAFETY COMES PREMATURELY
By The Weekend Warrior

My position on sex is Male Superior. And my favorite male superior position is called 68. You go down on me and I owe you one. That's as safe as sex gets and it involves sticking sensitive, irreplaceable components between sharp teeth. Safe sex is a myth! They want you to believe it's safe so they can use it to sell you worthless junk.

Listen, I'm no prude, for crissakes. I receive the ministrations not only of columnist groupies, but also the old, the young, the incapacitated, the begrudging, the easily duped, the elated, unrated, inflated, animals (both stuffed and previously unstuffed), vegetables, minerals, leather and several modern synthetics of arcane properties, machines, chains, chain letters, chain letter sweaters, footwear, underwear, everywear, anywear, hardware, software, artificial intelligence, intelligent artifice, unintelligible artifacts, milking parlors, prods (both stock and custom), mammaries, memories, murmurings, prostheses, French ticklers, German sticklers, and Oriental pricklers that give tickling a whole new slant.

In short, whatever gets you through the night. Lech and the world leches with you, kvetch and you kvetch alone. Not that "alone" is without erotic possibilities. Best not to rule anything out, is the rule of thumb. In fact thumbs themselves can be sugar plumb fairies: there are cults of digital freaks who spraypaint "Thumbs Rule" on freeway ramps. Find your personal fetish through the process of elimination. In fact, that process itself... but I'm sure you get the idea. Several maybe. If so, send them in care of The Week. If your obsession is chosen, you could qualify for my Queen For a Day Special, a ride on ol' Jumpin' Jack Flash, his own bad self.

It's not my job to educate anybody. I just wanna be your lover, not your limpdick fascist boss. I want you to have my multi-headed love child. I just want to give up all my crazed, retardo, muskrat love. I just wanna to be your everything, be your macho man, be your teddy bear, your handy man, your salty dog, your smooth-up criminal, your overnight sensation. I just want you to be my party doll, my inflatable date, my meat puppet, my lip-smacking, ham-slammin, joint-jumpin, nipple-nibblin', boogy-woogy foo' . See what I'm saying?

But don't try to tell me any of the above is safe! There's nothing you can put on to make it safe, no pills you can take, no advice from the wise. Most of those just make it more dangerous, actually. In a safe world condoms and diaphragms would come equipped with emergency airbags. Don't think "cybersex" is safe, either. The oxymoronically-named "Virtual" sex. Punching up smut on your laptop or fax machine. If all you can get on top of your lap is a computer, buddy, you've got problems. The micro, soft syndrome. But what pops up when you're browsing seemingly innocent sites like CatholicCradleRobbing.com? Click Here To Meet Personal Dates. Danger! Danger, Will Robinson!

It's the spot market for Proper Genitalia, eBay for biohazards. And don't even think about handing me that, "Oh, no. It's all about companionship." You can get companionship in a pet store. But they all play the game: "Friends First". Okay, sure, honey. "First" meaning, before *what*? Eh? All this platonic crap. To me, platonic friends are the kind you met in Plato's Retreat. But the game is to pretend that for platonic soul mates, Proper Genitalia doesn't matter. Well, here's the scoop. It *does matter*. Look at the top of the webpage: Men Seeking Women, Women Seeking Men, Transsexual Cross-dressing Masochists Seeking Highly Confused Dudes. But see, it's not like "Seeking Whatever". One touch of an Improper Genitalia and you find out It Matters. Don't search the engine if you don't have a clear idea of what you are ISO.

All those code letters are a bad sign, right there. But at least we know what ISO means. Interested in Sucking Off. Some of these little codes in the ads are like, what is it? What does this bitch want from me? Okay, SWF, we know that one, we saw the movie. Means she looks like Brigit Fonda. Or maybe it means Super Wack Freak. Just right for some AMF.

Here we got all these women looking for an LTR. What? Little Tickle in the Ribs?   Love Triangle Rumble? Lowdown Twisted Rutting?   Whatever, I'm there for it. Long as there's no commitment involved.   Another thing they're all ISO, is stable. Spelled just like sounds: $table. Very self explanatory.

Then we get to HWP. I figured that stood for Ho With Problems. Or possible Ho With... Hmm, what starts with P? How about Proper Genitalia?   Then I found out it means Height Weight Proportional.   Like this is a big deal. Whoa, that babe is really proportional! Look out sweetie, I'm proportioned like a horse. Hey, is Barbie HWP? Hell no. Would you have sex with her? You bet you did. Or Jessica Rabbit.   Or probably even Calista Flockhart. Hey, check out Wilt Chamberlain.   Far cry from HWP, okay?   And he apparently did a different woman every 9.7 minutes from the time he was nine.

The problem is, what do you say if you're *not* HWP? Shamu look-alike?   Roseanne Class Cruiser? Welterweight runt?   No, you've got all these vague categories like "Dieting".   "Pleasantly Plump".   "Big Beautiful Woman". You gotta hope for at least two out of three on that one. Or "Lots Of Me To Love". Great: Single, White, lots of me to obsess over and harpoon and drown your whole crew.

Here's a few guidelines for these displacement classes. Just try this simple test. Have her sit on your face. If she's "Dieting" you can't breathe. "Rubenesque" and you can't see. If you can't hear, she's a "Big Beautiful Lot To Love". If you can't survive, she's an obese pig and what the hell were you thinking?

What's wrong with a little truth in advertising here? Like, "SWF, sloppy fat, but I sure can cook and I've got a proper genital and know how to use it.

So tell me. *Does any of that sound "Safe" to you*? Or some treacherous bait/switch scam aimed at stringing you up, looting your finances and emotions, then gutting you out into societal fish sticks? While infecting you with some strain of incurable, transmittable, death-dealing cooties and serving you with papers to support a dozen ill-conceived little bastards brainwashed to call you Pappy?

Next time you're thinking stinky and assume you'll get away unscathed, ask yourself three questions approved by the Solana Beach Police Department:

1. Would Jesus do anything this disgusting?

2. Do you have an exit strategy?

3. What year was the Battle of Hastings?

That final question is a mere bagatrix for those lucky enough to have attended a reasonably cogent school district prior to the drugs and rap era. The rest of us (or what's left of us) share my personal experience; that those ignorant of history are duped to repeat it. Same deal with Math and English, I discovered.

The latter was a particular disappointment at the time, since I had assumed the course would teach me how to speak more like the Beatles and Rolling Stones. Fortunately, rock and drugs did that for me anyway, but by then I had slipped into one of those odd little psychic traps institutions lay for the underly wary and ended up becoming an English Major. That was disappointing, too, since I expected to get a short clipped accent and mustache to match, but I did learn how to say "Leftenant" and "Stand Easy". Not to mention the names of a baffling bevy of heavy old weirdos like Chaucer and Milton, who could barely write English themselves. That Chaucer was the hip-hopper of the day. Should have sung that gobbledygook and called himself Tew Lyve Crewe. Acid Chause, cuz.

But I digress. Or had you already noticed that? The important thing to remember is: sex is spelled Danger! At the very least it makes you sleepy and stupid. It causes babies, who are eating us out of house and home. You can catch disease, wives, lawsuits, your death. Bottom line: how safe can anything be if you have to do it with women? Never trust women. Without them, I'd be on top: have God-like powers and the reach of empires. Instead of working for some miserable rag, surrounded by itinerant gophers and forced to flog my priceless (or at least cut-rate) wisdom to any semi-literate dipstick who cares to pick it up for free.

So, you get the general idea. And about time. Remember that nothing is as powerful as an idea whose time has come. Except perhaps a bull rhinoceros just about to come. In other words, nothing, but nothing can stop the Duke of Earl. Layeth not boogie-woogie on the Warlord of Weekend.

Casey didn't know whether to be proud of what she had snatched from the jaws of a looming deadline or humiliated. The more she thought about it, the more alternative ways of feeling about it occurred to her. None of them self-actualizing.

CHAPTER TWENTY-FOUR

"We should talk," were Caitlin's first words.

Rollie, sitting in the sunstruck salt air and rolling a joint with his cell phone shouldered to his ear, thought it was a pretty lame way to start a conversation. If we shouldn't talk, why call?

"No good," he said.

"What? I mean, why not?" Caitlin backed and filled, trying to get it. "What's no good?"

""We Should Talk" was a regular column about six years ago. Some featherhead chick doing gossip and can-you-believe-it scandal. Good idea, though."

"Boy, you can kick the guy's ass out of the editorial desk, but you can't... you know."

"No, I don't. You haven't talked to me yet.'

A little of this whimsical stuff goes a long way, Caitlin thought. But what the hell? "Not over the phone. It's too important for that. They're on to us."

Rollie put down the joint and sat up, "You'd better tell me a little more."

"Ha! Gotcha back, joker. Now, can we do lunch?"

"Nope, "Can We Do Lunch" was a weekly restaurant review back in the eighties. But there was never one called Let's Meet At the OB Pier Cafe."

"I think it would be overly restrictive. But you're the ex-editor. Early afternoon? If your schedule permits. Ocean Beach, you say?" Caitlin subscribed to the image of OB as a grungy sixties flashback teeming with druggies and didgeridoos; where locals sported "U.S. Out of O.B." bumperstickers and menaced yuppies and citizens.

"I live in OB. I'm there right now, basking in front of a cute little bungalow looking right at the Pier."

"Is 'cute bungalow' doper slang for 'sleeping bag under the pilings' or something?"

Rollie grinned at that one. "No but it'll probably catch on. I moved back in with an old surfing buddy. It's like being back in college but without worrying about finals."

"So, Pier Cafe around one?"

"Make it one-ish. Wear something anonymous. We shouldn't be seen together."

"Look for a veiled Muslim woman on a skateboard."

"Sounds like a bomb scare," Rollie said as he turned off the phone and turned on the joint.

Caitlin's actual disguise was even better. A touristy scarf, baggy shorts and blouse, huge wrap sunglasses. Not only would she blend in, nobody would ever think she was the glamorous TV woman. You couldn't even see her cleavage.

Rollie had waited inside, the better to keep them from being seen together, but she took a table outside. She was further concealed by their table umbrella as she munched on a lobster burrito with side of fries. Rollie, lolling back in the sunshine, worked on clam chowder served in a hollowed-out sourdough roll. It was his favorite place to eat or drink iced tea. A nautical café a few hundreds yards off the California coast. Miles of waves underlining Mission to the north, Sunset Cliffs and Mexican Islands to the south. Surfers bobbing and waiting for a ride. Gulls, pelicans, dolphins. Seals begging for scraps. Skatepunks, grannies on trikes, hippies, casting rod duffers, bikers, *cholos*, people in ill-chosen bathing suits. The OB Riviera, adrift on a sympathetic sea.

"I got some information from Taylor," Caitlin told him between bites. She realized she looked like a Kennedy or Loren hiding from photographers, but didn't care. "He likes you, by the way. Just doesn't trust you. He even knows your name."

"Okay, okay. Taylor. So what's the scoop?"

"He says Ovarón never held all the stock. And it would be better for everybody if none of it was in his hands because the other stockholder is smarter and stronger."

Robbie slumped in his chair. Caitlin didn't really understand his reply, which was, "Aw, shit. The Walrus."

"Goo goo ga joob."

"Absolutely."

"So you know what all that means?" She hadn't expected her message to get more obscure as he explained it.

"It means I have to go up to Santa Cruz and kiss an ass that doesn't like me one little bit. But there's an upside."

"Ah, good. Share."

"They've got a really righteous break and a cool roller coaster."

Caitlin thought that over for awhile and decided to move on. "So, you turn up anything?" She was hoping for a total info one-up. But no...

"Yeah. I was going to call you in a day or two." Rollie had reached the age-old dilemma: was he eating the chowder bowl, or prosaically using the bread to sop up the last of the chowder? "I've spent a lot of online time poking around a real spaghetti can of links and subterfuges, but it looks like the station holds maybe a quarter of the paper's stock, swapped for five percent of station stock."

"That doesn't seem like a fair trade."

"Well, it looks like the deal was for half of the Week stock, but a quarter of it's held by small buyers, who are starting to look like tentacles of some unseen octopus behind the scenes."

"That," she said with a certain certainty, "Would be the Mysterious Owners."

"Oh, so you know who they are?" Rollie was more impressed than he let on.

"If I did they wouldn't be Mysterious." Caitlin tossed a french-fry straight up into the air. Rollie looked up in case he needed to evade a gory ketchup hit, only to see a sleek fat gull swoop up to nail the fry before it even hit perigee. Another gull stuka-ed in to grab half the fry and an aerial dogfight ensued, ending when the fry broke and both gulls dropped to the café roof bragging about it. Caitlin had noticed the gulls on the roof were all fat and sassy: reservation injuns, she'd decided Hanging out frenching fries.

Caitlin hefted another fry, then decided to eat it herself. She caught Rollie watching and released the fry, which hung from her mouth like a giant bloodworm until she slurped it in. Rollie seemed to bring out the little girl she'd never really been.

"Don't play with your food," Rollie scolded. "Do you eat your toys?"

"You did it first."

"If I jumped in the fire, would you do it too?"

Caitlin thought a minute. "What if your face froze that way?"

"It would all end in tears," Rollie said sternly.

"It all goes to the same place anyway. Give up, Rollie. Women are congenitally better at the Mom Within thing."

"Okay, but if you start throwing pudding you're going straight home."

Caitlin brushed her lips with a napkin and squinted out over the sparkle of open ocean. "We talked about it at the station, but nobody knows anything specific. They have this henchman who comes in and, I don't know... has meetings, gives orders, carries out sacks of money, dumps bodies? This really geeky Chinese guy named Yao."

"Wow, zow."

"No, Yao. He's always bugging me to get naked for him."

"That doesn't sound very geeky." Not to be outdone, Rollie flipped a french-fry up and caught it in his mouth. "Or even inscrutable."

"He's like the accountant for some investment group, is how he explains it."

"So he confides in you to some extent."

"Well, when you're asking a woman to take her clothes off, you can't very well refuse to answer questions. He always tries to steer it towards his Ferrari and some paintings he wants to show me." She saw Rollie's glance and put a finger in his face. "Oh, no. Oooooh no. Don't even think about it. I'm not Mata Hari. I wouldn't get near that little doofus for any amount of information."

"Did I say anything?"

"No, but it was your tone of voice."

She held up a fry, then tossed it up in a tall arc towards Rollie's face. He moved his head to intercept it, opened his mouth. A gray gull swept in and snatched it just inches from his nose, brushing his hair with a wing as it made its getaway. Rollie jumped back, slamming his chair into the wall and almost falling over. Passers-by and fishermen were laughing at him, kids pointing. Caitlin was bent over laughing. On the roof a dozen gulls yucked it up.

Very solemnly, Rollie restored his chair, brushed the seat off and sat down. He motioned to the waitress, who was laughing her butt off. "Two small orders of fries," he told her. To Caitlin he glowered, "This isn't over yet by a long shot, ya varmit."

Caitlin laced her fingers and cracked them. "Bring it on, bluepencil boy."

"So," Rollie went on as if nothing had happened, "Around a quarter of the stock is in the hands of the Mysterians and around a quarter in the flabby mitts of J. Danforth-forth. Well, trying to get hold of the ghost holders doesn't look very promising."

"And talking a billionaire maniac out of them looks better?"

"Didn't you say he hit on you? Might be some play there."

"Sure. I'd much rather compromise myself with The Sprawl than a nice Asian accountant with a Ferrari."

"I knew you weren't serious about this." Rollie huffed. "And it was your idea."

"When will you go to Santa Cruz? Or more specifically, get back?"

"I'd say I'll be back in about four days. Let's get together on Thursday, once your paper's in bed."

"You probably know my schedule better than I do."

"You're learning. Todai good?"

Caitlin wasn't so sure of that. All the Japanese seafood you can eat? Something she'd never wanted to find out. On the other hand, she did like shellfish. And nobody would be there. Besides, she really liked the Café so maybe she should trust his choice.

CHAPTER TWENTY-FIVE

Her success in diverting Wiley's scattergun attack to a purpose, however insipid, inspired Casey. What the man needed was an editor, a manager. Somebody who could direct his obvious genius away from the gutter and towards pathways leading to fame and influence. She could hitch her wagon to his literary star and cause it to rise in the East.

Her next conversation with Himself was in her own office, while he slumped in a chair, wild-eyed and shivering from the travails of producing another gem in the rough for her. She skimmed it and was a shade appalled. Fortunately there was little chance that Ovarón would read it.

"Wiley," she said gently. He continued to orbit, his eyes following some three-dimensional ping-pong match of his own device. "Wiley!" she barked more forcefully. He looked at her, performing the onerous docking procedures for intra-species contact.

"I love your work. But it seems very negativistic."

"But in a positronic way," he asserted. "It's a negation of negativity, if not relativity itself. The attraction of opposing ions, in case you missed that part. Unified Field and Stream theory. Catch as catch can. Release as a goal to be humped for. I'm aiming for the nuosphere, here. Annals of Agnoiology. Negatory, nugatory, nuggie noggin territory. It's all good, what I'm saying, Sistah."

"Well, just think about this," Casey said. Yeah, right. The way a reactor thinks about environmental impact as it melts down to the center of the earth. She thought she could see sparks flitting from his head to the file cabinet he leaned it on. "The Christmas season is painful and depressing for a lot of people. Maybe you could do something about that in your column. Show your sensitive side. Empathize."

She surveyed his non-reaction to her words, sighed. "Well, think about it."

Wiley came out of his chair like a rogue PopTart from a toaster. He stared at her, grabbed her hand and kissed it. Well, slobbered on it. He paced around the office tossing his hands and head. "Think!" he yelled. "About IT! My God, girl, you're onto something. If we could just think. Brush aside the tedious clamoring of renegade electrons buzzing our resolve like pheromone-crazed Afro-Cuban bees. Rumba lines of dissipation. How *can* we think? Ever think of that? Or course not, what I was just saying. But in spades. In epaulets and garters and bustiers. My stars, woman. If we could only think, of course we could empathize. We could be sensitive if we could only come to our senses. Write the US senses bureau. I'm a sympathizer. Report that, if you dare. An empathizer from way back. Just show me a plight and I'm on it like a sailor on leave. You want sensitive empathy, you came to the right fucking guy, I'll tell you that much. Good on ya, babe. Hoozah!"

He bounced down the hall, yelling mottos at alarmed staffers as he went. "Think Of IT!" "Think of what IT means!" "Think of your family, your dear old mother!" "Think IT ain't?" "Think this, motherfuckers. I'll empathize 'em back to the Stone Age."

At four the next morning, Casey stumbled across her living room, punting aside Arab cassocks, Indian tables, and Pilates geegaws. Wearing her sag-assed sweatpants and threadbare "Mandela For President" T-shirt, armed with her trusty graphite squash racket, she took minor notice of her ornate German clock, telling her in no-nonsense Teutonic that it was no time for this crap. Scrabbling at the door, she re-lived Wiley's Morning Electric column. It was like a prophesy she was living out. A journalistic deja-vu. She tugged the door open the full two inches allowed by her heavy-duty night chain, fully expecting to see the promised Jehovah's Witness family in the hallway.

Instead, The Prophet himself stuck his grizzled, bleary face into the crack between door and jamb, drooling and yammering like Nicholson in The Shining. "Heeeeere's Wiley!" he blithered, obviously out of control and losing it bigtime. Casey stared at him sorrowfully, twitching the squash racket.

"I *did* it!" Wiley screamed. "I fucking *did* it! I gotta give it to you now, because when I crash, I ain't coming back up until I see my shadow on St. Mlotokisierp's Day."

Casey had no idea what to do with that, but Wiley made it more obvious by thrusting a handful of typing paper through the crack. "I did what you wanted! Here it is. It's all sensitive and shit!"

Casey tugged the paper out of his hands just as his face sagged, sliding down the door crack leaving a trail of slaver. His descent stopped abruptly when his nose hit the safety chain. He hung there with nostrils displayed, dangling from the chain like a performance art tribute to Monmouth Caverns.

Making no move to do anything stupid like removing the chain, Casey flattened out the clutch-creased sheets and read the first page:

> All work and no play makes Jack a dull boy. All work and no play makes Jack a dull boy. All work and no play makes Jack a dull boy. All work and no play makes Jack a dull boy. All work and no play makes Jack a dull boy.

She reacted in horror, had to force herself to look back at Wiley. Not a reassuring look, since his face had skidded down the breach to waist level.

"Just kidding!" Wiley blubbered. "Shoulda seen your face. Should see my face, huh? Oh, yeah, you do. I'm pulling your leg, Mighty Casey. Twistin your arm, tweakin your tits, holding your mudville, boogiewooging your boogaloo down funky Broadway til the cows come home. Read on, MacDuffin."

Quaking inside, Casey dropped the page, looked at the second sheet in the sheaf.

"See?" Wiley crowed. "Huh? Huh? I did it!" He slumped all the way to the floor, lips to the carpet, only his scalp pressed into the crack between her guarded reality and Wiley-infested hallway. "Am I free now?" he burbled. Can I please go?"

She shut the door, nudging Wiley's head out of the way. She walked to her desk, put on the light and reading glasses, started reading the piece.

SOMETIMES A GREAT DEPRESSION
by The Weekend Warrior

As the equinox approaches and imagery takes a turn towards holly, mistletoe, decorated fir trees and other flora alien to the California landscape, you start to realize that 'tis, indeed, the season. The season, specifically, for Seasonal Affective Disorder. In case you've never heard of the appropriately-anacronymized SAD, it means Depression. Pop-shrinks coined the term in order to make naive laypersons aware of the fact that people get depressed during depressing seasons. And many find it oddly depressing to get bombarded with a flurry of seasonal expenses and ubiquitous media messages that if you aren't well-fed, beloved, and deliriously happy you're some kind of pariah freak. Call it what you will, it means The Holidays and it means Depression, so let's get on with it.

Our society offers its usual "cures" for being unhappy: denial and drugs. Prozac came within an ace of being the first chemical named "Time" magazine's "Man of the Year". Don't be taken in: Prozac is rivaled only by another nineties media star, the Wonderbra, at offering an illusory solution for problems that exist only in the minds of beholders and invoking a spurious sense of upliftedness. Maybe it works, but how necessary is it to the average Southlander?

Just as cleavage brinkspersonship is a bit ludicrous to people who spend so much time in bikinis, how practical is a Prosacian outlook when you live in Southern California? If we couldn't handle depression would we be living in a state without enough water to survive on, an unbalanceable budget, impending earthquakes, a homicidal robot for governor, and Mexico right next door; entering without knocking? Of course not. Prozac is for wimps that can't handle post-modern despair and lack of climate. Drugs are a cheap crutch that only appeal to those without the fortitude to tackle emotional bankruptcy with a straight face. Hip SoCal peeps just say "No" and look for ways to enjoy their depression with a little flair.

A perennially popular style of fashionable depression is existential angst... roughly expressed as a desperate lack of essential meaninglessness. Take a Gallic, Left Bank approach to it, smoking Galouises and sipping absinthe or bitter wine dregs as you read "Nausea" or some other bummer by French cyclothymiacs like Gide and Sartre.

Sartre was a sort of patron saint of depression, who propounded a philosophy of total freedom of existence before deciding that it would make even more sense to be a Maoist. Which may be an intellectual non sequitur, but makes perfect sense when viewed through the jaundiced eye of a depression aficionado.

Another traditional flavor of depression is romantic/poetic license, generally used to woo artistic success or members of the opposite sex. Wax very wan, get fey and cadaverous. Your skin should hover on the border of deathly and luminous. It's been a hit look from La Boheme to Kate Moss and the Cruise LeStat. Moon around and pine away; investigate "Love Story" wasting diseases. But call it consumption; so much more romantic than tuberculosis. If need be, go ahead and die of it. Dying for love is always the rage--just let word get around that dying or killing yourself for romance is your customary procedure and watch your social calendar start filling up. See, even suicidal depression can work to advantage.

Easier for modern suburbanites to master, perhaps, is post-quasi-modern, semi-demi punque, new age/wave nadaville. Recall that you are a pampered, middle-class American; overschooled but under-educated and member of the most privileged and spoiled class in history. No excuses; nowhere to go but downhill. Sit in a cold, sterile mall and contemplate the fact that you are lost and unhappy. In no time you'll be totally depressed and ready to sally forth and meet the seasonal emotional mugging on its own terms. A good depression, not a Great Depression.

Among the young, black-clad, and histrionically depressed, nihilism is popular to the point of becoming a cliché. Everyone's into being nihilistic for its own sake, apparently not realizing that if you don't put nothing into nothingness, you don't get nothing out of it. And out of it, need we remind you, is where depression is supposed to get you in the first place.

If, despite your best efforts, things persist in looking up, just repeat to yourself the phrase, "This, too, shall pass." Normality will reassert itself. Gloom is just around the corner, so have another cup of absinthe and another non-filter cigarette and hang tough.

Finished, Casey sat without moving. Her first impulse had been to scream, "He did it *again!*" then go cram the pages up Wiley's butt and kick him down the stairs. But something kept her still, kept her searching. She felt an eerie aura around herself, a feel she recognized from moments when spiritual epiphanies hovered over her, poised to strike. She read the final line again and looked up at the decades-old poster that had graced the wall of every American bleeding heart since the sixties: a cute kitten clawing at a tree branch, struggling to hang in there, baby.

She read the piece again, this time with a growing sense of what some guru or another had termed "serene excitement". Wiley had It. She could see it plainly now. He was an end run around the blandishments of religion and psychology: a chord struck deep in the rebellious inner self. Which would help more people cope, she asked the poster kitten. Reading Wiley with a cynical laugh and double espresso, or nodding off over the blandishments of Norman Peale or Dr. Phil?

Wiley, she realized, was more than just a baggy-pantless clown. He was a messiah sorely sought by the emotionally disenfranchised. He spoke to the potential suicides, pill-poppers, binge drinkers, and Grinch converts where they lived, injected his wisdom where they most needed it. They've awaited him, she thought, and he's come.

But more immediately, she discovered when she threw open her front door, he'd gone. Leaving a lock of hair that she'd slammed in the door and a small pool of vomit festooned with pepperoni slices and Kandi Korn.

CHAPTER TWENTY-SIX

Already depressed or not, city officials and the various perpetrators of the Union Tribune got a nice little lump of coal in their stockings the week of Christmas. Following up on the Brown Field story, "Dennis Schumann" danced out choreographed sugar plums about the city's remarkable malfeasance of that property. Refusal to use it as a freight terminal to take some of the crush of the downtown field. Denial of several offers to turn a profit on the field, including a firm that customized superjets for rich moguls and Arabs. The yearly rent paid to the city for the entire field by a collection of ragtag junkyards amounted to even less than was collected by the Sports Arena complex--which Dennis was gleeful to inform them was less than the total rent paid by the tacky 34 unit apartment he lived in.

The big question was--duh--"WHY?" A question that the UT had never even approached. It had covered some of these obvious bucket jobs once they were brought to public attention by the SEC and FBI investigating the city government and jailing half the counsel, but no tough questions were raised, much less answered. Everything got puffed off in a style Dennis referred to as the "inane neglect policy", and the paper moved on to weightier matters like starlet spawn and getting a new airport built on land shanghaied from the Navy.

Well Dennis had the answer to that one. A coterie of big realtors lusting after the Naval Station land. San Diego had already been handed several "peace dividend" windfalls by the Navy, including a waterfront complex and a massive recruiting station campus. Welcome had been trumpeted to both, great civic benefits were promised for both: and both ended up being scarfed up by the companies Rollie was talking about. He didn't name any names. Yet, as he put it. But the names were known. The second big question became: why would a major daily newspaper in one of America's ten largest cities ignore such matters? Readers were starting to wonder why themselves. Talk radio and internet forums were starting to fill with suggested answers to that question. And they tended to herd themselves towards the same conclusions.

Meanwhile, Casey endeavored to herd Wiley towards the Big Corral of humankind. She had noted that the paper hit the streets on December 26, which had occasioned early deadlines. While informing Wiley of this, she took another opportunity to mold him towards the light. He proved a reluctant heliotrope.

"It's a chance, Wiley," she pleaded with him as he sat in pie-eyed shambles in front of her desk. "A sort of rear-guard shot at doing something worthy and human for the season."

"I'm drunk, overweight and got a case of the crabs," Wiley retorted. "How human can it get?" His throbbing hangover and itching crotch made him less than amenable to the blandishments of secular humanism applied to religious holidays.

"It's a challenge that I think you're up to," she pressed on. "It's been done so often, but you're a special talent and I think you could find a very special way to express the True Meaning of Christmas."

"So what would that be, Virginia?" Wiley carped. "Mangy scenes? Dueling turkey basters? Rudolph the Red-Assed Rainqueer? Angels We Have Heard While High? Frosty the Fucking HoMan? Chestnuts! It's all chestnuts being roasted by Mel Torme while we frolic and play."

"I understand what you're saying," Casey said. "The real meaning got lost in the hubbub. But it's there and it's real."

She waited for Wiley to respond, but he obviously wasn't going to ask. Or even call humbug. "All is forgiven," she said.

That got to Wiley. "What?"

"That's it," she said, spreading her hands in earnest simplicity. "Strip it down, that's what you get to. Forgiveness. The whole world forgiven for a day. Is that a miracle or what?"

"Miracles," Wiley snorted, "What a scam."

"Have you ever tried forgiving, Wiley?" she asked. "It's not as easy as it looks. It takes a miracle. Under the tinsel and hogwash it's worth believing in."

"Maybe for you," Wiley shouted, lurching to his feet. "For them. What have you got to be forgiven for?"

He lunged to the door and yanked it open. He turned to her and growled. "You want the true meaning of Christmas? I've got your true meaning of Christmas right here."

He slammed the door and rebounded down the hall.

"And to all a good night," Casey said, and turned sadly back to her corrections.

MORE BLESSED TO RETURN
By The Weekend Warrior

While many unwary dupes of Third Millennium-style post-capitalism have their seasonal positions jerked grinchishly out from under them on Christmas Eve, those with a little *savoir laissez faire* focus on jobs that keep on giving and learn to master receiving returned merchandise. Returns (along with binge spending of gift money and certificates) form a sort of Second Season without greetings or niceties--kind of like the NBA. This mini-mall mini-season starts on December 26, the busiest retail day of the year and focal point of the True Meaning of Christmas. Namely: Only 365 Shopping Days Until Christmas.

Of course even the return counter jobs dry up right after New Year with few nods to auld lang syne (leading to the condition of Post Part-time Depression), but by then any seasonal de-retailer could write a book on which gifts have problems with acceptance. (Interested publishers may beat a path to my agent, care of this very publication). Suggested title: "What to Give Somebody That They'll Like More than Money." Order now in time for next Christmas.

A major category of returned gifts would be Inappropriate Technology. Now that you're not tearing through a mall with a long list of loved ones and a charge card in your teeth, do you really think a remote control for an automobile CD deck is such a great idea? Why not? (Answer: Because the technology is inappropriate).

What would make more sense would be answering machines for cellular phones. This would avoid a major trap of portable phones, namely that all that technology to give you immediate access also makes you immediately available.

And being available by phone is the number-one indicator of lack of status. *Real* power lies in having secretaries hint that you are occupied in unfathomably important things and require lesser souls to be available to be called back. When two players are competing for image they can't talk at all unless their secretaries manage to set up a meet. Cellulars are just electronic slave-bracelets to the very kinds of people who buy them. So they have to either have secretaries in their cars or have some way of having to get back to somebody later.

This would serve a human need, however vain and obnoxious that need might be. Car stereo remotes do not serve any human need except the need to take it back to the store and question their integrity for selling such a thing.

We see a lot of new computers so cleverly miniaturized that the keys are too small to be pressed by human fingers--lap tops, palm tops, finger tops, tiptoe tops. How many spread sheets can you do on the head of a pin? They are already talking about selling bottom tops--computers ergonomically shaped to conform to the derriere you are resting it on while working--like James Bond's telephone. And you will buy them, keeping our gift exchange hopping like a stock exchange.

That's why you've simply got to quit buying these things, people: to protect future gift recipients from even more stunning outrages to their intelligence and dignity. The Japanese are already planning on selling us televisions too small to be seen with the naked eye. We are constantly hearing about marketing Virtual Sex. Not only technologically inappropriate, but extremely dangerous in a world without Virtual Virtue. And probably something you can't return after it's used you.

Another reason for gifts finding their way back to the shelves from whence they came is that buyers have not cluttered their search for thoughtful presents with a whole lot of thought for the loved one in question. We are constantly importuned by parents and grandparents bearing Kenny G. cassettes and Mannheim Steamroller CD's and saying, essentially, "I need from New Age music?" They exchange them for Old Age music and go away happier and hipper than their kids think they are.

It's amazing how many parents get exercise videos as gifts. Why, so they can have Buns of Steel? They stream in saying, in effect, "Don't you have any workout tapes by *Henry* Fonda?" And who's to blame them? Not us...all we demand is a receipt.

Some of the problems here stem from some idiot advice that's been around for years--to give people gifts you yourself would like to get. Right. Do you enjoy those little mouse faces your cat brings home to you? Under that logic, every parent in the country would be getting Pixar characters carved out of Sponge Bobs. Forget it: if you want a true insider's tip to thoughtful gift-giving, here it is...give them something that's easy to exchange.

Nursing a beer at the far end of the bar and watching the Mimosans fulfill, Casey felt like Margaret Mead, observant among specimens. Or more like Diane Fossey. She was starting to get identities sorted out, put names with voices and faces. She couldn't see the shining noggin of "Strack", apparently a combat vet, and a proven resource--though it would have been hard to express exactly what he had proven. "Doc" was also some sort of ex-killer and the one they called "Joe" or "Smoke" depending on who was talking might not be all that ex. A bounty hunter, she was thinking, maybe hit man.

Jasper seemed harmless enough, mentally deficient and under the negative impulse of the various predators around him. Although "Smoke" had just bought him a drink and rubbed his shoulder in a friendly way. She didn't hear what a dowdy old-timer named Pruitt said, but Cathilda slapped him on the shoulder and brayed. "You just say that 'cause you rich." The term "rich" in Mimosa parlay, meant that he didn't have to hustle. Had a pension that paid for his sleeping room with washstand in a nearby SRO hotel, decent grocery bill, and enough left over to drink freely at the Mimosa, buy a few rounds. It was an enviable trove to the denizens and Pruitt was looked up to.

"Rich?" He spit our bitterly. "What good is that?"

"Beats the shit out of poor," Strack croaked from his chair.

"Yeah, yeah. I'd give all that money to be able to get a hard-on, so I could fuck."

The naked, simple declaration appalled Casey, who stared at him. It even stopped the japery a minute. Then Jasper said,

"Well, that's life. When it's soft you can't beat it and when it's hard you get fucked."

They were used to his reverse sequiturs, so nobody paid any attention. Goody thrust his vibrator to his throat and clacked out, "Two different things, Pruitt. You can have both, you could have neither. You got it made."

There were nods at the wisdom of that, then Cathilda laughed. "Shit, man can't make it and you tell him he got it made. You need to get your head out your ass and put that vibrator where it'd do more good."

Goody pointed the device at her and activated it, making a nasty buzz like Daffy Duck farting. "Easy for you to say," Strack rumbled.

Casey looked around this new tribe she had found, an unexpected culture living in a dusky pool of hourless shadow beneath the canopy of San Diego's sunshine civilization. They were as deserving of her sympathies as any other minority, she realized. How bravely they bore an existence as empty and punishing as any she could imagine. And without any identity tags or cultural items. She had re-discovered the Urban Barfly Peoples. They tore at her heart, but warmed it at the same time with their defiant good spirits and bold declaration of their own impotence and meaninglessness. Then it got brought home to her in a sudden yawp from down the bar.

"How about you, Honey?" Cathilda probed. "You work down at The Week, too?"

Startled to be included, Casey stammered a little. "Oh, yes, I... I guess... Yeah. I'm an editor."

"Whooeee," Cathilda trilled. "Damn. Must got some education on you, girl."

"Well," she said, as always, "Just State." Cathilda stared, blank. "San Diego State. University." Casey filled in.

"College girl." Cathilda made it sound like "working girl" instead of "whore". "Must be makin' big money down there."

Casey smiled uneasily. "Well, not as much as in real jobs."

"You gonna buy us a round?" Cathilda tossed it out as preemptory challenge, but Casey took it as an invitation.

"Sure." She motioned to Jerome. "Could I buy a round for the house?" Cathilda was tensed to pounce when Casey added, "You're all friends of Wiley, right?"

Cathilda unwound a little, took her in. "Yeah, we're his buddies, you might say."

Jasper spoke up for the first time. "It's kind of like a family here. So nobody has to really give a shit about anybody else."

"How about you?" rasped Strack. "You a friend?"

Casey opened her mouth, then closed it again. She looked around, then right at Strack. "I'm trying to be, " she said. "But I don't really know how."

Even the hardest cases in the Mimosa were touched by that one and knew exactly what she meant. And not just about Wiley, either. Their reaction was to break into raucous laughter. The laughs continued as Jerome distributed fresh drinks. Casey sat without moving a muscle, watching them hyucking and heehawing. Then she started laughing herself. Which flared up more laughs from the regulars.

Casey lifted her beer to salute them, and they lifted their free drinks to her. Jasper got up and moved down beside her, clinking his glass on her bottle. "Here's to not knowing how," he said. Which was a complete crackup.

When Wiley rolled in an hour later, desperately seeking alcohol, Casey sat with Jasper on one side, gooning at her like a sophomore, and Cathilda on the other, resting her enormous jugs on the bar as she leaned forward to punctuate some ribald tale that had Casey in stitches. He stood in the door staring. What's wrong with this picture? After a minute he made up his mind. Nothing a drink wouldn't fix.

CHAPTER TWENTY-SEVEN

Caitlin had not been aware of how the Week had been in the past, or how it moved among its fellow newsbeasts. When she ran the first piece by Dennis insinuating that the Union Tribune was culpable in the massive city corruption scandals, she unknowingly violated a long-standing unspoken truce--not to antagonize mutual papers. A truce largely in place because of Ovarón's craven conformity and normity. And, or course, the UT's unwillingness to lob stones around in the greenhouse.

She was unaware of the amount of attention it drew in upper echelons of the journalistic community, not only in San Diego, but in larger areas. Attention to her, for one thing. And of course an obsession for finding out who "Dennis Schumann" really might be. Rollie might have drawn scrutiny, except for his abhorred status at the Week, and the fact that "Dennis" wrote in a terse style of short words and simple sentences. Rollie had purposely created a style distinct from his own, as well as the florid tripouts of Wiley. But the scrutiny level ran high.

Caitlin actually happened to be present at the scene of one undercover feel-up. She'd dropped next door for a cameo appearance at a major soiree thrown by the actual Dennis and his long-smothering life partner, Jacob. They'd cozened her to come by and she was happy to oblige them because they were little dears. They were delighted at her entrance in glamour rags, but played her off coolly and left the gushing to others. Of whom there were some world class gushers. Jacob and Denny might not have a Craftsman bungalow up in the Hillcrest "Swish Alps", but they did have gorgeous media stars dropping by to say hi.

Doggedly circulating through the swarm of gay pride, Caitlin happened to spot Dennis standing on the lanai chatting with a good-looking man who was either almost too gay to live or just plain overacting it. Dennis caught her eye and subtly beckoned her close. As she approached she could tell that the interloper was probing into the stories in her paper. She crept stealthily nigh.

"Oh my *God*!" Dennis bleated, "Don't *ever* Google yourself, sweets. It's too horrible. The homophobe preacher in Oklahoma, that football gorilla in Nigeria, now this muckraker.

196

It's just too appalling. I should change my name to something that nobody else will have."

"Think something like Cynthia Schlongschlurper would live up to the billing?" Jacob, in a bit of a pet over the proximity of the studly snoop to Dennis's splayed railside stance, arrived and sniped.

"I said something *nobody* would have," Dennis simpered. "If you're going to eavesdrop, at least get the whole ejaculation."

Jacob opened his mouth to jump on the widest punchline of all time, then grinned and wagged a finger at his sweetheart. They both laughed uproariously, ostentatiously excluding the snoop, and quick-kissed before returning to circulation. When the spy turned, Caitlin stepped right in front of him. His take verified his intentions completely and she also started laughing.

Stepping close to the abashed gossipbait, she purred, "Tell them the real Dennis is more secret than they'll ever guess, cutie." Giving him a Myrna Loy turnaway, she spoke back over her shoulder past a shining blonde cascade. "A mole that dare not speak its name." That ought to send them into a tailspin, she thought. And oh, it certainly did.

She mentioned the incident to Rollie, causing them to laugh so loud and long they were in danger of getting bounced from "Mi Tierra", a Barrio Logan taco shop where few of the customers spoke English and none read the UT and Week or even watched Channel Nine. It was the day after deadline and it would be twenty-four hours before The Week hit the street containing the latest Jeremiad from Dennis, one of the most damaging so far because it didn't rely on documentation, just memory and common sense. The worst kind of slander, because the truth of it is so palpable and ubiquitous.

The piece rolled past the spectacular collapse and indictment of City Hall to broaden the image of the UT as working in collusion with inimical interests to prevent people from finding out just how inimical those interests were to the public well being. It recalled the extraordinary deadliness of the local police against citizens. No other force in the country shot as many civilians, and without punishment or even public comment. This tied in with memories of the previous County Sheriff, a

"Heat of the Night" character named Duffy who had ran a larcenous, intrusive, law-smashing department that would have been shameful in a small cracker community, much less a city with an NFL franchise.

Duffy had finally been outed and ousted. But, Dennis was obliged to remind, the story had been broken by the Los Angeles Times, not the UT. The image of a murderous, corrupt police culture that was never called to task was laid up beside the undeniable news silence regarding the unique civic swindles and nailed in place with a little reminder of what San Diegans apparently hadn't thought particularly noteworthy: that the Editor in Chief of the Union Tribune had previously been the police chief. The fact that this didn't happen in any other city was driven home, and the literate citizenry left with a broad, distinct mural depicting their monopoly local newspaper as being in cahoots with the cops and the robbers as well. With the results they were just starting to see laid before them as the SEC prohibitions, FBI arrests, and federal indictments piled up.

It was time, Rollie felt, to broaden his approach. Caitlin batted her eyes and asked, "Going after the Supreme Court and Security Counsel next week?"

"Worse," Rollie grinned. "Critics."

He had fumbled around with the concept and a name for the column. The idea was to be a critic of the local critics, who were critically lousy. Just turn about, Rollie said. Fair play. If you dish it out, you should take it now and then. In the shorts. He'd fiddled with something like Critic Squared, but it was too hard to make sure the superscript would be read right. He settled on "MetaCritic", then switched to "MetaBitch" before deciding to fit into the mode of Wiley and Savage with "BitchKitty." The logo was a cute, big-eyed Japanese restaurant puss holding a coin and waving hello with upraised middle finger.

The new column became popular very quickly. Some San Diegans had long suffered from the idiot commentaries of the UT's art and film pundits; not only two of the most ignorant reviewers in the country, but demonstrably the worst writers. Others just hadn't realized that it was possible to read movie reviews that made sense and showed some sort of understanding of what people wanted to know about films. Dennis filleted the film dolt, Saul Gould, reproducing some of his stupidest comments (though it was hard to choose). He showed examples of him writing off as "juvenile" films obviously aimed at young children. He excerpted from a review of "Big Trouble In Little China" citing "gratuitous use of special effects" (a standby comment for any film not shot with one camera in black and white) then asked: If special effects aren't useful in a supernatural, martial arts western, then where should they be used? The following week he shafted Germain McDuff, not just for his elliptical grasp of prose, but also a running scorecard of the films Germain reviewed in the last three months...none of which he liked.   If there are no films worth seeing, Dennis implored, then why have reviewers? And why bring them to our attention?

He went on to lay waste to the pretensions of the UT's art critic Bruce Erizo: possibly the single most despised writer in the city and deservedly so. Along with pointing out scores of actual errors in the reviews, Dennis skewered his criteria for dismissing public art that many locals liked (a fountain made of prisms, where kids and adults alike moved around to catch color-outlined profiles, was damned for being "too prismatic") while lauding Emperor's Clothesline praise on vacuous non-work at the Museum of Contemporary Art (what the hell, Dennis demanded, is a *museum* of *contemporary* stuff, anyway?) He crowned it with a picture of a corporate piece that had been lauded--a toppling heap of bulbous brown bronze residents had dubbed "The Turd"--and a contrast shot of a beautiful Faberge egg, which the critic had found "not even Art".   The lack of appreciation for actual crafting and accomplishment, Dennis sneered, was born out in the writing and conceptualization foisted on his captive audiences.

The attack on reviewers seemed to hurt the UT even more than the proofs of their corruption, complicity, and greed. That was just business: the arts was personal. But it would get worse: there were places even touchier than arts and entertainment.

CHAPTER TWENTY-EIGHT

"Listen, Wiley..." Casey looked up from scanning his latest Missive Impossible to note that close attention was unlikely. Wiley was slumped in an upright chair, his head lolling back, unsupported. His Adam's apple fluttered nervously, letting in just enough air to keep him alive in the supra-conscious mode he called "Stand By".

"Yo, Wiley!"

He snapped forward like a shrimp out of hell, his head snapping like a whip, then coming into an approximate alignment with her line of vision. He gasped, "Not my fault!"

"Yeah, right. Look, have you given any thought..." she scanned his face, reworded. "How does the idea of doing something romantic strike you?"

Wiley gave her the eye. The other eye was not his to give, wandering in orbit seeking vision. He stared at her, bringing things back into approximate parallax. "Sorry, Case. I'm not that kind of guy. If I were, though, you'd be first one on my list for flowers, chocolates, and a negligee with inscribed gift card. Ya little sweetie."

Casey shook her head. "I may be 'that stupid', but I'm not THAT stupid. I'm talking about your column, meathead. Ever thought of laying off the frathouse horndog thing for a week or two? Hit some hearts and flowers? You know there are people who spend their weekends on nice dates trying to please women of their fancy."

"I'm hip. The way to a girl's pants is through a fancy French restaurant."

"See, you at least understand the concept of 'Romantic'. And Continental Dining might be the perfect touch. Kyle would like it, too."

"You've done it again, Chones. I'm on it like *l'orange* off a duck's back."

"Shall I arrange for reservations?"

"Oh, I think I can handle that pretty well."

"All right then. *Bon apetit.*"

"No, *cherchez la femme.*"

TREU GRITS
by The Weekend Warrior

The recent review of Thai cuisine in this space was met with such a effusive swell of apathy that a review of French food seemed the inevitable encore. French cuisine being our idea of the queen of foreign dining and so influential on the diet of strip mall dwellers--witness the role of croissants in fast food joints--it's high time we passed judgment.

It's been said that the secret history of the world is that the French would take over places and then the British would conquer them in order to be able to get something decent to eat. But that was said by another and hence lesser writer, so why should I bother to mention him?. This is a fairly competitive field, you know, and I have to be ruthless. Unless, of course, Ruth comes crawling back on hands and knees. Which used to be a lot of fun, but I digress.

There seem to be three distinct kinds of French restaurant in Southern California. The traditional kind features vellum menus with punchline prices, the kind of atmosphere that suggests you should be impressed with yourself for just being there, and a cuisine based on smothering everything under heavy sauces loaded with cholesterol and subtleties (or perhaps it was subtitles--it's hard to read these calligraphy menus.) Dishes generally called by proper names and odd words like "*Ce'st*", "*Chez*" and "*Bleu*". (Example: Chuck E. Chcz)

Then there are the newer places specializing in Nouvelle Cuisine which, like so many "New" things--be they Journalism, Politics, Nixon, Wave, or York--is a total flop. Old hat is old hat, spell it Nouveau Chapeau if you please. If you took the New Math and never learned a cuisine from a cosine you know what I mean, albeit in a vague and fragmentary sort of way. These places have the same names as the perfumes you're always seeing copies of.

There are also a legion of foreign French restaurants that do some sort of Franco-American fusion, perhaps beans and francs. They are called things like "Le Petit Francais" and offer "*cuisine tridundante*" such as "French Dip Sandwich *avec* Au Jus Sauce."

The first type is the funniest, because they actually speak French and lay on all the traditional national color, such as hysterical chefs and surly waiters. They will look down their Gallic noses at you and suggest that you order escargot. Just try to get any French toast or French fries from these guys, much less the famous postcards, kisses, or ticklers. They will smirk at your pronunciation (or spelling) of idiotic words like "*ratouile*", "*bouillabaisse*", or "*bourguignon*." They reserve their snottiest of sneers for more common French words like "*coupón*".

Don't be intimidated by this (or by any representative of a culture given to talking through their nose, fighting with their feet, and making love with their mouths). A little-known fact about the French tongue is that it cannot be pronounced correctly by anyone. This affords Frenchmen cheap amusement and a sense of superiority otherwise almost impossible for them to come by, while their own patently absurd pronunciation goes uncorrected because most people feel unqualified to tell them they are garbling their own language. You might as well tell the Italians they don't know how to run their own government.

There are other secrets of the French tongue, but they are totally inappropriate to a decorous restaurant review, as witness the lurid conclusions to which your febrile mind has already jumped. This column is for the education of the consumer, I should remind you--not the titillation of the febrile-minded.

There was no sneering at Southcoast Week's table in the highly-reputed Ce'st Chez Bleu, of course. The heaping helpings I received had platoons of subservient waiters helping with the heaping, their service excellent, if not excruciatingly obsequious. Aside from my personal animal magnetism, I attribute this to the fact that they seemed to think I was reviewing for a major dining card publication. It was a mysterious misapprehension, which I finally traced to the business cards I'd printed up and handed around when I arrived. I've found in the past that this sort of thoughtful preparation saves a lot of time, embarrassment, and tedious necessities such as paying the bill.

Escargót, which I assumed to be flotsam or some other form of ex-cargo, turns out to be snails. Well, *outré* actually *is* a French word--presumably meaning something like "Totally gross". There's a bit of mystery as to where the snails come from. Do they just snatch them off downspouts, garden fresh, or raise them on little slime ranches? They keep us in the dark on such matters, which is probably just as well. Most of us already know they use pigs to hunt for truffles (especially the clerks at Nordstrom's candy counter after my recent understandable fracas there) but even a pig won't fetch a snail for you. Even a lawyer would hesitate. So we didn't sample the truffles that showed up on the desert cart, chocolate coated so as, no doubt, to cover up the pigtooth prints.

Fortunately the threatened snails never appeared, though I noticed a cockroach nipping along the wall at one point. Enough to knock a few stars off their rating, but at least nothing to leave a trail of slime down your throat and munch up the leaves of your nasturtiums. Not even the French would fry a roach to get attention. Snails and frog legs are about as freaky-deaky as they care to stoop. Though God only knows what's in some of those sauces.

Meanwhile, in an entirely different cuisine, Caitlin watched Rollie adeptly chopstick a couple of nigiri sushi onto his plate. "Very deft, there, Dennis," she said.

Rollie smiled and inhaled one of the rice lumps. "So you approve of the way things are going there?" he asked her once the last of the smoked eel had been processed.

"Absolutely. I'm getting the impression from, you know, letters and such, that people are more outraged at the picture you paint of the UT than at the city itself."

"Well, they should. You've heard the one about better to have newspapers than government?" Caitlin nodded.

"Well, see," Rollie went on, fooling with a ball of wasabi that was going to mess him up if he didn't watch it, "That only works if the newspapers are worth a damn."

Which had been the import of the latest Dennis blast. How could the UT snark about the unprecedented corruption and malfeasance in City Hall, he'd asked, if they hadn't reported it before it came to public notice through court and police actions? Had they been too incompetent to figure out what people in Washington and New York had sussed out, or had they known about it but kept silent while the bureaucrats pillaged pension funds, leased public property for a song, and spent millions that would only benefit realty speculators? A question the daily had declined to address.

But "Dennis", with a relentless flourish of documents and reports not reported in the UT, had shown the pattern of collusion. None of it actionable, but definite, incontrovertible journalistic malpractice.

"Damn good job," Caitlin told him, with a warmth and admiration that he found it pleasant to stretch out and bask in. "I assume you had similar success in Santa Cruz."

"That's a bit iffy," Rollie admitted ruefully, reluctant to leave the pedestal Dennis had built him. "And anyway, it's not enough. If we can't figure out a way to acquire or control Scorment's stock, it's over."

"A tall order," Caitlin said with just a pinch of irony.

"We won't know until we poke at it a little. It's obvious the controlling stock is split that way because of certain FCC and SEC nitpicking. But maybe Scorment isn't all that tightly aligned with The Mysterians?"

"If he wasn't a jillionaire, maybe we could buy him off."

"Looks like the Mystery men did. I've got some buyers lined up for some of it if we can get an agreement to sell."

"Really?" Caitlin gave him a 'good boy' smile. "You've been on the ball."

Rollie glared at the guy who'd bumped his shoulder while leaving the table behind him. He liked the food at Todai. And hard to argue with their "all the sushi you can eat" posture. But the tables were packed too close. Then again, nobody in their right mind would see them together here.

Caitlin was absorbed in the tricky task of separating a mussel from its half-shell without messing it up or flipping it onto somebody else's table. Her surgery successful, she popped the mollusk in her mouth and savored it. She looked at Rollie with a nicely furrowed brow. "But seriously, I just don't see how. We've got no idea of the situation. Or where he's coming from. Other than Creepsville."

"I don't know if we could even talk to the guy. He lives in a sort of money bubble, like one of those kids with no immune system."

"Oh, I could talk to him, I think." Caitlin strung him out a moment before adding, "He gave me his card."

"Really? Whoa. Have you ever tried the number?"

"Get real. The best scenario I can see coming out of that would be like, free phone sex."

"Well, it's a nice card to hold, so to speak."

"Oh, sure. When to play the dreaded Perv Card?"

"Well, we'll just keep thinking."

Caitlin looked at the far end of Todai, where a blue metal sculpture of a Sperm Whale breached out the wall. She suppressed a reaction to the alien feel of the place and nibbled another futomaki. Trying to lighten up her mood, she joked, "Maybe I ought to just marry him."

Rollie did one of those great smiles and she replied in kind.

"Just think," she gushed breathlessly. "A half-hour ceremony and we could both get our jobs back and I'd get to live a life of pampered luxury. Slash, revolting horror."

"It humbles me you'd make a sacrifice like that just so I could recover a thirty thousand a year job."

"You're right. Forget it. The wedding is off."

"Too bad we don't have some sort of roboslut we could fob off on him," Rollie mused. "Something totally sexy, but with no gag reflex, that we could control by radio."

Caitlin looked startled, then smiled a slim, satisfied smile. Her eyes shone as she stroked an imaginary villain's mustachio. She never did things like that. Rolling with Rollie was probably good for her. Cool and contained, she said, "We do. I mean, I think I know just the girl for the job."

Jammi glanced away from the task of applying eyeliner in a style that would have fit right in on the stage of the Peking Opera, to see Caitlin's reflection behind hers in the Makeup mirror. She jerked in surprise, almost converting her mascara job to Late Boy George. She didn't turn around to speak, just went back to laying out the carnival raccoon look, which the camera would translate into a slightly desperate sexual advertisement. But she kept an eye on Caitlin in the mirror. She never trusted that bitch.

"They hire you back?" was the best opening line she could think of.

"Nope. I probably should have spent more time in Makeup."

You got that right, Jammi thought. That bleached pine look just disappears into the flyback. "So how may I help you?" Was her tone just sarcastic enough, or did she overdo it, the way she so often did? "I've got about eight minutes until I'm in the Weather Picture."

"I'll just be a second. Somebody's been asking about you."

Great. Another station door Johnny. And this one got Caitlin to run his message for him. That should show her the natural pecking order right there. "Let me guess. Some biotech dickhead with enough paper value to drive a Porsche?"

"Close. A billionaire who's got enough income from owning this station that he doesn't have to drive at all. Everything comes to him."

Oops, that news caused Jammi to add a Pagliachi lick to her eye job. She stared at Caitlin in the mirror, then turned around for a straighter shot. Damn, she wasn't kidding.

Caitlin extended her fingers, Scorment's business card held between two perfect commas of fingernail that set off the ice-green of her eyes. Jammi looked from the card to her face, then back.

"Take it," Caitlin urged her. "He's been wanting to meet you for a long time."

Jammi grabbed the card and looked at it hungrily.

J. DANFORTH SCORMENT IV

SCION

206

With a La Jolla number on the back. That was the guy, all right. Holy schlamoly. She looked back at Caitlin, who was making a blotting gesture at the corner of her eye.

"Better fix that little teardrop there, Jammikins. People might think you're a gang member."

Jammi shot a look at the clock, spun around to the mirror. As she cleaned up her facial fresco, she mumbled, "Thanks, Caitlin."

"Oh," Caitlin said as she slid out the door, "Don't mention it."

CHAPTER TWENTY-NINE

"It's not without its creepy elements," Caitlin said, making the common mistake of trying to eat a Spam musubi with chopsticks as though it was just some huge sushi roll. "I mean it's like I just wound her up, pointed her at him and released her like some sexbomb Chucky doll."

Rollie nodded as he eyed the strip of surf visible from the outdoor deck at Da Kine. Decent size for Pacific Beach, but no real shape. He'd check the pier break later. Not that he'd get out there today. Damn. He looked back at Caitlin, stuck a plastic bowl under her chin just in time to catch a falling ball of rice. He set it on the table, told her, "There's no shame in using the fork. Chopsticks aren't Hawaiian, anyway. Hello, it's Spam cuisine."

"It took her what, three days, to get a date with Scorment?" Caitlin switched to the fork. "Four days later they fly to Cabo."

"I wonder if they make him sit in the middle of the plane?"

"He must have to buy an entire row. Maybe have a row of seats taken out, like they do for people on stretchers." She could sort of imagine that, actually. Grim.

"Well, she seems to have jammed herself in pretty quick. Hope she's cunning enough to play him a little."

"I'm not too proud of taking part in this thing."

"Why?" Rollie gestured airily with a Portuguese sausage. "Ideally, it'll be two people getting what they want. We just facilitated it. Sort of a Cupid merger role. Besides, he's not a guy I can work up to feeling sorry for."

"I was thinking more of her."

"Good. I think it's about time to have a chat with her." Rollie regarded the sausage, the Spam, the seaweed wrap. Hell, Hawaiian chow was fusion cuisine before fusion was cool.

Jammi couldn't believe she was hanging out in Caitlin's boring condo. She'd never liked her worth a damn. Blonde inflate-a-date who thought she was all that, was the way she sized her up. Basically, your condescending, superior twat. All she really had going on was those tits, and Jammi would run her own pair up against the much-ballyhooed Vanderkeller rack in a heartbeat. Mano a mano, aureole to aureole. She loved seeing the Platinum Witch of the North lose her show. Jammi might be just the weather girl, but she was still on the air.

Rollie, on the other hand, was just some hairball nebbish. She had a hard time seeing herself sharing anything, much less a goal or conspiracy, with these yo-yos. Case in point, Rollie was floundering around talking about Sacred Principles of Newspapers.

"It's more than that," Rollie told her, "There's the whole matter of what journalism is, or is supposed to be. Entertainment, too, for that matter. People need to be informed without being manipulated, they need to have more than one option of where to get their information from. They need to be entertained without being degraded. The world isn't really an MTV rap video."

Jammi wasn't convinced of that at all. Didn't these people ever get out? She was thinking it was about time to jerk the plug on this whole scene. But then Caitlin interrupted. Typical. But whoa, what was she saying?

What she was saying was, "It's criminal. To replace a great editor like Rollie with somebody totally inexperienced, to gut their staff. They're reducing their whole paper to the level of that Wiley germ."

"Wait, wait, wait. What does all this have to do with Wiley?"

Oh, oh. Caitlin remembered rumors that he and she had been some sort of item. She hadn't taken it seriously since she saw Jammi as an insatiable man-eater who could have any guy she wanted--at least for the duration--and Wiley was, well, Wiley. But both were obviously kinked, and Wiley was evil and cunning, so who could say? But look, Jammi's face, usually as placid and unrippled as a baby's, had clouded over at the very mention of Wiley. Caitlin struck out boldly. "He's their star writer now. He's a big reason behind this whole thing. He's got to be stopped."

Jammi now exhibited the face of a petulant, squalling baby, enraged by the universe at large and mustering all its infantile powers to grab, smash and bite everything in sight. Caitlin was a little alarmed. The girl was a physical dynamo, not to be taken lightly. She was glad Rollie was with her.

"Stopped?!?!" she howled, jumping up and stomping around. "He's got to be eliminated. Like, extincted. That little scuzzfucker! You saw what he wrote about me, didn't you? Did that suck, or did it just totally suck?"

Rollie and Caitlin shook their heads, wondering if this squall would blow up into a full-bore cyclone of destruction and remorse. Jammi stopped bouncing around and fixed them with a glare, fists on hips. "You didn't read the famous Italian Restaurant Massacre? I don't believe you."

"We're not huge fans of Wiley's work," Rollie ventured. Very true. Rollie found it depressing to even look at The Week anymore and Caitlin avoided anything having to do with Wiley. She liked being out of his entire perceptual loop.

That seemed to help. Jammi scanned them for a beat, zipped over to a bookcase to pull out one of several high-quality scrapbooks, then bounded back. She opened it and thrust it at them. They quickly read the clipping through the plastic cover sheet, Caitlin looking over Rollie's shoulder. Both managed to keep straight faces out of consideration for Jammi, who waited for them to partake in her outrage.

CIAO DOWN

By The Weekend Warrior

We overlooked the ghastly red/green/white decor at Cocina Italiano (which means "Italian Pig": probably a reference to the owner's wife, who we glimpsed blocking the garage door) After all, it's Italy's culinary signature; pasta, slopped with tomato sauce, salad on the side. They even designed their flag after it. Their national anthem is probably about tortellini.

The **WEEKEND WARRIOR**© respects tradition, and Italian cuisine is about as traditional as it gets. You think of Italy and what do you think of (other than irreparable cars and skinny mutant footwear)? You think of food, that's what. The great Italians of the past are all connected with eating: Caesar, inventor of the salads that bear his name; the Roman heroes and the sandwiches that bare their buns; Galileo, popularizer of the leaning tower of Pizza; Vivaldi, composer of the Four Seasonings; Mussolini, inventor of Mousse, (as well as the Lil Duce Coup). The great La Sagna. Martini, Rossi, Spumoni, the whole *antipasto*. Food and history are inseparable in Italian culture. Rome was the cradle of cuisine, as well as civilization. Well not civilization, exactly, but fascism, which is still something. Not as big a deal as civilization itself, but when did you last see a Mesopotamian restaurant reviewed?

Anyway Rome, to get through this history drivel, came into being in a single day (contrary to popular myth). It was founded by Romulans and Uncle Remus, who were abandoned as youths (but then weren't we all?) and survived by drinking wolf milk. Not to worry: Italian cuisine has gotten better since then. In fact, the better places don't even have wolf tit on the menu anymore. What replaced it was mostly carbohydrate.

Which was just fine with my dining companion of the evening, who can metabolize carbohydrate like a house of burning love. The waiters and patrons did a good job of not noticing her, although everyone has seen the perky weather girl on Channel Nine. Or checked her out in those ads for the body salon gym. The ads that told you how you could have a body like hers for only several thousand bucks in dues and years of sweat, pain and malnutrition. If you had different parents. Well, neener neener, I get to have that body for the price of a comped Italian dinner. What she calls "carbohydrate loading", a buzzword in the aerobics slums for an activity that would be called "pigging out" if done by a person without a lycra suit and subscription to "Your Gorgeous Own Little Self" magazine.

She and I are lovers (if that's really the word for such a demented, grasping relationship) off-camera. Generally off-camera, anyway: I have some interesting videocassettes I'd consider renting to discriminating fans. Electronic media people are a weird bunch. Many are not even really people. There are several pre-programmed androids in the business, looking human above the waist and a mass of circuits and relays below. And a few computer-generated refinements on Max Headroom. My pasta date is neither and therefore, though she doesn't realize it, on the way out. But don't tell her. Like most television types she doesn't read print media because she's a little vague on how the whole "reading comprehension" thing works.

As the waiter seated us, I was able to impress him with a well-turned Italian phrase or two, such as, "*Vini, Vidi, Vici*". Meaning, of course, "Get us some <u>*vino*</u> and put on a <u>vid</u>eo of Miami <u>Vic</u>e ." Little Miss Local Feed, who never studied Italic, was less impressed by my erudition, displaying the demeanor that caused her high school classmates to vote her, "Most Likely Competitive Little Bitch To Get Slapped Down With A Veal Scaloppini."

"This is the pits," she proclaimed, looking around the restaurant, "I mean, there's just the two of us, sitting here...eating."

"Well, at least you're being a sport about it," I said.

"And speaking of sports, what sort of night did the Padres have?"

"Will you quit doing that?"

"Sorry. Anyway, here's our waiter with a peek at what highly visible young media darlings are consuming these days."

"Keep it up, kid."

"Look I wouldn't even be in this dump with you if you hadn't told me it was a photo opportunity."

"I know. And you wouldn't have gone to bed with me if I hadn't convinced you I was scouting for talent in the Eastern market areas."

"That's not true. It was your camera. My therapist says it's because I've spent most of my life projecting my sex appeal into a camera lens and now that's the only kick I get. Live people bore me, really. I mean, they're just one person, you know? What kind of demographic slice is that? But the sight of a camera pointed at me gets me horny as hell."

"Well that sure explains a lot of weird things you do in bed."

"Probably, but as long as we're explaining away weird kinky stuff, why the hell can't you fully aroused unless,,,"

"Look, let's not get into that here and now, okay? I mean, there's a lot of people reading this column and..."

"Yeah, but they can't *see* me, can they? God, it's so frustrating! It beats me how print media people stand it."

"Well, it has it's compensations. For one thing, I can rewrite and edit, make you say anything I want to."

"You wouldn't."

"You've been sleeping with me for months and think there's something too rotten for me to do? Go ahead, say something."

"Look," she said, pulling open her dress and standing up in the Cocina wearing nothing but heels, a string of pearls, and her prosthesis, "Take me...right here on the table with my ass squishing the melons and *prociutto*. I want you to degrade me, fill me with vile filth in front of the world."

"Maybe later," I replied, nibbling at the melon and *prociutto*. They were passable, by the way. This is, after all, a restaurant review.

"My *God*!!! What am I saying....How did you *do* that?"

"Word processor. Weird, huh? Print media can warp reality any way I want."

"But... we're real people. I mean, more or less. You can't change what's in my mind by editing this three days from now."

"Come on, who cares what's in your mind? Or if? Admit it, your whole world is what all those people perceive. Isn't it?"

"Of course it is! I'm the token hottie on a local news show in a third-rate media market, for God's sake."

"So how's your *fettuccini carbonara*? Just so I can write this off."

"It's just wonderful. There's plenty of sauce in the picture, and you can see how these little vortices of olive oil are swirling in here. So it should be a pretty nice weekend."

"So, you approve?"

"Noooo.   It's   missing   something.   Excuse   me but...*pictures!*"

"Well, what should we say about the Italian restaurant?"

"I think we both have the same opinion. Details at eleven."

"That covers it. Could you handle the tip while you've still got your clothes off?"

"I do?"

"You do now."

Silence hung in the air like a zeppelin fart. Caitlin didn't trust herself to speak without betraying a giggle, snort or equally unproductive manifestation. Rollie was dealing with his surprise at the strange literary quality. He'd had no idea that Wiley actually had talent. Jammi's patience was not only wearing thin, it was starting to fidget and cast about for blunt objects.

Caitlin broke the ice. "See? He needs to be stopped. Or like you said, exterminated. We need your help to do that."

Jammi stared at her, then Rollie. Who had been leafing back through the scrapbook. It was the Second Epistle of Jammi: starting with Junior High baton twirling and cheerleader shots, dance recital, gymnastics. Serious awards for exercise, tanning, bikini contests. News releases on her hiring as weathergirl, studio glossies smiling in front of a storm-tossed Pacific Coast. He held her life in his hands. Little Jammi trying to get over. He looked up, right into her searching eyes. He gave her a warm, understanding smile and handed her the scrapbook.

Rollie's look blew Jammi's set. For a moment they had looked at each other at some level beneath the usual surface tension and she realized that he didn't want to screw her but liked her anyway. Mind-blowing. She didn't quite know what to make of Rollie but figured he could be trusted. And he seemed to have a handle on Caitlin, so...

"You need *my* help?"

Caitlin let Rollie do the talking. He said, "Yeah. We'd appreciate it."

"Well, know what? You got it, chumps."

CHAPTER THIRTY

Casey wallowed in knee-jerker heaven at the Mimosa. She'd progressed past the anthropological observer stage and was starting to enter the next phase of Liberal contact with downtrodden cultures: attempted assimilation. Of course, she could have actually become one of them by quitting her job and investing a few months in steady drinking, but like most in her class, she preferred to deny the psychic distance that preserved her.

Wiley had started answering letters by tacking little responses on the end of his columns. The first one, countering a retired Bosun's Mate's rabid litany of perceived offensiveness, was tucked at the end of a quickie extolling guzzling tequila as a means of combating illegal immigration from Mexico. The "answer" started with:

> Obviously it is not our purpose here to offend or shock people. Our purpose is to spout off, whine, get cheap revenge, and attempt an unruly access to easy money, glitzy notoriety, and cheap, unfulfilling sexual experiments. Shocking and offending people is a sort of sideline we just do for the fun of it.

And gone downhill from there. Casey had chuckled at the office, but felt a word to Wiley would be a good idea. And maybe in his secure environment of the Mimosa he would listen to her.

"You really think it's good for a highly visible media voice to be a proponent of drugs, crime, violence and drunkenness and sicko sex?"

"Yeah, who do you think you are, Wiley?" Jerome cracked as he tussled a rack of chips past them, "Fox network?"

Wiley himself was shocked wide-eyed at the very idea of that idea. "You think I'm some sort of proponent? No way. A product, maybe. But hardly a proponent. Not an opponent either, of course. More like an X ponent."

"You should give some thought to that stuff, Wiley. There's more out there for you than that. There's no reason you can't break though your walls and claim it."

"Things better than booze and drugs and kinky sex, you say?

"Things like love and security and fulfillment, Wiley. Caring about others."

A round of sarcastic applause swept the bar. Cathilda did a few appalling cheerleader moves, turning the bar (willy-nilly) into "The Wave". Casey ignored them.

So did Wiley. He leaned closer to her, speaking directly into her eyes for the first time since she'd known him. "You think I don't know that?" he asked her. "You think I don't dream of the day?"

This was a Wiley she'd never seen before, an inchoate earnestness pushing up behind the hard-bitten exterior, threatening to spill out of the mouth and eyes. And in the instant, he caught himself, looked around the bar. Into a dozen faces staring at him.

"One of these days I'm going to clean up my act. I swear it. Devote myself to good works. Settle down with a good woman and not abuse or cornhole her. One of these fucking livelong days."

Now *that*, the Mimosans could understand. They'd been there themselves, and they were touched. For the fifteen seconds before they damn near killed themselves laughing. Wiley sulked.

"Why doesn't anybody ever believe me?"

"Because nobody's that stupid?" Jerome hazarded.

"I believe you, Wiles." Jasper said.

"Okay, nobody but Jasper's that stupid," Cathilda hooted. "I mean *no*body."

"Wrong!" Casey snapped, standing. "I am, too. So just shoot me now."

Nobody shot her. But nobody disagreed, either. Cathilda smirked. "So send him a Valentine and hope for the best, sugar."

Jasper looked around questioningly. "Hey, yeah. What month is this, anyway?"

"Yep," Casey turned to face Wiley. "Valentine's Day is coming right up. Maybe you could do something even more romantic than that French restaurant farce."

"Romance," Wiley sneered. "Life is a box of chocolates. Or wait, is it a loop around your scrotum with the other end tied to a millwheel?"

"Great attitude, Wiley," Casey chided. "I can tell we're going to have some misty-eyed ladies out there when you finally sit your butt down and write it."

"An attitude," Wiley clarified, "Otherwise known as 'reality', often confused with 'experience'. Show me a woman interested in romance, and I'll show you a woman baiting the ultimate trap."

"Oh, like men aren't out there lurking with clubs and lassos."

"That's us," Jasper piped. "Dearstalkers."

"The difference," Wiley ground on, "Is that men lay simple traps where the goal is to claim an hour of a woman's time. Doing what she wants anyway." He tossed back a shot and cuffed off his lip. "Whereas all women are angling for is our whole damn life, doing what we'd never do in our most whipped-out dreams."

"Wiley," Casey said in a patronizingly teacher-like voice. "Not every woman you meet is interested in tying you down."

"No," Wiley replied, "You're the only one who's tried it in a long, long time."

Casey recoiled as if slapped. She stared at Wiley. Could he possibly mistake her attempts at guidance and friendship for grabbing control? She looked down the bar, where everybody was silently watching the interchange. Even Jerome stared poker-faced, thick arms across his deep chest.

"Wiley, I..." She didn't know what to say, or how to say it. It seemed so obvious. "I don't want anything from you."

"No? No angle? No strings, hooks, sinkers, wholly-owned statements of mutual operational concern?"

Casey looked at him sadly, slipped off her stool to face him directly. "No, Wiley. I don't want anything from you. You don't really have anything to give or anything anybody can take away."

He'd never thought of it that way. The rest of the bar took it as a given. Who among them was worth clipping?

Casey, possibly at the point of tears, went on. "All I ever wanted was what's best for you. To serve your talent. All I wanted is for you to have a life, feel good about yourself. Is that so much?"

She turned and ran for the door, now definitely in tears.

Wiley turned, looked down the bar. She was right about one thing. He didn't feel all that good about himself. He glanced at Jasper and got an emphatic nod.

"I'd say she's on the level, Wiley. She means it."

Jerome weighed in, as well. "No doubt in my mind. She's sincere and selfless and likes you for yourself. I've seen the same problem before."

Wiley sagged back on his stool. "Oh shit."

The bar erupted in a unison of advice. "Run!" "Run for it, Wiley!" "Ruuuun!"

He fidgeted a minute, then slipped off his stool and headed for the rear door. As he rounded the bar, Jasper called to him.

"Yo, Wilester. You dropped this." He held up a slightly damp white envelope.

Wiley looked at it sadly, "Crap, Blew another one." Then moped out to the alley.

Casey didn't even finish reading the Weekend Warrior column for Valentine's Day. Even before it veered off into scuzz, she had given up on it and blitzed it out to Make Ready.

THE VALENTINE'S DAY MASSACKWARDS
By The Weekend Warrior

Valentine's Day is, simply, Love Day. With the exception of your odd massacre, it's not about Valentine at all. Whoever he was. Some pussy-whipped Roman flit. It's all about Love. "Love" in the sense of "Having Somebody to Take You Out Somewhere Expensive and Give You Things".

Which would be a pretty simple transaction, except our entire concept of what Love means has gotten cluttered up with all those sayings people take as truth, leading to misunderstanding and the sort of homicides that misunderstandings justify. It's time to examine some of these seemingly benign maxims and weed out facts from foibles.

For openers, it's widely stated that All's Fair In Love And War. Not so. Let's examine this one in specific detail:

1. Poison Gas: unfair in both, although perfume is generally excepted

2. Lying about marital status: considered unfair in love, merely ineffective in war.

3. Surprise and sneak attacks: fair in both, though unsporting

4. Biochemical tactics: unfair in war/ widely advertised in love. Because warfare operates on the Geneva Convention, as opposed to the more conventional conventions of Paris. Or even conventions of Shriners.

5. Taking no prisoners: frowned on in war, merely cost-effective in love

6. Two-timing: unfair in love, OK in war, but difficult. The problems with wars on two fronts has been discussed, but not as widely as difficulties with the beast of two backs.

It should be obvious at this point that these homilies are not always what they seem. Let's just cast a cold eye on other saws, mots, and chestnuts that confuse our already sufficiently confused approach to the other sex.

--Love makes world go around. False. Love can make *your* world go wild. Or kablooey. But the rest of us will not be moved.

--Love don't last, cooking do. True. Where are preservatives when you need them?

--Love conquers all. False. Or there would be no soap operas. War doesn't conquer all either. That's the whole point. Half of it has to lose.

--Love is blue. False. This notion probably comes from "Blue Movies". Otherwise who knows what they were thinking? Actually, love is pink inside.

--All you need is love. False. It's like saying all you need is money. Or youth. Or looks. Or a ladder as tall as the well you fell into. Not a solution, in short.

--Love means never having to say you're sorry. False. Actually, it's superior firepower that means never having to say you're sorry. You hear people in love saying how sorry they are all the time.

--Love hurts. True. But not as bad as the lack of it. When you look down a calendar of American holidays and commemorations, Thanksgiving and Love Day really jump out as the least crazy reasons to celebrate.

* * * * *

I know this will come as a great a shock to the conscientious reader as it did to me, but it seems there are those who are taking a rather loose approach to these columns—scanning over them lightly, not really getting involved. Not, in short, getting much out of our wisdom for lack of putting much of themselves in. Now I'm not going to embarrass you by mentioning any names here in front of everyone, but you know who you are. Let me suggest the following:

1. Shape up punks, or ship out,

2. Read The Weekend Warrior© over several times—there are many nourishing nuggets of nonesuch that will otherwise escape you,

3. Use a highlighter pen to accent particularly sage phrases and salient truths (I realize this is difficult, because of their very number, but try—and remember, neatness counts),

4. Get together in small groups to discuss the column. Be prepared to defend critical viewpoints, preferably with your life. There will a test afterwards. We are creating pop culture here—you've got to expect an occasional pop quiz.

She slumped back in her chair, eyes wet, arms hanging, head lolling over the back of the chair. Know who I look like, she asked herself. She didn't really care if anybody saw her misery and resignation or not, but jerked erect at the knock on the door. There might have been other people she'd less expected to see there, but the apparition of Jasper in broad daylight was enough to trigger cognitive dissonance.

Jasper was no more assertive or articulate in the Week offices. He blurted, "You dropped this. I mean, Wiley dropped it. I mean, it's yours. So here it is."

Jasper's gauche fumblings rallied Casey's mother hen instincts to drag her out of her black mood. She smiled at him, waved towards a chair. "Here's what, Jasper?"

He blushed, rummaged through the endless pockets of his field parka, and pulled out a white envelope, now somewhat dog-eared and marked with circular stains from various glasses, like crop circles of uncertain import. He handed it towards her, then dropped it on her desk and bolted. Sure enough, there was her name.

Inside was a Garfield valentine, obviously intended for schoolkids. Which read, "If you don't have anything better to do, consider being my Valentine." But "anything" was crossed out and "anyone" written in. And in the same hand, "Your amigo, Wiley."

THIRTY-ONE

Jammi dressed out for her next date with Scorment. Which is something like saying a medieval knight put on some gear for a joust. She came to him arranged in layers, some bombproof, some hardly visible, most composed of fabrics designed to advertise and augment the shape of sensuality. She was colored, texturized, retouched, de-scented, re-scented. Beauty may be skin deep, but sexual craveability, Jammi felt, starts there and builds outward. She looked like the small fully-clothed "personality" shots of a Playmate feature. And underneath the shifting sheaths of peek-a-boo she wasn't far off the big eight by ten airbrushed chromes and folding shots they lead up to. Not that J. Danforth was going to find that out. Not tonight, by any means. Hooking is the short game: it's reeling them in and getting them into the boat that produces the big payoff. And Scorment was about as big as game could get. She'd researched it. She just hadn't been prepared for how big he was on the sheer physical plane. But she was a trooper. They got married in a little over two weeks.

A real wedding, too. Technically. Not, strictly speaking, a matter of dearly beloved gathering today. More like the cat and the mouse signing letters of intent.

Once the proposal had been received with the appropriate swoon and gush, Jammi started fretting about the wedding itself. Unlike most girls, she hadn't really thought about that, just focused on negotiating the bridge between enticing and coming across. Leaping the quantum between lust in the heart and bucks in the bank.

Feigning schoolgirl giddiness after dashing her name on a complex pre-nuptial agreement she couldn't read, she broached the topic of the formal nuptials. She hoped it wasn't some Big Church Ceremony. If this was Scorment's idea of a house, God knows what he considered a Big Church. She didn't like the picture of herself standing up in St. Peters wearing a long wig and wraparound shades because every paparazzo in Rome was packing the naves hoping for wardrobe malfunctions they could flog to "National Inquirer".

But it turned out to be one of the few matters on which they thought alike.

"I thought we'd just have it right here at the house, Cupcake."

Jammi looked at the baronial hall and imagined herself descending the gracefully curving staircase, overwhelmingly desirable in acres of white lace and flimsy promises. Then recalled, whatyoucall it? Oh, yeah... reality. She'd better keep a close eye on herself during this whole situation, she figured.

"What are we doing about guest lists?" She ventured. "Just family and friends?" She wasn't anxious to have too many witnesses to Danforth plighting his snout in her trough. But suspected he had as few friends as she did and just as messed-up a family. And was she ever right.

"Sure, sure. Bring in a justice of the peace and maybe two caterers," he waved expansively, populating the hall with justice, peace, and chow. He turned to face Jammi, which still gave her the queasies. "I think we'll keep this whole matrimonial situation our own little secret for now. That sound okay to you, Cutie-pants?"

"Oh, Christ, yes," Jammi breathed in relief. But wait... "Then why would we need caterers?"

J. Danforth howled like she'd told him the party joke of the month, slapping his bulging belly to make his point. "Now ask me a hard one, Sugar-poon!"

But Jammi wasn't completely nauseated until he added, "And speaking of a hard one, what have we here?" With appropriate hand signals.

She fled the room and house, wailing, "Not until we're married."

"Just an old-time girl at heart," Danforth chuckled. Boy, he just couldn't wait for the honeymoon.

Most girls would have been given pause by the sight of Danforth's body. Or given leave to dash shrieking into the night. But Jammi wasn't so much grossed-out as horribly fascinated.

She was seeing the Anti-Bod, the unholy antithesis of everything she'd driven to accomplish with her own flesh. His movements were like an ambulatory lava lamp. When he flopped onto the monstrous, reinforced bed, he flowed all over it, looked like a face sinking into a vat of lunchroom tapioca.

From that position he waved a hand at Jammi, ravishing in her Fredericks of Gomorrah negligee, and cackled, "Jump right in, sweetie-Jams. Get it while it's hot."

Jammi approached her conjugal bed with understandable trepidation. She surveyed Danforth and found the prospects of rapture unpromising. But this wasn't just some one-shot for a free bigscreen or modeling job, this was Holy Matrimony or Happily Ever After or something. She had to figure out a way to get things turned around.

"Do you have anything to sort of... you know... get me in the mood?"

Danforth howled in glee, pointing at a drawer beside the bed. Jammi slid it open as if expecting a little Mexican snake to pop out and stab a wire tongue into her hand. Instead it contained a mind-boggling pharmacopoeia. Plastic bags of herbs and powders, glass and plastic pill containers, injectable syrettes, popable ampoules... if you couldn't boggle your mind in here, you were either a candidate for canonization or a lost cause.

She poked at the amazing array of goodies for body and mind. She'd never cottoned to drugs very much, although steroids were a subject of interest. Gym rats might be dull conversationalists, but they tend to live clean. She pouted a little, gave Danforth a look from under her lashes. He squirmed and sloshed.

"I mean something you could, like, plug in and turn on."

Danforth dissolved in laughter, creating Perfect Storm effects throughout his entire physiology. He pointed under the bed, where Jammi could see the pulls of another, larger drawer. It was full and heavy, but she tugged it open. And stared into Little SexShop of Horrors. Vibrators, rotators, motivators. Stimulators, simulators, terminators, spaculators. Bindings, lashings, stingings, invadings. Gags, chokers, shutters, openers, imploders. Dildos, dildon'ts, steely dangers, squirmy rooters. Batteries included. Don't try this at home.

"They don't call me the Heavy Equipment Operator for nothing, Bootycakes," Scorment bellowed.

Jammi, lost in wild surmise, picked up a particularly wicked multiple warhead device. She couldn't figure out where the third ram was supposed to batter, but it looked rewarding. "Hmmm," she murmured as Scorment guffawed. She hefted a flashlight-sized device that writhed in about four different kinds of motion when she pushed the button, "Well, now," she muttered, feeling a little warm and giddy. She grabbed something at the bottom of the drawer, but it was big and buried under other marital arts paraphernalia. She yanked if free and gasped, "Oh My *God!!!!!*" She felt a rush of desire tinged with dread. Dan Fourth yelped and reached for it.

"Good eye, Pussycat. Plug it in right over there. And turn on."

Well, there's no point in dwelling on this scene for cheap, prurient indulgence. We're all adults: we know what honeymoons are like.

At the exact moment the circuit was connected and Jammi's consummation hummed to plunging life, Casey was nearing the end of her wits in her campaign to recycle Wiley. He could admit he was a worthless piece of shit, and there were times when that was his main topic for hours of booze-propelled recrimination. But couldn't admit that the booze and drugs might be the problem, not him. Admittedly, it was hard to draw the line.

As she sat on the comfortably curved rail at The Mimosa, watching Wiley put away a six-pack of Tequila shooters, she was willing to propose desperate measures.

"Haven't you ever tried some sort of detox facility?" she asked in pleading tones.

"I've been tried and sent to them," Wiley replied with obvious distaste. "Horrible places. Run by sub-human monsters, proctored by evil scientists herding us into nameless, obscene experiments. They put things in the food to make your skin crawl and give you the heebie-jeebies. It's a police state in there."

Actually Casey could see that as true to some extent. "Have you ever tried Alcoholics Anonymous, Narcotics Anonymous? Some sort of anonymous thing?"

On the other side of Wiley, Jasper piped up, "The Mimosa's about as anonymous as it gets."

Doc nodded, "No last names. No names at all, in fact. Know what I'm saying, Sister?"

Down the bar, Strack yelled, "Need to know basis."

Cathilda leaned over, gave her a look. "And ain't nobody need to know."

Jerome, squirting the siphon to check pressure of a new cylinder of gas, nodded sagely. "Who you see here, what you say here, when you leave here, who gives a shit?"

"Wiley, you need to get a handle on this before you destroy your talent, your body, your life." Rolled eyes and chuckles along the bar. They just might have heard that one before.

"Who am I to mess with that?" Wiley asked her. He thought it was rhetorical and self-evident, but she obviously craved a fuller explanation. "I'm just a vehicle here, baby. You understand?" Well no, probably not. He felt obliged to expand her awareness. He tossed off another shot, shivered, and turned on his professorial demeanor.

"Talent? What is that but a chemical reaction in the brain? Sertonin, adrenalin, the frequently maligned testosterone. All these and many more play their part. And chemicals have to come from somewhere."

She looked ready to object to that, so he hurried on, grooving into it as the so-called Tequila took hold. "My brain is just a vessel, an altar on which drugs are sacrificed, incorporated, liberated from their mundane physical confines. They go willingly, in fact insistently, to this immolation because only in concert with the various cerebral synapses, ganglions, and receptor sites do they come to actualize their true nature and purpose. Which, conversely..."

Casey stared at him like a rabbit at a cobra. He decided to shift from theoretical underpinnings to the applied side of the psycho-pharmaceutical alliance.

"My output, my writing and various public works, aren't something I create. Nothing I can take responsibility for. In fact... Well, let me put it this way. It's not me there on that newsprint. It's just the drugs talking."

A voice from down the bar amplified that, "And what they say is, 'Go get money for more drugs'."

"But you're a really good writer, Wiley," Casey expostulated. She didn't understand why he didn't see that, and why he didn't understand that it made other inadequacies irrelevant. At least to her.

Wiley rolled a jaundiced eye towards her and chuckled bitterly. "I used to date this actress. Well, more like I just used to screw her. She got it in her head I was an 'angel' behind some plays."

Casey was confused about what that had do with anything, but willing to listen.

"Anyway, I went to see one of her plays, which turns out was a musical. She sang two songs, nice voice. I was surprised because she never sang in the shower or anything. I told her I didn't realize she was a singer, too. Know what she said?"

Casey shook her head, expectant.

"She said, 'I'm not a singer, I'm an actress. The part called for me to act like I can sing.' "

Casey regarded him, befuddled but trusting him to tie it in.

"Don't get it? Let me remind you of something. I'm not a writer, I'm a two bit swindler."

"And a bargain at half the price," Jasper chirped.

"Not really, " Wiley demurred. "I'm tied into a setup with two idiot millionaires and all I've taken out of it so far is wages and a little strange pussy."

Turning back to Casey, he explained the whole thing. "See, this scam calls for me to impersonate a writer."

Casey's baffled look turned ineffably sad. She started to speak, but Wiley held his glass up for Jerome's attention and said, "Maybe that's what all those writers are doing. How the hell would I know?"

Appalled and saddened, Casey slipped off the stool, stared at Wiley like a hollow-eyed painted waif, and vanished into the gloom. Wiley heard the door close. He shrugged. "Yo, Jerome, my man. Does this glass look half-empty to you, or half-full?"

Jerome extended a bottle, splashed. "I'd say it looks full, Bro."

Wiley tossed it down with a single spasmodic snap of his spine and elbow. "Yeah? Look again."

CHAPTER THIRTY-TWO

"You lied about your age to get married???" Jammi screamed.

Her Morning After Glow seemed to work only if there were no men involved. Furious at the duplicitous Danforth, she battered the broadside of his barn with some sort of Siamese tickler device.

Whinnying under the attack, he repeated and expanded his post-nuptial revelation. "Yep. Not a day over sixty five. What, do I really look ninety three?"

Did he ever. Jammi's rage was stilled for a moment by sheer natural wonder.

"Yeah, but... incredible... how...?"

"Clean living, Honeypot. But forget that for a couple of weeks while we get down to Living Dirty."

Jammi jumped up and kicked him, but the sensation gave her the creeps, like Br'er Fox's assault on the Tarbaby. She ran to the door, turned to throw the Bangcock Bruiser at him. It flipped and twitched on the carpet like a worm on a hotplate as she slammed out and headed for the nearest phone.

"So I'm like... *Shit!*" Jammi tacked onto her story like an Aesop moral. Having heard the tale of her latest marital speedbump with operatic intensity and scale, Caitlin and Rollie were a bit of a loss for the proper reply. Caitlin couldn't risk a comment yet, and Rollie was nonplussed: he hadn't thought the stock scheme out to its logical mortal conclusion, but could immediately see how Jammi might have concerns in that area.

But she obviously expected some sort of response, standing there with her fists on the hips of her expensive new curve-clinging red catsuit. She'd called for this meeting and now here she was, pumping frustration and bitterness into Caitlin's living room, posture and expression clearly announcing, "Deal with it."

Caitlin tried to make nice. "On the other hand, you look really good, Jammi."

Jammi, derailed from her bitter disappointment regarding the Mortality Dividend to her favorite subject, was nevertheless wary.

"Seriously. Married life must agree with you. You look more relaxed."

Less borderline disordered, Rollie thought.

"More, I don't know... fulfilled."

Like a digesting python, perhaps, Rollie translated.

"You see what I mean, Rollie?"

"Aglow," he offered.

Caitlin trod out on the thin ice of the relationship by offering some light and happy. "So can we expect the patter of little feet pretty soon?"

"Eww," Jammi snapped. "It's not that kind of glow."

"Well, anyway," Rollie tried, "You're really rich."

"Sort of. Don't get me off on the whole pre-nup thing. Point is, I didn't sign up for twenty years on the Fat Farm."

"I just don't see what we can do for you, Jammi."

"Well, think of something because I've got a newsflash for you two editors. That stock you're so hot to get your hands on is only twenty four percent. And he can't vote it except the way those assholes tell him to."

"What makes you think so?" Rollie asked. This didn't sound good. They'd hoped she could use her wiles and more evident assets to cozen him into voting a new slate.

"What makes me think so? Mostly hearing it myself. He brags a lot, but he also talks on the phone a lot. To that creepy chink, Yao. I've got that place surveilled. Believe it, kids, he's scareder of Yao's bunch than he is of me."

"Not good," Caitlin said, chewing her lip. "We were really counting on you being able to control those stocks."

"*Stocks*? What do I care about a few damn stocks when the man's worth jillions in like cash and property and stuff?"

"I told you, Jammi," Rollie said, soothingly. "We need to vote those shares."

"Let me get started on my needs, here."

Caitlin spoke firmly, hoping it wouldn't be the straw that broke the camel's back and caused the camel to hurl a highball glass through her picture window. "Don't you think we deserve a sort of finder's fee on this?"

Jammi controlled her first impulse pretty well. For one thing, there was still vodka in the highball glass. And she had to admit the bitch had a point. She wouldn't have hooked into this bonanza without them setting it up. Maybe they could figure out her next move. She really, but really, needed an alternative to playing out her youth beneath the avalanche of Danny Boy's Viagra-stoked compulsions.

There was an uncomfortable pause, which Jammi tempered by stalking across the room and refilling her glass. Power may corrupt, but Absolut vodka corrupts Absolutly.

Caitlin first broke the oppressive, glaring silence. "Is he mentally competent, would you say?"

Rollie shot a startled glance at her, not expecting anything quite that Machiavellian to bubble up from Caitlin's sleek surface. Then he shrugged. It was probably a legitimate tactic. It's not good to have feebs and psychos running public information utilities. Just ask "Dennis".

Unfortunately, Jammi gave a negative snort. "He's as on the ball as I am."

Everything's relative, Caitlin thought. "What if he gave you the shares? Some sort of wedding present? Then he'd be out from under the gun..." Her idea petered out in mid sentence. That wouldn't be any different from a proxy in the eyes of the Mystery Mob.

Rollie confirmed her thought. "They don't care who owns the stock, or they wouldn't have given it to Scorment. But they'd react like vengeful vipers at losing control of the voting power. Maybe we should go straight to Yao, or even to Question Mark and the Mysterians. Cut a deal. We might have coinciding interests."

"I doubt it." Jammi was polishing off her second helping of vodka and getting morose about her prospects. Alcohol was fairly new to her and kicked her ass every time. "*Yao* is scared of them. You can tell. Their only interests are them."

"No way to get them in a divorce, I assume?"

"Hey! First you set me up to get married, now you want me divorced? Divorce and I get nothing. It's the old Death Do Us Part." She stopped suddenly. She couldn't believe she hadn't even wondered about this before.

"Wait. What if it did do us part? I mean, it could happen. He does some pretty crazy stuff." They'll never know just how crazy, she thought bitterly. Nobody ever will.

"Well, you'd probably end up in a classic court bloodbath against his kids." Rollie didn't use words like "family versus gold-digger" or "Anna Nicole's law" out loud.

Danforth's two seldom-seen offspring sprung off from a previous marriage that ended in his shapely young wife being beaten to bloody death by the fiery Nicaraguan gardener she was cheating with at the moment. One headline had been, "The Rake's Revenge." No pix, though.

Jammi knew about the kids. Her stepkids, come to think of it. Yuck. Well, she could step up to Evil Stepmother, if need be. What she said was, "Just leave them to me."

Rollie and Caitlin were both shocked as the full import of that sentiment hit them. They gave each other a look. Are we just both really naïve, Caitlin asked herself. Rollie's cheerful thought was, I think just sitting here might construe criminal conspiracy. He spoke to her as carefully as a man addressing a dog in his path with jowls foaming.

"What do you mean, Jammi?"

"Okay, sure. Play it like that." Jammi dumped the idea of these two muffins helping her out. She'd always gone with Numero Uno and this was The Big Chimichanga, no time for tossing a change-up. "But I think we all know there's only one way he's going to get out of our hair."

Oh, shit, Rollie thought. Then he thought again and came up with *Oh Shit!* He didn't want to, but said, "What way is that?"

Jammi had a smile on her face as she said, "With a smile on his face."

Rollie thought he felt a chill wind across his testicles. Caitlin just stared as Jammi tossed off the rest of the vodka and strode to the door with the fixed resolution of Rambo pulling on his bandolier and head scarf. Neither said anything about it. But both developed neck pain during the next few days, cringing from the drop of a big shoe.

Another colleague with a pain in the neck that eluded a satisfying scratch was Casey Chones. Her obsession with Wiley's

231

turnaround was getting to her. And his other support group, the various blind fish in the grotto of the Mimosa, weren't a whole lot of help. Jasper tried to explain, but was oddly unsuccessful.

"It's hard to figure Wiley," Jasper told her solemnly. "The man is deep."

And piling deeper all the time, Casey thought. But she said, "Yes. He is. There's something deep inside him that I'm responding to. He's obviously troubled and blocked. But I think he can work that out. Especially if he got some support instead of people just feeding on his sickness."

Eyes barely clearing the rail, Strack grunted, "That it? Or does he feed off other people's sickness? Think about it."

"Scavengers are important to the ecology," Jerome put in, not particularly comfortable in conversations involving the concept of drinking too much. "But listen, are you an editor or a social worker?"

"Is there that much difference?" Stack growled from below the bartop. "You just rearrange things a little, take out the screwups, mold in the right direction... "

"Cut a little off here and there," Joe added"

"That's what you think?" She didn't see Doc, Cathilda and Goody nodding.

"Casey, how many editors does it take to change a light bulb?" Jerome asked.

"Depends if you can use the "Undo" button."

"The answer is that the bulb has really got to want to change."

"Isn't that the first step? Wanting to change for the better?" Casey had spent a lifetime grasping at straws in the wind.

Jasper, familiar with the Twelve Steps from a lifetime of having them suggested to him by foster parents and fleeing spouses if not ordered upon him by mollycoddling judges, said, "No, the first step is thinking you have a problem."

Seeking some solidarity in helping a man cope with weakness, Casey looked around a group of people astronomically unlikely to provide it. "How about you people? Don't you see a problem?   Some of you are also struggling with substance addiction..."

Cathilda almost, but not quite, spilled her drink as she brayed, "Struggle? Honey, I think I got it down pat."

"No struggle involved," Jasper chirped. "I got took out by the first punch." Leaning closer to Casey he confided, "I'm pretty sure it was my cousin Randell who spiked it, but then it could have been his date, Diamond Relow. She liked having liquor to blame for whatever happened to her."

While Casey absorbed the coming of age story, Strack offered, "Shit, I got med-evacked out of the struggle. Tied down and shot full of the best shit in the world."

"It's only a struggle if you put up a fight," Goody clackered.

Pruitt mumbled, "The struggle is *getting* it up, not *giving* it up."

"True story, sweetie," Cathilda assented, vaguely waving her oddly dainty hands. "I just get a drink, cop a taste here and there. Only reason I drag my ass out of bed."

"Now *that* would be a struggle," Strack said, ducking as Cathilda caromed an ashtray off the bar and over his head.

CHAPTER THIRTY-THREE

The coffin looked like a piano crate designed by Liberace. Caitlin peered in apprehensively. J. Danforth had been hard to take when he was alive. Actually he looked better in death. Seemed to have lost weight. Better color.

The morticians earned every penny of their exorbitant bill. The removal of the corpse from the bedroom had been no picnic, one of them confided to a circle of colleagues at a popular funeral director hangout. The deceased had been on his knees on the floor, ass end up with his face pressed into the carpet. He'd looked like a quarter ton of snot and engineering him out had required enlarging three doors. But the real challenge had been getting the smile off his face.

An autopsy had revealed multiple entry wounds, but only in places they were to be expected, if not precisely normal. A cop at the scene had commented: "I'd guess Mrs. Scarlet in the Bedroom with Obscene Gizmos." His partner thought there must be some kind of law against what he termed, "cruel and unusual pleasurement".

Caitlin hurried back to her seat and watched the collection of millionaires, media moguls, civic corruptees, and the usual ghouls parade by the coffin and offer condolences of various natures to the stunning young widow. Who looked like, If Morticia Adams Had Been A Streetwalker.

As one executive turned away from her, Jammi called out for the entire "chapel" to hear, definitely including his wife, "Wait, you dropped this. In my hand. Oh, hey, it's a phone number." He might have had better sense if Caitlin or Rollie had told him that J. Danforth the Fourth had survived less than forty-eight hours after Jammi had hit upon the idea that his existence clashed with her agenda.

Yao wasn't looking forward to dealing with Jammi. He assumed that she would be jacklighted meat for him or anybody else with the power to advance her naked, throbbing yen to become. Unattractive men with money, influence and libido learn to gauge these things the way a hawk interprets movement in a wheatfield below.

But Jammi, though certainly the toasted muffin of many a masculine urge, was not his cup of chai latte. He worshipped clean, smooth and serene: she evoked muscle, sweat, odorous fluids, hairs, unrest. The girl was plainly all about pounding. Did not further to cross. To tell the truth, he was a little afraid of her.

But not in the sense of financial ledgermain. He was a black belt in fiscal skullduggery and she was, let's face it, a twit. Brainless breasts on wheels. So he sauntered into her presence at ease, figuring a half hour, tops, to line her out on the Week and station stock, among other items of interest to his employers.

One omen that it wasn't going to work out quite like that was the room in which Jammi received him, her spanking new home gym. It had previously been a home library, one of the finest in the state, though seldom perused by The Fourth. However non-intellectual he was, however, he had never had the books carted out and stacked in the garages. Which Jammi decided to do in a hot minute in order to accommodate her exercise equipment, another taste the late Danforth had neglected to cultivate.

Yao was wowed by the gym. It was lavish and complete, an indoor forest of shining chrome bars, burdensome black weights, oiled steel cables, businesslike molded seats and grips. Some of the machines seemed softer and more feminine with functions that were not quickly interpreted. Jammi stroked one of these affectionately as she ushered Yao to a seat on a bench. As in "bench press". She faced him from the seat of some sort of abdominal curl apparatus.

Though Yao didn't recognize it, he was seeing not only Jammi's favored environment, but evidence of a heads-up investment strategy. She'd been told by her financial adviser (a high-priced call girl she met during her three semesters at junior college and kept bugging her to get into the game, claiming that not to was a waste of resources verging on criminal) that contesting her entitlement to the estate could lead to accounts being frozen and assets commandeered. Her best bet was pouring cash into high ticket items she could take with her if it came to that. She'd become a popular fixture in the tonier La Jolla jewelers and carried a secret stash container with her wherever she went. She had paid cash for the gym stuff and figured there was nobody to ever say it wasn't hers all along. It was a hedge against future downturns, and a great fit for Jammi's interests. And not the only advice she'd picked up for the price of a meal at a ludicrously over-priced Del Mar restaurant where her advisor previously had never seated with another female.

"Yes, I have the certificates," she informed Yao. "They were in a little vault in Danforth's den, along with a lot of other interesting things. I moved them to a safer place." Meaning a place where somebody couldn't pay almost a thousand dollars for a pair of barely-English-speaking locksmiths to take damn near all day to drill the tumblers out of, like Jammi had been forced to do.

"Oh, wondahfuh. So now you bling them to me."

"Why?"

Ah so. More resistance than Yao had expected, and a tough question at that.

"Stocks ploperty of Danfought's cleditors. They own station, own stocks. He just keep safe. Now he gone, not so safe." I can say that again, Yao thought, sizing Jammi up with fresh eyes. How'd she get into that vault? Was Scorment stupid enough to give her the combination? However she did it, she'd also gained access to a lot of extremely potent information. Good thing she's too feather-headed to use it, he hoped.

"Well if they left it with Danforth, they must have had their reasons." She let that hang, but Yao didn't rise to snap it up. "But one thing I noticed about them was that they all had his name on them. Not some 'cleditor'. So I guess they're mine now."

Yao was seldom speechless in any language, even the ones he invented himself. But this wasn't working out and he didn't have a quick answer for it.

"So," Jammi said with wide-eyed innocence, "Did you come to buy them or something?"

"Not work rike that. You have name on car legistlation, but bank own car. Same, same. You see?"

"Oh, I get it. They actually own the stock because it's like, collateral?"

Yao's head bobbed happily. Finally got through to this airhead bitch.

"No problem, then. I always like to co-operate."

I'll bet you do, you little hooker, Yao thought. Now get off your hot ass and go get those stocks. He decided to confer, make a list of the other information in her hands and come back for it better prepared.

"Ah, velly nice. I wait."

"You have the loan agreement, contract, whatever you call it, right?"

Ah, shit. "I no understand."

"Yeah, you do. You say these aren't my stocks, prove it. That simple enough?"

"Not that simple."

"Well this is. No tickee, no stockee. Unless you want to ask me for them in good English? I know you speak decent English. You went to college, right? You've lived here for twelve years and they speak English in Hong Kong, too. Especially in Empress College prep school."

Yao's poleaxed look was worth every penny she'd paid the cybersnoop to turn him over for her. Another good tip from her on-call chum.

"So come on, say it right," Jammi wheedled, "Or the stocks stay right where you aren't going to find them in a zillion years."

"I no see what you..."

Jammi came off the padded vinyl seat like a striking snake. She loomed over Yao on the low bench, broadcasting anger and a terse, muscular vibe. Involuntarily, he leaned back. "Cut the crap, you two-bit Hop Sing!" she yelled in his face. "Fess up or piss off!"

Yao, leaning back and feeling completely threatened, adjusted his glasses, then took them off. He regarded Jammi's hard, demanding face for a minute and thought about not being able to get the stocks in time for the board meeting in June. He cleared his throat and said, "Okay, look. We want the stocks and sooner or later we're going to get them. Why don't you just do it the easy way?"

Laughing heartily, Jammi morphed back to Playmate and grabbed Yao by the armpit. With a lovely flex she effortlessly curled him up to his feet. She patted his back in a hale, friendly way, the last "pat" driving him a step forward. Towards, he figured out, the door. She walked alongside as he retreated in humiliation. At the door she faced him, smiling gently. With sparkling eyes and a girlish lilt she said, "Fuck the hell off, you Buddha-assed banana."

Yao was still in shock from that one when she grabbed his shoulder and rushed him out the door. "Benny will show you out," she said graciously. Yao noticed a very competent, muscular young man in a crested blazer standing by. He looked at Jammi, but she closed the door in his face. Benny motioned a willingness to show, toss, or punch him out; whichever. He turned tail and slunk out, not a happy camper. "Clazy Amelican cunt," he thought. The first time he'd pulled that accent jive on himself.

Yao's sensibilities were smarting smartly upon escaping from Castle Greyskull, and he had no appetite for calling anybody connected with his task. He couldn't believe he'd gotten handled by that aerobics twit. She was haywire, somehow. What did she *do* with all that equipment, anyway? Some of that stuff looked like it had been built for Auschwitz or Abu Ghraib.

He knew he has just been through exactly the sort of reversal that could deflate a man's self-confidence, soft-boil his hard-on, shunt him off the varsity hardball team to the noballs scrub lineup. He was risking a major setback to the minors if he didn't find a way to take hold of the situation and turn it around, humiliate that twat and come out on top.

But he never did.

CHAPTER THIRTY-FOUR

Once a spiritual quest is established, the seeker needs absolutely no evidence to reinforce the certainty that there is actually something out there to be sought. This is commonly observed in mystics and cultists, reformists and world-savers, scientific explorers, stalkers of grails and proofs and continents. So naturally Casey wasn't giving up on Wiley. It only required her finding the proper motivation.

And April's shewres did show her a bonanza: Earth Day. A celebration as recent, contrived, and flaky as Kwanzaa, it nevertheless stood for something monumental. Surely even someone as sunk in cynicism and self-immolation as Wiley could grasp the concept that the environment needed coddling. Confident that concern for the planet itself would inspire insight where motherhood, children, patriotism, love, God, safety, romance, and the sanctity of life itself had failed, Casey buttonholed Wiley through one of his misaligned buttonholes and pitched the Earth to him. Did she perceive a certain inner light flickering into life deep within those murky eyes? She thought it was just possible. So she waited.

50 WAYS *YOU* CAN SAVE THE EARTH

By The Weekend Warrior

If you've got absolutely nothing better to do this weekend, maybe you should try ganging along with the latest craze-- Saving The Earth. *Or should you???*

The unasked question (asked here for the very first time in another of the daring journalistic arabesques that distinguish this column from those who have to live with their mistakes) is: Save it for what? Undoubtedly unasked because the only possible answer would be: Save it for Later. You don't need to be a two-year-old with a cupcake to see the fallacy in that proposition. Now is "Sure thing", Later is "*Quien sabe*?". They'll try to reassure you that saving is a wiser strategy than enjoying on the spot, of course. Right. Remember "Savings and Loans"? Remember "save yourself for marriage"? If the long-term prospects of the planet are so bullish, why the big panic about saving it? You're probably already starting to appreciate the advantages of having the ol' Warrior around to put you wise.

Hey, if petroleum products are so awful for the environment, what's the big objection to getting rid of them as quick as possible? Use the crud up, make it easier for the younger generation to live in harmony with nature. It's just like AIDS, one of those problems that would solve itself if the alarmists would keep their hysterical little mitts off it.

That same toddler trying to keep his cupcake from being gobbled up in a blue sky investment scheme could probably articulate another squirmy little objection to saving. Namely, the suspicion that Some Other Time might involve Somebody Else. Even it you accept the idea that momma plans to return your cupcake Later (in which case I'd like your name and address for my investment counseling newsletter), who's to say that Somebody Else might not grab the cupcake while it's sitting around gathering the obscure virtue of getting older uneaten?

It's obviously a plot. And it's obvious who benefits. Who is so concerned about the ozone thing? You got it: Kids. Who else runs around naked in the sun all day? I'm supposed to crimp my lifestyle so they can save money on sunscreen? All these EcoSaviors want you to do is give up your claim to the Earth itself so there'll be more left for them. Not a new story: we've been brainwashed for years on the virtues of sacrificing for children. A perversion of tried, traditional sacrifice techniques, in which sacrificees have always been young. Or virgins, even, who must be sought out younger every year.

Best bet is to remember a memorable Weekend Warrior© proverb. Or motto, if you must. Or even bumper sticker, T-shirt or anodized keychain medallion if you just send $19.95 to Warrior Enterprises, care of Southcoast Week Please include size. (Of the T-shirt, idiot.) The proverb, in case you've already forgotten, is: Never trust anybody under sixty. In fact, it's not that great an idea to trust anyone except your periodical pal, The Weekend

Warrior.™ And even that should only be done under adult supervision.

And why do you think it's only kids sporting those "Save the Planet" stickers? Which usually have photographs of ol' Mother Earth on them; heavily retouched but still obviously taken when Mom E. was much younger and a lot more salvageable. Just this planet, you'll notice: nothing said about the erosion on Mars, smog on Venus, methane atmosphere on Neptune, Klingons on Uranus, and no ozone layer at all on Jupiter. Conditions as inhospitable for human life as any found around here. But do these creped crusaders care? Noooooo. Me first, as always. And why bumper stickers? Notice that? These earth saviors always have fossil-fueled pollutomobiles to use as billboards for their crackpot ideas. Maybe this makes sense to them. And maybe they're all missing a few bricks in their toilets, if you catch my drip.

So what can you, personally, do to Use Up the Earth and Get It Over With? Just cut out the handy little list below and staple to your nasal septum or whatever the current fashion might dictate. For that matter, you can take it, roll it up and stick it up into a moist, dark place to save for later.

1. Just be yourself. Any half-assed neo-eco-freako-geek will take about thirty seconds to accuse you of dozens of selfish, genocidal, geophobic behaviors no matter what you do.

2. Keep reading. There are scads of books, articles, periodicals, flyers, handouts, calendars, note pads, hang tags, and cereal boxes with valuable ecological information. All of it on paper made from acres of trees that manifested a desire to be ground to pulp in order to beg off from the boring chore of converting carbon dioxide to oxygen, then slathered with extremely toxic synthetic inks that seep from landfills into the water table, in order to provide an income for effete dorks in New York to spend on imported cheese and water that presumably crossed the ocean by windjammer.

3. Recycle Metal. For instance, have the next car you see with any of those "Fellate the Planet" stickers towed off

and scrapped. One less to pollute, one less to commute, and a few extra bucks to boot.

4. Organize. We need an ecophagic movement with concerts by dozens of washed-up musicians selling out to their own egotism, a lobby in congress, some tribute albums, and "Eat the Earth" bumperstickers. Maybe some good recipes.

5. Put bricks in cars. Just one brick through the windshield of a BMW or Hummer can save a lot of noise, pollution, and ignorant self-satisfaction. A few yards of brickbats and voila, another one rides the bus. Get rid of enough of them and there'll be more lanes free for you and, more importantly, me.

6. Pig Out. Do it now. Eat it all. Take seconds, take thirds, take cuts, take out, take home: but above all, take. If you're gluttonous enough, you probably won't even live to regret it.

7. Burn Rubber, Bitch.

8. Support toxic wastes. You can't get wasted without intoxicants.

9. Don't come crying to me. I'm doing my damnedest to run this planet so that nobody gets hurt or loses what's left of their mind. Okay, maybe I'm not doing the greatest job in the world. But I'm not getting much co-operation, am I?

Okay, so that's only nine. I'll give you the other forty one when I see you. If we're still around after the earth-savers have their way.

Casey's disappointment in the Earth Day column was manifest. It was a week or two before she dropped by the Mimosa, a chill that Wiley affected not to notice despite inquiries from the Mimosans, who were starting to feel that Casey was a sort of mascot, a goodwill ambassador from a Real World that had otherwise shown them little goodwill.

But towards the end of the month she put in an appearance, though much cooler to Wiley and his utterances than formerly. She brought up the environmental question, eliciting the

242

commentary of the Mimosa Mob. Their comments brought home to her that their idea of "the environment" was the environs of the Mimosa and adjacent grubby streets. They saw little need to improve or preserve. Alcohol, in fact, *is* a preservative.

Before giving up on the discussion entirely, Casey fired one last reproach across Wiley's yawing bow. "The Earth is a heritage and we are the stewards. You'd feel different if you had children." She looked at Wiley, lolling on the bar punting olives along the rail with his fingers and knew the full folly of her concept. With the bitterness of the barren, she told him, "Maybe you'd be a better person if you did have kids."

"Good idea," Wiley rejoined. "Let's see... they come in boys, who can't wait to get old enough to carve a piece out of your butt just to feel like men. Or girls, who turn into psychotic trouble machines at the age of thirteen, and/or get knocked up by surly dickheads. And any other possibilities are worse."

Cathilda caught some of the freight behind Casey's tone, but missed the main point. All she could see was that Casey was the only one at the bar even distantly qualified to be a parent. "So how about you, Casey? How'd yours turn out?"

Sparking, of course, her secretest sorrow. Being against population growth on the intellectual level was one thing, but not having no legitimate outlet for her brood mother instincts was crushing. But this was not a place where flimsy press-release answers would work. She simply said, "I can't have them."

Cathilda cackled, "And you bummed out? Know what having brats is like? Like shitting a bowling ball, that's what."

Nobody touched that line. So Cathilda continued, "Then they run off with your best clothes and worst boyfriend."

Casey tried to imagine somebody running off with an underage girl who could wear Cathilda's clothes, but was mercifully spared a cohesive image. She barely heard Wiley say, "I can't either." She turned to him, on the scent of soul kinship.

"It's made a vas deferens in my life," Wiley went on, in a flat tone. "I realized, somewhere along the line, that I just sort of shouldn't have kids."

Casey looked it over a moment and saw that "shouldn't" have kids was a much wider psychic disability than "can't". Softened, she told him, "Well, we're past worrying about that stuff now."

"It's all ass backwards, " Jerome suddenly tossed out. "Ya should be sterilized when you're young and dum and full of cum, then be able to have kids later when you're wise enough to deal with the little fuckers."

"Yeah," Jasper chipped in, "And you should have lots of money and shit when you're young and can do something about it. Then be broke when you get too old to need it."

After a long pause, Goody clackered, "That's about how I did it." There followed a round of "amens", clinking glasses and orders for more.

CHAPTER THIRTY-FIVE

Jammi thought it best to interview her the children of her sorely-missed husband (she just couldn't think of them as stepchildren) in the formal parlor of the mansion. She'd purchased clothing especially for the occasion. Dark and bereaved looking, she'd told the shopgirls. And modest enough not to shock the daughter. But she spent hours looking for something that would also be sexy enough to impress the son towards her camp. Was there some Freudian word for wanting to make it with your stepmother? She bet it was a pretty common obsession, probably a couple of porn sites. And bankable.

Jammi worried about a lot of things, but getting tired of being right all the time was never one of them. The male heir of her departed hubby preferred being called simply Jay. His willowy frame didn't even hint at his father's hulking bulk, while his sinuous movements and flowing silk outfit suggested that if he shared the paternal lust it was certainly directed towards other areas and genders. Worse, his waspy mannerisms made it pretty clear that he would not be moved by arguments, pity, or belligerence.

When Jammi, more out of reflex than desperation, moved up into vamping range he laughed like a brass wind chime.

"That stuff doesn't cut any ice with me, Ms. Thingies. To say the very, very least. But my sister's here, too." He turned and yelled at the door, "Daniella! Are you lurking?" He stepped back, smirked campily and told Jammi, "Try your luck with her."

A stocky woman around Jammi's age stalked in, motorcycle boots slamming the parquet. She wore jeans and a steerhide bomber jacket. Her wide leather belt had a saucer-sized belt buckle and her wrist bands glittered with studs like a Doberman collar. She had a bulge in her pants and a silicon Adam's Apple. She stopped beside Jay and cruised Jammi shamelessly. "Sure thing, Sugartits. Try me. You might get lucky."

"Well, okay, look," she dithered to the two cross-wired offspring. "Maybe we can work something out. You know." She met blank stares, one reminiscent of a spoiled Afghan bitch, the other recalling somebody who might be called upon to "lean on" the uncooperative. She flopped her last card. "Money?"

Daniella hooted like the pressure release on a steamroller. Jay clapped his hands and simply *shrieked*, dearie. "What, *our* money, honey? We're going to have that anyway. And all the stuff *and* your tight little ass." Daniella flashed a smile like a roadgrader grill. Hard to say which she'd enjoy most. Jammi was on the phone telling Rollie about her "step-tiles" before they were out of the house.

"I'm just not sure you being there will work for us," Rollie said, standing beside his Baja-ready Voyager and not offering to open the door for Caitlin, who looked terrific in a simple white summer dress and broad straw hat. "She obviously doesn't like you."

"I don't think men should be around that woman alone."

"Your lack of trust in male fortitude hurts you more than it does me, Blondie. You think I need a chaperone?"

"I think you need back-up. Should I bring a gun, or do you think the pepper spray would stop a charge?"

Rollie thought it over, opened the door. "How big a gun can you conceal?"

The meeting took place in the suncourt at Chez Jammi. Quaint rattan seats with green, bamboo print slipcovers, glass teacarts with refreshments, soft music, plants in huge Zapotec pots. Caitlin liked the looks of it. She didn't much like the looks of J. Danforth Scorment The Fifth. And presumably The Last, from the look of him. Or his sister Daniella, for that matter, sulking around the perimeter like Marlon Brando just off the waterfront. She sat close to Rollie on the sofa, dipping Milano cookies in her Lopsang Soochong tea. She had a feeling she'd ranged out of her depth. She hoped Rollie was up to it: table stakes loomed large in this one.

Rollie wasn't at all sure he was. Jammi was adamant that the world owed her big, big bucks for her marital cession, suffering and mental anguish: Jay Scorment was no slouch at pettiness and greed, either. It was going nowhere and starting to get nasty. And there was no doubt in Rollie's mind that though

Jammi was a talented amateur, Jay could be nasty at a professionally ranked level. And if not, his sister could always stomp over and start tearing new apertures. What was really frustrating was that the gender-switched-at-birth siblings, probably with an eye to legal costs and time factors, were making her a pretty generous offer. Generosity wasted as usual on Jammi, who was willing to shake 'em up and roll 'em for the whole pile. Trouble was, if the judge instructed the jury to Google "gold digger" it would probably find 187,945 images that looked an awful lot like Jammi. He really wanted to head off a major conflagration at least long enough to pull the Week stock out of the fire. He tapped his Frappuchino cup with an ornate Italian silver spoon.

"Jammi. Excuse me, Jammi. Can I point something out here?"

She threw him a look like a cornered badger, but nodded. Barely.

"Listen, do you know what a million dollars is? Way more than all the money you've ever had in your life added up."

That was a curveball to the Jamster. She mulled it a moment: Rollie pressed on, catching a glance of bitchy approval from the laxly lounging form of Jay. "You could just put it in a CD or offshore account and draw three thousand a month forever."

Her reach continued to exceed her grasping. Rollie did dumbdown. "A hundred dollars a day. For life."

That started to get there. Rollie switched to the slider. "Ten million and you'd be taking in a thousand dollars a day. A thousand a *day*. Sock away half in your Christmas Club and you'd have a million bucks in six years. Before you're even thirty." Well, you never go wrong underestimating a woman's age a little. And she was vague on math.

"I'd grab it and run, Jam. I'll bet they'd throw in a Mercedes to run with."

Jay's laconic nod and subtle smile endorsed that bet. He was starting to look at Jammi like she was a Mormon missionary kid who'd agreed to come in the door and expressed polite interest in the collection of prints he kept upstairs.

"I'll have to think about that," Jammi pouted. You could tell she'd already done some thinking and was already sick of it.

"Certainly," Jay crooned, suddenly the soul of effete charm. "Get advice, use your head. We're willing to work with you."

You sure are, Rollie thought. Like you'd be willing to work with a bunch of underprivileged Boy Scouts. But there it was, the opening he'd thought would never come.

"And while she's thinking and you're working with her, I'd love to discuss something here that's of interest to a lot of us, and even the community at large."

Jay's take on that indicated that he didn't owe the large community a lot of favors, but he maintained his reasonable air.

"The estate includes shares in Southcoast Week. Probably around a quarter of the outstanding stock. We were hoping you'd allow Jammi to vote that stock at the board meeting in June."

"Which we'd be glad to do," Jay purred, "If you could just give us a plausible reason why we should."

"I think I can do that," Rollie said, earning a look of surprise and admiration from Caitlin. Well hello Rolland, she thought. I knew that guy when he was sleeping on the beach in a sombrero.

"First let me lay out what I have in mind. You cede voting control of those stocks to Jammi. I've got a document that's sort of a provisional proxy. Essentially it says that you don't know whether you or she owns the stock, but you don't care if she votes them."

"Interesting," Jay said in a much less fruity voice you kind of suspected was how he normally talked. "But what do I get? We get, that is."

"I have another document here by which she cedes the stock to you at the end of a period of time to be filled in on the contract, but not to exceed one year. So you get the shares without let or litigation. Just so she can vote them in a meeting I'll just bet you don't give a damn about."

"Clever solution," Jay admitted. "To *your* dilemma. But in a year we'd own the stocks anyway."

"Would you?" Rollie asked bluntly. "I've covered a few little parties like this over the years. They buy yachts for attorneys, but I don't remember one ever getting completely hashed out in less than five years or so." It was an exaggeration, and he knew Jay knew it, but it invoked an undeniable reality. And... "You could also lose."

"You're damn right they'll lose," Jammi yelled. "What's in this plan for me? You're just milking me so you can get your stupid jobs back. What about me?"

Caitlin stuck her finger in the pie for the first time. "The stock isn't worth all that much, Jammi. Not money. But you'd have clout. As soon as Yao's Mao Maos hear about the proxy they'll be kissing your butt. You could play this up to a lot more than weather girl. You could be the anchor."

Jammi gleamed at that, then jittered. Rollie realized that the goal Caitlin saw as a living dream was something Jammi knew she wasn't up to, but wouldn't admit it. He blurted: "But you know what else you could do? That would work much better for you?"

That was the sort of thing that grabbed Jammi's interest, but she waited him out, non-committed. Rollie wound up and floated it right across her letters, her own personal creampuff. Three little words that mean so much to a girl.

"An exercise show."

Jammi was smitten into open-mouthed silence. Caitlin stared at Rollie in awe. Jay gave him a nod, and swishy hand salute. Even Daniella, sitting backwards in a chair by the door, couldn't resist curling a lip. Nailed ya, huh, cutie?

Caitlin mentally tacked an additional ten percent on Rollie's IQ score, as he followed his shot like a classy point guard. "Your Personal Trainer, with Jammi Jamison. The Week would push the show, promote it and you. You'd have your face on billboards and buses. Doing what you're best at."

Jammi's lips moved but nothing happened. She seemed to be experiencing a semi-religious phenomenon known to theologians as "The Adoration."

Caitlin tagged in for the knockdown punch, "That's a great idea, Jammi. You'd have a shot at a national show. DVD sales."

Relaxed, effortlessly, Rollie drilled in the KO. "Maybe even your own gym." Caitlin thought it possible that Jammi was suppressing the visible symptoms of a spontaneous orgasm. One symptom was nodding. Beginning slowly and progressing to an impression of a bobblehead doll on the dashboard of a pickup with shot suspension.

Jay applauded Rollie silently and somewhat mockingly. "Inspirational. But you're forgetting the main factor again. *Moi*." A warning grumble made him flip a hand in Daniella's direction. *"Et elle."* He sat up to confront Rollie. "Why should we?"

Rollie stood and walked over to the divan, sat down by Jay and spoke to him in low tones. Not even Caitlin could hear him, though she was doing her best.

"I think I mentioned saving money, saving time, right?" Jay nodded provisionally. "And a nice step towards maybe settling things over coffee instead of in court. But think about this. When did Jammi first date your departed dad?"

Jay knew from rhetorical queries, waited him out. "Now he's dead and she's got the house, cars, and bank accounts,' Rollie pointed out. "In two months. Do you really want her pissed at you?"

Rollie let that sink in while he moved back to his seat. "Besides, we're lining up a buyer for the stock. You'll come out better than you'd get selling tomorrow. And if it's tied up and the paper goes to shit, what will you own?"

Jay glanced at Daniella and, evidently reading some message in the clinched beef of her face, turned back to Jammi, beaming. "Let's do it; sign off for six months. The rest of the estate is still up for grabs."

Rollie's heart plunged when Jammi zipped back up to Red Alert.

"The hell it is, fudge-packer. Possession is nine points: how many points you have? It was a legal marriage. In California. Half of it's mine right now and there's nothing you can do about it. And I want the house."

That rolled off Jay in a tinkle of girlesque laughter. "The *house*? This dire old dungeon? Look, take it. But what do I get?"

Rollie dared to hope. Jammi studied Jay a bit. Hmm. He was an interesting guy. Give a little here to get a little there. Might be a workable concept. She glanced at Rollie, who waved his hands toward Jay in a "go for it" gesture. She looked back at Jay, who seemed amenable.

"Do you know what these "debenture" things are?" she blurted.

"I surely do. Why, they don't grab your interest? Little pieces of funny paper?"

"Okay, you have them."

Caitlin glanced at Rollie, whose teeth clenched like the first twenty feet of a roller coaster drop. Whew. And she had a clubhouse seat for this thing.

"The cars, no problem," Jay said. "The horses, too. What the hell?"

"There's horses?" she gaped. "You mean like real *horses*? How many?"

"A dozen or so, last I looked. Not like, race horses, you understand. Except old Jalapeño. He broke a leg and got put out to pasture."

"Where do they sleep?" Jammi asked. It wasn't unreasonable to think the mansion had a wing of suites for the equine set.

"Out on the ranch," Jay said, "But that's a separate transaction. Daniella is quite fond of it." Assenting rumble from the wings.

"Do they eat much?"

"Well, it's not chicken feed," Jay said straight-faced. Then he laughed and Jammi joined him.

"This is great," Rollie stuck in, like tossing a life ring to somebody caught in hopeless currents. "Co-operation beats slugging it out every time. But maybe you should do this with lawyers and financial advisers around."

"Oh, I think we're getting on just fine, aren't we Jammi?" Jay flashed warning looks at Rollie and Caitlin.

"Jammi..."

"No, he's right, guys. We can save a lot of money and trouble this way."

"You can also lose your butt because you don't know the color of the chips." Caitlin nodded her agreement with Rollie on that point.

"It's okay. Look, we're going to be doing this for awhile, I think." She looked at Jay, who nodded. "Why don't we catch up later?"

"Leave me your documents and we'll get them to you all signed and sealed." Jay stretched a condescending hand for Rollie's sheaf of legal-sized papers.

Rollie and Caitlin walked to the door, glancing back at Jay and Jammi's potlatch. "He's pitching her bright pennies and grabbing the greenbacks," Caitlin whispered.

"She's better off right now than when she started. This house must be sitting on seven million in real estate. Not bad for two months work."

Caitlin looked back once more before casting Jammi to her own devices. Jay had moved over on the sofa beside Jammi and was examining her face.

"Say," he said, "Would you be offended by a few cosmetic tips?"

"Well, I guess not."

"Look, honey, you've got good skin and don't need this much help. But if you do, you have to start at the base and work up, so to speak. You have a blusher? Let me show you. We'll talk clothes later."

Jammi took a closer look at Jay's clothes. Hmm. She said, "Okay, sure. Where'd you get that blouse?"

Taking the little foam brush in hand, Jay leaned in to begin delicately sketching something entirely less trashy. "This old thing? I'll show you some time. But I understand we share an interest in, what should I say, wind-up toys?"

CHAPTER THIRTY-SIX

Caitlin shook her head all the way to Rollie's heavily modified minivan. As he unlocked it, their eyes met over the roof. Both started laughing uncontrollably.

"The Billion Dollar Slumber Party," Rollie intoned in thirty point type. "By Dennis Schumann."

"I can't run it," Caitlin hooted, "The real Dennis Schumann would die because he wasn't there."

They got in, the doors closed on their laughter.

They relapsed into laugh spasms as Rollie drove Caitlin home, replaying highlights of the Shootout At Castle Numbskull; soundtrack provided by a stereo she figured cost more than the van. Some anthology of R&B or Gospel. She couldn't tell which. She recognized Ray Charles, but not many of the others. It was growing on her.

"Thing is," she told him, "What you bought her in with is all true. That could all work out for her. Well, if she can step up and handle it."

Rollie gave her an odd look. "Of course it's true. You think I'd lie to manipulate her into something just for our program?"

Caitlin stared at his profile for a long time as he drove and punctuated Aretha's "Oh, Happy Day" with finger moves and background vocals. Wait, was that James Brown on there, too?

But what he'd just said was obviously the unfeigned truth. That was the sort of thing, right there. Any man who wouldn't lie to manipulate a girl like Jammi just wasn't from any planet she recognized. She fully realized what she'd known when she first met him: that he wasn't like anybody she knew. He was finer, truer. Hairier. She leaned over, brushed her lips on his ear. "Let's make love."

Once the van was back under control and Rollie's emotional airbags had undeployed, he dared to look at her, a vision of all-American gorgeousness gazing at him raptly. Jesus. "That's an easy one," he said. "Marilyn Monroe in the movie. Covered by Kim Bassinger in "Cool World". Now I'll do one. Ready?"

She nodded.

"Go ahead, make my day."

Another funny/warm feeling moved over Caitlin. What kind of guy is this? Amazing. Leaning back to his ear, the murmured, "I want to get you all over me, let you infect me. I just need to... eat you up and be like you."

"Well, they say you are what you eat."

"Then I think I'm about to become a total dick." She was shocked to hear herself giggle. Then delighted.

Later, lying in pleasant exhaustion on the meticulously thread-counted sheets of her Ikea sled, she figured she'd gone through some sort of looking glass into an alternative universe. No trophies awarded, no reasons to get back to work, no posturing. Plenty of eye contact and snuggle. She would have been content to lie there indefinitely, playing with Rollie's belly hair and talking the kind of vapid nonsense single people employ to learn who it is they've just been screwing the brains out of.

"No national roots, actually," Rollie was answering her. "My dad was a rock musician. About as rootless as it gets. I got the brand name of his synthesizer. His main ax. My middle name would have been Rock but Mom put her foot down."

"Rolland Rock?" Caitlin chuckled. "So what was her idea of a middle name? I didn't catch it when you applied. It better not be "Unit"."

"Mom was more into jazz. So it's Kirk. Which is why it didn't make the résumé."

That was over Caitlin's head. As was:

"My college band called me Rahsaan. Even though I played bass. But enough about me, let's talk about my prowess."

"Talk's cheap."

"Yeah, but if you write it down it can go for a dollar a word. But hey, Caitlin isn't exactly a normal name either. What is it? Dutch? Irish? CryptoJewish? Yuppish?"

Caitlin's glib answer stopped at her teeth. She put her head on Rollie's chest and listened to the slow, solid meter of his heartbeat. Then said:

"My name's Katherine."

"Ah. So you took on a pen name. Well, tube name."

I took on a hell of a lot more than that, Caitlin/Katherine thought. And I suddenly get the feeling it didn't do as much for me as I thought. "My family back in Wisconsin call me Kate. When they call me."

"Kate's nice. Doesn't fit you as well, though. Get a little older and classier and you can drag Katherine out of the closet and get a Hepburn thing going."

"I've never told anybody out here on the Coast."

Rollie realized that the difference between Kate and Caitlin might only be a short syllable, certainly not as dramatic as the reinventions of Marion Morrison, Frances Gumm or Norma Jean Mortensen, but to her it was major and she'd entrusted him with it. He felt touched and oddly protective.

"And you'd better not, either," she growled. "I've got you by the balls."

"I've been told that before, but it was never literally true. Don't worry, I won't tell anybody about your *nom du pantage*. At least not until I get on at another paper. Ow! Owwww! Hmm. That actually hurts kind of nice."

His turn to feel touched and totally unprotected. He kissed her gently, "Your wicked secret's safe with me."

Which just might, Caitlin thought, be close to the kernel of why she'd brought him to her bed. Anything she might have hidden, been ashamed of, sought to push down or lock away, were safe with Rollie. She was in good hands. She just hoped he was, too. He was giving her a glimmer of the idea that maybe she could be any good for somebody other than herself. For some reason, she reminded herself to call home. Then she rolled astraddle ol' Rahsaan to start cranking things back up. All that hair felt better than it looked.

Casey returned from a daunting jaunt to the euphemistically termed "Ladies" room with a much warmer feeling for Wiley than she'd had an hour before. The man had his reasons, was what she was thinking. And would continue to exhibit completely different facets of his complex, if degenerate, makeup.

Thus her surprise at seeing Wiley leaning forward on his favorite stool, deep in a Spanish conversation with a weathered Latino gentleman, came as no surprise. She was pretty sure it was still correct to think "Latino". The Mexican was ageless, as gnarled as the flinty soil of the Sierra Madre, the stolid Mestizo face beneath his ancient white straw Stetson making him a good bet to portray the Grandfather of The Children of Valdez. He seemed very chummy with Wiley, in a depthless dignified way.

It was not without a certain pang that Casey, signaling Jerome for a beer and staying carefully aloof from the cross-national confab, watched Wiley's effortless command of colorful, colloquial Spanish. Like many a California liberal, she thought of herself as an international, trans-frontier type of person. Her heart was certainly one with the struggles of immigrants, migrant workers, and Chiapas peasants. She bewailed the Minute Men, knew the exact death toll of women in Ciudad Juarez, the current number of crosses depicting deaths of incipient Americans in the deserts. She loved to spice her conversation at meetings of the like-minded with perfectly pronounced Spanish words. Though she wouldn't have put it quite this way, she'd have blown a musk ox to have her living room designated as a Movement sanctuary for refugees from Central American genocides and ineptitude.

But in fact, and also like so many of her ilk, she couldn't speak Spanish beyond inquiring for beers and bathrooms, and felt chastised that Wiley, whose political attitude she so deplored, seemed comfortable with complex sentence structure and enjoyed an obvious rapport with this representative of *La Raza*. When Juan Valdez stood, held his fingers up in a pinching gesture indicating he'd return in "just a Mexican minute", and carried his worn old leather satchel into the men's room, she expressed something of this to Wiley. He wriggled his brows, made a very Mexican-looking deprecating gesture and said, "Well, you know what they say."

Of course he had to tell her, "Never trust a White man who speaks good Spanish."

That one set her head spinning. She was working on a probable derivation in the Old West, where racist sheriffs had to worry about renegades and desperadoes. But before she could treat the Mimosa Rail Scum to the guffaws that observation would have produced, the *Indio* was back, satchel slung over his shoulder and an old book in one hand. He set the book on the bar, slapped Wiley's shoulder and winked salaciously at Casey. Wiley didn't introduce them (so as not to be embarrassed by her shameful lack of Spanish and proper sub-border etiquette, she assumed) but pulled a sheaf of bills from his pocket and handed them to old-timer. He fanned them, showing twenties and fifties, and tucked them away in a leather vest dusted by many dry trails.

He picked up the book with a gravity that was not lost on Casey, handed it ceremoniously to Wiley. She had no doubt she was watching the transfer of lore, if not some precious tribal artifact. She stared at Wiley: what more was this remarkable man capable of? She hoped she would be allowed to peruse this volume, perhaps with Wiley's translation and guidance. Wiley nodded solemnly, placed the book on the bar in front of him, and exchanged a three-course handshake with the old man, ending with their two fists knocking together. The Valdez patriarch clasped Casey's hands in his own soulfully, turned his obsidian gaze on hers, and planted a wet kiss on her cheek. Then turned and walked out, a bow-legged strut into the rectangle of blazing white light that represented The Street. Casey felt a rush of inspiration.

"Wiley, it's so great you have that familiarity with *Español*," she gushed. "What a privilege to be able to penetrate our neighboring culture."

"Oh, he's no neighbor. He's up from Sonora."

Better yet. Don Juan's sacred book, lying right there. "I was just thinking," she hurried on, "*Cinco de Mayo* is coming up. You could take advantage of your... well, advantage... with language to write a column that expands people's awareness of the whole Latino/Chicano thing. You know, pointers, details, translations of items of Mexican culture. You could break down some fences, for sure."

"*Cinco de Mayo*?" Wiley quickly calculated. "Yeah, you're right. Coming right up on us like the sun from Mandalay. Might be a good idea for a column."

"I was thinking..." Casey said, but Wiley held up a hand, continuing the movement to lightly brush a finger across his lips. He turned his stool to face the door, taking on a smiling affability that caused Casey to swivel in search of what would make Wiley turn so amenable.

Anti-climatically, it was a heavy-set guy with long stringy hair and a facial resemblance to Tony Soprano, including a broad midsection that explained the long, untucked shirt. He looked around the bar, seemed reassured by its very sameness, and headed over to Wiley returning the cheesy smile.

"Right on time, Kenny," Wiley smiled.

"What up, Wilemeister?" he said quietly. You could tell he seldom said things quietly. "Everything on time, A-OK, green to go?"

"Hey, you know me," Wiley said, causing Casey to look at him, wondering if. "Show me yours, I show you mine." Casey had a momentary jolt, suspecting some sort of horrid homophile revelation, then flogging herself for thinking there was anything wrong with that.

Kenny nodded and pulled out another sheaf of twenties and fifties. He fanned it quickly, giving Casey the impression it was almost as large as the amount Wiley had just given to the old *vaquero*. The guy held the money hidden in his fist while Wiley turned and picked up the book. Casey felt somewhat disappointed that she had only witnessed some sort of go-between transaction.

Wiley opened the book, licked his fingers and thumbed back a page to reveal a hollowed-out compartment full of plastic bags rolled up around reddish leaf mulch and brownish powder. Wiley stuffed a bag of herbs in his shirt pocket and held out three of the brown bags to Kenny. They exchanged money and bags simultaneously. Kenny saluted Wiley by tapping the baggies to his forehead, and walked out into the sunshine.

Wiley turned to Casey, exultant. "Talk about a quick break-even point? The rest is pure gravy. Party time."

Casey, once again bummed out to witness Wiley's purported qualities elude the both of them, tossed off her beer and headed for the door. Wiley called after her, "Hey, thanks for the *Cinco de Mayo* idea. I'm on it like water off a wet's back."

As she faded out into the doorway, she waved a hand in what could have been farewell, dismissal, disgust or just resignation.

"Gonna break some fences, you bet!" Wiley yelled at her back. Then turned to the denizens, who were closing in on the lid in his pocket like a wolfpack surrounding a tethered lamb. Three packets of ZigZag papers, two small pipes, and bong appeared magically on the bar in front of him. Wiley pulled the baggie from his pocket teasingly, passed it under his nose like a cigar aficionado, then let it roll open to sniff deeply. "I can never decide," he said. "This... or strange pussy?"

As he rolled a couple of doobers and presented one to a ring of flaming Bics, he said, "*Cinco de Mayo*, man. I got it nailed."

CINCO SWIM
By The Weekend Warrior

Cinco de Mayo is one of those holidays like St. Patrick's day: folks back in the old country don't even get a day off, but their immigrant *paisanos* in the United States get to go out and get hammered. Cinco de Mayo is exactly the kind of holiday you'd expect to find located within four days of Mayday.

"Cinco" is a holiday whose origins are, perhaps deservedly, obscure. Originally the term meant what it sounds like--a sink full of mayonnaise. How this happened and why it should be celebrated is mysterious, but just one more example of how little we gringos know about our amigos South of the Border. Those who have elected to remain south of the border, that is.

Why, for instance are so many Spanish love songs about cortisone? Why the big deal about La Bamba, but not the Samba, Mamba, or Caramba? Why do rear license plates say "Front"? When the bull wins a bullfight, why not give him the matador's ears? It's all pretty perplexing, all right, so the Weekend Warrior © thoughtfully provides this little glossary to straighten out some of the terms you might come across at a Cinco de Mayo celebration.

Mariachis	Mexican equivalents of Pagliacci, but not as sad
Piñatas	Drink with pineapple juice and coconut milk
Cervesa	Cervix. Why this is mentioned so often at holidays is hard to comprehend
Marimbas	Maracas
Maracas	Macarenas
Mantilla	Diminutive of manta- a form of ray
Fiesta	An afternoon nap

Hope that helps. Of course San Diegans have the novel option of going over to Tijuana and celebrating the Mexican holiday in actual Mexico. In which case here are several phrases guaranteed to make your international visit a bit more memorable. Clip this out and staple it to butt cheek or whatever fashionable location. *Hasta Lumbago.* Baby.

THE WEEKEND WARRIOR'S™ TIJUANA PHRASEBOOK

Good morning	*Bogus Dias*
Good evening	*Bonus Nachos*
Thank you	*Muchas Garcias*
Please	*Poor Sabor*
Which bus to the border?	*Autobus por Guadalajara?*
Where are the mariachis?	*Me gusta maricóns.*
A lite beer, please.	*Doble tequila, por favor.*
I'm going to be sick.	*Mas tequila, con gusano.*
To the bullring, cabbie.	*Hasta un bordello, pronto.*
Buy you a drink, miss?	*Cuanto dinero, puta?*
What's wrong, officer?	*Chinga tu madre, cabrón.*
Why am I in jail?	*Vender mi favores sexuales.*
I'm an American citizen.	*Soy loco y con pistola.*
Call the American Consul.	*Soy traficante de drugos.*

Casey entered the column into the computer drives, read it over on the screen, then butted the monitor with her forehead. A couple of good, solid shots.

CHAPTER THIRTY-SEVEN

Whatever its political insights might have done for city, it was only when the umbrella of criticism was extended to include sportswriters that the already popular BitchKitty really caught fire with the town at large. San Diego is big on sports and the UT staff of writers on the subject was even worse than what Dennis called them: a bunch of punks. He documented their abuse and errors, compared with coverage in the LA Times. He brought up the concept that perhaps the meteoric career of top draft quarterback Ryan Leaf might not have crashed in a splatter of ego if the UT sportswriters hadn't heckled the young rookie so much in print and even followed him into the locker room to jeer and jape at him.

He dissected the continued howl from the UT to fire the coach of San Diego State for not winning more...even bitching about losing by one touchdown to then-fourth-ranked USC. Finally the coach, sick of it all, resigned. So of course his star Junior running back, who had committed to playing his Senior year out of respect for the guy who'd recruited him, immediately declared for the pros. Young lad named Marshall Faulk. With a rookie coach and without what would have been a spectacular season from the future NFL Rookie of the Year, SDSU sunk lower yet, a plunge was not soon arrested.

Finally, BitchKitty could only state that there was a good reason why Jim McMahon had blown his nose all over the UT sportswriters. He suggested that everybody else do the same. What was worse, after each of his BitchKitty columns, he listed lesser known publications and websites where much better reviews of the subjects could be obtained. People were starting to wake up to the fact that they were being shortchanged by their media monopoly. Just pick up a Sunday LA Times, BitchKitty suggested: Notice that it takes you longer to read the A&E section than the whole San Diego paper? And you suddenly know a lot of new things? Things that you are being kept in the dark about?

BitchKitty ignited a rebellion on the radio talk shows and small local papers. Sports fans, suddenly shouldered awake to how badly they were being gulled, howled in outrage. As usual, the UT shut the protest down or printed suspect creampuff letters about it and answered them in soothing tones.

The column became a vital part of the Week's new look and feel. The booming popularity and credibility of the paper was only fed by the hysterical denunciations that accompanied its new role as social irritant. It was fun for Rollie and exhilarating for Caitlin. She still ignored Wiley and Savage, but was greatly impressed by Rollie's work. They guy had been studying the town, she realized, even if he hadn't been allowed to do anything about it. Inside that shaggy teddy bear was a stainless steel barracuda. And she had released it.

Casey did her own share of unleashing. One of the suburban high schools had approached her about sending them a prominent journalist as commencement speaker, not a totally unusual request. Especially so late in the spring, when they were obviously having trouble lining up anybody else. Unfortunately, the secretary from the high school was a habitually supercilious, condescending snot. And displayed those characteristics to Casey, not one to suffer them gladly. Casey idly inquired if they were familiar with Wiley's column. When the snot said no, Casey poured on the oil. Not only would they provide a speaker bound to prove memorable, they would record his remarks for publication in the Week. She was as good as her word:

GREETS TO THE GRADS
By The Weekend Warrior

Students, parents, distinguished old farts. It's a dubious pleasure to be here today at LaCagia Falls High School. As I look out on all these bright and dilated pupils, I can sense the high ideals of this generation. Namely, that it's ideal to be high. When the older generation looks at the history-making actions of the students in Mexico City and Tien An Men Square it's hard not to think to oneself, "Gee, those Chinese and Mexicans really know how to deal with students." Here, of course, we have no better solution than to let obnoxious students (if you'll pardon the redundancy) graduate and become as normal as the rest of us. This system, though less dramatic, is probably more fiendish in the long run.

Because, in many ways, the world today is tougher than the one we elders graduated into. For one thing, it's crammed full of increasingly moronic and ugly kids, all hustling to get theirs and screw the world. We know you look to us, if not for leadership, at least for a piece of the action. We know you want to take your places among us, standing strong and proud on our faces. What you don't know is that we wish we were back in high school screwing around, partying, knocking each other up, and doing long drugs. So let's trade. We'll wear those dumbass robes and you work these mindless jobs, slaving to pay taxes to support free education for the unable, unwilling, and unpalatable. Well, all in good time.

There might be those among you who think the older generation hasn't left you much of a world. But in time you'll learn the wisdom of the old saying, "So sue us, kid." I know that each and every one of you wants to get the big picture. Or at least a piece of the big pie. To stand up and say for all the world to hear, "I'm all right Jack, get yer hands off my stack!" That's the spirit, but this focus on riches is not the whole story. More significant is debt. You probably think the world owes you a living. Well, speaking for the world, let me just say, "Hardy har har". Fact is *you* owe the world billions and billions if Carl Sagan can be believed (or even understood). You were born with a price on your head and your rear in arrears, a squalling little deficit-spent unit. And you will quickly start piling up new debt, wrecking the universe to protect your credit rating. You're screwed before you even start.

They will tell you that the educational process has no finish line, that life is a never-ending schooling from birth to death. Forget it, they're just trying to bum you out, as usual. In fact you never learn anything worthwhile, really. We tend to think of schools as vast repositories of knowledge; and to an extent this is true. Each frosh brings some little dab of knowledge in with them and nobody ever takes any out, so it gradually accumulates.

You are about to step from this huge suppository of wisdom into what jokesters like to call "the real world". You will learn new lessons there. You'll learn the value of a job done well enough to look right. You'll learn the importance of having a decent haircut and nice tits. You'll learn the powerful aphorisms (and euphemisms) of success. Like: When the going gets tough, it's tough to get going. Or: Don't be afraid to make mistakes, only to admit them. Never put off until tomorrow what you can delegate to a chump. Neither a borrower nor a lender be: the future is in leveraged buyouts. Know thyself: who else matters?

Perhaps the most famous comment on education is a telling parable from the Chinese: If you give a man a fish you have fed him for a day; if you teach him to fish, you have fed him for life. And, the saying goes without saying, if you start selling him fish you have him right where you want him. There is more than one way to handle a hook, line, and sinker.

Forget that lifelong learning junk: education is the preoccupation of the uneducated. Suffice it to say that you are leaving behind the joys of school, but the crapola goes on forever. Especially if you're dumb enough to go to college. Even if you haven't had up your ying-yang with papers, books, and dirty looks, think about this: If you haven't learned whatever the hell you want to know by now, four more years aren't going to do it either. Especially since you'll be older, more debauched, a step slower. Face it kids, this is the peak. It's all downhill from here on out.

The one thing I most hate to hear (other than that trash-ass rap music) is the idea that today's graduates face diminishing opportunities. Sheer twaddle! There are a myriad of opportunities for people your age. You could star in a Rob Lowe video, for instance. Even if you can't spell MTV, you can still Serve Mankind. In fact, McDonalds has served billions and billions (according to a census by Carl Sagan) and they don't even have numbers on their cash registers. I believe it was John Milton, the blind, arrogant, probably syphiliticly demented English poet, who said, "They also serve who only stand and wait." And today, over 300 years after those words were minced, there is still demand for waiters.

Some of you will want to work in a field that has growth potential, to be picky, to get to the roots of things, to grab hold with both hands, and reap ripe results. And for you, there are hundreds of strawberry fields. Forever.

I'm sure there are those who will seek careers in the arts: future musicians, painters, authors, ballerinas, authors. Let me give you two heartfelt bits of advice: "Get real," and, "Don't make me laugh." Not everyone can be cowboys, astronauts, football stars, junkbond manipulators or porn actresses. Worse yet, almost nobody can be award-deserving weekend columnists: only a select few of the very cream of the gene pool. A state of affairs scientifically known as Tough Titty.

Some will tell you that your diploma is just a piece of paper, worthless in the real world. No big; when you go job-hunting, they won't look at your diploma or grades or your athletic letters, or your four color salt and flour tortilla map of the principal iron-producing areas of Europe. In fact, they won't even look at your application. Why should they, when they can get somebody with four years work experience instead of four years sitting around some jerky campus putting on airs and getting weird ideas? It's not too late too start working on your hairstyle and tits.

But in closing, I would like to remind you that life is more than money. The true value of education lies in learning that material things are immaterial; that what counts is having a hearty heart, a spirited spirit, some lovely love, sensible sense, and credible credit. So follow your dreams; the ones you've never dreamed of. Dare to be what you wouldn't be on a dare. Be compassionate and caring to those you don't give a damn about. Be practical and honest, or at least practically honest. Have a sense of fair play, even if you don't play fair. Above all, it is important to have something to believe in. I, for instance, believe your haircut sucks. The most important thing is to remind yourself that you shall pass this way but once. In fact, it's a miracle you passed at all. Don't be another cog in the machine: be unique. That's what everyone else is doing.

Be all you can be. Do all you can do. Eat all you can eat. Dream the impossible dream. Right the unrightable wrong. Believe the unbelievable bullshit. Like the unlikely event. Do the undoable dude. Go forth and multiply. If you didn't learn to multiply, learn to add fast. If you can't go forth, go for a fifth, young man. A fifth a day keeps life insurance agents away.

In closing, I'd just like to remind you that only an hour ago you were students, an hour from now you will be has-been students. You'll bop happily off to whatever kind of future starts out with rented robes and a dorky square hat with dingleballs dangling off it. Well, you can't spell "diploma" without the d-i-p. Good luck. Congraduations. Welcome to a classless society. Pop a champagne cork. Pop several. Might as well graduate "Magnum Come Loudly".

In closing, I want you to remember three things as long as you live, or at least as long as your memories hold out. One: Get a job, twerps. Two: Do something with that damn hair. And last but not least on the list, Three: Shut the hell up and make yourselves scarce. Grads should aspire to being unheard, unseen and unsmelt.

So now, at long last, little Junior is a Senior. Ya freaking hoo. I can think of no finer closing words than to echo the sentiments I see reflected in your parents' misty eyes. And I'm sure they would join me in saying to you, "No more free ride, punks." In closing, I would like to leave that thought with you as a remembrance of this day, which I hope you will always think of as the last day of the best part of your life. Now, get the hell out of my face and take those stupid dingleberry hats with you.

CHAPTER THIRTY-EIGHT

The congenial little get-together officially termed the Southcoast Publications Quarterly Shareholder's Meeting but which Rollie and Caitlin had come to think of as The Lowdown Showdown, was held in a large, nicely appointed conference room in what was nominally Yao's office. Independent accountants don't usually have big meeting rooms. But this one was the *de facto* headquarters of a coalition of clients that brought Yao to bear on the Scorment accounts. Stark and corporate, but recently adorned by a large painting behind the head of the table, drawing attention mostly because it was shrouded in black cloth, the room came in handy on occasions when high-tech virtual hookups just wouldn't replace actual butts in actual seats. Several butts were already parked when Caitlin walked in, her hand on Rollie's arm.

Yao, at the head of the table, and Hollis Ovarón at his right hand, registered astonishment at the sight of the new version of Caitlin. Her face no longer had the glossy perfection of fine porcelain baked on stainless steel. Now there was a softer resilience to her, not hard but firm like a classy breast during its formative years. The tight, sculptured upsweep was also gone; her hair hung loose to her shoulders with a slight upturn at the ends. At the other ends were evidence that her dye jobs were lapsing: roots the color of dark chocolate. Her eyes were no longer contact emerald, but a warm brown. She showed signs of suntan. She wore flat shoes! Yao mourned the waste of such a close approximation to his visual ideals, but was consoled by the fact that it didn't really matter. He had her now. Forever.

Ovarón merely thought she looked more approachable. Which he didn't realize was his own internal screening code for "more fuckable."

"Good morning, Caitlin," he chirped, "You're looking wonderful."

"I feel wonderful, too, thank you Hollis." The unspoken content of her look at him said, Not that you'll ever know what I feel like. She nodded, "Mr. Yao."

"Prease," Yao remonstrated, "Call me Boo."

"And I think you know Mr. Moon."

Ovarón had clocked mild surprise at Rollie's presence at the meeting, but now that she mentioned it, it was a bit of a puzzle. So he puzzled.

Yao definitely thought Rollie being there was fishy, but couldn't see any reason why. He shrugged at an inquisitive glance from the man to his left, a slim dapple-gray who looked like he'd told a fairly expensive tailor that he wanted to look anonymous and soul-less. Yao motioned towards the functionary. "And this Herr Ottmar Kunitz. He heah to leplesent..."

Kunitz, who found Yao's pidgin ploy tedious, cut in smoothly, "...voting representative of Timberlake Associates of Hong Kong, London and Berne, holding a major block of shares."

Then the whole introduction thing had to be repeated, including a few lawyers whose names nobody gave a damn about, because Jammi swept into the room.

The change in her appearance was as great as Caitlin's, and geometrically more aggressive. The bouncy weathermap kid had been swallowed up from inside by a new organism; a slinking, feline creature whose lush promontories were no longer flaunted by her clothing, but hinted at maddeningly. She was a swirl of Autumn in gypsy silks and leather, from her knee length boots to a spiky tiara embedded in her newly springy cascade of curls. Elements of fortune teller, belly dancer, and hippie rock star swung around her as she glided to a seat without making eye contact with any of the servile drones who awaited her. Her face had an exotic hauteur, expert feathering bringing cheekbones forward from the babyfat, her eyebrows tilted as though deciding whether to pleasure herself or order a pogrom. Her uniformed chauffer... Bodyguard? Gigolo? Hitman? held her chair as she settled into it like a fall of October leaves. She barely acknowledged the introductions, including her own. He swept an icy gaze across the principles, bestowed a slight smile for Caitlin and Rollie to divide among themselves.

She looked around the silence of stares and made a duchess gesture. You may proceed. Her manservant, standing behind her with clasped hands, nodded. Yeah, so proceed, already.

"Gentlemen," Kunitz said softly. "Ladies," he nodded to both. "Our purpose here, as you know, is to ascertain if the majority of shareholders approve the current management philosophy or propose alternatives. This shouldn't take much of your valuable time: I'll require certain signatures after we confirm our agreement by a vote."

"Actuary, may be quickah than that," Yao chirped. The glory of his latest acquisition and his return to control, after having his ears pinned back by Jammi, made him quite chipper. "Mistah Ovalón, you got forty-nine puh cent of stock, light?"

"Well, actually I don't," Ovarón said, distracted by his examination of the veiled canvas on the wall behind Yao. "I doubt it matters, but my partner holds half of my... well, half. You know."

"You never say this befoah!" Yao was running quick mental math and getting a little unsettled, especially when Kunitz turned to him with one eyebrow elevated a centimeter. But there should be no problem.

"Well, no," Ovarón stumbled on, "There's never been outside shareholders before."

Yao relaxed. "So you got ploxy, same-same."

"Well," Ovarón said, drawing it out, "Not really. I founded The Week with a partner, see."

Yao nodded snappily, trying to get on with it.

"And she had twenty-five percent and I guess that leaves me with let's see... twenty-four." The hairs on Yao's nape were starting to pop erect, one by one. Nothing else was even close to coming erect. He forced himself not to look at Kunitz. This wasn't going as smoothly as planned.

"You don't have that proxy at present, Mr. Ovarón?" Kunitz asked calmly.

"No, but my partner came down from Santa Cruz to be here with us. She doesn't like meetings. But if it's time to vote, I suppose I should call her in?"

"Please do. She'll vote her own shares, then?"

"Of course. She's a very strong, independent woman."

Oh God, Yao thought, not that. He wanted to spin around and clutch his Goddess's knees in supplication. Ovarón was putting away his cell phone and the door opened. His secretary ushered in a chunky, beaming, post-menstrual woman wearing a straw-colored hemp smock, surrounded by bands and bangles of metal and smiling under a bushy mustache. Yao stared at her. What was happening here?

"Eudora Ovarón," Ovarón announced, "I mean, Whitely, now. Eudora Whitely, my co-founder, friend, and loving family."

Caitlin looked at Rollie, who nodded. "The Walrus," he whispered.

"I thought the walrus was Paul?" she whispered back.

"No, John was just saying that to be nice." Rollie replied, leaning his chair back on two casters. He wished he had some popcorn.

"Hello, Mother." Ovarón rose to kiss her cheek and be engulfed in an Earth Mother hug. He seated her and sat beside her. He'd be happier sitting on her lap, Caitlin observed, or even womb. Ovarón seemed more secure at her side. Still a nitwit, though.

Yao couldn't help it. He had to know. "How you vote? How you going vote?"

The Walrus ignored him, turned to face Ovarón with a motherly hand on his shoulder. He smiled at her sheepishly. "Hollis," she said gently, "How did you ever let these sorry pimps get their hooks into you?"

Ovarón fidgeted. You could almost see him scuffing his feet. "Well, it's all complicated, you know. Financial."

"Listen, Hollis." He was definitely listening. So was everybody else. "Do you ever actually read a copy of The Week?"

"Well, actually, my other duties..." he stopped dithering, touched his glasses. "Well, no, not really."

"Do you have any interest in it aside from the money it brings your ministries?"

"Not really. It's all so... so itsy. There's greater work to be done."

"Then why not just let someone else run it, take the money and forget about it?"

"That's what I was going to do, but you..." He saw the sorrow that crossed her face and backed up. "I mean, I appreciate it. But you said it was my paper and nobody should push me around."

"What do you think these jackals are doing?"

Ovarón looked at the table around him with a new perception. She was right, by God. But wait... "But if I'm not around, they'd be in charge."

"So? Delegating authority is what good executives do. Then it becomes *your* decision."

Caitlin frankly doubted Ovarón was qualified to decide what color socks to put on, but the Walrus's tune seemed to be working.

Kunitz cleared his throat discreetly. "Actually, Ms. Whiteley, it is your decision that concerns us here today."

The Walrus squeezed Ovarón's hand and turned her attention to the table. The Whole Earth Mama thing fell away, leaving the stern visage of one tough old broad. "I will vote to support any motion that returns control of this paper to," she raked Caitlin with a dismissive glance, "Qualified hands and independent operation."

Caitlin stepped right up to that, speaking softly, but with the steel certainty Hard Copy viewers had come to know. "Since we're here to vote, I have a motion to propose." She drew looks ranging from curiosity to dread to cloaked interest in her blouse. "I submit that The Week needs the guidance of an experienced professional publisher, to exercise all day-to-day decisions of management, editorial content, and staffing."

Ovarón leaned over to The Walrus. "I thought I was the publisher?"

She patted his arm and shushed him with a finger. "Let's just see."

Kunitz, in a chilly tone, asked, "Do you propose any specific person?"

You bet, Herr Sauerkraut, Caitlin thought. My boyfriend. Don't you love it? She said, "As a matter of fact, I am putting forth the name of previous award-winning editor Roland Moon. Perhaps you'd like to say a few words on your plans, Rollie?"

"A campaign speech? You bet." Rollie stood up, fervent and fiery, spreading his arms with a finger "V" on each hand. "I am not a suit! Vote for me because I'm always right and I never lie," he rolled out in forty point Rally Stentor. "A Golden Retriever in every pot, a pot in every pipe. Anarchy is just around the corner, so let's have a bigger piece of pie." He started to sit, but Caitlin rabbit-punched him and he straightened back up, leaned forward on the table.

"My plans include returning to the editorial quality of the past, maintaining the new advertising base of the present, and expanding into new formats of the future."

"Very admirable, Mr. Moon," Kunitz klipped. "But perhaps something a little more specific. For instance, what do you mean about advertising base?

"We should have been taking all those "vice" ads all along, and I see no reason to discontinue accepting them. Most weeklies have them. But there's only so much you can milk them for. There is more to be made as a legitimate source of local news, features and investigation. We can tip in stories the Union Tribune wouldn't notice for five years, as you've seen in the last few months. Build legitimate confidence and fulfill a genuine role in the development of this city. Which builds a readership that will attract ads for stock firms, financial advisors, high-end real estate and automobiles. That sort of stuff."

"And the future you mention?"

"Can you believe this paper has no web presence? I mean a real internet entity with features and news feeds and feedback forums. I've already identified two technicians who could implement that change and an addition to the sales staff with experience in selling online, click-pay ads. With that squared away and another hire-away I've been talking to, we can move into some truly innovative areas of untapped potential such as podcasting and segments for cell phones and satellite radio. We can chew ground right out from under the Union-Tribune and forge some new territory ourselves. Any further questions?"

"I think you have informed me, Mr. Moon," Kunitz said tonelessly. "Is there any suggested alternative to this motion?" Not a one. "And I would assume Ms. Whiteley endorses this motion?"

Whiteley gave Caitlin another glance, this one much warmer. "Well done, dear. I think this will work out wonderfully. I cast my shares for the proposal to create a position combining Publisher with CEO and installing Mr. Moon."

Yao's stomach fell out from under him. His temples throbbed in dark pain. His hands jerked violently. He couldn't lose like this. Three women, and all three of them busting his balls? No, no, no, no, no, no, no. And he hadn't even hit bottom yet.

Kunitz nodded at Jammi, "Ms. Jamison?"

"I'm going the straight reform ticket, Boo Baby." She laughed loud and harsh, "Your evil masters are going to have your heinie for this."

"Mr. Ovarón?" Kunitz asked blandly.

"Well," Ovarón dithered. He looked at Yao and Kunitz, avoided his mother's eyes. "Same as usual, I guess."

"Meaning that you oppose the motion?" Ovarón nodded at Kunitz unhappily. Yao unclenched. That was it, then. It was over.

"So we have Ms. Whitley's twenty-five percent and Ms. Jamison's twenty-four percent in support of this motion. Forty nine percent total. Is there more to add?"

Caitlin raised her hand demurely. "Just one thing." She looked at Kunitz.

"Yes, Ms. Vanderkeller?" he motioned with a Prussian gesture.

"May I ask about the new painting that Mr. Yao has behind those drapes. It must be quite impressive."

Kunitz stared at her as if he had been entirely remiss in his notions of her basic intelligence. He glanced at Yao, who immediately bailed out of his chair and stroked the drapes lovingly. His long-awaited moment was at hand. "Since ask, Caitrin," he said, took a deep breath, and tugged away the fabric.

Every eye in the room, once finished with devouring the oil on door-sized canvas, turned to Caitlin for dessert. She stared them down, waved a hand at the picture, made a self-deprecating moue. The huge oil featured a full-frontal view of her in the nude.

CHAPTER THIRTY-NINE

The painting was either by Soroyama himself or an extremely good wannabe. This was Kuan Yin not just as Goddess of Mercy, but also as deity of Beauty, Order and Repressed Sexuality. She had pendulous earrings in extended lobes, an upswept hairdo, the traditional lotus and mudra. Other than that it was Caitlin Vanderkeller's spitting image, naked except for the kimono draped over her shoulders and falling open to encase her stunning breasts like a pod split to reveal its peas. Oh, except that from the waist down, the smooth alabaster of her torso subtly changed to gleaming steel, giving way to articulated joints at the knees and a sort of robotic access slot in the domed mound at the crotch. It was not an apparition that invited a lot of idle comment. Yao accepted the strained silence as an accolade.

Rollie recovered first, because he was privy to certain knowledge indicating to him that this was not an artists conception, but hyper-realism based on discovery. He turned to her and said, louder than he meant to, "You posed for that?"

Yao was quick to be modest. "No, no... Master paint. I just take photoglaf."

"You posed nude for *Yao*?" That was exactly as loud as he meant to.

Caitlin smiled at him, laid a hand on his cheek. "Your lack of faith in my devotion hurts you more than it does me."

"Lucy, you got some 'splainin' to do."

"Do you trust me?"

"Yeah, okay. I do."

"Good. Because this thing isn't over by a long shot."

She leaned over, almost touching her lips to his ear. "He's been bugging me to pose for years. Always that same pose. So I took him up on it."

Rollie nodded with a total lack of expression, something more males should attempt in such situations.

Caitlin darted her tongue out to touch his earlobe, murmured, "For a nominal fee." Rollie smiled.

While they whispered and cooed Yao extolled the painting to Kunitz and Ovarón, who were pretty nonplussed. Ovarón finally ventured, "Nice. I wonder if I could get him to do one like that of

Our Savior?" He had never, understandably, faced up to his attraction to Jesus being largely homoerotic. He had four kids, but one of these days... just watch out, that's all. He stood up to better admire the seamless technique, shook his head in admiration. "So, what'd you give for that, anyway?"

"A very timely question," Caitlin announced briskly. As she pulled a multi-paged document out of her attaché case and plunked it on the table. "It's a proxy document. Allowing me to vote Mr. Yao's two percent of Southcoast Week stock."

Kunitz rapped the table once with his knuckles, a slight sound which instantly cornered all attention. He dropped the pretense that Yao was in any way in charge of anything. "Shall we proceed, here?" The attorneys all nodded. Some of them passed the proxy around, tisking at the inelegant language they could have done much better.

Rollie, this time, leaned to ear-licking distance. "You didn't have to do that for me, Darlin'. I was head over heels anyway." Caitlin smiled, moved her hand to his thigh.

Yao reacted to the situation as though electrified. He had discounted the proxy, sure of the Week's forty-nine percent and assuming that Scorment's shares were in the bag or hung up in escrow. Staring at Kunitz, he screamed, "Two puhcent! How I know? Two fucking percent!"

That last ejaculation, in pure Southern Cal English, surprised everybody but Jammi. Who yelped, "See, he speakee Engrish, numbah one."

Caitlin turned to Rollie, her brow creased. "Why do they always learn the potty words first?"

"I hope this means further conversations will be in standard English, Mr. Yao," was all Kunitz said.

"Good guys fifty-one, buttholes end up forty-niners, Stevenson," Jammi gloated. "Ya needledick."

Ovarón pulled at his mother's sleeve. "Don't they care how I vote? I'm the publisher."

"It doesn't matter now, Hollis. And you're not the publisher anymore. You're the beneficiary. And benefactor."

"Well that doesn't sound so bad."

"It's perfect. Shall we go to La Jolla for lunch?"

"Wow," Ovarón said as he held her chair. "Benefactor. Do you have to do anything?"

"No. That's the best part."

"That's great, Mother. Should we go to the Top of the Cove?"

"An excellent, choice dear. I'm so glad this month has an 'R' in it."

Rollie, smiling through his thatch, had whipped out his cell phone and made a quick, surreptitious call in the moment of embarrassment following Jammi's comment.

Yao was considering *seppuku* (forgetting that it was a Japanese thing, not Chinese) when Kunitz again rapped the table and announced, "For the record, then, Mr. Moon is now the publisher and sole executive officer of Southcoast Week. Any questions?" Oh, many of them, in several heads, but all held their peace.

"Are there any other matters to be tabled for vote?" He scanned the table with the precise rotation of a barcode reader. "No? Then we will await results until our next meeting in December? Date to be announced. Until then, gentlemen. Ladies."

"Just a minute, there, Mine Herr," Jammi called across the table. Kunitz looked at her blandly. "When's the little sitdown where we vote the Channel Nine stock?"

Yao looked at her in horror. He hadn't thought of that, he'd already been bummed enough. Of course, she'd have to have the majority of Week votes... He looked at Caitlin, Jammi, and Whiteley bleakly. And Ovarón, for that matter. Shit. But could they put together enough station stock to control anything? He looked at them again. If they'd pulled this one off... *Fuck!* He wasn't paying attention as Kunitz calmly announced a date in September and returned to passing documents to Jammi, Caitlin, and the Walrus.

So for the second time in two weeks Stevenson Yao got fucked by a beautiful woman, and not in the nice way. His collapse was complete at that point. His Goddess would now forever be a rebuff to him, his penis would shrivel as he waited to see what they would do to him. And the worst part was, they really didn't all that much give a damn.

The "Mysterians" ended up with a quarter of the stock in a well-performing small company. And a legitimate newspaper, enabling them to belong to several interesting organizations, which was what they wanted all along. But the way Yao fell apart over the vote shook their confidence a little and his business dwindled as his self-possession imploded. He became involved with causes, went to marches and protests, sat on committees. He became a sort of "professional Chinaman" until even non-profit groups started avoiding him. He was reduced to pedaling a pedicab in the Gaslamp, wearing black pajamas and a coolie hat, finally collapsing into a paranoid recluse sleeping with a cheap knockoff samurai sword in case they came for him. His painting of Caitlin was auctioned and passed through several collectors before being enshrined in the "Peace Temple" of a cybernetic spiritualist cult of the sort obviously headed straight for communal suicide.

Rollie buttonholed Kunitz as he was snapping shut the ultra-slim attaché that had held the documents now being distributed for signature, notarizing and return. He felt this was a guy you could talk to. And who had made it clear to him from the start of the meeting that the whole schmear had not been an earthshaking matter to him, just one small item to check off a long list of bigger ticket concerns. "Jeez, what a mess, huh?"

Kunitz regarded him with a flat stare. He said, "Congratulations on your new position, Mr. Moon."

"Thanks. It's kind of ironic." Rollie was every bit the rambling hippie now, just tripping away. "I was starting to wish I was still a reporter, watching all this. Great story. Big name firms, local kingpins, sex, death, big bucks. Photogenic chicks. And by the time it's over, wow man, I *am* a reporter again. Far out, huh?"

Kunitz carefully laid the case down and faced Rollie, his head cocked like the little Master's Voice dog. Rollie kept jamming, "I can see how it wouldn't make certain people look good, especially over on the TV side of the whole thing. But it's got some socko dirt and you know how inquiring those minds are."

Flat and colorless, Kunitz cut him off. "You sound as if you want something from me, Mr. Moon."

"Oh, no, nothing like that. It's more like I want to give you something. A suggestion, actually. Something that will do you more good than it would me.

"I'm always eager to hear things like that. But so often disappointed."

"This town is really tired of Barry. Really, really tired. And doesn't like that fake news show. You could use a new anchor and some grass roots guts over there."

"You may be right. A younger, classier person, perhaps?"

"Now that you put it that way, it might work."

"A woman, I think. To increase female viewership."

"But maybe attractive enough to keep men interested. Somebody of proven intelligence and resourcefulness. Previous local on-air exposure, of course."

Kunitz smiled. Rollie got the feeling he didn't do that as much as he'd like to. He said, "But where would we find such a person? You're describing, well, some sort of goddess."

Rollie smiled and stuck out his hand. Kunitz gave it two crisp shakes. Rollie held on for a moment, spoke to him in a level tone. "You didn't lose anything today. I'm going to get the paper moving again and increase revenue, the value of your shares. For one thing, I'm hiring back the old staff, which should save huge bucks in legal fees and probable payouts."

Kunitz liked the sound of that one. Rollie went on, "The Week won't take political sides, just try to promote solid, sensible leadership."

Kunitz actually laughed. "Good luck in finding such as that. Enjoyable to meet you." He turned on his heel and left. Rollie was almost knocked off his feet as Jammi slammed by him. She sprinted down the hall, her heels sounding like a teletype on the granite floor, and caught the elevator door just as it was closing. The door jerked back open and Jammi stepped in, already talking at Kunitz.

Caitlin had been straining to read what Rollie told Kunitz. She came up behind him and touched a breast to his upper arm. He turned to give her the smile she'd just known he had for her. "Great job today," he told her. "You're fired."

CHAPTER FORTY

Caitlin and Rollie parked the minivan in a bus zone in front of the Week offices and ran to the door hand in hand. She felt they should be riding a chariot through a stone arch surrounded by dancing girls tossing rose petals. They had conquered a superior foe and were returning home trailing glory and joy to all people. The scene inside the office was not quite all that, but impressive enough. Rollie's call from the meeting had triggered a chain of calls to disgruntled ex-staffers, who had flooded into the office in anticipation of possible regruntling.

Rollie's appearance was greeted by cheers, applause, and a shower of copy paper. He held his hands up in the swirl of confetti and frivolity and proclaimed, "I'm back and I'm pissed." He grabbed Caitlin, reeled her in and slapped a power kiss on her. The applause swelled. Breaking the kiss, Rollie pointed at her and proclaimed, "She's fired."

Caitlin threw her hands over her head, exclaimed, "O thank you, massah!" The applause was heartfelt and uproarious.

The festive air broke into whistles and raspberries as Jammi swirled in. She had tailed along, ghosting behind them in a powerful black Mercedes roadster previously owned by an aging La Jolla mogul who only drove it on Sundays to sniff out ever stranger stuff.

She did a haughty runway stalk right up to Rollie and Caitlin, gathered eyes, and announced. "We had a deal."

Which they did. And like most of Jammi's deals it benefited everybody more than her. Rollie had seen very clearly the flash factor that Caitlin had noticed in a vaguer way. He had already slotted Wiley, Savage, and some of the syndicated trashtalk columns to be dropped in favor of city hall voyeurism and solid ombudsmanship. Dennis Schumann would ride again.

"We do," he told Jammi. "You can count on it. First thing."

"Right now," Jammi snapped. "I want to be there when you fire him."

Newsy noses around the room sniffed spoor in the water and liked it. A re-instated political cartoonist slapped a mousy news editor on the back, yelling, "Sounds like somebody's getting their office back!"

"I want to see this, too," Caitlin told Rollie, "I've soooo earned it." She broke away from the crowd, plunging down a hall with Jammi right at her heels.

"Yes!" Jammi exulted. "I wouldn't miss this for a million more bucks."

"Okay," Caitlin cautioned her, "But no scissors or box knives or anything. Look, don't touch."

"Hoo hah," Jammi replied enigmatically.

Rollie caught up, half the staff trailing behind him out of affection, gossip-sniffing, curiosity, and bloodlust. Caitlin paused at the door to Wiley's office, looked back down the hall. Rollie shrugged. "Sorry, I couldn't line up a bunch of villagers with torches."

Caitlin reached for the door handle, but Jammi leaned into a sideways kick that blasted it open.

There was nobody there. In fact, there were few objects there. The computer was gone, along with the wall art, chairs and file cabinets.

Casey Chones picked her way through the staff and looked around the room. In a sad, muffled voice, she said, "He's vanished."

She shuffled over to the stripped-down desk and picked up a sheaf of paper laid in dead center with a shotglass as a paperweight. She looked at the top sheet, stared around the circle of staffers, then motioned for Rollie to read with her.

GOING... GOING... GONZO
By, Of ,and For The Weekend Warrior

The time is upon us, my friends, countrymen, amigos, and tomadachis, for Famous Last Words. This will be my last column for Southcoast Week, a column richly in the tradition of fifth column thought as well as the spirit of Eisenhower's farewell to the troops, in which he warned of the military-industrial complex. For all the good it did: it's way more complex now.

Since then we've learned a lot more about nogoodnik govbiz conspiracies that lay waste to everything from helpless foreigners to our savings accounts. And they've learned a whole lot more about us. None of it good. And the worse thing is that it's largely your fault. Yeah, you. What you looking at?

You are scarier than the military, actually. Modern wars aren't fought for land or freedom or even money. They're about Life Style. We want them to govern the way we do. We want to keep enjoying our perks, toys and blissful ignorance. Armies are only one head of the beast. Much more complex and deleterious than Armed Forces are Sales Forces. Critics of capitalism don't seem to get the connection that it's all about sales. Salesmen are the only ones who can increase revenue. Sales departments dictate product design and development. The military has the Stealth Bomber because the industrialists sold it to them.

The military doesn't really just take things without paying for them. Examine American history and you'll notice that when they decide to take Panama or Indian Territory or VietNam or Iraq, they end up paying for them afterwards, generally much more than they could have gotten them for up front. Then generally lose them or give them back. And why do they do these things?   They get sold on the idea. Generally by, you guessed it, the media. Who do it so they can sell more advertising. Because you respond to it by buying more crap.

It's all a pernicious pyramid resting on a massive base known as The Consumer. Okay, now you're starting to see who I'm talking to, huh? You make the whole nightmare come true just by consuming. You are idiots told by a tale, apes that antic before the reflection the Great God Gotta holds up before you. If your lameness were known, you'd all be murdered in your beds, rounded up for monoxide trains to camps, made into soft soap for washing the skin off their ass.

You are gulls, marks, targets for cons bigger than I could ever pull.   We grifters know our limitations,   they apparently have none. If their swindles can be contained it is only by you, the sheepish fodder which feed the principalities of lies. You are not innocent victims. No mark is.

And honestly, why do you suckers suck? Why do you bite the lures dangled before your glazed eyes? Mere childish pleasure in bright sparklers and sweet nummies is one thing, but aren't these crazed purchases mostly about advantage? Isn't the real motivating factory all wrapped up in looking more employable than somebody else, providing better entertainment than your sexual rivals, packaging your goods to further impulse, sending forth your DNA to more fertile fields than Them Others?

It may take a breathless minute for you to fully conceptualize this, but nobody on the planet needs a BMW, much less a Lamborghini. Nobody needs a motorhome, except possibly the homeless, who can't afford them. Which is why they're homeless. Show me one person so sunk in silliness as to actually need a wine cellar or a face lift or six-pack abs or chocolate truffles or a stretch Hummer or even a hummer from an "escort" over their cell phone. Your needs are simple and limited, but your desires are simple-minded and infinite. And more desire can be engineered in you by the experts, which is how the scam works.

Don't blame any of this on "capitalism", which is really nothing more than the mechanical physics of wealth. There's nothing wrong with the law of supply and demand. Until econo-lawbreakers figured out they could artificially pump up demand. By using your greed, your dishonesty, your genital stimuli, and your blatant obliviousness to the situation. You had me coming.

And now I'm going. This is the ultimate expression of Gonzo journalism: to be Gone. Doggone, long-gone and bygones be bygones.

I gratefully accept the little perks and gold watch. Not as such, of course: an office inventory will reveal the actual scope of my gratitude. Meanwhile, The Weekend Warrior© will continue the struggle against Culpable Consumption from the field, on all fronts. Back into the woodwork, back under the rock. Back in the box until the next unexpected rube turns the crank and plays the tune. If skulls need duggering, I will not shy away from a dire dugger or *deux*.

If you miss me (or even notice I'm not around every week to keep you together) do yourself the ultimate favor: Be your own Weekend Warrior. Here's a strategy for you: don't spend any money this weekend. Goof off, go to the beach, pick up chicks in the laundromat instead of someplace with two digit drink prices, walk on the beach with somebody you love. If you can't find anybody but yourself to walk with, try loving yourself. It's a love you can't buy or wheedle into the backseat with promises of candy. If you can't actually love yourself, you can always just go screw yourself. In fact, I wholeheartedly recommend it.

FINIS

Well, not quite the end. Within the following weeks there were shake-ups all over town. The old Week staff would settle back in, releasing an army of temps to return to Starbucks jobs and beach attire. The Week would do a big feature about the refurbishing of Channel Nine News and welcome Caitlin back, predicting she could build a gutsier news team. In return, Caitlin herself would mention various improvements at the Week, including a revamp of their now Wiley-less approach. Channel Nine viewers might miss Jammi, but would be able to catch her in much more provocative presentation on her morning exercise show--or stop by her new gym for the full impact of her dynamism. Corelle would also be missed, but could occasionally be glimpsed on chic magazine covers or Italian commercials. Nobody would miss Barry.

Guys might mourn the loss of all that eye candy but would be far from disappointed to have their weather forecasted by cute-as-a-bug newcomer Vicci Nuys. And the ladies would definitely take a shine to the virile new co-anchor, Ramón Castillo, who showed signs of wit and sensitivity under those caressable curls. His first impression on Caitlin was as a macho jerk, but after evaluating his abilities and personally picking him to work with her, she would take pains to keep him in enough benefits to resist offers from Los Angeles while forging the two of them into a team as seamless as any double-play combination. Their market share would zoom, even nibbling into the Hispanic stations' bailiwick.

Upon Rollie's return to the Week masthead, and Ovarón's increasing invisibility, there would be pointed inquiries, some more pointed than others, about Dennis Schumann. Especially regarding his possible future contributions to the Week. Rollie professed a profound ignorance of the man, who had been handed his checks directly by Caitlin and was never seen by

283

anybody on the staff. He liked to tease them along a little, decrying Caitlin's policies and bragging about changes in the lineup. But when they specifically asked about Dennis, he would whack them with the news that if any future Schumann manuscripts appeared in his mail, he would certainly run them. He would keep Dennis as a cocked right fist, and would occasionally let fly.

CHAPTER FORTY-ONE

A choirboy opened the door. On second thought, judging from the rouged cheeks and skillful eye makeup, it might have been some kid wearing a choirboy's robe. Probably so, judging from the saucy way he sang out, "Somebody to *seeee* you, 'Father O'Malley'," while sizing up Wiley's points.

Jay Scorment sauntered to the door, wearing a priest's surplice over harem pajama pants, a primitive and barbaric crucifix gracing his smooth chest. "Sorry, old chub. I don't do ugly."

Wiley stepped in anyway, shouldering past the strawberry blonde altar boy, who markedly resented the intrusion until Jay spun him around by the shoulders, slapped him on the butt and said, "Scat! *Pax vobiscum.*"

Jay watched the aggrieved little bait twitch his butt down the hall and sighed contentedly. "I swear, there's no such thing as a bad boy."

He reluctantly returned his attention to Wiley. "So come in, come in. I've got a nice check with your name on it."

He waited for Wiley's reaction, then cracked up at his expense. "Just *kidding*! Come on in the rumpus room and I'll hand you the drearily overdone black briefcase. Would you like handcuffs with that?"

"Rumpus room, huh? Can't I just wait here?"

"Don't be such a prude. There's not a rump in sight. Just that briefcase and some Scotch that doesn't look a day over twelve years. You can critique my seraglio décor."

As Wiley sipped the Scotch, soothed by the wisdom of its age, he cased Jay's playpen, shuddered. "I don't think 'seraglio' does it justice. Do you keep eunuchs?"

"Not for long," Jay retorted from his stylized odalisque on the rich brocade of a museum-quality love seat. "But listen, if it's not some trade secret you swore a blood oath not to reveal, I'm simply dying to know how you *do* these things? I see where it worked best for me not to know your plan. But how could you have predicted that your writing would be popular?"

"Not a big deal. Everything is so bland and emasculated anymore that anything different would score a hit. The problem's not writing, it's getting somebody to publish it. Which in this case was in the bag. Plus, I majored in Journalism at Iowa."

"I thought you said you were a Marketing major at NYU."

"Yeah, and Theology at Baylor, something at Hawaii... that whole period's very fuzzy... and Drama at Washington... I changed majors a lot. And schools and addresses and names."

"Ah, a couple of years each."

"If that. I gave that whole thing up when I got burned out on screwing college girls. They're cute and tight enough, but it's like lying down with magpies."

"Which reminds me. How could you possibly have predicted that Pops would marry Jammi?"

"Trick question, right? Kind of like I jumped to the conclusion that you're playing organ in the vestry of Freckleface the Doorman."

"Deduction's way easier than prediction," Jay scoffed. "Come on, the Popmeister was a billionaire. You don't think he's beaten off, so to speak, campaigns by top-rated fortune-fuckers? La Jolla is like a Homeland for vampire man-eaters."

"Yeah but any chick from his set knows what he's like, and his real age, and the kind of pre-nups he does. Most probably figure your Mom was happy to get weeded out. Besides he'd had years of watching Jammi on TV and getting hot for her."

"If you say so."

"Okay, okay, there were drugs involved."

"Another novelty."

"Oh, I think I had some stuff he never scored before. Military grade."

"Well, I certainly hope you share. But look, how could you know she'd screw him to death? Believe me, that's been tried, too. Mostly by himself."

"No, but it stood to reason. I had about four plans in place for shaking him down. That one just worked out best. And soonest. That's one scary chick, brother."

"I'll tell the world. A real mongoose. But she seems happy and better adjusted these days. Enjoying what she seems to think is wealth."

"You keep in touch?"

"Oh *fuck*, no! But Daniella does. They get along famously, go figure. Once she figured out she didn't have a place to put those damned horses, they worked out a boarding deal on the ranch and she goes out there a lot. Taking *dressage* lessons and looking pretty good at it I hear. She's fairly human when dealing with animals... isn't it weird how some people are like that? Sis is the same way, so they're actually becoming sort of stable buddies. Dani's been pumping iron over at that gym of hers."

"You mean Slam Jam?"

Jay made a face. "How did I forget a name like that? I don't think she's completely abandoned all hope of strapping Jammi on, for that matter."

"That sort of goods, you never know when you might hit the jackpot."

"You *must* be a master of bucking the odds."

"Playing the field, shading the percentage, doubling down."

"Like you say, you never know what's going to pay off. Which reminds me, and just out of scientific curiosity, now. That Hard Look woman? Ice Barbie? Are those bazooms really real? Is she even anatomically correct like mortals?"

"Keep your eye on The Nine. She's got this, like, softer look now. Probably get a bigger share of female viewers. As far as her entertainment areas, you'd best ask Rollie."

"Oh, right, the editor. Say, for such a Boy Scout he's a pretty sharp cookie. I'm sure he'll do better with the Week than that simp Ovarón will do on his crusades. Too bad I didn't hold onto the stock." He and Wiley snickered at that one. "So they're lovebirds, are they? Boy, there's a mixed doubles for you. Well, you know what they say about opposites attracting. Fortunately, so do certain of us same-o same-o's."

Jay cocked an eye at Wiley, looking ahead. "So if I need your services again, God forbid, I assume you'll have moved up from that ghastly gin mill where I found you."

"For a rich fag, you've got some pretty common acquaintances. But no, I'm moving down, actually. Down Mexico way."

"Why, for Pete's sake? They don't have any money."

"You'd be surprised. Ever see inside a Cathedral?"

"Stop, you're making me all wet. Hundreds of macho little acolytes, and all uncut stuff? Maybe I'll just come with you. So to speak."

287

"You're a really creepy guy, Jay. And there's not many I can say that to."

"I'll bet. But flattery will get you nowhere except out that door and off to the airport. I've got afternoon Mass coming up. Klaus will drive you." He turned a wave into a wristy slap on Wiley's chest. "No, no, not like *that*. In the car to the airport, silly."

EPILOGUE

Casey picked her way carefully down the path to the beach. It was so steep she couldn't even see any sand, just the insistent glitter of turquoise sea laced with dark purple shadows of reef crossed by lacy lines of wave.

She had her suitcase with her and was sweating profusely in the clutching humid heat. A breeze teased her Hawaiian shirt, cooling her somewhat as she stopped for a breather and drank in the view. Then she saw the people standing out in the surf. Around Wiley. It had required pressure and money at the Mimosa and some heavy leaning on Rollie, not to mention a slice of vacation time and chunk of savings, but she was almost there.

She left her suitcase and camera with a darling little girl in one of the thatch restaurants at the base of the cliff. She threaded past primitive fishing canoes adapted for battered Japanese outboard motors. She picked her way through the crowd of short, stocky Mixtecos in white cotton clothes standing waist-deep in the gentle surf. She stood watching as Wiley held a slim young girl underwater.

He raised the girl's head. She gasped air, rapturous as she floated on Wiley's hands in her thin, clinging shift. Wiley handled her familiarly as he set her feet on the sand. She joined her tearful parents and accepted the soulful hugs of a dozen other youngsters with soaked shifts sticking to their torsos. The adhesion looked best on her.

Wiley tossed his head back and spread his arms to heaven, intoning in Spanish as the flock murmured along with him. He then bowed his head and stepped deeper into the sea while they drifted away to shore, their attention focused on the newly baptized. When they were all out of earshot, Wiley turned to look at her.

His hair was longer, but better kept. His skin was browned, his eyes clear and healthy. His stubble had grown into a short beard, trimmed in a way that resembled artistic renditions of, well, you probably have the picture. In his white robe with rope belt he really claimed the role. All you need, Casey thought, is a crown of thorns. Maybe a little flogging and a handful of nails.

He smiled at her, and lo, his countenance did shine forth upon her and bring her peace. He said, "Come my daughter, let us break bread together."

Sitting in plastic *Toma Coca Cola* chairs that sank into the sand, Wiley broke up a nice crusty *bolillo* and handed her half, using the other half to mop up garlic butter from around his shrimp. Casey had tried to pay for the meal, but her money had been waved away by the *Señora,* who patted Wiley's shoulder and made the sign of a cross. Which explained a lot, Casey figured.

"So this is another scam, Wiley? Or whatever your name is." She'd done her best to find out, and she was damned good at research and fact-checking. She had turned up diddly-squat. The man was innocent of electronic footprints, if nothing else. "Another plunder job like getting Rollie and Caitlin their jobs back and that Jamison girl her show and all?"

"I took a couple hundred thou out of that caper, " he grinned. "And here in *no-extraditionlandia* I can discuss it."

"So you baptized those kids as part of a get-rich scheme?"

"Window dressing. The real con is up there in town. It's beautiful: straight to the heart of everything, past all the symbols and tokens and monetary resemblance to take total control."

"Wouldn't Catholic be better yet?"

"Maybe, but that takes longer. Besides, these hick Indians have acquired some resistance to that whole grift. The Born Again thing has more energy, and sinks a harder hook. Old wine in new bottles, is the theological expression."

"So you did read those tracts Ovarón sent you."

"You bet. That's where I came up with the fake orphanage. A real money mine."

"You mean the fake orphanage where they directed me down here? The one with all the kids mixing cement and the big stack of new metal windows?"

Wiley waved away her cynicism. "Of course you have to maintain a certain amount of layout for credibility. It's called "setting up the store" in the trade. I have a nice house up in the grove behind it. They bring me food, treat me like a king. Little girls worship at my knees."

Casey felt like slapping him over the head with a plate of *cameron*, but still had a little fact-checking to do.

"Ovarón's orphanage?"

"Well, it was being run by his church. You saw the pamphlets. Turned out to be a real pigsty. But it got purchased by some anonymous non-profit. I weaseled in and starting hooking it up to really soak up the alms amid the palms."

"A latter day non-profit?"

"God, no. I wouldn't come near a Mormon. It's one of those, you know, NGO's."

Called God's Coyotes, Casey thought. Linked to United Way, wholly owned by the First Church of the Latter Revelation out of Belfair, Delaware. Founded twelve years ago by the Reverend Will Bechamel Dunne. Another guy with no known details.

"Sounds like they could use some volunteer help."

Wiley eyed her closely, "You've got a suitcase, right?"

She nodded.

"In that case," he said, "Suit yourself."

As they walked up the path to the orphanage, two barefoot tykes happily hauling her suitcase, Casey spotted the bungalow back in the trees. A bright yellow surfboard stood by the door, decorated with *Dia De Los Muertos* skulls. A stream of kids ran out of the buildings, mobbing Wiley.

Casey yelled over their delighted jabbering, "So it's just another con?"

"Yeah. I gotta million of 'em." Wiley hoisted two laughing *chamacos* and tussled them around. "Just waiting for someone to pull them on."

"Like maybe even yourself?"

He turned, a squirming kid on each shoulder, and favored her with a blinding smile. "How the hell would I know?"

ABOUT THE AUTHOR

Linton Robinson was a free-lance writer for many decades, working for top national magazines and winning awards for articles in urban weeklies in the American West, ranging from Seattle's Weekly, Stranger, Rocket, and Sun to San Diego's Weekly, Revolt, and City Beat. Those years took their toll.

One of his more successful (or at least cult- idolized) columns was "The Weekend Warrior", started up at the Weekender in San Diego and eventually synicated as far north as Vancouver and as far west as Denver. In keeping with his new career as a novelist, Robinson has turned many humor columnists green with envy by figuring out how to convert The Warrior into a work of allegedly real fiction.

If you didn't like "The Weekend Warrior", well, to hell with you. What do you know, anyway, philistine? If you *did* like it, however, you're very fortunate. And not just for being wise, perceptive, and able to read between the lines—there are more works available from this blazingly talented, questionably domesticated writer.

For more titles by Lin, as well as pictures, videos, and the usual smartass attitude, take a look at his website at http://linrobinson.com

If you want to be notified of new titles and events as they happen, sign up for Lin's mailing list (not to mention the famous slangster, Cabo Bob's) at http://linrobinson.com/mail. If you don't want occasional fun mailings, don't sign up. Duh.

MORE TITLES

By Linton Robinson

For instance, there is "Mayan Calendar Girls", a team-written serial arguably directed by Lin and now available in paperback, Kindle, and all sorts of truly bizarre ebook formats.

Sexy, wild, adventurous, satiric, even romantic at times—but don't get any ideas—romp through the Yucatan and modern mythos, one of those books building a buzz. Probably the bees. Or maybe the amorous dolphins, stoner crystal skull, jetski chases, presidential antics, or just the pre-Columbian cheesecake factor.

For a more serious look at the San Diego/ Baja area, take a look

at the much-acclaimed "Imaginary Lines", published essays by two border writers. Gamblers, gigolos cockers, bullfighters,—an examination of the subtle and brutal lines of nation, culture, language, belief, and sex that divide us from each other, yet bind us together.

Lin's "other column" wasn't funny: in fact, often characterized as "lacerating". Fellow Colorado columnist Hunter Thompson called it "yuppie noir". Collected in book form without attempt to further blur the queasy lines between reportage and fiction, these letters from the understrata continue to have impact. These are missives from a world that reciprocates brutalization and penetration, but not without a subtle backtaste of redemption.

Lin's years writing newspapers in Mazatlan, Mexico were obvious influences on this murder thriller set during the mania of Carnival and involving dirty politics, journalism baseball, and some highly memorable *femmes fatale*. A cultural travelogue as well as an engaging anti-romance, Mexico style.

www.ingramcontent.com/pod-product-compliance
Lightning Source LLC
Chambersburg PA
CBHW071300170626
46809CB00001B/293